my first lo...
my second l...

Darling Venom

WALL STREET JOURNAL BESTSELLING AUTHOR

parker s. huntington

In memory of Khanh Võ.
For Chlo, Bau, Rose, and L.

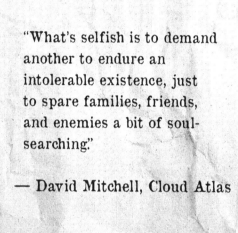

"What's selfish is to demand another to endure an intolerable existence, just to spare families, friends, and enemies a bit of soul-searching."

— David Mitchell, Cloud Atlas

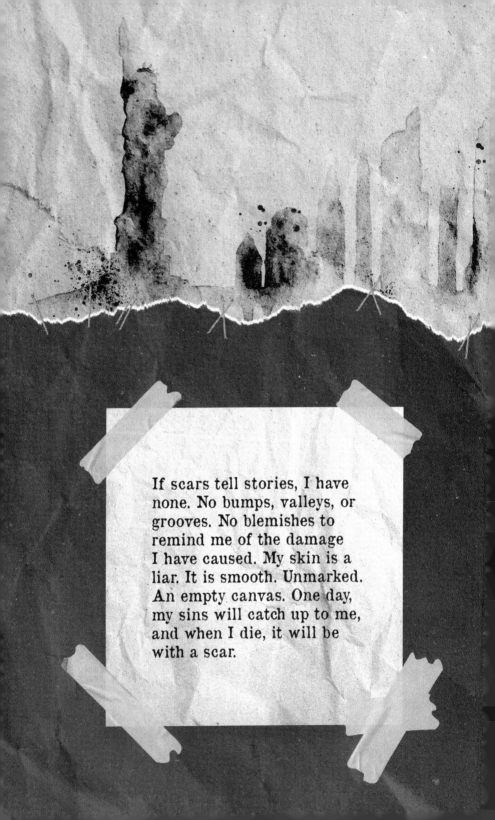

If scars tell stories, I have
none. No bumps, valleys, or
grooves. No blemishes to
remind me of the damage
I have caused. My skin is a
liar. It is smooth. Unmarked.
An empty canvas. One day,
my sins will catch up to me,
and when I die, it will be
with a scar.

Prologue

CHARLOTTE, 13

"Please don't go out tonight. Puh-leaseee." I pressed my palms together, flashing Leah my best puppy-dog eyes from my position on her multicolored quilt. "Pretty please with a cherry on top." I crawled across her bed. My big, goofy smile hid the ball of panic hiking up my throat. It felt like the world would end if my sister walked out that door.

In front of the mirror, Leah finished curling a lock of ebony hair with a flat iron. It bounced past her shoulder like a spring. She ran her tongue over her teeth, wiping off a lone lipstick stain, glued to her flawless reflection. "No can do, kiddo. It's my first college party, and Phil is super pumped. Raincheck for next weekend?"

Phil was Leah's boyfriend. Things Phil liked: One—hogging her time. Two—calling me Plan B in a totally serious way. Three—glaring at me until I was sure he saw beneath my skin whenever Leah wasn't looking.

Leah grabbed her clutch. Her hips swayed as she exited her room. She wore a miniskirt that would garner a heart attack from Dad and indefinite dishwashing duties from Mom. Luckily for Leah, they were both asleep.

"Penny!" I burst out, jumping to my feet, sounding as desperate as I felt. How'd I not think of it sooner? "Penny, penny, penny. Don't go."

Penny was our safe word. It meant business. Penny trumped boys.

And parties. And losing your virginity to a sociopathic tool. I wanted so badly for Leah to not lose her virginity to Phil tonight. I'd overheard them discussing it on the phone the other day and hadn't slept since.

Leah didn't even slow down. My heart was a kaleidoscope of glass shards. What was the point in having a secret word if it meant jack shit?

"Sorry, Lottie. Next time, boo."

I noticed she'd forgotten her pack of menthol cigarettes on her vanity. Out in the open for Mom to find. My rage simmered, spilling over the surface. Screw this. *I hope Mom wakes up and sees you.*

Leah stopped on the threshold, swiveling her head in my direction. "Oh, what the hell." She shoved a hand into her clutch, rummaged through it, then flicked a penny into my palm, humoring me. "Hey, Lottie, a penny for your thoughts?"

Accepting defeat, I twisted it between my fingers. I hoped she didn't get pregnant. I would've told her to be careful, but last time I'd broached the subject of Phil, she'd nearly decapitated me. She knew I hated him. They say love has no eyes or ears. They forgot the brain. That's missing, too.

"I hope I never fall in love. Falling in love makes you so dumb."

Leah rolled her eyes, ambling back into the room and dropping a kiss on my head. "I hope you do. Falling in love makes you feel immortal. Don't you want that?"

She didn't wait for me to answer, charging to the hallway. Her steps turned into thuds as she torpedoed down the stairs before Mom could catch her leave. She blasted past the front door, straight into Phil's arms.

I poked my head out her window, knowing seeing them together was going to hurt, but looking anyway. I watched him lean over the purring Hummer as he caught her. He grabbed her ass, shoved his tongue into her throat, and raised his eyes, staring right at me. A smirk formed on his face as he devoured her. I gasped, turning off the lamp and sliding under Leah's colorful quilt. The dread I'd felt all night rocketed, seeping out of my pores.

Falling in love makes you feel immortal. Don't you want that?

No, I thought bitterly. *Death doesn't scare me.*

Part One:
THE FALL

Chapter One

Charlotte, 14

I'm going to die without scars. Without experience, battle wounds, signs that I've ever lived. Without ever bungee jumping, learning a second language, or being kissed.

The thought lodged in my brain as I scowled at the couple in front of me on the subway. They'd been making out since I'd hopped in the car in the Bronx, and I was willing to bet they would continue until I got off in Manhattan.

He cupped her inner thigh, leaving scarlet dents on her flesh under her minidress. I pretended to read a book, watching them above the horizon of the softcover I held. *On the Road* by Jack Kerouac. Their kisses were dirty. Greedy slurps laced with the unbearable screeching of the pink heart-shaped balloon he rubbed against her leg.

My eyes glided to the other passengers. Young professionals. A few corporate guys holding flowers and wine. Women reapplying their makeup. A couple in the corner in matching cherry-colored *I'm With Stupid* shirts.

Some were short, some tall. Some large, some thin. Some old, some young. They all shared one thing in common, though—they didn't give a crap if I died tonight. Not that I'd tattooed *I'm suicidal* on my forehead before I left the house. Still... I was a kid, alone, and I looked like a mess with my hair, which hadn't seen a brush in weeks, haunted eyes, and the tooth gap Mom used to insist was endearing so she didn't have to pay for braces.

The mascara streaks under my eyes were courtesy of my five-hour meltdown prior to hopping on this train. I wore striped knee socks, a short black kilt, hand-me-down Doc Martens, and a denim jacket on which I'd scribbled quotes of books I loved with a Sharpie.

"Her future needed her, so she turned her back on her past."

"Perfection is profanity. Icy, hostile, and unattainable."

"She believed she could, so she did."

Bullshit, bullshit, bullshit.

I changed trains. Platforms. Stations. The underground clung to my clothes. A whiff of earthy engines, cheap takeout food, and sweat. Hot wind blew from the train as it approached, fanning my hair over my face.

The idea of hurling myself onto the tracks and getting it over with crossed my mind. I *tsked* to myself. Nah. That'd be hella basic. First of all—worst, most painful death ever. Second—I loathed people who did that. Especially during rush hour. What was up with assholes who insisted on launching themselves down the rails when everyone was either headed to or leaving work and school? Every time I got trapped underground, crammed between human sardines, their sweat so tangible I could taste it on my tongue, and the driver said we were stuck due to a person under a train, I wanted to bash my head against the plastic windows. Third—I'd gotten the idea of plummeting to my doom off a roof from a Nick Hornby book, and I liked the literary touch. Yup. Back to the original plan.

I hopped onto the train, pushed my AirPods knockoffs into my ears, and scrolled through my phone. "Watermelon Sugar" drowned the outside noise. I wondered if Harry Styles ever thought about committing suicide, decided that he hadn't, and rolled *On the Road* into a cone, tucking it into the back pocket of my skirt.

I'd told Leah I was going to a party, but she'd been too wiped out from her double shift at the bodega down the street to notice fourteen-year-old girls weren't supposed to go to parties on Valentine's Day at ten at night.

She'd also forgotten my birthday today. Or maybe she'd pretended not to remember because she was mad. Not that I blamed her. I didn't know how she could look me in the eye.

Don't worry. She doesn't.

It wasn't the only reason I was killing myself tonight. But it was one of them. That was the thing about despair. It built up like a Jenga tower. Higher and higher, on shaky ground. One bad move, and you were toast.

My sister hated me. She hated me every time she looked in the mirror. Every time she went to a job she loathed. Every time I breathed. Coincidentally, she was the only person in this world I had left. My death would come as a relief. Sure, at first, she'd be shocked. Disturbed. Sad, even. But once those feelings began to fade...

My suicide was a tightly knit constellation of tragedies, sewn together by bad luck, circumstances, and despair. But not having my birthday acknowledged this year? That took the cake. Which was actually kind of punny when I thought about it.

I climbed the stairs out of Cathedral Parkway. Arctic wind slapped my damp cheeks. The soundtrack of the Manhattan traffic, car horns, and drunk fuckboys filled my ears. I strode past corporate buildings, fancy apartment blocks, and historical monuments. Dad used to say I was born in the best city in the world. Only seemed fair that I'd die in it, too.

Breaking off onto a side street, I arrived at my school. This was my first year at St. Paul, a K-12 college prep in the better part of town. I rode a full scholarship, something Principal Brooks had enjoyed shoving in my face until The Night Of happened and it suddenly became unkosher to be a dick to a kid whose parents just died.

Basically, the scholarship rewarded me for being the best student in the mediocre elementary and middle schools outside this zip code. Some random-ass, couture-loving lady from the Upper East Side had agreed to pay my way through private school until I graduated, as part of some charity event. Last year, Mom had forced me to write her a thank-you letter. She never replied.

7

I hadn't been at St. Paul long enough to actively hate it, so that wasn't why I'd chosen to off myself from its roof. But it was hard not to notice the railed stairway on the side of the six-floor Edwardian monster, leading to the rooftop. Such a convenient suicide venue, it'd be a crime to choose anywhere else.

Apparently, the staff of St. Paul knew giving overstressed students access to the roof was not the brightest idea, but the stairway had to stay. Some health and safety BS. They'd put a chain around it, but you could climb over easily. Which I did, ascending the stairs in no hurry. Death could wait a few more minutes. I'd imagined it so many times, I could almost feel it. Static silence. Lights out. General numbness. Utter bliss.

When I reached the top, on the last stair, I made a split-second decision and nicked the inside of my wrist over the rusty rails. Blood materialized on cue. Now I would die with a scar.

My hands were clammy, and I was out of breath as I wiped the deep scarlet over my kilt. I stopped in my tracks when my feet hit the ink-colored shingles. The roof was slope-ridged. Three chimneys curled skyward, their mouths blackened with ash. New York stretched before me in its morbid glory. The Hudson. The parks, churches, skyscrapers partly covered by clouds. City lights danced across the dark horizon. This city had seen wars and plagues and fires and battles. My death wouldn't even make it to the news, probably.

I noticed something. Something I hadn't expected to see here. Actually, it was a someone. Clad in a black hoodie and track pants, he sat on the edge of the roof, dangling his feet, his back to me. His shoulders hunched dejectedly, he peered down, ready to jump. He leaned forward, one inch eating the other. Slow. Determined. Steady.

It was a knee-jerk reaction, the decision to stop him. Like flinching when someone threw something in your face. "Don't!" I barked out.

The figure froze. I didn't dare to blink, too stressed he'd be gone when I opened my eyes. For the first time since The Night Of, I didn't feel like a complete piece of shit.

Chapter Two

Kellan

I bet they'll ask why. Why did he do that? Why did he dress like a weirdo? Why would he fuck his brother over like that?

Well, allow me to en-fucking-lighten you. I was doing it because Tate Marchetti was a sonuvabitch. Trust me, I lived with the guy. He'd torn me from my father and didn't even stop to ask me what I wanted to do with my life. If I could die twice just to rub it in my big brother's smug face, I happily would.

Anyway, about my suicide.

It wasn't a rash decision. Suicide had built its case over the years. Then, last week, I'd jotted down pros and cons (cliché, I know—sue me). I couldn't help but notice one part of the list fell short.

PROS:
- Tate is going to have a coronary.
- No more school.
- No more homework.
- No more getting my ass whipped by rando jocks who watch too much *Euphoria*.
- No more Harvard vs. Yale discussions during dinner (can't get into either with my grades, even if Dad donates three wings, a hospital, and a kidney to these schools).

CONS:
- Will miss Dad.
- Will miss my books.
- Will miss Charlotte Richards—side note: I don't even know her. So what if she's pretty? WTF?

I plucked a can of Bud Light from my backpack and chugged it down. It was foamy from the journey here, and my fingertips were freezing, and I should just get it over with. I was about to do just that when it caught my attention. The *tap-tap-tap* of feet coming up the stairs.

What in the...?

Tate didn't know I was here, but if he'd found out by some miraculous chance, he worked a night shift Morgan-Dunn Hospital. Which left someone else from St. Puke who'd noticed the same hidden metal stairway. Probably a drunk couple sneaking in for a quick lay.

I leaned forward to jump before they could see me when I heard, "Don't!"

I froze, not turning around. The voice was familiar, but I didn't let myself hope, because if it was her, I was definitely hallucinating.

Then there was silence.

I wanted to jump. I hadn't come this far only to come this far, so to speak. I hadn't chickened out. But I was curious to know what she'd do next because... Well, because she'd just walked into a shit show.

The person behind me spoke again. "Crass doesn't sell hoodies. They're anti-capitalism. Nice brain fart, dude."

Dafuq?

My head bolted in her direction.

It was her.

Holy hell, it was Charlotte Richards in the flesh.

With the thick chestnut bangs and big green eyes and emo anime attire. Which was basically American-porn attire. Kilts and AC/DC shirts and knee-high socks under Dr. Martens.

She was not a popular kid, nor a hermit. But she had this air about her. I don't know. She made me want to get to know her.

Pacing toward me on uneven shingles, she shoved her fists into her jacket. "You made this hoodie yourself? That's lame."

I pretended to ignore her, hurled the empty beer can into the dark jaw of the school's backyard, and grabbed a fresh one from my backpack, cracking it open.

It pissed me off that she'd called me out on my bullshit, even if I was crushing on her. People our age were too dumb to know British anarchist punk bands from the seventies don't sell merch. But of course, I had to go and want the one chick who actually had brains.

"Can I have one?" She plopped down next to me, hugging the chimney with an arm for security.

I blinked at her. Nothing about this situation rang real to me. Her being here. Talking to me. Existing beside me. She must have known that I was a social pariah. Nobody spoke to me at school... or out of school, for that matter. And I didn't mean that as a figure of speech.

I wondered how much she knew about my circumstances. Not that it mattered. It wasn't like I'd date her or even deal with her tomorrow morning. That's the beauty of quitting life—you don't have to hand in a notice.

Hesitantly, I offered her the Bud Light. Charlotte released her death grip from the chimney and took a small sip.

"God." She poked her tongue out and passed it back, wrinkling her nose. "Tastes like feet."

I swallowed the rest of the lager, feeling an unjust sense of superiority. "I suggest you stop licking feet."

"And drinking beer, apparently."

"You get used to it. Nobody likes the taste of alcohol. Just the way it makes you feel."

She raised an eyebrow. "You get drunk often?"

The only light illuminating us came from nearby buildings. Charlotte freaking Richards, ladies and gents. Up close. So pretty I would smile if I could still feel anything past the numbness.

"Often enough."

Translation: Way more than I freaking should at my age.

"Do your parents know?"

I pinned her with a what-the-fuck? look. I didn't normally feel so easy with people, let alone those with boobs, but the beers had loosened me up. Plus, in my head, Charlotte and I had spoken to each other plenty.

I popped a brow. "Do your parents know you're getting hammered tonight?"

"My parents are dead."

It came out flat. Monotone. Like she'd said it so many times, it no longer held weight. But she rendered me speechless for a moment.

Sorry seemed too small a word. I didn't know anyone our age with two dead parents. One dead parent—sure. Happens. My mom was six feet under. Two—that was some Oliver Twist shit. Charlotte Richards just out-tragedied me.

"Oh."

Really, Kellan?

Of all the fucking words available? Oh?

"How?" I added, not that it reinstated my right to speak the English language.

She rocked her leg, glancing around. "There was a fire in our house. Everything burned down."

"When?"

When? Why did I ask that? I sounded like an insurance inspector.

"Just before Christmas."

Thinking back, I'd noticed she wasn't at school before and after Christmas. Sure, I bet kids talked about it, but seeing as I was a little less popular than a lone, used tampon in the girls' restroom, I wasn't in any danger of being on the receiving end of gossip. Truth be told, I'd become so invisible, people bumped into me by accident.

"Sorry," I grumbled, feeling lame. It made me resent her. I wasn't supposed to feel lame tonight. "I don't really know what else to say."

"Sorry's fine. What pisses me off is when people hear about it and say I'm lucky I survived. Yay, lucky me, orphaned at thirteen. Pop the champagne."

I made a popping sound, drank straight from the imaginary bottle, then held my neck, pretending to choke on it.

She offered a tired smile. "I could've gone upstate to live with my uncle, but St. Paul is too good an opportunity to pass up." She grabbed the beer from my hand, and our fingers touched. She took another sip and handed the can back to me. "So, why are you here?"

"Why are *you* here?"

She winked. "Ladies first."

Charlotte Richards had jokes. Damn, she was cool up close, too.

"I needed to think."

"Hashtag lies." She let out a humorless snort. "I saw you leaning over the edge. You're here for the same reason I am."

"Which is?"

"To end it all," she declared dramatically, slapping the back of her hand to her forehead.

She lost her balance, lurching forward. I shot my arm out to stop her from falling. She clutched it with a yelp, unlike someone intent on ending her life. I was kind-of, sort-of cupping her boob now.

I REPEAT: I'M KIND-OF, SORT-OF CUPPING CHARLOTTE RICHARDS' BOOB.

I pulled away frantically, but she snatched my hand, tearing into my skin, and it was awkward, and there was a ninety-nine percent chance I had a semi, and Jesus Christ, why hadn't I jumped minutes ago when my pride was still intact?

Her heartbeat thrust against my palm. She loosened her grip on me, and I withdrew, snapping my gaze back to the Hudson. My jaw was so tense it hurt.

"Wanna die, my ass," I muttered. She'd almost shit herself a second ago. "That's cool. Not your fault. Statistically, you're now less likely to want to off yourself."

This was my area of expertise. I had straight-up mad knowledge when it came to suicide. I'd done my homework. Which was ironic, considering I never did my *actual* homework.

I knew, for instance, that people were most likely to kill themselves between the ages of forty-five and fifty-four. I knew the most common suicide method was a firearm (fifty percent), and men were more likely to succeed in it.

Most importantly, I knew pretty, smart Charlotte didn't really want to kill herself. She was having a moment, not a year.

I looked down at my future demise, then up again. I'd come here to die because I wanted everyone from school to see. To scar them the way they'd scarred me, leaving an ugly dent inside them that couldn't be covered with makeup.

Other than Charlotte herself, ironically.

She hadn't been nice to me per se, but she smiled when we passed each other and once picked up a pen I'd dropped. Her niceness was cruel. It gave me false hope, which was dangerous.

Staring past the rafters, she tucked her hands beneath her thighs. "I'm serious about this. I just... I don't know... Wanna die on my terms, I guess? I can't bear living without my parents. Then, there's my sister. Leah. She works full time at a bodega to keep a roof over our heads and dropped out of college to raise me. She hasn't even realized it's my birthday today."

"Happy Birthday," I mumbled.

"Thanks." She inched forward on the sloped shingles as if testing the waters before leaning back. "I wish I had cancer. Or some other grand battle. Dementia, stroke, organ failure. If I lose those fights, I'm brave. But the thing I'm battling is my mind. And if I lose, they'll just call me weak."

"It's a good thing it doesn't matter what anyone else thinks once we're dead."

"When did you figure out you wanted to..." She jerked her thumb across her neck, then rolled it sideways, playing dead.

"After I realized I prefer my eyes closed than open."

"Meaning...?"

"When I sleep, I dream. When I wake, the nightmare begins."

"What's the nightmare?" When I didn't answer immediately, she rolled her eyes and took something out of her pocket. She flicked it in my direction. I caught it. It was a penny. "A penny for your thoughts."

"Fifty bucks would be more lucrative."

"Life's not about money."

"Uncle Sam begs to differ. Welcome to America, baby."

She laughed. "I'm broke."

"That's the rumor," I confirmed. I just wanted her to hate me like the rest of school, so she'd stop looking at me like I was fixable.

"Whatever. Don't change the subject. Why do you want to jump?"

I decided to skip the social part of why I was here—the name-calling, the loneliness, the fights—and focus on what had thrown me over the edge tonight. "I see your orphan status and raise you a fucked-up family situation with a side of broken legacy. My dad is novelist Terrence Marchetti. You know, *The Imperfections.*"

She couldn't not know.

It'd released last month and already entered its third printing. Think *Fear and Loathing in Las Vegas* meets *Trainspotting* in a very dark alley. *The New York Times* had named *The Imperfections* the biggest book of the decade before it even came out. Three different adaptations in the works—film, television, and stage. Translated into fifty-two languages. Record for fastest-selling paperback in America. Word around town was, it'd win the National Book Award this year.

I continued, trying to keep a monotone, "Mom was model Christie Bowman. You may remember she died of an overdose with her face smashed into a broken mirror from which she snorted cocaine in her family home."

I didn't mention I'd found her dead. I didn't mention all the blood. I just didn't. Now it was Charlotte's turn to look at me as if I'd fallen from the sky.

I soldiered through. "I have an older half-brother. Tate. From Dad's eighties fling. He ripped me away from Dad on some bullshit excuse, and Dad is too frail to fight for custody."

"For real?" Her eyes were very big and very green, and I wanted to jump into them and run like they were a rural field.

Looking down, I nodded and pushed my ass up, suspended by my palms. "At least your sister took responsibility for you because you don't have parents." This was not the victim Olympics, but it kinda was, seeing as, if one of us would be granted the right to die tonight, it needed to be me. "I do have a parent, but my brother is keeping him away. I think it's because Dad wasn't there for Tate when he grew up. He got all fucked-up about it, and now he is punishing him through me."

"He sounds like a real piece of work."

I sat back down, wiped the roof grime on my hoodie, and nodded, realizing I probably looked too eager, but no one, except maybe Dad, ever had anything negative to say about Tate, and this was Charlotte Richards, and she'd just called my brother a real piece of work.

"Tate's a demon. I could've lived with Dad, transitioned to homeschool, gone on book tours around the world. I want to be a writer like him. But no, I have to go to this nightmare of a school and come home to nothing because Tate works eighty-hour weeks."

"You said want." She bit her lower lip. "Not wanted. Present tense."

"So?"

"Bet your dad will be super bummed when he realizes you offed yourself."

"Don't try to convince me not to do it," I warned.

"Why?"

"Because I'm going to."

There was a pause, then she said, "I bet when you're midair, you'll regret it."

I whipped my head her way. "What?"

Charlotte Richards, my eighth-grade crush, was telling me not to kill myself. I didn't even want to process that.

"When your body is no longer on this roof, you're going to realize what a stupid mistake you've made. Not to mention, I don't think we've thought this through all the way. It's not that high. You can break your spine and spend the rest of your life in a wheelchair, drooling into your chest. You have too much to lose."

"Are you high?"

But I was surprisingly and horrifyingly tempted. More than anything, I didn't want her to see me do it. I don't know. What if I shit myself? What if my head explodes? I didn't want her to remember me like that.

Totally. It's going to ruin your chances of dating her from the grave.

"You have a family who loves you. A rich, famous father, and a dream to chase. Our circumstances are different. You have so much to live for."

"But Tate—"

"He can't keep you from your dad forever." She shook her head. "I'm Charlotte, by the way." She stretched her hand toward me. I didn't take it. Her presence had a presence, and she confused me. Then she said something that threw me off guard even more. "We're in the same class, I think."

"You've noticed me?"

And the Most Pathetic Bastard Award goes to... me.

"Yeah. I saw you reading on your Kindle during lunch like some kind of animal." She took a paperback out of the back pocket of her skirt. I couldn't see what it was in the dark, but she slapped it on my thigh. "I think you'll like this book. It's about sadness, madness, and dissatisfaction. It's about us."

Chapter Three

Charlotte

I knew his name, too. Kellan Marchetti. He was the son of America's newly minted literary legend. I'd googled Kellan first thing after I arrived at St. Paul. The elephant on the roof was that Kellan is unpopular. Radically—and deliberately—so. It was weird, because based on his looks—tall, lanky, cute, athletic—and last name, he should have had good social standing. He chose to be a loner. He dressed Goth at school. All black, safety pins everywhere, eyeliner, leopard patches, and painted nails. He once showed up at St. Paul with fishnets for gloves. He walked with his back hunched, like Atlas, carrying the weight of the world on his shoulders. He picked up cigarette butts at lunch and pretended to smoke them, and Sandy Hornbill once caught him licking a frog in biology. Okay, the last part was a rumor. Point was—Kellan wasn't a freak. He *wanted* to be one.

I didn't know what made me so distressed about him jumping. I was going to do it, too, right? But somehow, for Kellan, it seemed like a waste. He had shabby, overgrown auburn hair and eyes the color of a thunderstorm. The more I looked at him, the more I realized he was kind of boy-band gorgeous.

"Don't jump," I repeated, curling his fingers around my book. They were icy, and I wondered how long he'd been up here, working his way toward death.

"Kinda hypocritical of you to say, everything considered."

"My situation is different."

"Yeah, it is. You have hope."

"I have no parents, money, or prospects. Hope is not really in my cards."

"Just a sister who agreed to sacrifice her life for you," he said. I recoiled, his comment hitting home more than he'd ever know. "And now you want to leave her alone. Real nice, Lottie."

I bit back a flinch at the nickname, throwing him an exasperated look. Even though he said really harsh things, he did it in a nice way. As if he actually cared about me.

"We're in the same situation," I pointed out. "With our siblings. If I don't jump, neither should you. They love us." As I said this, I realized the truth of it. Leah loved me. Even if she hated me now, she still cared for me. That was why she'd made the sacrifice. That was why she'd dropped out of school. My chest was jam-packed with warm epiphany.

Kellan shook his head. "Not my brother."

"Humor me. I'm not saying don't kill yourself. I'm saying, think about it tonight. You haven't even read *On the Road* yet. What a way to go."

He drank more beer. "Yeah, no."

"Wheelchair," I reminded him.

"This shit is six stories high."

"People jump this height from yachts and slice through the water like a knife. You might just break all your bones. If that happens, you'll never live it down."

He stared at me. "You're relentless."

"I know!" I said cheerfully.

He smiled. Actually smiled. It wasn't a huge smile, or even a happy one, but it was a start. "Fine, let's see what the fuss is all about." He picked up the book and squinted at the sleeve.

I wanted to laugh, but I didn't. It seemed too easy, but maybe what we were doing right now made complete sense. Hearing that someone else is going through something shitty is comforting. Even the devil needs a friend.

"How do I know you'll keep your side of the bargain? You could do it as soon as I leave here."

"I could," Kellan agreed. "But I won't. I gave you my word. I'm depressed, not a lying jerk."

"Then what?"

He shrugged. "It was your idea to bail." His eyes glittered, and for a brief moment, I thought he might be truly happy.

I snapped my fingers. "Let's make a pact. I read about it in a book."

"*A Long Way Down.*" Kellan nodded, rolling his winter-in-London eyes with a smile. Nick Hornby was the guy who made contemporary literature great again in Britain and cemented the coolness of soccer to the middle-classers. I shouldn't have been surprised Kellan knew this. He came from a house where people actually read. The books. The punk-rock music. It was like Kellan and I shared a secret language. Locked in the same orbit, completely in sync when everyone else around us was off key. Kellan's eyebrows jumped with surprise, maybe realizing what a pact would mean. "You want to stay in touch?"

My cheeks burned. "I do." I thought about all the crap I would get for befriending Kellan Marchetti, but somehow, I didn't really care.

Kellan did, apparently, because his face shifted from hopeful to agonized. "Sorry, I don't do friendships." He nudged my shoulder with his, his voice almost kind. "Better for both of us. Don't take it personally."

"I don't care what people say."

"That's because you haven't heard them saying spiteful shit yet. Let's make sure it stays that way. I'm not saying no to friendship." He shook his head. "I'm just saying... Well, ours would be adjusted. Fri-end-ship."

"Every Valentine's Day." I grinned. "On my birthday, we meet."

"On this rooftop." He looked up to the sky, at the vastness of the universe.

Shoulder-to-shoulder, we star-hunted for a supernova that would crash and burn. I felt more alive than I had since Mom and Dad died now that I'd decided not to join them.

"Same day, same rooftop, same time." I checked the clock on my

20

phone. It was close to midnight. I'd arrived here at eleven.

We sat here for an entire hour?

"And if one of us decides to do it..." he trailed off.

"We give the other a heads-up," I finished.

Kellan nodded in agreement. "I know the drill."

"Oh, and don't forget to give me back my book. It's from the library. I don't want to get fined."

"Rock 'n' roll, Charlotte Richards." He saluted me. "Before we leave, I want you to promise me something. Like, really promise." I stared at him, waiting for him to continue. I knew better than to agree before I heard the fine print. "One, don't talk to me publicly. Like, ever. Trust me, it's for your own good. Two, this pact is from freshman to senior years. Once we turn eighteen, we no longer need to babysit one another." He dropped an invisible microphone, signaling that he'd finished.

I knew he was doing this for me, for my reputation, my chances of surviving this school. It made me want to cry. I wanted to fight to be his friend—his real friend—but I didn't want to push him too much, either.

"Agreed."

Kellan got up. He offered me his hand. We shook on it, me from the shingles where I sat and him standing. He pulled me up. I felt dizzy and disoriented. He tugged me deeper to the roof, away from the edge, then stuffed *On the Road* into his backpack, slinging it over one shoulder.

"You're bleeding." He jerked his chin toward my wrist. I looked down, not surprised. "You should probably get a tetanus shot for that."

"I'm afraid of needles." I realized how ironic my words were.

He did, too, because he filled the chilly night with hoarse laughter. "Your funeral."

"Funny stuff."

"Until next time, Charlotte Richards." He took a small, regal bow and strolled away, leaving me to stand there, my blood dripping down my thigh.

Did I just save this guy's life?

Or did he save mine?

Chapter Four

Charlotte, 15

I arrived on the roof famished. Leah had been dodging my ass for days. She went straight from work to her evening classes to become an aesthetician and slept on the trains in-between. I'd wanted to get something from the Dollar Tree on my way here, but I'd spent all my money on books this week. Better to feed my soul than my body.

Five minutes past eleven, and I wondered what made me think he would show up. True to our pact, we hadn't spoken to each other all year. I'd seen him every day at St. Paul, barring summer break. He'd gotten a lip piercing. Dyed his hair platinum. And he was pretty much the star of fistfights around the hallways. Kellan now wore kilts and ripped women's pantyhose to school. I'd heard from Cressida and Kylie that he wrote short thrillers for online fanzines and took E and Oxy. I pretended not to care.

I did care.

But I had my own social problems to worry about. Namely, how I'd turned from Charlotte Richards to Lots of Dicks (Lottie Dicks) overnight after I'd pointed out in Sex Ed that it's unfair to expect women to have fewer sexual partners than men do. Everyone had laughed. Everyone other than Kellan. His bloodshot eyes zoned in on his phone as he sat in the back row, pretending he wasn't there. He was getting scarily good at not being in places that he was physically in.

My suicidal thoughts had gotten less frequent. Or maybe just more manageable. There were moments when life overwhelmed me, and it was hard to breathe. When the guilt became too much. When my classmates, my sister, life became too much. Sometimes, I lay in bed, listening to my own heartbeats thudding against the mattress and willing my heart to stop. It seemed so easy. I could instruct my limbs to move, my eyes to blink. I could even hold my breath. Still, my heart was steadfast. The defiant little creature. It was a lesson I'd started to get used to: I had no control over my heart. It would do what it would do with no regard to the rest of my body. I guess that was the whole fascination with this organ. It could be your ruin, your salvation, your friend, and your enemy.

At night, I stared at the wall and thought about Mom and Dad and what they'd do or say to make it better. I thought about Leah and her pennies. About sticky summer days, splashing each other in fountains. Cartwheeling in our backyard and eating ice cream together. A part of me was glad I'd stuck around to hate myself every day for what happened to my parents. To Leah.

It was ten past now. Kellan wasn't here yet. I sat down, rocking my right leg back and forth. I was so hungry I was lightheaded.

The only signs I'd gotten throughout the year to indicate that night on the roof wasn't a hallucination were our secret exchanges. Three weeks after Valentine's Day, I'd found *On the Road* on my desk. I'd opened it and discovered a note inside, a few bucks to cover the library fine, and a USB.

I feel like your soul and mine are made of the same stuff. The black slug. You make me hopeful, but that's the last thing I should be. Let me know what you think.

When I got home, I plugged the USB into my dying laptop. He'd left me a Word document. Ten pages long. A short story about a boy who falls in love with his pet spider. I cried when the boy's mom killed the spider. I wondered what it meant. A few days later, I left another book on Kellan's desk. *Don Quixote*. Tucked inside the first page were his USB and a note.

> **The more I think about it, the more I realize I don't want to die before I fall in love. Before I lose my virginity. Before I make up with Leah. By the way, I cried when the spider died. More, please. – C.**

We ping-ponged through small notes, and books, and short stories. Kellan said he'd already had sex, already fallen in love, already made peace with the fact that he wouldn't make up with his brother. So, for him, he had nothing left to scratch off the bucket list.

Kellan was a friend without being one. A dark, clandestine cave I slinked into when I bothered to get my nose out of my textbooks. I didn't think anyone in my class knew what my grades meant to me. Why I broke down crying when I saw an A-minus. Why I chased teachers in the hallways and always arrived everywhere fifteen minutes early. I was the designated brainiac, but only because I couldn't afford to be anything else.

I was about to go downstairs when I heard it. Tap, tap, tap. *I'm going to kill you for being late.* The thought made me chuckle.

He showed up on the edge of the rooftop. He wore a kilt over black skinny jeans, a distressed hoodie, and a denim jacket on top with patches from punk bands. Wordlessly, Kellan took off his backpack, unzipped it, and threw something into my hands. "Happy Birthday, Dicks."

I unwrapped the doughy, round thing. A blueberry muffin in a Costa paper bag. My mouth watered, my stomach growled, and I resisted the very serious urge to hug him. Maybe because I was delirious with hunger. Maybe because Leah "forgot." Again.

"Thanks." I played it off, plopping down and tucking in.

Kellan settled in front of me. Seeing him here out of context reminded me he was a boy. A cute one at that. Even so, we were kinda pathetic. When we'd made that pact, we'd both assumed we would have nothing to do every Valentine's Day for the rest of high school. No dates. No celebrations. No one in our lives. And we were right. *Pathetic.*

He watched me eat, cracking open a can of Bud Light and guzzling the beer. "How's the black slug doing?" *Subtext: Do you still want to jump?*

I shook my head, my mouth full. Kellan watched me in amusement, producing another muffin from his bag. He threw it at me like I was a feral animal he needed to feed through bars. I was too hungry to care. I felt subhuman as I ripped into the second muffin.

"Are you not tempted? Not even a little?" He was going for mischievous, but I could hear the disappointment in his voice.

"I'm a long way from happy, and there are still moments when I want to do it, but I think I'm okay."

"And your sister?"

"Still hates me. Mom used to tell us, 'Don't shrink yourself to help others grow.' When I'm with Leah, I feel half my height, but she doesn't look taller, either. I hate being home, so I end up at the library often."

"What are you reading these days?"

"*The Astonishing Color of After. The Bell Jar.*"

"Suicide books."

"Yeah. You know the plastic paper on a new album? It's like suicide had that same glossy shine, and once I ripped it off and listened to the music, it didn't live up to the hype."

"The problem with books about suicide is they're written by people who are alive."

I jerked my chin toward him, throwing him a penny I'd prepared before he'd come here. "A penny for your thoughts?"

"I still think about committing suicide."

"And your brother?"

"I don't believe he wants to kill himself, although I strongly hope he reconsiders."

I rolled my eyes. "Kellan."

"The past year's been a shit show. Dad did a stint in rehab. I think he misses the hell out of me. He gets so lonely, Dicks. We only visited him twice the month he was there. Then Tate got himself a girlfriend. She practically lives with us now. Cooking plant-based rabbit food every day, buying me crocheted pajamas from Whole Foods, replacing my vintage leather jacket with vegan leather. She even tried to limit my time with my dad after he got discharged."

"That's bullshit." I scrunched my nose. "Did you put her in her place?"

He ran his fingers through his new platinum hair. "I'm putting them through hell. I barely talk to Tate anymore. He fights with Dad all the time. I heard him telling Hannah, his girl, that he's thinking of moving away. He got a job offer in Seattle. As much as I hate this school, I'd have nothing to live for if I moved away from New York. Dad's all I have."

"He'll do anything to keep you away from your father," I mouthed. I hated his brother without ever meeting him. "What a tool."

We stayed on the roof for another hour, catching up. I told him about my physics project, the books I'd checked out, pieces of gossip about my friends. He told me how he'd started writing for a few fanzines, and I pretended it was news to me. He also began working on an actual novel, but he didn't elaborate when I fished for details.

This time, we took the stairs down together.

When Kellan turned to leave, he groaned, "Yeah, yeah, I know the spiel. Same day, same time, same roof."

"Try not to die this year." I punched his arm. Nerd with a capital N.

"No promises." I made a sad face. He rolled his eyes. "I'll give you a heads-up if I decide to."

I offered him a thumbs-up as I continued walking backward to the train station. I parted a cloud of helium-filled, red, heart-shaped Valentine's Day balloons knotted to two street vendor carts. It felt like I'd stepped out of a dream, back into a reality I didn't want to deal with, that didn't want to deal with me.

The only thing keeping me from crashing down was Kellan's half-moon smile. Reluctant, but there.

"It's a date."

Chapter Five

Kellan

Charlotte Richards got under my skin. No question about it. Maybe because she was pretty. Maybe because she cared. Maybe because she wasn't just another beautiful face to look at. She was also great books and funny notes and encouraging words, praising the short stories no one else knew I wrote. All I knew was, I'd started to see this little arrangement as the worst thing I could have done to myself. The only thing to keep me going this year was knowing I'd get to hang out with Charlotte.

And when I did, I didn't even tell her all the important things that happened. Like that time Mark MacGowan shoved my head in the toilet after I'd almost broken his nose in a fight, and how all the other sweaty bastards in the locker room watched and cheered him on. Like the fact that I'd started having wet dreams about her. Like how I didn't feel anything anymore other than confusion.

No, I basked in her Charlotteness, because she was rare and sweet and sunshine. Then went back to my existence.

Too angry to listen.

Too jaded to care.

Chapter Six

Charlotte, 16

I arrived ten minutes early.

Kellan and I had kept the books and short stories tradition alive throughout the year, but lately, he'd been looking disinterested. More so than usual. The circles behind his eyes had become more prominent, and a dark energy crackled around him, threatening to electrocute you if you got too close.

Still, I found myself trying to reach him, subconsciously or not.

Almost talking to him.

Almost touching him.

Almost hugging him.

I always ended up taking a step back, coward that I was. Kellan had made it clear that I shouldn't—couldn't—get anywhere near him. I didn't want to break the rules. I feared losing him. Not just as a friend, but lose-him lose him.

It occurred to me on multiple occasions that I should probably tell someone more qualified than me about the situation. I even got as far as waiting outside the student counselor's office. But then I'd remember every time they forced me to talk about The Night Of with adults and how each conversation only made it worse.

One thing that had changed this year was that I'd started hanging out with some boys at school. We grabbed a slice of pizza or walked the High Line or washed our hands in Sabon in SoHo. I'd even let one of them kiss me.

Mark MacGowan.

Full disclosure: the kiss sucked. Another full disclosure: that hadn't stopped us from trying again (and again and again). We'd been making out for a couple of months now, but we were both happy to keep our relationship secret. Mark was probably ashamed because I wasn't a rich heiress like everyone else around here, and I was embarrassed because, frankly, I'd met cans of Diet 7UP more intelligent than this guy.

Tap, tap, tap.

I clicked my lock screen off when I heard Kellan pounding up the stairs and shoved it into my pocket, turning around to face the rusty metal door.

He appeared on the roof. His gauntness hit me with the weight of concrete. He looked ghost-like up close. But the thing that struck me most was that he was stunning, even more so than before. It was as if his face used to be a blurry picture, and now it'd finally come into focus.

It'd been said—whispered—that he was hooking up with girls from school in secret. That, despite the fact that he was a hermit, he slept around often. I didn't want to think about these rumors. They made me nauseous.

I caught myself holding my breath and smiled when I realized he'd arrived early, too.

"Happy Birthday, Dicks." He unzipped his tattered backpack, throwing something into my hands.

I unwrapped it, unveiling an entire block of spongy, carroty cake. "Dang." I squashed it in my fingers, laughing. "Setting the bar high for next year, Marchetti."

He advanced toward me and plucked out two Bud Lights. I wondered if he'd heard I'd started drinking or just figured it out because everyone drank these days.

We clinked cans and sat crisscrossed. My right leg rocked.

He ran a hand through his hair. "How's the black slug doing?"

"I don't think it's in me anymore," I admitted, almost sadly, because the black slug was what glued us together.

Leah hated me. No doubt about it. I'd ruined both our lives. But I knew my parents would be devastated if I killed myself. Leah, too. Despite her resentment, she didn't want me dead. She just wanted me gone. I'd respect her wish. I planned on taking an early registration, any full scholarship offered to me, and getting out of her hair as soon as I graduated.

"You?" I asked, playing with the clinging plastic wrap on the cake. For some reason, I felt shy about eating in front of him now. I didn't know what had changed, but stuffing my face was definitely not on my agenda tonight.

"My black slug is alive and kicking."

I took a penny from my wallet and threw it in his lap. "A penny for your thoughts."

He caught it midair, rubbing it between his thumb and middle finger. "Everything just seems pointless."

"You haven't tried to..." I trailed off.

"I'm still here, aren't I? When I try to kill myself, I'll succeed. I'm a perfectionist, Dicks."

When.

I cleared my throat, smashing the carrot cake with my tight fist. "But... why?"

"Giving up on porn and beer is harder than I thought."

I swatted him on the chest. "Have you tried talking to someone?"

"Yeah. Talking to a therapist just makes it worse. Either I'm stuck with someone I don't click with, so I just fake it and spend an hour making shit up and dragging them around, or I do click with them and start surfacing shit I don't want to think about."

"You know it's only temporary, right? Tate won't have custody of you forever."

"It's not just Tate. I hate everyone at school."

30

"Everybody hates everyone at school. Not peaking in high school is an accomplishment. What a sad existence our popular peers are going to have. We only have two and a half years to go."

He fell silent for a moment, peering down from the roof. "Tate and Hannah are getting hitched. They're staying in New York, but Tate told me he's sending my ass to an out-of-state college. I'm not talking New England, either. Berkeley or UCLA or some shit. Somewhere far. He doesn't want me anywhere near Dad. He flat-out told me so." I groaned, covering my face with my hands. Kellan added, "He also stopped giving me any allowance or lunch money."

"Monster." Surprisingly, I meant it. And I normally wasn't the mean type.

Kellan scratched at his chin, which was now coated with a layer of light-brown whiskers. Suddenly, I really wanted to kiss him.

It made no sense. I wasn't into him. And yet, he appeared perfectly kissable right in this moment. More so than Mark, who I actually did make out with frequently.

Come to think of it, I sometimes thought about what Kellan was doing while I was with Mark. Not sexually, but what he was reading, where he was going, what he was thinking…

The stupid penny I kept tossing Kellan's way seemed to finally drop.

Charlotte, you idiot.

Something swelled in my throat.

I wanted Kellan.

I really, really wanted Kellan.

"Anyway." Kellan lit a cigarette, tipping his chin upward, sending a ribbon of white smoke to the dark universe. "Tell me something about you. Something real. Something intimate."

I told him about Leah and about visiting my parents' graves and working a summer job as a busser at an Italian joint that specialized in events. We had to break up drunken fights at least twice a week, but the tips were awesome.

31

My mind had fixated on kissing him the entire time, so I finished by saying, "Oh, and I started getting frisky this year. So underwhelming."

"Frisky?" He grinned. He liked this new topic, which annoyed me. "Is that what you youngsters call it these days?"

I swatted his chest. "You know what I mean. Making out sucks. I want my money back."

He threw the penny my way. "Here. But don't sell yourself short. A girl like you is worth at least…" He gave me a meaningful once-over, raking his eyes over my legs, boobs, then face. "Five bucks, easy."

I shoved at his chest again. He chuckled, tickling me. I squirmed, flattening my back against the roof as I tried pushing him away. He was on top of me in no time. It felt calculated without it being calculated.

We breathed heavily as his fingers poked my ribs and side boobs, and I belly-laughed. I pretended to kick him without really making an effort.

Kellan stopped abruptly. We stared at each other, panting, his entire weight on me, our lips inches from one another. Something in the atmosphere changed. Everything became heavier, thicker, sweeter.

The wind still blew on our faces, but I didn't feel it anymore.

I wondered which girls he'd been with. Their names. If he liked any of them. It horrified me that he had a secret life I wasn't aware of.

Kellan leaned over me. Condensation skulked from his mouth when he spoke. "So, tell me about your bad first kiss, Dicks."

I licked my lips, my throat bobbing. It occurred to me that I was going to kiss him.

He is going to kiss me.

We are going to kiss.

This might change everything. I wanted it to. Not necessarily in a boyfriend/girlfriend type of way. I just wanted to be a constant in his life. To have my finger on the pulse. His pulse.

I scrunched my nose. "It was very wet."

He groaned, his eyes dropping to my lips.

I rolled my eyes. "The kiss, you pervert."

My mouth magneted toward his.

Slowly. Tentatively. Maddeningly.

His gray eyes held mine prisoner. "Continue," he croaked.

"And kind of messy, but not in a good way."

My breath was short and heavy. Our lips were an inch from one another. My stomach flipped like I was on a rollercoaster. My body was rioting, my senses heightening. Everything was warm and gooey and right.

"Who was it with?"

His lips hovered over mine. His hot breath made my cold face tingle. He smelled of beer and leather and cigarettes and trouble. Like a bad boy. I wondered what he'd taste like. I was about to find out.

"Mark MacGowan," I rasped, leaning the last inch to kiss him.

And just like that, I felt the coldness and terrible emptiness as his body left mine. I looked up, scrambling to my knees. Kellan stood, sneering down at me.

I blinked. "K...Kellan?"

"This is not working for me, Dicks."

"Okay." *Oh my God. What is happening?* "That's fine, I just..."

"Nah. Don't sweat it. Listen, I have to run, so..."

Never in my life had I been so humiliated. I thought I might puke the minute he got down from this building. I nodded and mumbled something about wanting to leave, too. Clearly, Kellan felt some kind of way about Mark. I guess I hadn't noticed. I'd never seen them talk.

Kellan stalked away, leaving me on the roof without a second glance. I took the train back to the Bronx, eating the smashed carrot cake without tasting it. The crumbs decorated my thighs like sad snowflakes.

By the time I got home, the clock hit past midnight. It was no longer my birthday.

Leah snored softly on the couch, a book about self-love propped open, covering her face.

I slammed my bedroom door, not caring if I woke her.

"Happy birthday to me."

Chapter Seven

Kellan

Fuck. Fuck. Fuck.

Anyone but him. Anyone. Even Toby Watts.

But of course, it had to be Mark MacGowan. The dirtbag who'd caught me stealing a glance at Charlotte in French class at the start of the semester and had made it his mission to get into her pants since.

"Hot shit, right?" He'd matched my steps when I walked to the subway. I pretended to flick dirt from under my nails. "Lots of Dicks. Bet you fifty bucks I could get mine in her little mouth before the end of the year."

I said nothing.

There was nothing to be said.

Mark was on the rowing team. Big, burly, widely popular. He looked as if he'd stomped his way straight out of those one-dimensional teen shows where everyone talked like they were thirty.

Mark's dad worked as a morning show presenter and shared a decade-long beef with mine. He'd invited Dad to his show to promote a new book ten years ago. It flopped, as all the others did before *The Imperfections*, but that wasn't the point. In fact, Dad got one line of promo out before they moved onto politics, and things escalated from there.

In a nutshell, James MacGowan was the most traditional, uptight person on planet Earth, and my father was just a few slip-ups shy of being a complete anarchist. Nasty words were exchanged, followed by a headline about how paparazzi caught Terrence Marchetti sneaking into a hotel with James MacGowan's wife—Mark's mom.

My guess was Mark wanted to sleep with Charlotte for the same reason my dad had slept with Mrs. MacGowan. Revenge.

But I knew where to pick my battles. Charlotte wasn't one of the girls who snuck after hours into my room and watched in wonder as I rubbed them off and made them come. She was smart and well-read and hot in a reserved way. Neither Mark nor I could have a chick like that.

If anything, Mark ruining her for me would save me the stupid hope she'd pumped into me in small doses every time she left me a book or a note. All in all, a bulletproof plan. Now I saw through all the holes in it. How much of an idiot I'd been to believe it would work.

The minute I stumbled down from the roof, I reminded myself that I didn't, in fact, care. Charlotte had never been a part of my plan. There was no plan. There had been—offing myself—but now that was a bust, thanks to Dicks.

Even though I missed the last train home for another half hour, I walked in the opposite direction from the subway. I couldn't chance bumping into her. Not after chickening out on our kiss.

I didn't regret not kissing her. I felt irrational resentment toward her for fooling around with MacGowan. Any girl willing to touch the jerk ought to be a waste of time.

Yeah. Right. Keep telling yourself that.

Manhattan was ugly and dirty and rich and a total mystery to me, just like Charlotte. I got why I was lucky to grow up here. This city was as complex as a person—full of contradictions.

I collapsed against a gray stone monument.

A ruined kiss with Charlotte Richards was not even in the top twenty worst things that happened to me this year. To name a few:

- Dad hit a writer's block and fell behind on his deadline. Again.

His publishing house is threatening to sue him. Also again.

- I got fired from the fanzine I worked for because I punched an intern in the face for saying Dad plagiarized *The Imperfections*. Okay, maybe it was also 'cause I slept with the editor-in-chief's girlfriend.

- Tate no longer allowed me one-on-one visitations with Dad. Now he got to play bad cop all the way. He supervises us when we meet.

- Mark and I graduated from fistfights to trying to kill each other. Last month, he tried to push me onto the rails while I waited for the train. No one was there. We fought it out, and I broke his rib.

I didn't return home, aware it would drive Tate mad not to know where I was. Hannah was probably telling him to send me to military school right about now. She'd been trying to get me out of the picture.

Couldn't blame her.

Not after I'd propositioned her in the bathroom to scare the shit out of her, so she'd leave. She cried to Tate afterward for hours.

I heard her hiccupping from across the hallway, sniffing and repeating, "But I'm trying so hard. I'm so good to him, Tate." Because, apparently, everything was about her.

I checked my phone, and sure enough, I had fifteen missed calls from Tate and twenty text messages. Why I'd expected to find Charlotte's name there was beyond me. We never exchanged numbers.

I slept on the streets.

When I woke, it was four in the morning, and I was covered in my own puke. My half-brother tugged on my sleeve, hoisting me up to my feet and dragging me to his gross white Lexus RX350.

"I'm going to kill you," he muttered. He sounded tired and pissed off.

Not if I kill myself first.

Chapter Eight

Charlotte

The breakup with Mark was a total shit show, and everybody got a front-row seat.

Even though we weren't officially together, Mark insisted on making a public scene in the middle of St. Paul's cafeteria. Kellan read a book on the far end of the room (*The Human Stain*), stealing glances at us every once in a while.

Mark called me a cheating bitch and spat in my face for dramatic value. The spit was warm and disgusting and slugged down my cheek.

I took a deep breath, knowing I couldn't afford to get into trouble. "Sorry, Mark, I didn't realize it was more than a fling for you." I pretended to examine my nails, my heart beating so fast, I needed to throw up.

More than I wanted to kiss Kellan, I wanted to please him, and it was obvious he hated Mark with a passion. That was what gave me strength when the entire school stared and laughed at me.

"You know damn well it wasn't a fling."

"It was for me. Besides, for a big schmuck, your actual schmuck is not so impressive."

It was a blow to my already slutty reputation, but it humiliated Mark to the point where he released a growl and punched the wall. Then he yelled even louder, covering his fist with his other hand. If I had to guess, he'd broken at least three fingers in the process.

After the public cafeteria breakup, I'd officially become an outcast. But it was worth it, because Kellan and I were back to exchanging books and short stories. He never thanked me or referenced our almost-kiss on the roof.

But for me, something was better than nothing.

Another year passed in a blur of exams, busser shifts, and days tiptoeing around Leah. I felt like I was preparing myself for real life without living it.

Chapter Nine

Charlotte, 17

"Happy Birthday, Dicks."

I heard Kellan behind my back. I turned around. He dropped his leather jacket on the shingles and threw something into my hands. I looked down at it. A Valentine's Day teddy bear. The type you squeezed in the belly, and it started singing.

A peace offering?

I tucked it under my armpit and shoved my hand into my pocket, flicking something of my own at him from across the roof. He caught it.

"A penny for your thoughts."

"Fuck your money."

He stalked toward me.

Slow. Deliberate. Feral.

My right leg jerked nervously. I popped an eyebrow, resisting the urge to step back.

Another step.

Then another.

He was freaking me out.

I refused to appear freaked out.

I tipped my chin up, feigning defiance. He strode closer. I could smell him, feel him, taste the leather and cigarettes and beer on my tongue. Chills skated up my spine. My blood bubbled and my body buzzed.

"Cut it out," I huffed. "What're you doing?"

He didn't stop when he reached me. In one swift movement, he scooped me into his arms.

I let out a gasp, wrapping mine around his neck, clinging to him for dear life. We were on a steep roof, and Kellan was not the most muscular guy in the world. But he made me feel surprisingly light.

He looked down at me. Every time I stared into his eyes, it felt like meeting him for the first time. I always found something new in them.

Today, I found promise.

My heart was pounding so hard, it must have been the only time I'd felt alive since The Night Of.

"This is not the beginning of something," Kellan warned. "If anything, it's the end."

Chapter Ten

Kellan

She tasted like sweet venom.

Warm and cottony and dreamlike.

Deadly toxic.

Gorgeously addictive.

I kissed her hungrily, my tongue thrusting into her mouth, erasing Mark. I wanted to do bad things to her, and it frightened me.

These thoughts had started last year, after Mark MacGowan. My desire for Charlotte had laced with something else.

Something darker.

Maybe they were in this together. Charlotte and Mark. To make me lose my mind.

I don't know.

I was pretty paranoid these days.

Maybe not.

Fuck. Was it pathetic that I didn't even care that she might have been doing this for shits and giggles?

Our tongues swirled together. She tasted of bubble gum and coconut. I wrapped her in a vise grip and thought, *if we could just stay this way forever, maybe it wouldn't hurt to breathe.*

I had so much I wanted to say to her. Hannah had dumped Tate. The wedding was off. He was pissed at me for ruining yet another thing for him.

This time, he'd found a great way to retaliate.

Tate dragged me to therapy twice a week, sitting outside the door like a guard dog, glaring at the wooden barrier to make sure I didn't sprint out of there. He got it all wrong. What I wanted to do was jump out the window, but it was usually locked.

In answer to his BS, I'd started doing drugs. I might not be good at math, but I sure as hell was good at meth. The drugs made me cold all the time, but nothing killed Tate quite as much as the knowledge that he was not in complete control over something.

Dad didn't answer my calls. Tate had finally scared him off. And catching even more feelings for Dicks was a bad idea. Guys like me never got the girl.

Everything seemed so final.

At a boiling point.

As if life was simmering and about to spill over.

Charlotte groaned into my mouth, and I cupped her neck, putting her feet down so I could rub myself against her. I was so hard, and she was so soft.

I never got hard anymore.

Probably a gift from the drugs.

Our kiss grew deeper, more passionate. I allowed myself ten more seconds before I broke it off. I burned her taste into my memory: fresh, sweet, innocent.

Another tongue stroke.

Another nibble.

Another kiss.

Then I let go, shoving the penny back into the front pocket of her jacket, a blasé smile on my face.

"See you next year, Venom."

Chapter Eleven

Charlotte

Turned out, all it took was one kiss for me to break all the rules. Suddenly, I cared too much to pretend I didn't know him. That I was oblivious to what he was going through. Kellan constantly straddled the edge of disaster, and I was done watching from the sidelines, hoping he didn't take the leap.

One day, I strode over to Kellan during lunch break. Everyone stopped what they were doing and watched. I was a nerd, and he was a freak, and that was the sort of fraternization that was even worse than popular kids and losers. He read a wrinkled paperback, frowning at the pages.

I planted myself in front of him, fists curled over my hips, and cleared my throat. "Hey."

He ignored me. Panic rose up my chest, and my cheeks heated.

"I said hi."

Still nothing. Some people whispered. Others chuckled. Cressida recovered from the shock of seeing me speaking to him, took out her iPhone, and recorded the whole thing in my periphery.

I raised my voice a notch. "I'm talking to you, Marchetti."

Giggles ricocheted against the walls. Kellan lifted his eyes from his book, then stared right through me, yawned, and got up, walking away.

Though my pride screamed at me to quit, I chased him out of the cafeteria. I was making myself look ten times more pathetic than I already felt.

I placed my hand on his shoulder. He didn't stop.

"What the hell is wrong with you?"

"Everything," he said, point-blank. "And you know that firsthand. You're breaching a contract, Venom."

Venom?

But I didn't have time to dwell on the small stuff. Like why the hell he called me that. Why he'd called me that the night we kissed.

"I don't care about the stupid contract."

"Shame, because I do."

"You're not okay."

"No shit, Sherlock."

"Kellan!" I stopped in the middle of the empty hallway.

He stopped, too. He turned around, and his face was so pale, I thought he was about to faint. I took a step toward him, but he raised his palm up.

"Don't fight my wars for me, Venom."

Again—who is Venom?

I was about to ask him just that, but he stalked off. Right out the double doors and out of school. He was skipping, leaving me here to deal with the consequences of being snubbed by the most unpopular guy at school.

I stood rooted to the ground, staring at the wooden doors. I fished out my phone and sent him a text message. One of many he hadn't answered since I'd gotten my hands on his number in not-so-kosher ways.

Who is Venom?

Who is Venom?

Who is Venom?

Answer me, goddammit.

Mark materialized from one of his classes. His minty breath fanned the hair blanketing my ear. "Why didn't you say you like your dick the way you like your life, Dicks? Extra trashy."

Chapter Twelve

Charlotte

I left a four-page letter for Principal Brooks the following week. I detailed all my reasons to believe Kellan was suicidal and slipped the envelope into the box outside her office. Two weeks later, I got an answer from Kellan's number.

> Kellan: You breached our contract. Twice. You talked to me. You wrote a letter to the principal. Next Valentine's is off.

I called him.

He didn't pick up.

I texted him.

He didn't reply.

I called again.

He'd blocked my number.

I kicked the wall beside my bed and screamed. "Fuck!"

Even though Leah was there, in the other room, she didn't ask what happened. She never did.

Chapter Thirteen

Charlotte

Six months after the kiss, I found Kellan's address. I showed up at his place on a Saturday morning when his brother would most likely be there.

I mustered every bit of my courage to do this, as there was a good chance I'd be airing Kellan's dirty laundry to anyone willing to hear about it without his permission. He said he was suicidal, but so did a lot of teenagers who never followed through with their threats. Hell, I still felt suicidal sometimes.

He's never tried anything—has he?

So why couldn't I let it go?

Kellan and Tate lived on Pomander Walk on the Upper West Side. I'd always imagined a loaded Kellan tucked in an icy, futuristic skyscraper on the Upper East Side. This street, however, resembled a charming English village.

In the middle stood Tate and Kellan's home. A red-brick brownstone with pea-green shutters, overflowing flowerpots adorning the windowsills, and cozy yellow light seeping through the windows. Normal, warm, and inviting. The exact opposite of the men who resided inside.

A stab of jealousy found my gut. I couldn't help but compare our lives.

The narrow road brought the houses near, facing each other closely like two people on a date. I had nowhere to hide, so I sat on a stairway across from his house, in front of his closed door. I produced a book from my backpack and pretended to read. I slapped my right leg to stop it from rocking.

Get your shit together, Charlotte. It's not about you.

I didn't wish to talk to Tate Marchetti, but I also didn't want to wake up every day with a headache, praying to see Kellan at school just to know he was still alive. I started playing out scenarios of how it would go down when I finally met this Tate guy.

I imagined myself bursting into a lecture when he arrived. Yelling at a faceless Tate. Putting him in his place. Balling my fists and hitting his chest. Ripping him to shreds with my sharp words. Bringing him to his knees with the truth of what was happening to Kellan.

I even imagined myself chickening out and running for my life when he appeared.

Nothing prepared me for the third option—the one where Tate never showed his face. An entire afternoon of my staring at the Marchetti entrance passed before I saw their living room curtains flutter open.

Kellan peered out from inside.

Fuck.

Our eyes collided. My throat worked around a swallow. I didn't wave hello. There was a limit to the amount of awkwardness I could endure. Fifteen minutes later, a police officer parked at the end of the street and approached me while tugging his belt over his beer belly.

"We received a call from a resident that someone has been sitting in front of their door for a few hours now. Everything all right, miss?"

This felt like the deepest betrayal.

Me trying to narc on him to his brother.

Him calling the cops on me.

I nodded, smiling weakly at the uniformed man as I uttered the lie that slipped through my mouth so easily these days.

"Yeah, sorry. I'm absolutely fine."

47

Chapter Fourteen

Charlotte, 18

"Sometimes I wish you were never born. Does that make me a bad person?" Leah finally said it. Well, whispered it.

It came out of her mouth in a rush. Just as I scooped my keys from the bowl by the door, about to go to my last meeting with Kellan. Technically, he'd canceled. But I still hoped he might show. I knew I would. I had to.

I twisted my head. Leah stood before the darkened hallway mirror, staring at her face. Guilt was a monster, clawing at my skin. Before The Night Of, Leah had been the pretty one. Her huge, vibrant eyes a few shades darker than my green ones and raven hair gave her a striking look guys fawned over.

I stopped, but I didn't turn to her. "You think I don't know that? I live with that knowledge every single day."

A few months ago, Leah had finished studying for her aesthetician diploma and started working sane hours. I'd thought it would improve her mood, but it'd only made things worse. Now, once-beautiful Leah was the freak with the long sleeves, who had to cake on makeup each time she left the house.

"Phil called me today."

We shifted to face each other at the same time. Her, from the mirror;

me, from the door.

Phil and Leah had broken up shortly after the fire. It was connected to what had happened.

When he finally left, the last thing I heard her scream at him was, "No one asked you to touch me. No one asked you to stay. Don't feel guilty because you want to leave me. Feel guilty because you're shallow enough to be turned off by scar tissue. Now get out!"

He stormed out, pushing me when he found me eavesdropping in the hallway. "Catch you later, Plan C."

I was no longer next in line. I was the bottom of the barrel, in case he couldn't find a replacement for my sister.

I shook my head, ridding myself of the memory. "What did he want?"

"Just to check in. He's a banker now. Morgan Stanley."

I pretended to gag. I had nothing against banks. Or money. But I had a boatload against Phil.

She continued, ignoring my reaction. "He's dating Natalie Moseley. It's serious. Two years I gave this man."

"Don't say that."

I thumped the back of my head against the door, closing my eyes. I hated that phrase. It implied women sat around and waited for men to pop the question while wasting their fertile years. A relationship version of Russian roulette.

"You've given each other two years," I added. "Whatever time you lost—or gained—he did, too."

"Well, he's not on the losing end anymore."

She looked at the mirror again, brushing her hair absentmindedly. I wanted to wrap my arms around her shoulders, nuzzle my face into her neck, right where her scar was, and tell her it would be okay, even though I had no idea if it would.

Leah and I had been best friends before The Night Of. She'd literally walked through fire. For me.

I didn't move from my spot.

"Leah..." I started.

She shook her head. "It's fine. Forget what I said. Obviously, I'm happy you were born. I don't know what you do every Valentine's Day, but I hope it's better than sitting here watching *Grey's Anatomy* reruns. Because that's what I've been doing since Mom and Dad died."

I rocked my right leg back and forth, struggling to breathe. "Let's do a marathon. After I return. I promise. Raincheck?" I sounded exactly like her the night things went down.

She snorted, twisting her hair into a topknot. "Know what? Before you go to your mystery date, make yourself useful and get me a pack of menthols."

She threw some money my way and disappeared into the kitchen. Of course, she still smoked. That was the great irony. I picked up the bills from the floor. Checked the clock on my phone.

I was already late, but I didn't want to refuse her. More than that—I couldn't refuse her. I made a run to the 7-Eleven at the corner, waited in line, then came home, gave her the cigarettes, and hopped on the train.

By the time I got to Manhattan, drops of cold sweat flew from my brow as I zipped down the street toward St. Paul.

I was forty minutes late to a meeting I hadn't been invited to. But if I knew Kellan at all, I knew he expected me. He wanted someone to fight for him. And that person needed to be me.

I ran so fast my feet burned. My lungs bounced in my chest. I took a sharp right and reached campus. I stopped dead in my tracks when I saw the lights.

Red, white, and blue, swirling together like a carousel in the darkness. There were two police cars and an ambulance.

No.

No, no, no, no, no.

Kellan...

Did he think I wouldn't show up—that I gave up on him—and jump?

I launched forward.

An officer blocked my way, raising a hand. A colleague behind her walked around, stretching yellow tape across the scene. "Sorry, honey, but you gotta stay clear."

"What happened?"

My teeth chattered. I'd forgotten to put a jacket on when I'd left the house. I'd been in such a hurry. The only reason I didn't cry was that I wasn't certain what I was seeing was even real.

The cop replied. A fellow officer joined her. Their lips were moving, but I couldn't hear them.

I looked past her.

I didn't see him.

He must've jumped from the other side. Where we used to sit every year.

I'm going to throw up.

"... so young, so sad. Still investigating."

I could finally hear through the pounding in my head. I wanted to scream. To rip my hair out. I'd told him this was not a sure death, and he still took the chance.

He proved me wrong.

He won.

He lost.

He broke our contract.

I had, too, but only to save him.

I fell down on my knees. My hands hit the concrete, and I felt something. I picked it up, squeezing it in my hand.

A penny.

He'd left me a gift.

His very own version of goodbye.

Part Two:
The Imperfections

Chapter Fifteen

Charlotte, 22

"Charlotte, do me a favor." Reagan poked her head out of her glass office. She cradled her baby bump with pointy manicured fingers, her dress matching her flaming scarlet hair, courtesy of Manhattan's finest hairdressers. Her hand always laid on her stomach.

I couldn't blame her for being so protective. If I were a forty-two-year-old woman who'd spent the last decade trying to get pregnant and finally got my wish, I would live in a bubble until the babies popped.

I jerked my head up from the manuscript I'd selected from the slush pile a few minutes ago. I could use a distraction—any distraction—today. A bright smile spread across my face. "Of course."

Heart-shaped balloons and flowers filled the room, sent to my colleagues for Valentine's Day. My cubicle sat closest to her office. The only one clean of any love declarations or romantic gestures. I had my laptop, my pens and highlighters organized in two separate mugs, and my planner and Post-it notes stuck in neat, militant rows.

I was pretty sure whatever she was about to say had nothing to do with it being my birthday today. Nobody paid attention to my birthday. I'd learned to accept it, to a point where, when people mentioned it, I was taken aback.

"My ob-gyn is not picking up, and I need to see him later today. The line at the clinic is busy. He's not answering his phone or email. It is so unlike him. Could you please drop in there and deliver my message personally? Thanks!" She didn't wait for me to reply. Instead, she breezed in my direction, grabbed a Post-it from my arsenal, and scribbled the address down, slapping it on my keyboard with complete disregard to my tidy environment. "And don't come back until you get me that appointment, okay? I'm extremely gassy. I think the babies might resent me for that once they're here."

Right. I'd almost forgotten—Reagan was having *twins*.

My boss dashed to the break room, waving the tips of her fingers like a fairy godmother.

I'd started working for Reagan Rothschild Literary four months ago, two months before my early graduation, and had already moved up the ladder from office coordinator to literary agent assistant. The end game was to become a literary agent. I'd have to push myself to make it, but I was used to hard work.

I plucked the note from my desk and ordered an Uber. I spent the car ride glued to my phone, answering emails, ordering printer paper, and confirming Leah's annual checkup with her dermatologist tomorrow.

I assured myself I was okay.

It's just another Valentine's Day. You've survived three of them since Kellan did what he did.

This would be the fourth.

Of course, nothing screamed "I'm not okay" more than telling yourself that you were okay.

The sedan stopped at the curb of a neo-Gothic building. Tall and looming. The driver tossed me a pearly smile. "That's you. Happy Valentine's Day."

"Fat chance," I mumbled, tipping him on the app before my butt left his polyester seats.

I walked into a boutique hospital on 57th Street called Morgan-

Dunn. Supposedly, the city's elite liked to have their babies here because the rooms were more luxurious than in the Waldorf Astoria.

To secure an ob-gyn at this in-house facility, you needed to take your place on a three-year waiting list. This information had come courtesy of Reagan. My twenty-two-year-old self had nothing to do with babies, pregnancies, or—hopefully—hospitals.

I signed my name at the security area, took the elevator to the fourth floor, and poured myself into a sleek clinic. I'd never seen anything that screamed RICH so loud in capital letters, and I'd lived in New York my entire life, save for my college days in Kentucky.

Black-rimmed, shadowy glass doors complimented cherry accents, upholstered brown leather couches, and plush recliners. The reception desk was wave-shaped, made of curved, dark wood. Rows of baskets held loose-leaf tea, snacks, and bottled water in the luxurious lobby, along with prenatal gummy bears and a variety of goodie bags.

A stick-thin woman in a suit stood behind the glossy desk, her brunette hair pulled back so severely, it stretched her forehead tight. She greeted me with a barely tolerating smile. "How can I help you?"

"I'm here to set up an appointment on behalf of my boss, Miss Reagan Rothschild." I passed her Reagan's insurance card.

The receptionist's frozen smile remained intact as she scanned it, clicking away on her Mac. She handed back the card. "I'm afraid I'm not at liberty to schedule any appointments for Dr. Marchetti today."

Dr. Marchetti? I tried hard not to let his name rattle me.

Marchetti is a common last name, right? Besides, I assured myself, *everything reminds you of Kellan. Especially on Valentine's Day. You're just reading into things.*

"Miss Rothschild has been trying to reach him all day. It's kind of serious, which is why I'm here." My right foot started rocking. I'd yet to let Reagan down, and I definitely wasn't about to start today.

"I understand that, but Dr. Marchetti is currently unreachable."

"Is he not in the office?"

I knew that the doctor was a he because Reagan once shared with me and the other girls she employed that every time she came from an exam, her panties looked like the bottom of a birdcage. Apparently, he was out-of-this-world, Hollywood hot.

"No, he's here. He just doesn't take appointments or calls on Valentine's Day. Only urgent cases."

Spoiled brat.

For what Reagan paid this clinic each visit, he should not only be at her disposal on an hourly basis but give birth to the babies himself.

I lost my patience. "Well, consider Miss Rothschild's case urgent."

"Is she in labor?"

"No."

"Does she have any cramps? Spotting? Is she feeling weak or lethargic?"

I considered saying yes, but then remembered that if I lied, I could snag an appointment from someone who actually did have these symptoms. And since Reagan had dubbed this guy Dr. Miracle for his specialty in high-risk pregnancies, this scenario wasn't farfetched.

But what could I say? That my boss was super farty?

"No." I cleared my throat. "However..."

"I'm sorry. You will have to wait until tomorrow."

"But he's here." I wanted to throttle her. Him, too. I couldn't fail Reagan. I had to get this appointment for her.

"Yes, but he isn't done."

"Done with what?" I resisted the urge to stomp, exasperated.

"I don't know."

Instead of strangling her, I smiled. "Fine. I'll wait. Which one is his office?"

The receptionist pointed at the middle of the three doors facing the lobby. I nodded, grabbed my bag, and sat with it in my line of sight. I excelled at the waiting game. Bonus points: I got to work while I did it.

I ignored her wrinkled nose as I produced the manuscript from earlier and continued reading the small-town, tragic novel a prospective client had sent us. My eyes drifted to the office door of the mysterious Dr. Marchetti every few seconds. He was probably playing solitaire, the jerk.

Forty-five minutes after I'd arrived at the clinic, the receptionist twisted her face in my direction. I could tell she hated my presence, but she couldn't kick me out.

"I need to go to the bathroom," she announced to the empty room.

I looked up from the manuscript. "Good luck?"

She shot me a dark look. "I'll be right back."

"I'll be waiting."

She pointed a manicured nail at me. "Don't knock on his door."

"You have my word."

The minute Brunette Barbie was out of sight, I jumped up from my seat and practically lunged myself at the guy's office. A golden sign hung on the wall, but I couldn't read it when I was all the way across the room.

Now I could.

Tatum Marchetti, MD.

The name descended on me like the entire sky, hammering me to the ground.

Tatum.

Tate Marchetti.

As in, Kellan's brother. As in, the asshole who had a hand in making Kellan hurl himself off of St. Paul's roof exactly four years ago.

What were the odds?

Not horribly bad, a vicious voice inside me snapped.

In high school, I'd never bothered checking who Tate was or what he did for a living. I'd never googled him or asked Kellan. I just knew he worked insane hours and night shifts.

Now it all made sense—he was a doctor. And he was here. A door away. The man I'd wanted to strangle from the moment Kellan entered my life. Eight years and counting. My hatred for him had time to stew, build, simmer, and flourish.

My throat rolled with a swallow, and my eyes narrowed at the door.

I was not a reckless person. Everything I did was planned to the finest detail. Especially since The Night Of. But the realization that Kellan's brother was here undid every single positive trait I'd honed after that fateful night.

My fingers curled over the doorknob. I waited for my sensible side to tell me to stop. To turn around. To come to my senses.

Silence.

I flung the door open without knocking (I'd promised Miss Bitch I wouldn't).

Took a step inside.

Froze in my spot.

I blinked, trying to digest the scene I'd walked into. A sheet of long blonde hair cascaded down a deep-cherry desk in waves. The owner of the hair had her mouth open in an O-shape, her eyes squeezed in pleasure and concentration as the man between her legs thrusted into her ruthlessly. One of her tan legs wrapped around his waist. The other extended over his shoulder.

He was fully clothed in dark cigarette pants and a matching cashmere sweater that highlighted his insanely muscular physique.

He was also looking straight at me.

I met his eyes disobediently. The woman he was screwing was still oblivious to my presence. After all, I hadn't knocked.

Blood rushed up from my neck to my cheeks. My face grew impossibly hot. A slow, taunting smirk spread over his lips. I realized two horrific things at the same time:

1) He looked exactly like an older version of Kellan. Unruly auburn hair, tousled and glossy, light gray eyes, and the angular cheekbones of a titan. No, he was not Hollywood hot. He was deity-hot. He was screw-your-life-up hot.

And 2) He enjoyed me being here, watching. A lot.

Every bone in my body screamed at me to turn and run away before I got arrested. Or maybe he'd be the one getting arrested for sexual harassment. I didn't know, but I felt strongly that one of us should be handcuffed and not just for funsies. Only, I wanted to rattle him like he rattled me, so I stayed rooted in my spot.

"Yes, Tatum! Yes! I'm coming. Fuck, I'm coming. Oh. Oh. Tatum. Tatum," the woman screamed, her eyes squeezed shut in pleasure.

Tate brought his hand between the two of them, sliding his thumb into her. He slipped it into his mouth, sucked the juices, and freed the finger with a pop. "You like that?" his husky, low voice snarled.

Chills ran up and down my arms. My eyes narrowed at him.

No, I hate it.

"Yes!" the woman wailed, but it wasn't her he'd asked.

He thrust harder and deeper, hitting a spot that made her whimper again and again. To my horror, I felt myself squeezing my thighs against nothing. My nipples were hard, and for the first time in years, I thanked my lucky stars I was so flat-chested I had to wear a padded bra.

"Fuckkkkk," she cried, obviously not satisfied until everyone in this zip code knew she'd reached her climax.

She is coming. I am watching her come.

What was wrong with me?

Everything.

Everything was wrong with me.

But turning around would be letting him win, and I didn't want to let Tate Marchetti win.

She became limp as he pumped into her, finding his own release. His climax hit different. Straitlaced and unruffled. He didn't let go. Just released a little, polite grunt, then moved a few inches away from her, yanked the condom off, and tossed it into the trash at the side of the desk.

He reached for a silver tissue box, wiping himself off—her privates shielding his—and tucking himself back in. He was still staring at me. Our eyes had never wavered from one another.

The woman opened her eyes slowly. Her hazel pupils found my green ones. "What the hell?" Her brows shot skyward, body jolting upright.

Tate stepped aside, fully clothed. He didn't look like he'd just had sex. His cheeks weren't flushed, his clothes not rumpled. He looked like he could step into an operating theater and perform an open-heart surgery with steady hands. She, on the other hand, looked like she'd just gotten back from a weekend-long orgy and had forgotten to shower.

Tate leaned against his desk, sliding his fists into his front pockets as he crossed his ankles. "Can I help you?" He raised an eyebrow, bone-chillingly nonchalant.

There was no point in telling myself I was okay anymore. I was one-hundred percent about to blow a gasket. I opened my mouth to yell at him until I lost my voice when the receptionist stormed into the room.

She pushed me aside as if I were racing in his direction with a weapon. "Dr. Marchetti, I'm so sorry. She said she wouldn't knock on your door. She gave me her word!"

"I didn't break my word." I glowered at her, crossing my arms over my chest. "I walked right in. There was no knocking involved."

Shockingly, it made him chuckle. A deep chuckle I could feel in my stomach. I wanted to kill this guy.

"You asked if you can help." I turned back to him. "You can."

He threw me a half-moon smile of the Kellan variety. I was drowning in nostalgia. It was hard to breathe.

"Ever heard of sarcasm?" He spoke around that easy grin.

"Yeah. It's the lowest form of wit."

That awarded me another amused chuckle. "Watching two strangers fucking is the lowest form of etiquette. I'll take cheap wit over bad manners every day of the week."

Yup. He's just as horrible as Kellan said he was.

I ignored his jab. "I'm here on behalf of my boss, Reagan Rothschild. She wants to schedule an appointment for today, but can't seem to reach you."

And your receptionist is as cooperative as a suicide bomber.

The blonde woman behind him, who was currently arranging her designer dress in place, huffed. "Are you for real?"

I shot her a leveled look. "Totally real. Are you?"

I might or might not have been referring to her breasts.

"I'm calling security." The receptionist stomped her heel, but she still looked at Tate for confirmation.

He cocked his head sideways, assessing me like I was a delivery box with no return address. Suspicious in a thrilling way. "Don't. She amuses me."

Which, in addition to the used condom visible through the metal basket, told me everything I needed to know. That he didn't give a shit about whether he maintained a professional appearance. Reagan had authors like that. Too talented to care about manners.

I bared my teeth. "I'm not a circus monkey."

"No." He drummed his long fingers over his desk. "They are trained. You are not."

An hour ago, I'd thought I couldn't possibly hate Tate Marchetti more than I already did based on what had happened with Kellan. Now, I knew I could. It's true what they say. Sometimes the sky really is the limit. In Tate's case—he was unfathomably unlikeable.

I jerked my finger at the iPad in front of him. "Just book Miss Rothschild an appointment and let's get it over with."

"Sylvia, go back to your station. Allison, it's been a pleasure, all puns intended." He dismissed the two women with a wave of his hand.

It surprised me how quickly they slinked away. He obviously enjoyed the treatment of a king inside these walls. Mainly, I felt glad for that Hannah chick he'd been about to marry several years ago. She'd dodged a deadly bullet.

The door closed with a polite click. It was just the two of us. My panic danced behind my ribcage like a fly caught in a cobweb.

"All right, let's see, Miss...?" he trailed off.

"Richards."

"Do you always burst into places where you are not welcome?"

I thought of Leah. I was never welcome anywhere. "Only when I

61

don't care what the people inside them think of me." I smiled sweetly. "And just for your information, holding someone's gaze when you are inside someone else is ill-mannered."

He smirked. "I'm sorry. Did I give you the impression I was trying to impress you?"

I put a hand to my heart, pretending to swoon. "Such a gentleman."

"Darling, you cannot afford the sum people pay to see my gentlemanly side."

How had Kellan survived him for four years? I couldn't even stand him for ten minutes.

Tate grabbed his iPad, his eyes on the screen. I hoped he'd finally decided to do us both a favor and book Reagan an appointment, but after long seconds where I stood there and he ignored me, he clipped, "Get out of my office, Miss Richards."

"But the appointment..."

"I don't take appointments today. Tell Ms. Rothschild to call me tomorrow."

"You have to." But I knew he didn't, and that caused the panicked fly in the cobweb to make the mistake of thrashing uncontrollably, losing energy as the spider dove in for the kill. "I've waited here for over an hour."

"You also walked in on me balls deep inside someone else and didn't bother apologizing, not to mention you made a Netflix special out of it. Leave."

"Tate..."

"Dr. Marchetti," he amended. "I'm not your playdate."

My eyes widened at his chiseled face. He didn't return my gaze.

"You're shocking." I sounded like my mother. Well, my late mother. But it was true.

"I am?" he asked, not an ounce of interest in his dry tone.

"Yes."

"How so?"

"You're a doctor who is doing amazing things, but you're a complete bastard."

"I wasn't always a bastard, but the alternative fell short." He shrugged, his eyes still on his iPad.

I tried not to cry, but these weren't sad tears, which were manageable. These were angry tears, and they burned the backs of my eyeballs.

"Would it help if I apologized?"

I really had no desire to, but pride aside, I might not have a choice. I wanted this job. I wanted to keep Reagan happy. And I really didn't want her to not have this appointment because I'd somehow screwed this up.

As much as I hated Tate Marchetti, being rude to him would not bring Kellan back.

Finally, he dragged his eyes up from his screen, a scowl on his face. He looked like a perfume model. His eyes were fossil gray, like foamy water.

"It wouldn't help if you sucked my cock and sang the alphabet backward simultaneously, Miss Richards. Now, let me repeat myself for the third and final time: Get. Out."

One tear betrayed me. It slid down my cheek, exploding on my upper lip. I threw caution to the wind and did something else out of character for me—I said whatever was on my mind, consequences be damned.

"I can see why he hated you so much. You're loathsome. Doesn't matter how many women you go to bed with every night. I hope the last thing you think about when you close your eyes is the fact that your brother hated you enough that he chose death over living under your roof. Happy Valentine's Day, asshole."

I turned around and slammed his door, not waiting for his reaction. I took the stairs down to the ground floor. I didn't even care about the assignment Reagan had given me.

All I cared about was my hate for Tate Marchetti.

I hailed a cab and headed straight home.

Buried my face in my pillow.

Cried myself to sleep.

Chapter Sixteen

Tate

Iwoke up every Valentine's Day thinking today would've been an excellent day to not wake up. Not in a suicidal way. I could read the signs accurately—in fucking retrospect—but in an I-don't-want-to-deal-with-this-shit resignation.

Usually, the feeling subsided by four or five when I had a few drinks in me and my dick had been sufficiently wet. Not today. Today, I would happily put a bullet through my head and not even care about the crème Persian carpet the Dutch interior designer had placed in my office last week that cost more than my car.

Little Miss Richards knew Kellan.

The writing was on the wall, smeared in her glittery goddamn lipstick. First, she'd called me Tate. Kellan had been the only person to ever call me Tate. To everyone else, I was Dr. Marchetti, Dr. Miracle, or Tatum.

Second, she looked to be around the same age Kellan should have been today. Twenty-two. Someone from his school. But it was the third thing that made me jump out of my skin and chase her like a cheetah. The thing she'd said about Kellan hating me.

She knew him.

Over the years, I'd come to terms with the fact that my brother had no friends at St. Paul. I'd been aware of his social issues, but he'd downplayed them, and I'd been too self-absorbed to read a parenting book or watch Dr. Phil to see the signs.

Kellan had made up people he hung out with—whom I later found out didn't exist—so I would get off his case. It was only after his death that I learned how truly lonely he was in high school.

I'd thought he didn't have any friends. What if he had one? What if he had her? What if he confided in her? If she was my in, my opening, my connection to him?

I hunted Miss Richards after she stormed out. Sylvia called after me when she spotted me hitting the elevator buttons like I was trying to knock the lights out of them. Allison was nowhere to be seen. Not surprised. She knew the drill.

"She took the stairs," Sylvia cried out. "Did she steal something?"

Yeah. My goddamn mind.

I tailed Richards' ass, taking the steps two at a time. I almost got to her. Almost. I even caught the wisp of her chocolate hair as she breezed through the automatic glass doors of the building. She wore a long, black-and-white striped dress and army boots.

Like a fucking kid.

She is a kid, and you just spent the last five minutes of your fuck pretending it was her you were inside.

Before I could reach her, she slid into a yellow cab and zipped away.

"Dammit," I growled, stomping on the concrete and punching the building for good measure. My knuckles bled, but the pain didn't register. I fished my phone out and dialed Reagan Rothschild's number.

She answered on the first ring. "Good afternoon, Dr. Marchetti! I assume you've met my assistant?"

Sure as hell did.

"Correct."

"Great, so when is my appointment today?"

Her appointment. Right. That was why Miss Richards had burst into my office, guns blazing. Gotta hand it to her—it took ovaries to torpedo into a room uninvited and outstay your welcome while watching two people going at it.

I ran a palm through my hair, tugging at the roots. "How's early tomorrow?"

"Not a problem."

"Come see me at ten."

I was one-hundred percent certain I had a C-section scheduled for ten. I'd figure it out if I made it till tomorrow without committing a murder.

"Fantastic! Is there anything else you wanted?"

Yes. Your assistant in a cage, so I can cross-examine her in ways that'd make the Spanish Inquisition look like Sesame Street.

"I think your assistant forgot something at my clinic. How can I get it to her?"

"You can send a courier to my office. Have your receptionist email her the invoice."

"The thing she forgot is of a personal nature." It sounded like bullshit, even to my own ears. What could she have forgotten that was so private I had to hand it over in person? Her goddamn vibrator? "What's your address?" I used my cordial, sane, doctor voice.

"Hmm. That's weird. She just texted me that she's working from home for the rest of the day. That is so unlike her."

I didn't care what she was like. I cared that she apparently had answers to questions that had been brewing inside me for four years. "Will she be there tomorrow?" It took every ounce of patience I had left not to snap.

"She better be." Reagan snorted. "Let me text you my office address."

"Thanks."

"Are you sure I can't pick it up tomorrow when I see you?"

"Positive."

"Are you maybe a tiny bit infatuated with my little anime princess?"

I didn't know what anime was, and I definitely was not interested in finding out. "She's young enough to be my daughter."

"Not quite."

"I assure you, I have no romantic interest in your assistant."

"Should I be concerned about what she left behind?"

The word *yes* rolled on the tip of my tongue. I could screw Miss Richards over the way she had me. But at the end of the day, I couldn't risk her resenting me even more than she already did, because I needed answers from her.

"No. It's fine."

"She's a gem, isn't she?" Reagan purred. "I love her. Such a sweet girl."

"Sure," I said, tromping back to my office, hitting the red button on my phone to end the call. My knuckles dripped blood all over the limestone floor. "Such a fucking delight."

Chapter Seventeen

Tate

Here's a lesson I learned at an early age—if there's a rabbit hole to fall into, a Marchetti man would find a way to get sucked in.

Later that night, my poor excuse for a father sat across from me for our annual Valentine's Day meal. One of the rare times I saw him unless he ran out of money, blow, or people to cry to.

We'd started the tradition after Kellan died, and I'd be lying if I said I found it comforting. It was more of a checkup to make sure we were both still alive. Misery, like self-destruction, ran in our genes.

"He ever tell you he had a girlfriend?" I asked Terry, cutting up my turkey patty. I used a company that pre-prepared meals for me to heat.

I needed something packed with nutritional value, vegetables, and protein, and I needed it fresh. It cost three hundred bucks a week, but that was not a problem, seeing as I no longer had to put Kellan through college. Lucky me.

Kellan never got to discover just how broke our father had become. One less embarrassment to carry to his grave.

Terry didn't glance up from his plate, either. "No." He cleared his throat. "Pretty unlikely, though. We would have known."

"Would we?" I cut the meat into more tiny pieces, dismembering it until it became inedible. "We made quite a pair raising the poor guy. I ran into this girl today. I think she knew him. At the very least, he seemed to have confided in her."

That made his head shoot up with interest. "What did she say?"

Guilty much?

"Nothing yet. I'm going to look into it."

"So you should." He bit into... whatever the hell it was I'd served us both. Food was like sex. I pretended to be interested in it to save face.

I took a hard look at my sperm donor. He'd changed. More so after Kellan died. He looked older. Big and pasty, with a pink nose and ruddy cheeks, courtesy of years of alcohol abuse. Crazy white hair sprung from his scalp in every direction like snakes. Protective black braces covered his wrists, from decades of writing millions of words and deleting them. He needed a brush, a shower, three years in rehab, and a clue. If he'd been useless when I took Kellan from him, now he was one thousand percent toast.

"All of this wouldn't have happened if—" he started, like I knew he would.

I cut him off, dropping my knife and fork on my plate. "Don't go there. You dumped him on my doorstep and ran to Miami with one of your whores."

"Her name was Nadia."

"Her name could be the Duchess of Sussex, and it still wouldn't change the fact that you left your goddamn kid to raise your other kid." I slapped the table. The utensils rattled. The wine glasses danced across the tablecloth.

He stopped eating and looked up at me, his eyes wide. I saw my reflection in them.

I bulldozed forward. "You made me step into your shoes when I was fresh out of med school, doing my residency. You let me do your job while you chased tail and got hammered like a frat boy. I wasn't perfect, but if someone's gonna tell me where I went wrong, it sure as hell won't be you."

We both knew it didn't really matter. I carried the guilt with me like an honor badge. That was why the girl's words sliced so deep.

I didn't accept any calls or make any appointments on Valentine's Day because it was a day for me to take a long, torturous vacation in Guiltville. Today's menu consisted of day-drinking, followed by fucking my ex-fiancée's best friend Allison, followed by being a world-class douchebag to Miss Richards (side note: what's her first name, anyway?) before figuring out she knew Kel. Spending time with my parasitic father was the undigested kernel of corn on the shit cake.

Terry pushed his plate away. "Do you have anything stronger to drink around here?" He sniffed the air, scratching behind his ear. "Wine's not cutting it." He should go back to coke. It always put him in a merry, good mood. He would, too, if he could afford the habit. Alas, bailing on the three-book contract he'd signed had made a hole the shape of a middle finger in his bank account. That was what happened when you blew all your movie-deal money on hookers, drugs, and wild weekends with actresses who got paid triple what you made in your life for a coffee machine commercial.

"Knock yourself out." I gestured to the bar in the corner. If he wanted to ruin what was left of his liver, it was his funeral.

Standing, I retired upstairs. I passed Kellan's room. Still untouched from four years ago. I stopped, putting my hand to the door without opening it. I wondered who would be the first to set foot in it. The realtor when I finally sold this nightmare of a house? A new housekeeper who would forget about my no-touching-anything-Kellan-related rule and vacuum the place? A goddamn earthquake? It didn't matter. Could be a rat, and it'd still hurt like a motherfucker.

Kellan was good, and he died too young. I was bad, and every day I lived was a middle finger from the devil. I turned away from the door, slipping into my bedroom. My head hit the pillow. I gaped at the ceiling like I'd entered a staring contest, knowing I wouldn't win. Sleep wouldn't come.

They say time dulls the pain.

They lie.

Guilt is pain's fuel, and it rekindles it every time the flame fades.

Chapter Eighteen

Tate

She left her office at six thirty-five, waving the doorman goodbye with a smile.

I sat in a coffee shop across the street, watching the building like I didn't have a twelve-million-dollar-a-year practice to run. I'd been here since five, just to be on the safe side.

For the pleasure of stalking young Miss Richards, I'd pushed back a check-up appointment, along with two IVF treatments, and there was a thoroughly upset heiress three centimeters dilated in her room in Morgan-Dunn, wondering where the hell her doctor was. Watching a barely-out-of-puberty agent assistant get off work was probably the answer she was not expecting to hear.

I dropped a few coins into a fund-my-backpacking-trip tip mug and made my way across the street to catch the little firecracker before she sizzled into the subway. My eyes didn't waver from her frame. It gave me the opportunity to assess her.

Miss Richards wore her brown hair in a purposefully messy, trendy, fuck-you-I'm-from-New-York way, with side-swept bangs. Thick, dramatic eyebrows framed her green eyes. A black beret perched on her head, tilted sideways, like an artist. I wanted to tell her she was not, in fact, an artist. Although I didn't know. Maybe she was.

Did I want to pick a fight with this woman?

Yes. Yes, I did.

She was curvy and small and kissed by youth's beauty—smooth skin, delicate neck, and dainty ankles. Her hot feline reading glasses, black dress, and red plaid leggings made her look like she'd stepped out of a No Doubt music video. She was the kind of girl Kellan would have liked.

A whole-fucking lot.

I crossed the street at a red light before the subway entrance swallowed her. A car nearly slammed into me, stopping at the last minute. I slapped the hood at the same time the driver honked for ten seconds straight.

"Learn how to walk, moron!" he roared.

"Learn how to drive, dipshit." I gave him an unsolicited tip of my own, saluting him with my middle finger.

His mouth dropped open, but I was already gone. Running in Miss Richards' direction. Hoping the fact that I'd seen her boss earlier this morning—albeit after Reagan had waited an hour and a half while I performed a C-section—had been reported back to her.

My little showdown with the driver had caught her attention, along with half the street's. She stood in the entrance of the subway, staring at me with a mixture of shock and disgust.

Join the club, kid. I'm not my number-one fan, either.

"What are you doing here?" She scowled. A beauty spot sat between her nose and lip. Very film noir. Artistic Kellan must've had a hard-on for this girl.

"I didn't know you owned Manhattan. Mind giving me a map of streets I can walk on?"

My answer defied all logic. I needed her to warm up to me, not reach atomic levels of resentment. It was hard to be nice once you fell into the habit of being a dick.

Her hate-o-meter dinged as her eyes narrowed at me. She pivoted, resuming her journey toward the subway. When she descended the stairs,

I followed her. I'd started feeling like a creep about an hour ago after I'd showed up in front of her workplace, challenging my inner Joe Goldberg. But now the feeling bled into full-blown pervert territory, thrusting me deep into the Jeffrey Dahmer zone.

I couldn't follow her home.

Correction: I preferred not to.

It appeared to be exactly what I was doing.

"Fine," I said as she breezed through the turnstile.

I hopped over the one next to her, committing my second misdemeanor in the last ten minutes. The first was jaywalking. I'd lost my damn mind. I should be pinning a photo of my brain with cutouts of my number on trees around my neighborhood right about now.

And still, I continued, "My behavior yesterday might have been uncalled for."

"Your existence is uncalled for."

She hopped on the escalators. I stood beside her. She shook her head, scrolling through her phone. People grunted behind us.

I dropped my voice. "Look, I have questions."

"The answer to all of them is no."

"Then one of them is, 'Would you mind it very much if we talked about Kellan for a few minutes?'"

"Ha. Ha," she deadpanned, but I wasn't laughing. "Go. Away."

The grunting behind me intensified. I never took the subway, and now I remembered why. Other than the fact that it smelled like a public toilet, BO, and clinical depression, it was also a hostile environment.

"Not until you give me some answers after the bomb you dropped in my office yesterday."

A guy in a hoodie tapped my shoulder. "Hey, can you hit on this fine ass standing on the right side of the escalator like a goddamn New Yorker? People are trying to pass through."

I shifted to the right side, two steps below Miss Richards. Which reminded me...

"What's your name, anyway?"

My nose was level with her head. She smelled like sugar cookies and cypress. Maybe even coconut. More importantly—not like stale piss.

"None of your business."

"Cute name. Artsy parents?"

"Dead parents," she gritted out. "You're bothering me."

I told myself her parents were not really dead, so I could keep pestering her with a clear conscience. "Give me what I want, and I'll leave you alone."

Her head snapped in my direction, her dramatic eyebrows pinched together in anger. "Kellan was right."

It hit like a bullet to the gut, but I smiled through the pain. Cocky and unaffected and everything I was known for. The aloof, charming ob-gyn with the bronze heart.

She stormed to the platform.

I tailed her.

My patience, already a rare commodity, evaporated. Her train arrived, and Miss Richards stepped in. I did the same. I had no idea where we were headed. Hopefully Hell, so I could have the home-field advantage.

I realized on the train that, excluding the month after Kellan's death, I hadn't done anything out of character or off my schedule for at least a decade. Yet, I took the seat next to her.

She tugged a stack of papers from her leather briefcase. A manuscript. She uncapped a yellow highlighter with her teeth and struck a line on the page in her lap.

"If I were you, I would cooperate," I said through a tight-lipped smile, aware of the fact that people were watching us. Getting arrested for harassment would be the kiss of death to my career. Living without answers, however, seemed like a bigger punishment.

She flipped a page in the manuscript, forcing me to switch to the not-so-nice method. Clearly, I should have gone that route the minute I'd found her. There were not a lot of opportunities to salvage a relationship that began with you staring into a woman's eyes while coming deep inside another.

"I guess you leave me no choice but to tell your boss you flung my door open yesterday, caught me having sex, and decided to make yourself comfortable and watch." I took out my phone and began texting Reagan Rothschild.

Miss Richards snapped her head up in horror. "Wait."

Bingo.

My thumbs kept flying across my iPhone. She should have knocked on my door as soon as I'd lost him. No one had come to talk to me and Terry, other than Principal Brooks and a couple of guilt-ridden teachers who'd hardly even remembered anything significant about my brother.

Kellan had died, and not one of his peers came to offer their condolences.

She slapped her hand over my phone. I dragged my eyes up to meet hers. She averted her gaze.

Guilty.

"Where can we talk?" I demanded.

She flinched. I wanted to shake the answers out of her. I didn't even know why I cared so much. Finding out what made him do this wouldn't bring him back. A part of me just wanted to punish her for not offering her condolences.

Her forehead crumpled. "About Kellan?"

"No, about your fabulous beret. Your fashion choices charm me." I bared my teeth like a beast. "Of course, it's about Kellan." The way she stared at me, with enough hatred to freeze the sun, made me want to laugh in her face.

She thought I cared about her opinion of me. She thought I cared, period. I'd stopped caring the day he died. Threw myself into my work, not bothering to build a life outside of it.

"Well?" I popped an eyebrow.

"Fine. But not today."

"Why not?"

"I have plans."

What could be more important than Kellan?

"Elaborate."

She tipped her chin up. "I don't want to."

I fished my phone out and resumed my text to Reagan. Miss Richards slapped it away. It fell in my lap, and the lock screen image—of Kellan hiding behind a book, grinning—flashed.

I flipped the phone on its screen.

She sucked in a breath.

She saw.

"I'm taking my sister to the dermatologist," she answered, more softly. Which didn't make sense.

Most dermatologists in my building closed by five. Six, at the latest. But I didn't press on account of the fact that I didn't want to give her any reason to change her mind.

"Then when?"

"Tomorrow. There's a little café right across from my office—"

"I know the place," I shot out. "Time?"

I noticed her right leg was jumpy, rocking up and down. A nervous tick.

"Six."

"Now let's start over. Do you have a name, Miss Richards?"

"Charlotte. My name is Charlotte." She licked her lips. "I would say it's nice to meet you, but we both know that's not the case."

I got up and off the train without looking back at Charlotte.

"Wait," she called. "Shouldn't we exchange numbers or something?" I could practically hear her blush.

Rather than turning around, I exited the doors as I answered her. "No. I don't want anything to do with you after tomorrow."

Chapter Nineteen

Charlotte

"Yo, Char, what's good?" Jonah, my neighbor, offered me a fist bump when I hit the intersection between our respective doors. I was going in; he was going out.

I lived in Morris Heights. A far cry from dodgy Westchester Square, where Leah and I had moved after our parents passed away. Our new place was bigger. We had enough money for life not to suck majorly. We weren't swimming in it, but we didn't have to think twice before paying the bills or getting our weekly groceries.

Anything other than that was a luxury, but most of the time—between my salary and Leah working as a master aesthetician at an eyelash parlor in Times Square—we got by.

I bumped Jonah's fist, still shaking from my showdown with Tate Marchetti. "Seen better days. You?"

"Can't complain." He frowned, jerking my beret aside and ruffling my hair like I was a toddler. "Everything okay?"

He wore a broken-in leather jacket, ripped jeans, and biker boots. The light goatee, mechanic job, and muscles threatening to tear his tee gave him an overall Charlie Hunnam appeal every girl in the neighborhood was painfully aware of. He shared joint custody over his daughter

Rowling—yes, after the author—with his ex-wife.

"Nothing to worry about." *Just being stalked by a gorgeous, furious doctor.* "How about you? How's Rowling? Need someone to watch over her?"

Sometimes Jonah got called for special jobs over the weekend. When he did, he dropped Rowling at our place. We made sugar cookies and read books and went to the library together when Leah felt like putting her makeup on. Then Jonah came back with takeout food, a fizzy drink for Rowling, and beer for us. I hated to admit it, but weekends with Jonah and Row were the height of my social activity these days.

"Nah. It's Luanne's weekend. She's taking her somewhere fancy with her new boyfriend. Heard there's an ice-skating rink involved. Row's pumped for it. Actually, there is something I wanted to ask. There's this vintage car festival in Jersey this weekend. I have free tickets from work. I was thinking of hitting Leah up. If she's into that kind of thing, obviously." He ran his fingers through his longish hair. Black stained the insides of his nails.

I knew it was a test. Jonah wanted to know if it was even worth asking Leah out. It was no secret she wasn't really big on dating.

I slouched against my door, sucking my cheeks in. "Are you asking me if it's a good idea to ask her, or if she is available?"

He mimicked my body language, resting on his door, thumbs hooked inside the loops of his Levi's. Leah should be here any minute now. We were going to her dermatologist, who saw us after hours because my sister was too ashamed to show her face in public without makeup.

"Both."

"My guess is she doesn't have any plans for the weekend, but I can't tell you she'll go out with you. You know how it goes with Leah."

Jonah had never seen Leah without makeup. He'd never witnessed the gnarled skin under the coats of foundation, or the way the fire had nibbled at the tip of her ear, giving it an elf-shaped, pointy look.

He'd probably noticed the discoloration behind the foundation. The faint, purplish hue that adorned the right side of her face. But he didn't know what it looked like without the war paint.

"Has she gone out with anyone since the fire?"

I shook my head. "Not that I'm aware of."

"Hell."

"Pretty much."

"She's gorgeous." He tugged at his goatee, screwing his mouth sideways. "Hottest woman I know. No offense."

"None taken."

Leah was—and always would be—stunning. I guess people have two faces: the face the world sees, and the face they see in the mirror. The only thing Leah could see when she looked at herself was that night.

The jingle of keys two floors below announced Leah's arrival. The door whined open, then slammed shut.

I heard a small, familiar groan. "This baby fox is going to be the end of me. I'm the only bitch in the universe dumb enough to feed an urban fox," she muttered.

Jonah and I exchanged looks. I bit down on my lip to suppress a laugh. Jonah straight-up howled. That was the other thing about Leah. She was wonderful. Genuinely good-hearted and sweet.

We heard her ascending the stairs. She appeared on the third floor, clad in a canary turtleneck that hid as much of her skin as possible and tight leather pants. She held an empty container where she must've kept the food for that baby fox that had been roaming the park behind our building at night, searching for its mom.

She glanced between us, frowning. "You look like you're up to something fishy. Jonah, you know I will make a purse out of your nut sack if you get my baby sister into trouble."

Jonah snorted. "If anything, your baby sister will land my ass in trouble."

Leah raised her good eyebrow. The right one was nonexistent because of the scar. She did a good job painting it on when she left the house. You could hardly tell.

"My sister is a nerd," she said, with just enough malice. She loved me, but she didn't like me. "Anyway, you're too old for her. She's only twenty-two. You're what? Thirty?"

"Thirty-one. And you are twenty-seven," he replied.

For some reason, I thought about Tate. He should be in his mid-thirties. Then I thought about how much Leah would hate the idea of my dating someone in his thirties.

Not that I would ever date Tate.

"What does that have to do with anything?" Leah scowled. Like her being single or female had nothing to do with our conversation.

"Figure it out yourself, Teacup." He winked at her, looped his keys around his finger, and bolted down the stairway.

I turned to look at my sister. In the four years that had passed since I'd graduated from high school, we'd perfected the art of pretending we were okay. But deep inside, she would always resent me.

Resent me for making her take my parents' place when she was only eighteen.

Resent me for walking through fire to save me.

Resent me for killing Mom and Dad.

For looking less than perfect when she could have had her pick of any guy in the world before the flames ate at her beauty. Before the fire consumed her.

Leah rummaged in her fringed shoulder bag for her pack of smokes, tucking a menthol cigarette between her lips as we poured into our apartment.

"Did you notice he called you Teacup?" I asked.

Leah shrugged as she swaggered to her room, returning with makeup removal wipes. Her face needed to be completely bare when the dermatologist assessed her. She applied a ton of medical creams each day to minimize the damage to her skin and prevent it from falling apart.

She started shedding the caked makeup, the cigarette dangling between her lips. "Not really."

"I wonder why he'd call you that."

"Because I drink six cups of tea a day," Leah deadpanned. "Mystery solved. Leave the check in the mail."

I put the kettle on, making her some tea to-go before we left. "But how would he know that? You don't really hang out with him one-on-one, do you?"

"Maybe Row told him. We spend a lot of time with her."

"Why would he ask Row?" I fought a stupid grin, my heart swelling in my chest. For the first time in forty-eight hours, I was able to concentrate on something that wasn't Tate Marchetti. "I think Jonah's into you."

"I think you're high." Her healthy eyebrow curled into a question mark. "He's just being nice because he gets ten hours a week of free babysitting. The least he can do is be sweet and get takeout food." She ambled deeper into the long, narrow kitchen and opened the trash cabinet, disposing the wipes she'd used. "Anyway, I don't want to talk about Jonah. Let's hit the road."

The kettle whistled.

My right leg rocked.

"But don't you think he's... cute?"

"I think he's a gorgeous biker who is used to having women fall at his feet regularly and he wouldn't want to date a monster."

"You're wrong," I said with conviction, pouring hot water into her unicorn thermos. "He wants to ask you out this weekend. Should I tell him not to?"

Leah tilted her head, shooting me a look. Like the idea of her dating in her horrid physical condition was no less than appalling.

She puffed on her cigarette and shook her head. "Just make the damn tea, Charlotte."

Chapter Twenty

Charlotte

The next day crawled tauntingly slow. I wondered if Tate had thought about today as much as I had (probably). Then I wondered if Tate thought about what I thought when I thought about him (no chance whatsoever).

When the clock hit six, my stomach did an Olympic flip, and something heavy sank inside it. I looked around, trying to find reasons to stay at work. Reagan had left. So had Abigail and Irene, my other colleagues. I'd done all my tasks, everything remained tidy, and I knew that, no matter how hostile my feelings were toward Tate, he deserved answers about Kellan. It was time to face the music.

My legs were stone-heavy as I made my way to the coffee shop across the street. Guilt and rage swirled inside me like a whirlpool. Guilt, because I knew this meeting with Tate had been a long time coming. I'd never forgiven myself for not contacting him after Kellan died. I figured he and Terry would at least find it a bit comforting to know Kellan had one friend at school. But I never could bring myself to contact Tate because I was furious.

Which brought me to rage. I was angry with him. Angry about how he'd made Kellan feel and how he'd acted when we'd met each other at his office. It was like he'd validated every terrible thing Kellan had said about him.

The overhead bell jingled as I entered the coffee shop. It was a neighborhood joint, inspired by Central Perk from *Friends*. Cozy couches, bucket-sized colorful mugs, and posters of local bands and standup shows around this block.

I untangled my scarf from my neck and glanced around. I didn't have to look long to spot him. He sat alone in the far corner of the room. A dark, formidable force perched on a ridiculous yellow recliner, his hands bracing the armrests like a king on his throne. So tall, his knees brushed the round coffee table in front of him.

He wore a black turtleneck that clung to his ridiculous biceps and gray cigarette pants. He looked like porn in loafers.

When he caught sight of me, he stood and motioned me over. My eyes dragged up to his face. He didn't look cocky or nonchalant. None of the things he'd oozed the first time I'd seen him at his office. The fuck-you air electrifying everything around him.

No. He looked like a shadowy cloud that was about to crack and hail directly on me.

I made my way toward him, ripping the beret from my head and dumping it on the table. My mouth was so dry, my tongue stuck to its roof. Should I shake his hand? Hug him? As weird as it sounded, it felt like we had something that connected us. Kellan.

"What can I get you?" Tate asked.

"Coffee is fine."

"How do you take your coffee?"

With a side of heart attack if we don't finish this soon.

"Americano. No sugar. No cream." I definitely took my coffee with both. But it felt wrong bothering him with mundane things like Sweet'N Low when we were about to have such a heavy conversation.

I sat in front of his recliner. Tate returned with a steaming cup of coffee and the barista's number, which she'd scribbled on a leaflet. He placed the coffee in front of me and balled the digits, throwing them into the trash. I rocked my right leg and avoided his gaze as he took his seat.

He cut right to the chase. "Were you ever going to come forward and tell me about him if we hadn't met through Reagan?"

"Probably not," I said honestly, remembering that he enjoyed my rebellious streak. "He wasn't your biggest fan. I didn't think you deserved it."

He nodded, surprisingly mild about it. "What about my sperm donor? Was Kellan not fond of him, either?"

I shook my head, unsurprised he referred to his father by that nickname. "No. With Terry, I didn't come forward because I decided he was an asshole all by myself. It was an executive decision."

He almost smiled. Just a ghost of one. "Let's start from the beginning. How'd you guys know each other?"

"We met at St. Paul." I cupped the mug of coffee in my hands, stealing its heat. "I met Kellan around February of eighth grade. We clicked."

I'd decided last night, while tossing and turning in bed, to be selective about what I said to Tate. I wouldn't lie, but I planned on bending the truth where appropriate. It didn't matter whether Tatum was an ass. If yesterday had proved anything, it was that he cared for Kellan. The man chased me down a subway.

"How'd you two meet?"

On the roof.

"In a classroom. He came there to..." *End his life.* "... think, and I came there for the same reason. We got to talking. We were both pretty down at the time. We weren't expecting each other. I guess we forgot our armor in the hallway."

I couldn't tell him we'd met on the rooftop. Not when Kellan had taken his life there. Tate was smart. He would put two and two together and figure out the symbolism of it. My place in this.

But also, allowing Tate a deep-dive into Kellan's life felt like an invasion of Kellan's privacy. A betrayal of his trust. It wasn't like I could ask Kellan for permission to spill his deepest, darkest secrets, so I made the choice for him to share the least amount possible while still giving his brother closure.

"How bad was it? His depression?" Tate asked. The pain marring his face was so raw, it sucked the breath out of me.

"He wasn't happy." I took a sip of my coffee. It tasted like sewer water. Bitter and muddy. I put it down. "After we met that first time, we became friends. I would give him books to read, and he would give me short stories he wrote. He was a magnificent wordsmith."

Tate stared at me like we were still at war. Maybe we were. "He hated me," Tate said. A statement. Not a question.

I shrugged. It was not untrue.

Tate sat back, running a hand over his chiseled jaw. There was something very dark and decadent about him. Like if I unzipped his beautiful skin, his impossibly light-gray eyes, kissable mouth, and the body he'd worked so hard on, all I'd find was ice.

"He thought I tore him and Terry apart," Tate said, more to himself than to me. He called him Terry, not Dad. Somehow, I wasn't surprised. Still better than Sperm Donor.

"Didn't you?"

Tate frowned. "A couple of years after Kellan's mother died, Terry called me at four in the morning. Said raising a kid was above his pay grade. He just wasn't made for the whole parenting gig. It was either him dropping Kellan off at my place or shipping him off to boarding school. I wasn't close to Kellan—we're half-brothers, over a decade apart in age— but I knew he was majorly hurting because of what happened with his mom. I was just starting out my residency, working insane hours. But I couldn't let Terry dump this kid at some fancy-ass institute upstate. The next day, I broke the lease on my apartment, found the closest thing I could to a single-family house, and moved Kellan in. Our sperm donor dropped him off on my doorstep on his way to Miami to party with a European model who promised to suck his cock for a small role in one of his movie adaptations. Spoiler alert: she didn't get the gig."

His words cut me into ribbons of hurt, and my body folded like origami. I tried to cover up my cough by taking a sip of the disgusting coffee. Kellan hadn't known that.

"Why didn't you explain this to Kellan?"

"Lies hurt. Truth slays. It would've destroyed him to learn the truth about his father."

"If you weren't the one who asked for him, then why did you file for full custody over Kellan?"

Tate stared at me like I was wearing a fruit bowl on my head, and something clicked.

Of course.

"I didn't."

"That's what Kellan told me."

"That's what Terry told him." If looks could kill, I'd be getting out of here in a body bag. Tate's stare-game was no joke. "Terry's always been a cop-out. Not that I wouldn't have gotten custody had I needed to. As it happened, Terry never showed any interest in raising Kel."

I wasn't sure if he was telling me whatever he wanted me to hear to squeeze more information out of me or if this was his honest truth. I knew Kellan wasn't a liar. But I also knew Kellan had been a teenage boy hurting badly. He'd seen life through dark-tinted glasses, smeared by the consequences of being the child of two messed-up cultural icons.

"Kellan said you started monitoring his time with Terry."

I pressed my lips together, but my resentment toward Tate started to dissolve like smoke. Everything he said made sense. Why would a young, hungry doctor doing his residency be so hell-bent on winning custody over his half-brother, whom he barely knew? It made no sense.

"Did Kellan also mention Terry gave him pot and E?" Tate's brewing-storm eyes turned a shade darker.

"No, he didn't mention that."

He ran his tongue over his bottom teeth. "Yeah. Didn't think so."

"There were rumors around school that Kellan was using drugs," I admitted, "but I never confronted him about it. I knew he'd cage in on me, and I didn't want to lose him as a friend."

"He got high frequently. The first thing I did when I got home from work every night was raid his room, bathroom, and kitchen to find his stash. I'd flush it down the drain. His toilet bowl saw more drugs than Ozzy Osbourne. I'd monitor his phone with apps and drive around the school after a double shift at the hospital, eyes bloodshot, just to see where he was. Worst part was, Terry helped him score. After I realized Kellan was paying Terry lunch money, I started sending him to school with prepackaged meals. Thought maybe if that parasite didn't have the money incentive, he'd stop feeding his son drugs. The more I tried to help Kellan, the more he pushed me away."

I hadn't expected any of this. Learning how much Tate cared. How it wasn't his fault. I could see why Kellan had wanted to pin this on him. Being rejected by your only parent was a tougher pill to swallow than hating your control-freak half-brother you barely knew.

He stared at my mug, then flicked his eyes back to me. "I gave him everything I could."

"You dated a woman he loathed," I snapped, finally finding a hole in his version of things. "He hated Hannah."

"I broke up with Hannah because of Kellan." Tate bared his teeth, jerking forward like I'd physically hurt him. The fire in his eyes threatened to smother me. "Dated her for him, too, for that matter. She seemed like a good idea at the time. A nurse. Sweet, nice, caring. Came from a big Southern family. All about matching plaid pajamas on Christmas and baking casseroles. I thought she'd be able to replace Kellan's good-for-nothing mother, who OD'd when Kellan was asleep in the next room. Did you know Kellan found his mother when he had a nightmare? He ran to her room and tried to wake her up. She never opened her eyes."

I collapsed backward and pinched the bridge of my nose. Everyone in Kellan's life had failed him. His mother. His father. His half-brother. *Me.*

"For a while, Hannah tried," Tate explained. "I think she knew why I kept her around. Why I chose her. She made an extra effort to be there for Kellan."

"His version of things was different. Kellan said she was nosy and a pushover. He always complained about her trying to tell him what to do, what to wear, how to act."

Tate's mouth quirked up. "She was feeling the heat. I was growing impatient once I realized my instant McFamily wasn't fully cooked and ready within a year. Kellan wasn't cooperating. I was young with a new job, a chip on my shoulder from carrying the last name of a notorious drug addict, and raising a fifteen-year-old. I was a sour piece of shit. Both Kellan and Hannah suffered. After it became apparent that Kellan wasn't going to warm up to my fiancée, she changed tactics."

"Military school." I pinched my right leg to stop it from rocking. I remembered how much I'd hated Hannah for suggesting it.

Tate's jaw ticked. "He told you?"

I nodded. "He was upset."

"I didn't know he knew. She always brought it up when she thought he wasn't listening. It grated on my nerves. Even though, at that stage, my relationship with Kellan was strained, I still thought he would come around. Get a better perspective once he grew up. When Hannah began to push for military school, I cut her loose."

I looked down at my lap. "He thought she dumped you because she hated him. I wish he'd known how much you cared. He painted a different picture. Hence why I thought it would be a good idea to burst into your office and serve you a generous piece of humble pie."

"Is that what that was?"

A half-moon grin graced his lips. It marked the first time I'd seen him truly smile, and I momentarily lost my breath. He looked so much like mischievous, charming Kellan and yet a completely different entity. I wanted to reach out and touch him, but that would be insane.

"I wanted to make you feel uncomfortable," I admitted.

"Ditto."

"Mission accomplished." I chuckled, remembering how he had stared at me defiantly when he was inside Allison. "Sorry for interrupting."

"Sorry for..." he trailed off. I knew what he was sorry for. Holding my gaze while inside her. "For what it's worth, I'm always a poisonous piece of shit, but on Valentine's Day, I'm next-level asshole."

"Those days are hard on me, too. Truce?"

I curled my fingers, offering him my pinky. He took it in his. We looked comical together, since he was so much bigger than me.

"Truce."

Silence stretched between us, forming an invisible line I knew not to cross. Our eyes did the talking now. Something passed between us. Acceptance of sorts. I forgave him for being a douchebag, and he forgave me for things he was not even aware of. Horrible things.

For not giving him the comfort when I could.

For hiding the whole truth from him.

For feeding him the lies I'd gotten so good at telling myself.

"He never told you he wanted to do this, right?"

Tate didn't ask.

He *pled*.

He wanted to believe this had come out of left field. That none of us could have known. That he hadn't ignored the glaring billboard signs. My conscience told me one more blow to his shattered soul wasn't going to make a difference, but the cowardly truth was, I didn't want him to hate me. He was the only thing Kellan had left behind, and I couldn't stand the idea of him going back to despising me.

I shook my head, but I didn't utter the word *no* aloud.

Lie number one.

"I guess he wouldn't." Tate rubbed his jaw. "Can I ask you a personal question?"

"I guess."

"Were you friends or something more?"

"Just friends."

Lie number two.

This one I counted as half a lie. The only thing we'd done was kiss, but I'd rather Tate not know that. Adolescent love is the greatest pain of all. It teaches you the power other people have to destroy you. I didn't want Tate to look at me and see another person who'd put a hammer to Kellan's heart. Still, the words felt ashen in my mouth. I was not a liar.

You are now.

"Thanks for your time." He slapped his knee. "It's appreciated."

Maybe it was because Tate had apologized, or maybe I just didn't want to go back home and meet Leah's face, marred with scars I'd put there in a moment of recklessness... But suddenly, spending a few more hours with this man was all I wanted. Just until I made sure he was okay.

"How about we go to the bar down the block?" I suggested, my face growing impossibly hot.

"How about I call you a cab?" he retorted, flashing that rare Marchetti smile that turned women inside-out. "I think it's past your bedtime."

Jerk.

"I'm twenty-two."

Well. Barely.

"Still at least six years too young for me to be seen publicly with you."

"We're in public right now..."

"Coffee equals friendship. Alcohol equals face-riding," he deadpanned.

I choked on my disgusting coffee. It splattered all over my lap. Tate stared at me, at ease, like he evoked this reaction in people daily.

"How old are you?"

"Thirty-four."

"Not that old."

"No. And still..." He stood, shouldering his perfect frame into his black coat.

I jumped to my feet, a rush of panic coursing through my veins. I finally got it. Tate's presence gave me comfort. It made me feel like I was with Kellan. *Phew. That's natural, right?* It wasn't like I liked him or anything. I didn't.

Tate collected his phone and wallet robotically. "Thank you,

Charlotte Richards. Goodbye."

He was walking away. I couldn't let him walk away. Not after everything he'd told me. Not after learning he'd given up so much for Kellan. I scrambled, sorting through my brain to try to find something to make him stay. Something that would ease the pain he was in.

Because I felt it, too. Every day, I woke up knowing I'd failed Kellan by being late that day. That I'd ruined my sister's life by making a colossal mistake. I couldn't even imagine what Tate felt when he opened his eyes each morning.

"I wrote a letter to Principal Brooks, you know. About Kellan," I called out after him, knowing what I'd just risked. That if he thought hard enough, he would realize what that meant, and my lie—that Kellan had never told me his plans—would dissolve like dust.

Tate stopped in the middle of the buzzing coffee shop. The backdrop of a lit-up Manhattan glowed through the windows, illuminating his lean frame. All in all, he looked like a fallen angel, which was completely insane, because he was this hotshot doctor and I was a mere agent assistant. He could find so many other willing women to save him.

He still had his back to me when he spoke. "What's your drink of choice, Charlie?"

"Charlie?" My heart hitchhiked its way up my throat, just about ready to land on the floor with a thud, grow little legs, and run toward him.

"Charlotte is too formal for you." His back was still to me.

"It is?"

He nodded.

I liked it.

Charlie.

"Bud Light. Kellan used to steal your stash and share it with me."

Tate turned his head, fighting one of his bring-down-the-stars-and-hang-the-moon smiles I knew he hid behind his stoic expression. "I knew that. That's why I always bought extras. Oh, and he would've kicked your ass for narcing on him, Charlie."

Chapter Twenty-One

Charlotte

We headed to a bar I passed by every day on my way to work but had never visited. Even though I remained friendly with my colleagues, I wasn't big on socializing. I wasn't a fan of beer, either. But for Kellan's brother, I cradled a bottle of Bud Light as we slipped onto two high stools.

"The Cut That Always Bleeds" by Conan Gray bounced against yellow neon walls. The interior made me feel like I'd teleported inside a submarine, and I would feel claustrophobic if it weren't for the calming force of Tate's gray eyes. He sipped a Rusty Nail, bending the coaster in his huge palm. His hands were too distracting, so I stared at the wooden counter.

"I had my suspicions." I tried to ease my way to the truth. "About Kellan wanting to commit suicide, I mean. But every time I broached the subject, he took it as criticism and shut me down. It didn't help that, as time passed, we went through different changes. I was coming to terms with my baggage—sort of, anyway—while he continued piling more and more stuff into his. So, I turned to Principal Brooks."

"Did you talk to her?"

"No, I wrote her a four-page letter. But I signed it under my name and told her I was ready to talk when she was. Never heard from her."

Tate tipped his head back and finished his drink in one go. He slammed the glass over the counter. "She dropped by after what happened. Gave me some cop-out, ass-covering speech about how she encouraged all of her students to seek therapy and talk openly about their feelings. Said St. Paul had two counselors at the students' disposal at all times."

"She knew," I mumbled. At the very least, she must've talked to Kellan, because he found out I narced on him and blocked my number.

"Unless she didn't read the letter."

"How can you not read an intimate letter? It's too tempting, I think."

Tate shrugged. "Not for everyone."

I believed him.

I believed he took an interest in nothing and no one. He had this untouchable air about him, of someone who had once loved and lost and wasn't about to make the same mistake twice.

I arched an eyebrow. "So, if you found unsent letters Kellan wrote and you knew he didn't want you to read them, you wouldn't read them?"

Tate didn't miss a beat. "I wouldn't."

"Even if they were about you?"

"*Especially* if they were about me."

I nibbled at my lower lip. "You're weird."

"And you're stalling. Tell me more about Kellan."

I granted his demand.

I confessed I was the one who went to Kellan's grave and left roses every Valentine's Day. Tate had always wondered who that person was. He told me things I hadn't known, too.

For instance, Kellan used to be a star athlete and pretty popular as a kid, just as I'd suspected. Swim team member and track star. Then his mother died in a very publicized, very embarrassing way.

From that point on, kids taunted him about his screwed-up family. Their parents canceled playdates with him, and with his mom gone, Kellan didn't have anyone to take him to see friends after school, anyway.

His father was stuck in his room writing or partying his life away, and his brother was up at Harvard, studying medicine.

Tate had grown up with a normal mother, who'd been separated from Terry Marchetti since before she gave birth to Tatum. She'd ingrained in her son all the normalcy in the world, but Kellan was born right into the eye of the storm of a troubled model, a tortured artist, and their public love story.

Tate told me Kellan had the same substance abuse issues Terry had. He'd looked up to his father and tried to mimic him in everything. Even his bad habits. We exchanged notes for God knows how long until, suddenly, when we hit our third drink, we fell silent.

Tate stared at the bar.

I stared at him.

"I have an early morning tomorrow." He held his credit card between his index and middle finger, handing it to the bartender.

I fiddled with my bag to take out mine, too, but he covered my hand with his. A jolt of electricity made the hairs on my arms stand on end, and I sucked in a breath.

He released me. "Your money's no good here."

The bartender returned his card with a receipt, plus a napkin with her phone number on it. I watched carefully as Tate tipped her thirty percent, removed the napkin, and crumpled it in his hand when she turned away.

We poured outside. I wrapped my arms around myself, but not because of the cold.

Tate started flagging down taxis. "I'll hail you a cab."

A quick glance at my phone showed me it was already half-past eleven, and twenty-two-year-old me was much more careful about wandering around the streets of New York in the middle of the night than teenage me.

Did we really spend five and a half hours together?

A taxi stuck at a red light blinked at us, signaling its pending approach.

We turned to each other at the same time.

"Thanks for doing this." He squeezed my hand mechanically. Just like the way he'd plowed into that woman.

He did everything in such an offhand way, I wondered if he was capable of showing any feelings that were not Kellan-related.

"Sure. I'd give you my number in case you want to talk about Kellan some more, but I noticed you're not big on taking numbers." I was referring to the barista and the bartender from tonight.

"Sharp."

I tapped my temple, ignoring the faint sting in my chest. "Weapon of mass destruction."

"Keep that weapon locked and safe." He raised his hand, rubbing his thumb over my forehead. Zero emotion in his eyes. "Goodbye, Charlie."

"Goodbye, Tate."

The car stopped at the curb. I climbed into it as Tate stuffed money into the driver's hand, taking the cab company card from him and assuring him he'd call them to make sure I made it home safely.

I produced Kellan's last penny and rolled it in my fingers as Tate disappeared back into the bar we'd just exited.

Why would he go in?

To seal the deal with the bartender, you fool.

I shouldn't feel jealous.

I shouldn't.

But I did.

Chapter Twenty-Two

Charlotte

I found a wrapped box and a note by the door when I got back to the apartment building. The note hung from the parcel, kissed by black fingerprints. Unlike Tate, I couldn't refrain from reading private things, especially when they were in plain sight.

I unlocked the door, carrying the box with me. The note read:

Leah, Can I take you out this weekend? There's somewhere special I want to bring you. - Jonah.

Slipping the box under my arm, I made my way to Leah's bedroom and knocked on her door. Light poured from the crack under it, so I knew she was still awake. I always trod carefully when I approached her. Like I had the ability to make her burst into flames if I said or did the wrong thing.

"Leah." I cleared my throat, hating how unnatural I felt around my own sister. "Open up."

She answered after a moment, wrapped in her satin white house robe, her hair knotted in a towel. "What's up?"

"Look." I hovered just outside her room and handed her the box and note. She didn't take it, her eyes bouncing from me to the box. "It's from

Jonah."

"Yeah." She huffed, playing tough. "I saw when I got home."

"You did?" I faltered. "Why didn't you bring it in?"

The expression on her face didn't change. It remained blank and resilient and apathetic, like someone who had come to terms with her own existence but didn't plan on actually doing any living.

She hadn't taken it in because that would mean making a decision. I knew my sister.

A part of Leah wanted to go out with him, but a bigger part worried that he'd done this because he pitied her.

Or because she'd become some elaborate joke to him.

Or maybe the most vicious blow of all—that he'd asked her as a friend.

"Leah..."

She shook her head. "Leave it, Charlotte. Okay?" She shut her door just as a text message came through my phone.

Jonah: I saw you take the gift. Well?
Me: :/

I tore the box open with my fingernails. He'd gifted Leah a beautiful teapot, complete with a set of two matching floral teacups.

A red label stamped the top corner of the box: *Cracked*.

And another label, in green: *Full Price.*

My chest hurt as I decoded the not-so-subtle message he'd tried to give her. I took a deep breath, grabbed my phone, and texted Jonah again.

Me: Hey, Jonah?
Jonah: Sup?
Me: Please don't give up. She's worth the wait.

Chapter Twenty-Three

Tate

"I need a loan."

Terry leaned against my doorframe at ten o'clock at night, about as welcome as a flaming bag of dog shit. He didn't smell much better than said bag. The mixture of piss, cheap alcohol, and his own impending demise gave him the exclusive scent of a nineteenth-century brothel.

His nose had turned a permanent shade of Santa red sometime last year, and I wondered how many rock bottoms he'd hit before he finally took a hint. By my count, he'd plowed through at least six of them in the past decade. Clearly, rock was not a hard enough material to stop him from plummeting down the abyss of self-destruction. He was so far gone, I was surprised we were still in the same atmosphere.

I propped my shoulder against my wall, finger-shooting my own temple as my cheeks popped. *Boom.*

"Very funny." He staggered back. "I need help."

"Please enlighten me as to why you think I care?"

"You're my son."

"Right. Your son who has already paid your rent for the past couple of years. Get a job, Terry. I'm not social services. You can't ask me for money and throw your children at my doorstep when shit gets tough."

I slammed the door in his face. Another knock invaded my space, followed by a loud burp.

God-fucking-dammit.

Full disclosure: I'm not exactly the happy-go-lucky type.

Today, I was in a particularly sour mood. One of my patients had delivered a stillborn six months in. She'd been through hell and back trying to conceive, and this marked her last-ditch attempt. It was supposed to be her rainbow IVF baby.

Last month, she'd turned forty-five. We both knew what that meant after I delivered the baby, blue and small and pulseless, curled into herself. There would be no going back to the drawing board for this patient. Her lifelong dream would not be fulfilled.

When I'd left the operating room, dumping my medical mask into the trash, her husband was there. He looked out the window of the tall building, and I knew what he was thinking. I knew, because the same thoughts had swirled in my head in the months after Kellan had taken his life.

The thump on the door became a kick.

I opened it again, scowling. "What?"

"You know..." He pushed past me, shoving at my chest as he wobbled inside. I could knock his ass down with a finger, but I let him in anyway. I didn't need my neighbors talking about this tomorrow morning. "One would think you'd at least be a bit more remorseful about killing the only son that meant something to me."

This old tune again. I felt one hundred percent responsible for what had happened to Kellan. I carried it with me every day. But if Terry thought his first-grade psychology mumbo jumbo would work on me, he obviously hadn't gotten the memo that I held the puking green slime emoji's opinion of me higher than I did his judgment.

"See that hole you walked through when you got in? It's called a door. See yourself through it." I turned him in the other direction, pushing him out.

He spun with surprising nimbleness, balling the fabric of my shirt as he jerked himself forward, so we stood nose to nose. "They're going to kick me out of the apartment, you hear?" The stench of his alcohol breath fogged around me. This marked his sixth eviction since he'd defaulted on the mortgage of a Central Park high-rise condo he'd never been able to afford. "I'm going to be homeless."

"Downsize. Move to Brooklyn. I'm not paying your rent anymore."

As it was, the only reason I'd paid Terry's rent so far was because I knew his ass would land on my couch otherwise. He didn't have anywhere else to go. Turns out that, without the money, movie deals, and prestige, women were not so keen on sharing a bed with him.

I liked my privacy. I also liked not sharing a roof with a man I hated just a little less than Hitler.

"I can't." He lost his balance a little, stumbling back before jerking himself into my face again. "I have two hundred and thirty bucks in my checking account."

"Time to dip into your savings."

"I have no savings. Emptied 'em all out last week." He hiccupped, collapsing onto my couch and nearly pulling me down with him. Terry threw an arm over his head. "Maybe it's time to give up the apartment."

"Ya' think?"

He belched. Classy AF. Hard to figure out how he was single. Kicking his leg on the arm of my sofa, he added, "You do have a spare room here."

"No, I don't." I stood in my living room, hands parked on my waist, knowing the only things stopping me from kicking his ass were social etiquette, the remainder of my sanity, and the slight chance he'd slap me with a fruitless lawsuit in the hopes of funding his drug habit.

Terry removed his arm from his face, frowning up at me. "Whaddaya mean no? What about Kellan's room?"

"No one's walked in there for four years. Your sorry ass is not about to change that."

He whistled low, shaking his head. "Still, huh? His room must reek."

"So do you."

"C'mon, son. I need to sleep somewhere." His usage of the word "son" whenever he needed something made me violent. To be fair, watching him convert oxygen to carbon dioxide was enough to put me in a shitty mood.

"How about the street?"

I ambled toward my kitchen. I lived in a small house, only eighteen-hundred square feet and in desperate need of a remodel. It cost a fucking fortune, being smack in the middle of the city, on one of the most picturesque streets of New York.

Around the time I'd taken Kellan in, I'd been young and dumb enough to have high hopes about what we'd be. I'd planned to work on the place as I moved to the private sector. Rip the walls out. Start from scratch. Make it a sick bachelor pad Kellan and I could share.

Now, there was no way I'd start moving shit around. Not when Kellan's room still remained untouched. Exactly as he'd left it.

"You have to move on with your life." Terry's voice floated around the room like a green toxic cloud.

"I have. You're the one stuck in place, still trying to ride the wave of success from a book you wrote almost a decade ago. Get out."

He shot up from my couch, outraged. "You're going to let me live on the streets?"

"Yup." I popped the P, opening and closing the cabinets, not looking for anything. I hated this place. I wished I had the balls to move, but turning my back on this house felt like letting go of Kellan completely. "I'll throw in a nice sleeping bag as a housewarming gift."

"You're a monster," Terry cried out.

"I *am* yours."

"I've never been this—"

"Please." I raised a hand, already bored. "There's nothing more embarrassing than people singing their own praises. Are you done?"

He looked around at his surroundings. It wasn't a dump, but it was a far cry from the glamorous life he'd led since writing *The Imperfections*. I made great money, but remodeling the house required moving shit

101

around, and everything needed to stay exactly how it'd been the day Kellan did what he did to himself, down to the grandfather clock that no longer worked. Even the ugly clay mug Kellan made for his mom for Mother's Day in third grade still held my morning coffee every day.

It'd be great to get rid of this house and move to a clinical, soulless skyscraper with a cleaning service and a doorman.

"I'll take the couch," Terry said with conviction.

"Hard pass. I like it in my living room. Gives the place character."

"I mean I'll sleep on the couch."

"Hmm, that's a no, too. I'm not in college anymore. My days of sharing space with drunken, shady roommates are long gone."

"You have to help me." He clutched my shirt again. "You must."

"I beg to differ."

"If you don't help me, I'll be on the streets, then what do you think is going to happen? Someone's gonna notice, and before you know it, it will be all over the news." His hands framed the headline in the air for emphasis. "Literary legend Terrence Marchetti is homeless when, just a few miles away, his hotshot doctor son lives in a glitzy Manhattan brownstone."

He wasn't wrong, unfortunately, which was why he was still in my life in the first place. With my wholesome reputation, I couldn't let him die on the streets. However, the days of my paying his fifteen thousand-a-month rent were also over.

I bit my inner cheek, suppressing a chain of curses. "There will be rules to abide by."

"I can do rules."

"Rule one—no alcohol or drugs. Not just inside my house, but at all. I mean it. I don't want this shit anywhere near me. I find it, I hurl you to the curb, my shoe still deep inside your sorry ass. It will actually be perfect, because when the press comes knocking on my door, I'll have the perfect excuse—you brought into my house the same shit you fed to your late son."

"I gave him the clean stuff to keep him away from the poisoned drugs off the street. Rat poison, talcum powder, laundry detergent..." Terry trailed off. I hoped he wasn't waiting for his Father of the Century Award to arrive in the mail. "What else?" he asked through gritted teeth.

I didn't think he realized how serious I was about the drug and alcohol clause. I was counting on him to fail so I could kick him out before he even moved in, and he was counting on me to turn a blind eye.

"No bringing anyone here. No smoking indoors. You have to work every single day—I'm dumping your ass at the local library on my way to work and picking you up when I'm done—and above all..." I raised a finger in the air. This part was crucial. His eyes followed my movements religiously. "Don't you dare set foot in Kellan's room. Don't touch anything. Don't look in its direction. Don't even breathe in its direction. Am I understood?"

"Yes."

"Louder."

"Yes!" he boomed, throwing his arms in the air. "Heaven help me, yes."

"When's your lease over?"

"Couple days."

"You're not allowed to bring any of your possessions here other than clothes, your typewriter, and laptop."

I watched Terry stomp out the door, muttering profanity. He slammed it in my face, like a teenager who had just found out he'd been grounded for eternity and beyond. Just like Kellan.

I went upstairs, passing by Kellan's room. I stopped at the door, took a deep breath, and cracked it an inch. Terry was right. The room smelled like death. The sad mixture of dust and fungus and neglect. The windows needed to be opened. The sheets changed. A three-inch layer of dirt lived on just about every surface.

I clicked the door shut and proceed to my room.

Maybe next week.

Chapter Twenty-Four

Tate

Two weeks after bidding Charlotte Richards goodbye, I walked into a smoothie bar post-workout. It was pissing rain, the roads were empty and slippery, and ice coated everything around me, heart included. No way in hell I'd hail a cab back home if it meant waiting outside for a minute.

My black leather duffel bag was thrown over my shoulder, and I wore sweatpants, a bomber jacket, and a scowl. I ordered a protein shake and tapped the counter as the scent of sugar cookies and cypress assaulted my nostrils.

It was too sweet. Too innocent. Too...

Charlie?

I glanced behind my shoulder at the table by the window. What were the odds of crossing paths with her? Pretty goddamn good, considering Ralph's Gym was only two blocks away from her office.

She sat by the window, reading a hardcover and flipping what looked to be a penny between her fingers. She rolled the copper coin across her arm before tossing it in the air again. She licked her thumb, turned a page, then reached for something on the table. A piece of cake.

Carrot cake.

The memory sucked all other thoughts out of my damn head, and I could see it sharply. Valentine's Day. Five or six years ago. Kellan had called in the middle of my shift (three premature births, one C-section complication) and asked me to get him a cake.

"What do you need a cake for?"

"Not with the questions again. Can't you just do me a solid? I'm broke as hell."

"Damn straight you are. You'll get your allowance back when I trust you won't spend it on drugs."

"Just buy the damn cake, Tate."

"I'll see what I can do."

"How hard can it be? You go to a place, buy a cake, bring it home."

"I have a job, dumb shit."

"And I have a date, dickwad."

I hung up on him. I bought him half a pound of carrot cake from the hospital cafeteria just before clocking out, knowing damn well no one in the universe liked carrot cake, but that was the only thing they had left so late in the evening. It looked like a bald chia pet and probably tasted much the same.

Kellan huffed as I dropped it into his hands when I got into the house. He was on his way out, pushing his floppy emo hair aside so he could examine it.

"Wow. A carrot cake."

"What's that? Thank you, Tate, for making the effort. Why, you're welcome."

"Lame."

"So. A date, huh?"

"Just kidding. I'm seeing a friend."

"On Valentine's Day?"

"She's going through a rough patch."

"So it's a she."

"You know, some of us see a woman and don't instinctively want to stick our fingers in her pussy." He was referring to my job.

I grinned. "Spoken like a kid who's never stuck his fingers in a pussy." I chucked the back of his head, ignoring his scowl. "Good luck, kiddo."

"Go to Hell, Tate."

"Sir? Sir?" The dudebro behind the counter waved his hand back and forth.

I snapped my attention back to him. My mind was a million miles away, at home with Kellan. I should've driven him there. Should've asked him who she was, what they'd planned, what hobbies she liked.

"Do you sell carrot cakes?"

"Yeah." He puffed his chest out proudly. "The only place in this neighborhood to sell them."

She'd come here on purpose for the cake.

"Your smoothie, sir."

I took it, paid, and sauntered over to Charlie. Her leg was rocking again. Always the right one. Never the left. I wondered how the hell I'd noticed that. Hannah got mad every time I'd failed to notice a new haircut, dress, or piece of jewelry.

"I could walk into the house missing a limb and you wouldn't care," she'd say.

To which I'd reply, "Of course I'd care. Especially if I have to sew it back together myself."

I took a seat next to Charlie without asking permission. We'd said goodbye on good terms, but I still didn't trust her. Something about that chocolate hair, big green eyes, sexy reading glasses, and freckles that made me want to connect the dots between them didn't scream platonic friend. And I really didn't want to think about a scenario where she'd broken my brother's heart and hadn't even bothered showing up on my doorstep to apologize for it.

I banged my smoothie on the white table. "You lied to me."

She looked up from her book, her cheeks flaming when she noticed me. I peered down to see what she was reading and realized it was *The*

Imperfections by Terry Marchetti. My already sour mood took a further nosedive.

Charlie's mouth hung open. "Tate," she whispered throatily.

"In the flesh." I picked up the icing-coated Saran Wrap that once held her carrot cake as evidence, hooding my eyes. "You said Kellan was just your friend. But he saw you on Valentine's Day and brought you a cake."

I could tell she hadn't expected to be confronted. Her body jerked backward like I'd slapped her, and her red face turned pale. Whatever happened that Valentine's Day, she remembered it clearly.

And now I remembered something, too. Kellan had never made it home that night. I'd found him lying in his own puke not too far from the school grounds the next morning.

I crumpled the plastic wrap and bounced it in my hand like it was a ball. "Time to come clean, Charlie."

"There's nothing to come clean about." She slammed the book shut with a huff. "We always hung out on Valentine's Day. It was my birthday. Big deal."

I raised a skeptical brow. "You were born on Valentine's Day?"

A bitter smile slashed her face like a scar. "That's the first question you've ever asked about me. Yeah, I was."

Why would I be asking her personal questions? I had no romantic or platonic interest in her. The only thing tying us together was the fact that she knew my late brother.

I studied her carefully. "You failed to mention that."

"Why would I? How does it relate to Kellan?"

"He killed himself on Valentine's Day."

"He was not heartbroken. Not romantically, anyway." She looked like she was about to say something more, but then thought better of it.

I put on my invisible Captain Obvious cape and told her what she already knew. "He brought you a carrot cake for your birthday."

"Yeah." She rose from her seat, scooping up her things and shoving them into her bag. Her body tensed. "As I said, it was my birthday."

107

"Did you fuck him?" The question tore out of my mouth before I could stop it. It was quiet in the smoothie bar, just the two of us, and in the glass window, I could see the reflection of the guy who'd served us. He choked on his bagel, as outraged as Charlie about my prodding question.

Charlie glared at me for a second. Rather than answering me with words, she raised her hand and whirled it in my direction to slap me in the face.

I snatched her wrist an inch before her palm hit my cheek. What can I say? Killer reflexes. Came with the territory of a steady-hand profession.

I tsked, slanting my head sideways. "It was a yes or no question, Lottie."

She flinched, clearly not a fan of the nickname. I didn't know why I called her by it, instead of Charlie, but it threw her off-balance.

"How do you know that nickname?"

"Kellan's eighth-grade yearbook."

Yes, I checked.

And yes, I hate myself for admitting it.

"Don't call me that. It's my sister's name for me." She jerked her wrist back. The flames in her jade eyes turned to cinder. She was back to hating me, and she was in good company, because I hated myself, too. "And no. I told you, we weren't dating."

"Fucking and dating are two different activities."

I'm living proof.

She raised an eyebrow. "Should you be wondering about my sex life when I was underage?"

Touché.

"He didn't come home that night."

That made her mouth slide open in shock. She had a great mouth. Her body was curvy and full and very close to perfect. It enraged me that I noticed those things. She was too young, too complicated, too Kellan's for me to notice.

"He didn't?"

I bit my inner cheek. "He slept on the streets."

Her face twisted. A wall of tears covered her eyeballs. "God." She cupped her mouth. "Kellan, no."

"So, you can see why I'm a little hesitant to take your word for it. Especially since you were perfectly content not coming forward and sharing any info about him for four fucking years. So, Charlie? What did you do to him?"

Wrong choice. I knew that as soon as the words left my mouth. There were a million different ways to present the question. What happened that night? Was he upset? Can you tell me what he was going through? But no, I'd chosen to pin the blame on her.

I didn't even know why. He'd been pissed at me when he left. Him not returning home that night could have been solely my doing.

She slung her bag over her shoulder. "You know, the other day, when we got to talking, I actually felt bad for you. I thought about you after I went back home. Wondered how you were doing. I even had to stop myself from shooting you an email a few times just to make sure you were okay. But every time I start feeling sympathy for you, you go and prove that you are just as infuriating as Kellan said."

With that, she pushed the door to the smoothie bar open and ran outside. The rain pounded the concrete like bullets, coming in thick white sheets. Pitch-black darkness swallowed Charlie, and I couldn't see if she'd taken a left or a right.

I sat back in my seat, my stomach hollow with annoyance, and sucked on the paper straw of my smoothie when something to my right caught my eye. I turned to it fully. She'd forgotten her coat.

As much as I wanted to be that asshole—and I did, I truly, honestly wanted to hurt her for a reason unknown to me right now—I could not have pneumonia on my conscience. I grabbed the coat and dashed out of the smoothie place, leaving my drink behind. I looked around, but all I could see were the curtains of rain I blasted through. I got soaked in seconds.

The streets had emptied, but I spotted a figure running toward the subway. I stalked after it. "Charlie!"

She didn't stop, but I knew it was her. I'd already eaten a good portion of the distance between us—she was not a great runner—and she flinched when I shouted her name.

"Goddammit, Charlie. Stop."

The rain pounded harder, weighing her down. The fact that I'd been the star of the track team through high school and college didn't help her odds, either.

She rounded the corner. I grabbed the hem of her sweater and jerked her to my chest, spinning her around. I didn't hug her to comfort her. I trapped her in my arms because I didn't want her to fling herself into the street and get run over in her effort to avoid me.

And I hugged her because I was tired of running.

After Kellan.

After normalcy.

Running out of time and happiness and hope.

Running away from myself.

I cupped the back of her head and brought her close to me. Her sobs wreaked havoc through her body, her shoulders quaking with each cry that ripped through her mouth. Her hot tears mixed with the cold rain on my shoulder, and the clothes on our bodies stuck, gluing us together. Her coat still dangled from the edge of my fingers, kissing the ground.

We stood in the rain for I don't know how long. I normally had a good grasp of time, but this was so far from the realm of my normal, it could've been a minute or an hour. She was falling apart in my arms, and I knew I was the bastard who'd made this happen.

She was right. I hadn't asked her anything about herself, even though, in all probability, what had brought Charlie and Kellan together was the fact that they were both stuck in adolescent hell and only had one another for company.

"I just wanted him to be happy." Her words bled into my chest. "I swear, I tried."

I dug my fingers into her skull but didn't say a word. After Kellan had died, I'd tried to get over it. It wasn't an intentional decision, to become this bitter and fucked-up. Support groups depressed me, and volunteering with troubled kids just reminded me how inept I'd been at raising my own brother. Everywhere I went, empathy had the synthetic taste of fakeness. Like icing on a cake—too sweet, too colorful, too perfect.

Charlie was the only person I'd met since Kellan died who grieved ugly. With leg ticks and a dirty conscience and sloppy meltdowns. She was real, and vulnerable, and consumed by whatever had happened to her.

At some point, her quaking became full-on shaking. I knew she was freezing. I walked and cornered her until her back pressed against a building. A balcony above shielded us, so at least we weren't whiplashed by the rain anymore.

"I'll call you a cab."

She snagged her coat from my hand, looking away from me. "Thank you."

"I believe you when you say you weren't together."

Not really.

That made her head snap in my direction. She didn't look happy or relieved to hear that. "Whatever, Tate."

I ordered a cab on my phone, then tucked the device into my back pocket. "What's with the penny?"

"My sister used to throw a penny my way and say, 'a penny for your thoughts' whenever I was down. It kind of stuck with me. Every time I feel bad, I play with a penny. I got Kellan into it, too. I think he liked it. We had this rule where, whenever I threw him a penny, he had to confide in me. It was practical."

I stared at her. She was pretty when wet. Nose and cheeks peppered with freckles. Big full lips. I wondered why Kellan hadn't made a move on her. Sixteen-year-old me would have ravished Charlotte Richards and demanded seconds.

Great timing to let your mind wander there, asshole.

"You miss him," I said. That dull ache in my heart intensified.

"Yeah." She rolled her eyes, but only to suppress another wave of tears. Her nose pinked. "You're such a dick. No wonder you're an expert at knocking people up." She shook her head. She was weird in ways I wasn't yet sure were adorable or annoying.

I didn't offer an apology. "Yeah."

"But you can't be like that with me," she warned. "I won't have it."

"Okay."

It was an easy promise to make.

It wasn't like I was about to date her ass.

An idea popped into my head. A terrible idea. A great idea. A brave idea. An idea that might get me one step closer to getting rid of the damn house I'd hated since the day I bought it. And by default—help me get rid of Terry's presence on my couch.

"Have you ever been to his room?" I asked.

She shook her head. "We weren't that close."

This was the first time I believed her when she said they hadn't fucked. If they weren't even at each other's houses, bumping uglies would be difficult. For some reason, that made me relieved. Thinking Kellan must've been heartbroken over some chick was too much to handle.

"You think you're up to seeing it now?"

"You mean, now-now?"

"Soon-now. I need to clean it up. It hasn't been touched in four years, and I think maybe it's time. But I need help."

"To clean?"

"To set foot in it."

She lapsed into contemplative silence.

"So? What do you say?" I watched her, waiting for a reaction. Some sign she'd budge.

Her taxi arrived. The headlights blinked, blinding us. We squinted at each other. Charlie sure was taking her goddamn time making a decision.

"I'll pay you," I snapped.

"I'll do it for free," she said flatly, then frowned. "Actually, I'll do it for a signed paperback of *The Imperfections*."

"Terry's a dick. You said so yourself."

Really laying it on thick in the charm department, Tate.

"I don't care what he is. He can write the hell out of a book. If I had to boycott assholes out of my artistic menu, I'd be starved for movies, books, and songs."

I knew she knew I hated my sperm donor, so I concluded she did this for the same reason well-fed cats preyed on mice. Blood sport. "I don't talk to him."

The cab blinded us again. The driver was impatient. I didn't budge.

She smiled sweetly at me. "Looks like you're about to."

I glared at her with quiet hatred. I was going to have to face the idiot anyway, since he was coming to live with me. "Fine."

Fuck.

She ran to the cab, yanking the passenger door open. Before she got in, she stopped, turning her head in my direction. "I don't have your number!" she shouted through the rain.

"We're not exchanging phone numbers. You know the rules." I felt like a tree, planted in place, alive but unmoving.

Do I know the rules? Are there even rules?

Yes. In fact, there is one—don't fuck your dead brother's best friend, who is twelve years your junior.

A solid plan.

She was broken. I was destroyed. This had disaster written all over it.

"Fine, jerk. I have your address. Friday at six?"

Didn't she just say she's never been in Kellan's room?

"Friday at six," I confirmed.

I turned around and walked back to the smoothie bar to collect my duffel bag, jacket, and sanity. The rain still pounded on me, but with no damsel to save from pneumonia, I was in no hurry.

Chapter Twenty-Five

Charlotte

Did you fuck him?

I let the question spin in my head like a coin. I'd said no, and that was the truth. My truth, anyway.

But there were some things I should've mentioned. I had kissed Kellan. Kellan had kissed me back. And in another life, an alternate universe where I hadn't lost my parents and Kellan hadn't been devoured by his ghosts, maybe we could have been more. Either way, this one would go to the grave with me.

I didn't think Tate realized how he came off once his guard was down and he was not Dr. Miracle. He looked split down the middle, flirting dangerously close with depression.

I'd lost one Marchetti brother—I was not going to watch another one ruin himself. The realization struck me as I knocked on Tate's door, feeling like an intruder.

Last night, as I'd tossed and turned in bed, I'd committed to trying to be there for him. He was callous and hard and indifferent and cold, but he'd also suffered through a great loss—of a sibling who hated him and lived under his wing.

My being here for Tate was hardly selfless. I'd spent the past eight years searching for an opportunity to help me come to terms with what I'd done to Leah. To Mom and Dad. If I could redeem myself in my own eyes, prove to myself that I was actually a decent human, maybe I'd love myself again. I'd like that.

Tate opened the door. Jesus, he was tall. Abnormally tall. He filled the frame like it'd been designed to fit his measurements. Which was insane, because doorframes usually towered over people, not vice versa.

His eyes were fossil gray, naturally hooded, and screamed menace. His carved jaw was square and hard as stone. His Robert Pattinson hair begged for a tug, and I wondered how come he was single, because whoever the woman in his office was, she wasn't his girlfriend. Reagan always banged on about Tate's refusal to settle down.

I sucked my stomach in, straightening my spine. "Hi."

His beauty intimidated me.

"How do you know where I live?"

Hello to you, too.

Also: crap, crap, crap.

"Contact sheet from school. I had it printed out." I lifted a shoulder. "Nerd on a scholarship."

The tips of my ears burned, and my mouth had dried. Tate raised a skeptical eyebrow and stepped aside, letting me in. The mountain of lies on which I'd started off our friendship rose higher and higher every day.

The first thing I noticed was that the house wasn't as impressive from the inside as it was from the outside. It was still pretty nice, but definitely dated. Blankets and pillows had been stacked in an untidy pile on the couch. Peeling wallpaper from the eighties covered the walls, and the kitchen consisted of honey-oak cabinets with a heavy trim, mustard laminate countertops, and yellowed backsplash. This place looked like a *Three's Company* set.

I followed Tate's wide triangle back. The house might not look it, but it smelled fresh. Exactly like Tate. Sandalwood and citrus and bonfire and sex. I was no expert in what sex should smell like, but I swore he smelled dirty and clean at the same time. Mouthwateringly delicious.

I was glad I wasn't one of his patients. It must be so awkward to spread your legs in front of a man like that when the end game was not an orgasm.

"Who's crashing at your place?" I spoke loudly to drown my deranged thoughts.

"Terry."

"Where is he now?"

"I threw him out tonight so we could do this."

"Nice way to treat your father."

"He is not my father. Just a man who screwed my mother. Not the best thing to be admired for."

"It's still conception."

"It's just fucking."

I whistled, circling around his small living room and pretending to admire the mostly bare shelves with just a few small frames, the stock photos still inside them. "Ob-gyns don't have the best dirty talk game in the world, huh?"

My back was to Tate when he answered me. "Bet you all the pennies in your cheap little purse that I can make you drip cum on my face in less than ten seconds—before I even use my tongue or cock."

I swiveled around, my mouth hanging open in shock. Tate stared at me with a flat, almost disinterested look, arms crossed over his chest.

"What did you just say?"

"You said my dirty-talk game isn't strong. You were wrong."

"How do you know?"

Tate positioned himself behind the counter, producing two glasses. "I know because you're wet. Orange juice okay?"

"Actually, wine would be good." I decided to ignore his rude comment. There was no point bickering with him before we even started. "Considering I'll have to deal with you all evening."

He shook his head. "Threw out all the alcohol the minute Terry hauled his ass here. Water?"

"Sure."

"Coming right up."

We climbed upstairs with our water and stopped by a door. A roll of trash bags, a broomstick, paper towels, and cleaning products lined the wall like toy soldiers.

He turned to me. I turned to him. He was stalling.

I stared at the simple wooden door like it could swallow both of us into oblivion. "Do you want me to do it?"

Tate shook his head, took a deep breath, and pushed the door open. We sauntered into a dusty, messy room. The realness of Kellan's kingdom hit me like a punch in the gut. It looked like he was still here.

The sheets were wrinkled, the print of Kellan's lanky body outlining the linen. Posters of Black Flag, Poison Girls, and Subhumans hung on the walls. Hundreds of books stood piled up on the floor, soaring into three twisted towers all the way to the ceiling.

This room was so Kellan.

"I miss him." My words were barely audible, even to myself.

Tate groaned. "Should I put it all in storage?"

I shook my head. "You're never going to use these things. We need to give them away. Kellan would have liked that."

For the next three hours, we scrubbed Kellan's room clean and threw away seven trash bags' worth of stuff. Tate had been literal when he'd said he hadn't touched the room in years. The trashcan under Kellan's desk still had an empty Cheetos bag and a can of Diet Coke.

We dusted, scrubbed, vacuumed, and opened the window in silence. The only thing we couldn't get our hands on were the two drawers in Kellan's desk. We needed a key to unlock them and couldn't find it anywhere.

It was a nice desk, made of real oak. Tate shook the handles a little, but when he realized they wouldn't budge, he didn't snap and break the drawer, even though we both knew that he could.

His eyes drifted to mine, asking if I had any ideas. He was the most confident, formidable man I knew, but right now, this evening, he seemed as lost as his baby brother during our school years.

I shook my head. "We can find the key later. Let's tackle the books."

Tate reached for the top row, bringing them down for me to sort through. I started wiping them of dust individually. Poor books. It wasn't their fault their owner had passed away. Tate handed me *The Picture of Dorian Gray* by Oscar Wilde. A slow grin spread across my face.

"What's so funny?" Tate asked.

"This book holds one of my favorite quotes: *I am too fond of books to care to write them.* It's true. Once your art becomes your job, it loses its elusive, sexy charm. It's like seeing the behind-the-scenes of your favorite movie. The cables and green screen and latex-wearing stuntmen and scripts lying around. It desensitizes you. That's why I never wanted to become an author."

"Terry had that problem. When the cash flowed, the muse dried up. Art and prosperity don't play nice together."

Tate flipped through a book absentmindedly, still on his feet. I sat on the carpeted floor, legs crisscrossed, running a damp wipe over the covers. All the books were coated with wooly silver dust that looked like gray hair.

"No. I can only imagine what the pressure would do to him."

"Don't hold your breath for a feel-good ending." Tate set the book down. "Here's a spoiler—he became a drunk, a drug addict, and a shit dad."

"At least now you know why. He probably hates himself."

"Good. He should."

Tate handed me more books to clean. His citrus-sandalwood-bonfire had a fourth undercurrent. Musk. He smelled musky, and it made my stomach clench almost violently in a way I'd never experienced before.

"What's your Big T?" Tate asked.

"Big T?"

"Tragedy."

My throat constricted. "I don't really talk about it."

"You think I go around talking about my brother's suicide as an icebreaker?" He let out a bitter chuckle. "We're way past small talk, Charlie. Never been there."

I said nothing.

I didn't think it was the same. What Tate had done was destructive in a roundabout way. He'd tried doing a good thing and something had gotten lost in translation.

What I did was...not.

"C'mon. I could use a distraction," Tate coaxed. His low voice seeped into my gut, though it had no business going there. "This room is giving me a panic attack I can't afford. I'm on call tonight, and there are approximately seven babies due to be delivered this weekend who'd be very grateful if you could pull my head out of my ass."

We'd neared the end of the book pile.

"I think I can out-shitty you."

"I find it hard to believe."

I dropped a copy of *The Witching Hour* on my toe, but I couldn't even feel the pain. "Wanna bet?"

"Sure."

"When I was thirteen, almost fourteen, I found my sister's pack of cigarettes in her room. It was nighttime. My parents were asleep. My sister was out. She went to NYU and was at an off-campus party. She was riding a full scholarship, just like I did at St. Paul and in college. Leah was gorgeous and funny and crazy smart. Total catch. Her boyfriend Phil foamed at the mouth every time someone so much as spoke to her. He talked about marriage three months after they started dating. Anyway, she was so amazing—I mean, she is still so amazing—that all I really wanted to do was be like her. So..." I took a deep breath, squeezing my eyes shut. I didn't know why it still felt like the first time every time I talked about it. Over eight years had passed.

"You lit the cigarette," Tate whispered. He was absent of reaction, which was, perhaps, the best reaction he could give me.

I could feel his gaze on the top of my head. I swore my hair moved as his eyes dragged down from my crown to my face. I didn't know why, but his eyes on me were reassuring. Like a blanket.

"Yeah." I rocked my right leg back and forth, thinking, *Leah, Leah, Leah.* "To be honest, smoking turned out to be gross. I coughed a lot. I put the cigarette out after three puffs. At least, I thought I did. I threw it in her trash after I was done. Little did I know, that night Leah had finally done the cleanup my mom had been bugging her to do for weeks. She threw everything flammable in the trash, Tate. Dry nail polish. Half-empty hand sanitizer bottles. Nail varnish remover. I would've been better off throwing that half-lit cigarette into a bucket of gasoline."

Tate took a deep breath but said nothing. I saw him watching my jumpy leg. I couldn't bring myself to stop. He sat down in front of me, even though we had six more books he needed to hand me for a cleanup.

"I went back to my room and fell asleep. The next thing I remember is coughing and waking up to a temperature that didn't make any sense for December. I looked around, and the crack under my bedroom door was lit in orange. Smoke crawled from the other side. It was unbearably hot. I couldn't breathe. Mom and Dad's room was farther down the hall, so if I was feeling like I was burning alive, they were..." I sucked in a breath. My eyes remained pinned on my ankle boots. I couldn't meet his gaze.

Surprisingly, I didn't cry.

I'd been forced to recite what had happened that night so many times—to the police, insurance company, firefighters, relatives, curious neighbors—that I'd learned how to tell the story as if I hadn't even been there. Like it was a Grimm Brothers tale.

But with Tate, it felt different. I felt raw and exposed. I was frightened of what he'd think about me once I finished. It was bad enough that I'd committed to keeping all those other things from him. The kiss I'd shared with Kellan. The suicidal thoughts I'd known consumed his brother.

Here's a life lesson I'd never wanted to learn. Our secrets are nothing but a string of memories we wish to forget.

Tate placed his hand on my shoulder. "You don't have to continue."

I clasped his hand in mine. It was warm, rough, calloused, male. Perfect. "What about the babies?"

Tate rubbed at his eyebrow. "We have good nurses and a few more doctors who can deliver them if I lose my mind."

I took a deep breath. I needed to finish this story. For him.

For me.

"Leah arrived minutes before the firefighters and the police got there. I think, in a sense, I knew the fire was my fault as soon as I woke up. When I jerked my door open, the handle was so hot it left an imprint on my palm. All I saw was fire on the other end of that hall, and I knew my parents were gone. Maybe it was just my imagination, or maybe it's something I added to my memory in retrospect, but I swear I smelled raw, burning meat. You know, like at a barbecue shop. The smell of peeled, burnt skin and hair set on fire."

Tate closed his eyes and pressed his lips in a hard line. "Charlie."

My fingers curled into fists. When I shut my eyes, I still felt the heat.

"Then I heard Leah's voice. She called for me. Not for Mom and Dad. For me. She was standing at the end of the hall, near the stairway. I guess she went inside and wanted to see who she could save. She said she could see past the flames because her end of the hallway was clearer, and that I could run through it." My voice broke for the first time. "I was so scared."

Tate let his head fall into his hands, his elbows on his knees.

"She begged me to run into her arms until the fire became too much. Then, she just jumped into the flames to drag me out by force. She put her coat around me and protected me with her arms, shielding my body with hers as we ran through the blaze, down the stairs, and out of the house. The wall of the hallway collapsed onto her. It stamped her entire right side with a purple scar."

I remembered the screams. The tears. The way I'd frozen. Zoned-out. Leah had to drag me with all of her strength. I remembered the wall crumpling against my sister. Her body pressed against mine. Her weight searing my right leg with pain. I'd been rocking my leg back and forth ever since. A nervous impulse I couldn't get rid of when the weight of my Big T weighed me down.

"As soon as we got out of the house, we both realized she was literally on fire. She rolled on our damp front lawn to put herself out while I screamed hysterically. But it was too late. The fire devoured half her face. And to this day..." I took a shaky breath, closing my eyes to stop the tears from falling and moving on from the mark I'd left on Leah's face. "Dad took the batteries out of the smoke detectors when they started beeping and forgot to replace them, so we got very little from the insurance company. We were lucky to get anything at all."

I cleared my throat. "The house was gone, and we moved from Brooklyn to the Bronx. Leah dropped out of college to support us, and instead of becoming this hot-shot marketing executive with a prestigious degree like she'd dreamed, she went to beauty school and became an aesthetician. Not that there's anything wrong with that, but she never wanted it. I think she learned it because she became fascinated with ways to hide her face." I paused. "Phil, by the way, took a hike soon after. He's dating someone else now. Their mutual childhood friend."

"Asshole," Tate muttered. I nodded. "At least she managed to save you. The alternative, of not getting to you in time, would've left a scar that is way worse. I know, because I'm there. I'm there every day, and it's Hell on earth. To search for a face in every crowd you push through, knowing you will never see it again."

I don't know how it happened, but I let my face collapse onto his shoulder. He cupped the back of my head, and I let out a ragged, tearless howl. It was ugly and gutting and not at all something I would feel comfortable doing in front of a stranger.

Tate's arms wrapped around me. It transported me back to the hugs Kellan used to give me; I could count all of them on one hand.

In Kellan's arms, I'd felt like I was wrapped by a thin film.

In Tate's arms, it felt like nothing could touch me.

Not even death.

He was strong and big and tall and impossibly invincible. Only I knew that, inside, he was anything but.

I didn't know how long we sat like that. It was definitely not a comfortable position. But we seemed to be frozen in time when the door to Kellan's room creaked and a face poked inside. Just the face.

I didn't need to ask who this was. I recognized him from the back sleeve of *The Imperfections*. Terrence Marchetti. Had I not known what an asshole he was, I would've been star-struck.

"I... I thought... I mean..." He looked around us as Tate slowly peeled his arms from me. "Well, fuck me. Look at this place."

Reality descended on me like a cloud, slowly and with a chill. I realized as we untangled from one another that I was nestled between Tate's legs. We were a ball of misery, arms locked together, my head buried under his chin, and it might have looked more intimate than it was.

"Terry."

"Tate."

"Get the fuck out," Tate ordered flatly.

His father didn't even seem to flinch. He looked very much like someone who had fathered Kellan and Tate. The height. The deep-set blue eyes over tan, Italian skin. The full Mediterranean, brown-sugar hair with merlot highlights. Only his had grayed at the edges and in thick white streaks that he hadn't bothered to comb, and he looked worn out, wrinkled, and exhausted with life.

"How did you... you never even..." Terry Marchetti looked around the room in wonder. "You said you were going to keep this place intact forever."

"Plans change," Tate clipped.

Terry swept his eyes over me. "I can see."

My cheeks flared with color.

"Get your mind out of the gutter. She's a child. Now leave us alone." Tate stood abruptly and slammed the door in his face just to be on the safe side. I stayed on the floor, watching as Tate yanked the door open again as an afterthought. "Actually, make yourself useful and grab a copy of *The*

Imperfections and sign it to Charlotte."

"Got no copies here," Terry hollered from downstairs. "You said I couldn't bring anything other than my ass and my typewriter. Sorry, Charlotte."

"It's fine," I yelled back.

Tate slammed the door again, tugging at his hair. He didn't turn back to me. He was deep in his own head, and I wanted to get him out of there. Fast.

"Anyway, I found some real gems here. Those *Wizard of Oz* books, for instance, are first editions and signed." I picked one of them, clearing my throat. "I think if we donate them to the local library, they'll agree to taking on all the other books. It'll be Kellan's legacy." Honestly, with a full set of first-edition *Wizard of Oz*, I'd be surprised if they didn't name one of the floors at the library after him.

Tate's eyes snapped to me like he'd forgotten I was there.

I cleared my throat. "Or you could sell them. You'll get a good deal on them, I believe."

"No," he said. "We'll donate."

"I can do that for you if you don't have time. I've been at the library three times a week since I was thirteen." Way to tell him I had no life. Not that it wasn't the truth. "I'll be sure to give you the donation form so you can get the tax deduction for it." I just didn't want him to think I'd sell them myself or keep them. But now I'd made things a thousand times more awkward. Tax deduction? Really?

"Nice of you to offer. I accept."

It came out stiff and formal, and I didn't know why disappointment settled in my chest, considering we weren't friends. We weren't even acquaintances. Just two passing strangers who happened to be mourning the same person.

"Okay."

"Okay."

I looked at the hour on my phone. It was almost ten. I hadn't eaten dinner. I'd thought maybe Tate and I would order something since we'd spent the evening together. But he never suggested it, and I never asked.

My stomach growled loudly. I wanted to cover my face and disappear and crawl under the carpet. He couldn't not hear that.

He was still standing by the door. "Thanks for the help."

What are you waiting for, Charlotte? Get up and drag your ass home. He doesn't want to hang out. He made it clear that you are too young for him.

Not that I wanted him that way. I just wanted to talk. And maybe eat. Well, definitely eat.

I scrambled to my feet before he was forced to kick me out. "I'll take the books now and drop them off at the library some other time. It's late, and I don't want to—"

"I'll call you a cab."

"You don't have to—"

"It's the least I can do," he snapped.

I nodded. It occurred to me that he always called me cabs home. If this was not a great metaphor for our relationship, I didn't know what was. I pulled; he pushed. I popped up at his door; he sent me away like a rejected puppy. Seriously, it was a good thing we wouldn't be seeing each other after this.

We didn't hug or even look at each other as I piled into the taxi with the stack of first-edition books. Tate had said he'd call a company to get all the rest. It was just the expensive ones he wanted to see getting a good home.

"I'll send you the tax whatever in the mail," I said, tired. "Since I don't have your number." I had the decency to cringe at myself when I said this. Subtle much?

"Sounds good."

When he slammed the door shut after me, I noticed that he didn't even wait on the curb to see me off as the taxi slid back into traffic, disappearing among silhouettes of other vehicles under the twinkling New York lampposts. I hugged the *Wizard of Oz* set to my chest.

In the end, this was all I had left of either Marchetti brother.

125

Chapter Twenty-Six

Tate

I charged upstairs as soon as Little Lottie left. Little. Lottie. As in—teeny, tiny, twenty-two-year-old Lottie. Who used to hang out with my baby brother. I didn't need her to be illegal to be completely off-limits.

You did not have an erection after she shared her Big T with you.
You did not have an erection after she shared her Big T with you.
You did not have an erection after she shared her Big T with you.

Spoiler alert: I did.

Fuck my life sideways, she'd cried in my arms, and I'd popped a boner like a thirteen-year-old. The worst part was that Terry had caught me being a scumbag. He saw the bulge in my pants when I jumped to my feet to shut the door in his face. His eyebrows shot up as if to say, *it's not my mind that should be getting out of the gutter.*

Whatever. Shit happens.

It'd been nearly a month since I'd had sex. Since I had Allison in my office, to be exact. After Charlotte had stormed into my life like a contagious disease, my mind had been elsewhere. Namely—on Kellan.

I was sure Charlotte had felt like shit when I all but threw her out—especially after she'd helped me clean my house for four hours. Then her stomach began to growl, and I remembered I probably should have fed her. But spending more time with her seemed counterproductive to, oh, I don't know, NOT GETTING INTO HER PANTS.

Terry stopped me by placing a hand on my chest as I marched back inside. "Tate. Talk to me."

I peeled his hand off my chest, charging up the stairs. I felt like a fucking kid. He followed me. Why was I running? He couldn't ground me. It was my goddamn house.

"What's going on? That room is wiped clean."

"Yeah, well, as you said, it's been a long time coming."

"Can I at least crash there? I won't bring anything in. I'd be grateful to sleep in an actual bed." His words jarred me.

"No. It's Kellan's bed."

He stalked to my room after me. "I'm proud of you."

"I don't care."

"Look, I've dated them old, and I've dated them young, and I can honestly say, nothing brings you back to life more than a young, attractive, fun—"

I whirled toward him sharply when I reached my bedroom door, seeing red. My eyes were dead as I hurled him against the wall. His back crashed into it so hard, a painting dropped to the floor, its frame cracking.

"You don't know what you're saying. I don't want you to talk about her, think about her, or refer to her in any way. Am I understood?"

His eyes widened.

Mine, too.

I was not that guy who used his physical strength to put a point across. But I couldn't stress it enough—I didn't want my piece-of-shit father around Charlotte.

"I wasn't insinuating anything. Just trying to make you feel better."

"You could have made me feel better by taking care of your own kid."

He bared his teeth. "How much longer are you going to hold this over my head?"

"Until you stop blaming my ass for what happened," I snarled back.

"I was drunk that night!"

"You're drunk every night."

"Not since I moved here. Damn, son, I've been sober for a few days now. You haven't even paid attention. I came here to help."

"You can help by dying." Just as the words ripped out of my mouth, my pager started beeping. I pulled it out of my pocket and frowned. "I have a baby to deliver." I pointed at the cracked picture frame as I stalked downstairs. "Clean this shit up."

It'd always been like this for me.

Life laced with death.

On the night Kellan died, I'd delivered triplets. The mother, who had been trying to conceive for two decades prior to the pregnancy, listened to me bitch and moan about my brother throughout her weekly checkups right along with the three heartbeats.

She'd decided to call one of her sons Kellan.

I was going to tell him when I got home that night. That he now had a legacy, that someone was named after him, that I know the world is cruelly screwed up, but there are reasons to survive.

I never got the chance.

Chapter Twenty-Seven

Charlotte

The past is a hunter, and she never stops chasing.

I read the same line for the tenth time, unable to process it. My mind was stuck in a different place. Kellan's bedroom, to be exact, my body between Tate's legs. I gripped the highlighter tighter, slid the tip past my teeth, and bit the head.

"Charlotte." Reagan poked her head out of her door. "I need you to order a courier service for me."

I tossed the manuscript back onto the slush pile, grabbing a Post-it pad and pen. A distraction. That was what I'd been missing. "Address?"

She leaned against the doorframe, one hand on her belly and the other holding a thick cream-colored envelope. The fancy kind, laser-cut and wax-sealed. "Dr. Marchetti's office," she said with complete disregard for my mental state. "Everything is on the envelope."

I froze, pen hovered over the yellow Post-it, before standing to collect it. "When would you like it delivered?"

"As soon as possible. It's for the gender reveal party next weekend. The rest of the invites went out three weeks ago."

Seeing as I'd never tried nor wanted to have a baby, I didn't know when most gender reveals happened, but seven months in felt pretty late.

With an advanced-age pregnancy and multiple miscarriages under her belt, however, I couldn't blame Reagan for wanting to wait out possible complications before making any major announcements.

I opened my mouth to speak, but she stopped me with a raised palm. She plucked her phone from her desk, pointing the head of it at me. "And before you judge, I am well aware baby reveals are tacky. But I've waited a long time for a baby, and damn it, I want the whole shebang."

My lips curved into a smile. "Not judging. I'm looking forward to the party." I uncapped my pen. "What do you want on the recipient note?"

"Write..." She tilted her head, taking her time to answer. "I'm sorry for the last-minute invitation. I meant to hand-deliver it during our last appointment, but the pregnancy brain fog hit."

I scribbled on the pad, not really focusing on what I was writing. "Got it."

When I returned to my cubicle and peeled the sticky note off the pad, I realized I'd only written one word. *Tate.*

His name stared at me from the yellow square. Once I donated the *Wizard of Oz* first-edition set and handed over the donation receipt, nothing would tie me to him. I'd have no reason to see him again. My only living connection to Kellan severed.

I traced his name on the envelope.

What to do, what to do, what to do.

Before I could talk myself out of it, I darted to Reagan's office and knocked on the glass door.

"Come in."

I hovered behind the doorsill, half-convinced she'd sniff out the lie if I came near her. "Our normal courier is booked up through today and tomorrow. Would you like me to send it two days from now? Or I can find another courier."

Reagan winced, reclining in her wingback chair. "The last time we tried a new courier, the package ended up in Jersey. Can you deliver it yourself? You can take an Uber and put it on the company card."

"Of course."

Reagan called an Uber for me on her app. I waited by the curb, trying and failing to feel guilty about the lie. Trying and failing to think about anything other than seeing Tate Marchetti again.

I'd had years to build my hate for him, and he'd unraveled it in less than a month. If Kellan had seen me last Friday, nestled between Tate's thighs, arms around his neck, chin resting on his shoulder, would he call me a traitor?

Duh. If hating Tate Marchetti were an Olympic sport, Kellan would've medaled. He considered it a job, hobby, and lifestyle.

I'd left a thumb-sized dent in Tate's invitation by the time the Uber pulled up to his clinic. The driver coughed a few times, attempting to kick me out of his car without getting docked a few stars. I slipped him a cash tip and crept my way to the dark oak revolving doors.

There were a lot of things I should've been doing—reading a manuscript in the office, clocking out of work to donate Kellan's *Wizard of Oz* books, cutting ties with the brother he hated—none of which included lying to my boss and finding an excuse to visit Tate Marchetti. But here I was, riding the elevator to his office. And it was too late to stop.

The receptionist's head popped up as soon as the metal doors slid open. Since I'd last visited, she'd touched up her roots, upgraded to a balayage, and traded her contacts for trendy reading glasses. But she wore the same scowl on her face, recognition in her eyes, and a rectangular name tag that read *Sylvia*.

"Do you have an appointment?"

She knew I didn't.

"Yes," I lied through a smile, but only because I spotted Tate exiting a back room and knew he'd intervene.

He held a clipboard tucked between his bicep and an unbuttoned doctor's coat. His hair sat in styled waves, his fitted dress shirt bore no wrinkles, and his pants fell at a perfect quarter break.

And unlike me, he looked well-rested. Unbothered. It threw me off-balance. It made me dislike him a little more than I already did.

He is everything Kellan hated.

My words surprised Sylvia, because she paused for a bit, fumbling at her keyboard. "I don't see you on the schedule, Miss..."

"Richards," Tate finished for her, shooting me a leveled look. He clearly didn't want to see me. Yet another reminder this wasn't my finest idea.

Sylvia darted out of her chair. I half-expected her to curtsy at him. Instead, she gripped her wrist with the opposite hand, issuing a rushed apology like she expected him to behead her for poor service. "I'm so sorry, Dr. Marchetti. She said she had an appointment, but I can't find it in the system and don't remember making one. I can call security right now."

"No need." Tate hooked the clipboard he was holding onto a nearby door and continued to his office without another word.

I followed him, ignoring Sylvia's laser glare on the back of my head. He swung the door open and closed it behind us after I slipped through.

The last time I was here, other, more carnal things had distracted me. This time, I cataloged every inch of the room, more interested in figuring out Tate than I'd like to admit.

The space suited him—all dark woods and sparse furnishings. A clinical void. It looked like the kind of place where you delivered bad news. Two chairs sat before a heavy maple desk for the recipients and one tucked beneath for the deliverer.

Thick textbooks filled a built-in bookcase. Wall-to-wall windows offered a view of the city, high enough to render people faceless but low enough for them to still look like people. The lounger in front blocked most of the mini-fridge beside it from view.

A row of Ivy League diplomas, certifications, and awards decorated the opposite wall. I fingered the deep blue Yale frame before moving on to the crimson Harvard one. "Which did you like more? Harvard or Yale?"

I was clearly stalling, and naturally, Tate didn't let it slide. "Why are you here, Charlotte?"

"Kellan said you and Hannah used to argue at the dinner table over whether he should apply to Harvard or Yale, as if he could get into either."

"He could, and he did," Tate clipped, voice as thin as his patience. "Why are you here?"

"What?" I stilled. My thumb left a print on the frame's glass surface as I pivoted to face him. "He said he didn't have the grades."

Actually, he'd said he didn't want to apply. I believe his exact words were—*no way in hell.*

"Why are you here?"

"What do you mean *he did*?"

"He received an acceptance letter from Harvard that December. Early-decision. Special concentrations. I'll ask again. Why are you here?"

I reeled back as if he'd slapped me.

Kellan Marchetti—who hated school, structure, uptight historical institutions—applied to Harvard.

I didn't know what shocked me more—that he sent in an application or that they admitted him with his grades. He once mentioned Terry took over the inheritance from his mom and blew it on drugs, leaving him with barely enough to fund St. Paul's tuition through senior year.

So, who would've paid for Harvard? Tate?

Kellan had three months left until he graduated and escaped the bullies. Two weeks until he turned eighteen and escaped Tate. He wouldn't blow it on another four years shackled to his brother, relying on him for tuition money.

But still...

He also wouldn't have applied if he didn't want to get in.

The Why hovered between Tate and me, something I hadn't wondered in years. I thought I'd come to terms with Kellan's death, figured out the reasons he'd chosen to go, and known everything I could about the circumstances. Wrong, apparently.

The envelope crinkled in my grip. At this point, it resembled something from the two-for-one clearance bin at the 99-Cents Store.

My confidence evaporated. I stared at the hardwood panels, looking everywhere but at Tate. "I have to go."

Tate blocked my path, steadying me when I collided with his chest. My pulse thrummed against my neck. His scent invaded the small gap between us and left me dizzy.

I felt drunk. Unsteady. On a downward spiral I'd never recover from.

He lowered his voice, but it came out rough. On edge. "Why did you come, Charlotte?" He still had his hand beneath my elbow.

I stepped back, waving the envelope in the air like an idiot. "Reagan sent me over to give this to you. It's an invitation to her gender-reveal party."

He stared at the wrinkled envelope, my thumb mark on it, and the hand that held it before plucking it from my fingers. I hiked in a breath when our skin touched.

My hands curled into fists. I tucked them into my dress pockets and picked at the loose threads of the lining. "There's a ninety-nine percent chance you'll be the only man there. If you go."

That's it. You did your job. Stop talking. Leave, Charlotte.

Tate flipped it over, read his name on the front, and tossed it onto the foot-high pile of thank-you cards on his desk.

I flattened the skirt of my dress. "Her dad died two years ago. She has no siblings. And well, the babies came from a sperm donor, so there's no father in the picture." Tate's medical degree glared at me from its spot on the wall. "Oh. Right. You're her doctor. You knew that already."

Oh, God. It got worse the more I talked.

He settled into his chair. "Why are you still here, Ms. Richards?"

Yeah, good question.

My feet remained rooted to the floor. I pinned my gaze on the rows of textbooks behind him and blurted, "You owe me a signed copy of *The Imperfections*."

"I'll send it to your office using a courier service." He raised a brow, eyes flicking to the invitation. "Those exist, by the way. Reagan has sent me several things through a courier in the past."

I had no answer to that, so I said the only thing I could think of. "Don't forget to RSVP." It sounded like something my mother would have said, which made my cheeks flame.

"Will you be there?"

"Yes."

Tate grabbed a pen and checkbook from the drawer, tossing it back inside when he realized it was out of checks. His finger descended on the intercom button. "Sylvia, grab me a gift from the storage room."

It occurred to me that lying to my boss at a job I'd worked hard to get—a job I wanted to keep—was not worth seeing Tate Marchetti again. Not when he was back to being cold and distant and not the man who'd comforted me on Friday after I'd spilled one of my deepest regrets.

I crossed my arms, sudden waves of bitterness crashing into me. "I haven't had the chance to go to the library and donate the books. I'll get the tax donation form to you soon."

"Bummer. My bank account will take a hit in the meantime."

It seemed that, outside of Kellan and Reagan, we had nothing in common. Nothing to talk about. And I didn't know why, but I refused to swallow that truth. Call me stubborn. Or idiotic.

"How are babies one through seven?"

He leaned against the wingback chair. "Pardon?"

"The ones that were due to be delivered over the weekend."

"One through five made it out okay."

"And the other two?" My voice hitched. Tate saw life and death every day. How could it not remind him of Kellan?

"Stubborn. But I don't think you came here to discuss the upcoming induced labors. I don't think you came here to deliver Reagan's invitation either."

An abrupt knock interrupted us.

Tate never took his eyes off me. "Come in."

Sylvia entered with a tall, skinny gift bag. She set it on Tate's desk and left, but not before giving me major side-eye. Thin tissue stuffing wrapped around what was undoubtedly an expensive bottle of booze.

Tate snapped off the tag with his name on it, slipped two fingers inside, and pulled out a card, tossing it in the trashcan in front of me without reading it.

I stared down at the paper, tilting my head a bit to make out the slanted font.

Dr. Marchetti, you are our saint. Thank you for making our dreams come true. — Louisa and Tim Miller

Dreams. Tate Marchetti fulfilled dreams. I almost told him this. Just to see if his broken pieces could be fixed.

It's not your problem, Charlotte.

He *is not your problem.*

Tate slid the bag forward for me to grab off his desk. "I don't attend parties my patients throw, especially gender reveals of babies I already know the gender of. But please deliver my gift to Reagan, along with my sincerest congratulations."

Sincere.

The word didn't fit any part of him. And I decided, with unbreakable resolve, that nothing about Tate Marchetti and the chip on his shoulder was fixable.

I snatched the bag and headed for the door.

"Oh, and Miss Richards?" My hand stilled on the knob, but I didn't turn to face him. "Tell Reagan good luck with the twin boys."

Tate returned to his work, skimming through some files on his desk. I pivoted and gaped at him, more shocked that he'd earned such an angelic reputation as Dr. Miracle than I was that he'd blown the gender reveal surprise for me.

Something Kellan once said echoed between my ears.

Don't expect anything from Tate. If he's not happy, no one else can be.

Kellan had gotten it half right. Tate took pleasure in his own unhappiness. He saw it as penance, and he never noticed when it bled onto others.

Chapter Twenty-Eight

Tate

Here's a fun fact I remember every time I help a child enter this world—for nearly every birth in this country, there is a death. On the night the Omri triplets were born, Kellan happened to be one of those deaths. And every delivery since, I tried to put a face to the faceless. Kellan's. Which was why I never exited the hospital in a good mood, today included.

Tracey Wallingford's labor had lasted sixteen hours. She had an uninterested husband I'd bet my left nut would have no hand in raising the child, and she managed to use every curse on Urban Dictionary once I told her the spinal block only lasted an hour or two. By the time I grabbed a cab, light blanketed the city again.

Tracey's husband stood in front of the hospital, sucking on a Luxury Black. When he spotted me, he pressed a finger to his lips. "Hey, man. Keep this between us, okay? Tracey made me quit for the baby."

Tracey has a functioning nose and a mouth to match it. Enjoy divorce, child support, and losing fifty percent of your assets.

But for the privilege of returning home a minute quicker, I shut up, nodding past the thick smoke he wafted in my direction.

I slid into a cab and rattled off my address to the driver. "Wake me if

I fall asleep. Please."

I came home to an empty house. Terry had left the blanket in a twisted heap on the corner of the couch and a mess in the kitchen. I dumped the half-eaten box of cereal into the trash, unwilling to tempt fate when it came to anything Terry-related, and popped one of my meal-service cartons in the microwave.

It dinged about the same time I heard a sound drift down the staircase. There was no doubt who it'd come from. To his credit, I'd expected the rule break to occur sooner. Terry Marchetti possessed the willpower of a dog with a treat, which explained decades two through six of his life.

I followed the noise to Kellan's door. Snores thundered into the hallway through the crack. I swung it wider and caught the edge just before it slammed against the wall.

Terry lay on Kellan's bed, a pillow on top of his chest. His hand hung over the mattress, clutching onto something. A thick stack of paper, bound together at the top with a binder clip.

I paused in my perusal, knowing what I'd find when I continued and that I was liable to explode. Inches away, chunks of wood from Kellan's locked desk drawer were scattered all over the floor. It had splintered down the center as if someone had yanked the lock out.

It was just like Terry to ignore every rule I'd set. My anger rose. An impressive achievement, considering it was already riding high. It'd simmered all night, spiking every time my patient had to beg the nurse to call her husband in from a cigarette break. Fourteen times, by the way, as if he was the one who needed a break from the nine-pounder ready to tear a new hole in his mother.

I stalked to the window, jerked open the blackout curtains, and ambushed Terry with sunrays.

"Oh." He groaned, releasing the paper to shield his eyes from the light. His hair shot up from sleeping in an odd position. "You're home."

"Yes," I bit out. Fucking brilliant, my so-called father. "I'm home. *My* home."

Did I often want to pick fights with Terry?

Only when the sky is blue.

"Found a manuscript." He yawned, pointing to the discarded one on the floor. "Kellan wrote it."

The sound of Kellan's name from his lips sparked the typical reaction. Anger. Then, like clockwork, the guilt came to flush it out of my system.

I leaned against the doorframe, refusing to step back inside the room. "As I recall, a condition of your stay is that you do not set foot in Kellan's room."

"I was looking for a lighter." He scratched his arm. Bare, I noticed, and free of fresh track marks. Not that it meant jack shit. Terry preferred powders, pills, booze, and cigarettes.

I dragged my eyes to his bloodshot pair. "You broke his drawer."

"Hey, I left the other one alone. It's not like he's using it anymore."

This Terry—sober Terry—sucked as much as the other version of him. If anything, I preferred him coked up and out of my life.

When I'd started this conversation, I had no idea where it was going, but since he'd opened his mouth, I knew exactly where I wanted him.

I straightened and held the door open for him. "Leave."

"What? Why?"

"You broke the rules. You're out."

"I can't sleep on the couch. It's cold down there."

"It's colder on the streets. Which is where you'll be, since you broke the conditions of your stay and are no longer welcome in my home."

I stripped him of the comforter, staring at the brand-new, Terry-shaped dent on the mattress. Nothing in this room screamed Kellan anymore. Four years later, and I'd finally managed to clear all traces of my brother from my life.

Visible ones, anyway.

The situation must've finally sunk in, because Terry clutched the edge of the mattress as if he expected me to pry him from this place.

"I need the warmth," he insisted.

"Try Hell. I hear the weather's warm."

"But the couch—"

"Is no longer available to you." I followed him down the stairs to the foyer, jerking the front door open. "Out."

The fact that he had nothing to his name made kicking him to the curb quick and convenient.

"Did you make food?" He tipped his head up, sniffing the air. "Is that lasagna? I'll leave after I eat."

I strode to the kitchen, collected the microwave tray, and planted it in his hands even though it needed at least another three minutes on high heat. "Leave."

He hesitated, lingering on the threshold. "Permanently?"

I slammed the door shut as soon as he cleared the frame.

From the other side, I heard him yell, "I'll go to the press! Hot-shot doctor leaves his elderly father starving in the streets. See if you like the negative attention for a change."

I didn't respond.

"What about the manuscript?" he shouted.

I stomped my way back to Kellan's room.

Collected the shards of wood from his floor.

Ignored the piece that pierced my skin.

The manuscript stared at me. I picked it up, letting the heavy pages sink the splinter deeper into my flesh. I stared at it without really seeing. My eyes burned with the effort.

I never read.

And I'd certainly never read anything Kellan had written.

In the end, I managed to catch the title page before I slid the manuscript under Kellan's bed, right before throwing up in his trashcan.

Darling Venom.

Chapter Twenty-Nine

Charlotte

I found myself sandwiched between my colleagues at Reagan's gender-reveal party. Abigail spat when she talked, but I'd managed to dodge the liquid trajectory thus far.

Irene spoke so loudly, any sensitive subject needed to be broached in a soundproof bunker unless we wanted the whole tristate area to know what it felt like to have a man between Reagan's legs. Which, unfortunately, happened to be the hot topic of the night.

"I'm telling you, having this man touch you is a curse." Reagan propped her legs on the lounger across from us. "I don't know how I don't reach an orgasm the minute his fingers are between my legs. I think I'm going to have five kids just to have him deliver them."

I shifted on the butterscotch Victorian sofa. I hadn't gotten much work done today. Just shuffled things around and rearranged some paperwork, trying my best to block her voice when she sauntered out of the teleconference room, cradling her baby bump, and gushed about Dr. Marchetti's expert fingers on the exam table.

The conversation had carried over from the office to the cab to Madame Wade's, a bougie tearoom in the Upper West Side.

"I've been on his waiting list for years." Abigail sighed, biting into one of the fresh-baked vanilla scones. "He doesn't take any new clients."

Irene tipped a shoulder. "I just go somewhere local. In Williamsburg. Getting checked by a man—hot or not—is too weird for me. Dr. Waxman is a gem. The nicest woman I know."

All three women looked at me, waiting for me to chip in. Considering the intimate subject, I guess it felt weird that one of us had decided not to overshare.

I balanced a finger sandwich on my thigh and stalled, drinking basil oolong tea from a tiny cup, pinky jutted in Reagan's direction. There were fifty or so people scattered around the room, and I would rather be talking to any one of them than here, trapped in this conversation.

I plastered a weak smile on my face. "I've never visited an ob-gyn."

"Never?" Irene frowned. "As in, you've never been checked?"

I shook my head.

"Not even in college? When you started having sex?"

I'd never started having sex, but I had a feeling that admitting to being a virgin in a room full of educated, outspoken alpha females would be seen as a con.

Anyway, I was well aware most urban, single twenty-two-year-olds these days had popped their cherries. I'd just never had time for the dating stuff. Since my parents died, I'd prioritized maintaining my scholarship and earning money.

I felt myself blushing. "Yeah, not even then."

Abigail gasped. "This is unreal."

"What about a Pap smear?" Reagan sipped her blood orange tea. "Don't tell me you've never thought to have one done. Anyone twenty-one and over should."

I shook my head again. "I will rectify that, though. I'll schedule something soon."

"No, you won't." Abigail laughed. "Look at your face. You're frightened."

"My Aunt Jessa died of cervical cancer. She was very dear to me." Reagan tapped her mug with her fingernail. "I won't have you walking around the world untested. After this party ends, I'm making a call to book you an appointment myself."

"Please, that won't be necessary—"

"It is actually the definition of necessary," Irene pointed out.

Reagan replaced her teacup with her phone. "It's settled, then. You are going to get tested. I won't hear another word about this."

I eyed the device, worried she'd do something crazy like call Tate right now when he hadn't even bothered to show.

Relief sank into me when Reagan set down her phone, but then she waved her hand. "Hannah!"

I flinched, nails sinking into the finger sandwich. A crowded room seemed like a poor place to realize the name triggered me. Even though, well, it couldn't possibly be her...

A tall blonde materialized before us. She wore a cocktail dress, heels higher than my credit score, and long hair pulled back in a French twist. The room suited her with its elegant gold-leaf paintings, embroidered wallpaper, and cornice molding. Suddenly, my patchy skater dress, striped knee-highs, and combat boots left me feeling like an outcast.

Reagan scooted over, offering the extra couch space. "This is Hannah. She's the nurse who helped me after I had a miscarriage my second round of IVF. She referred me to Dr. Marchetti, and the rest is history."

My mouth dried.

It *was* her.

Tate's Hannah.

My heart jackhammered. I could hear my own pulse. A new song started playing overhead. Something about finding your way back home, which seemed like the universe's attempt to tell me something.

I felt like I'd teleported to my past. To the moment I'd gone from Charlotte Richards to Lots of Dicks. Should I introduce myself? Admit I knew Kellan? Admit I knew *Tate*?

In the end, I stayed silent, sipped my tea, and studied her, trying to see what Kellan hated and Tate liked. Abigail and Irene offered warm greetings, which I mimicked, but I wore a snowman smile. Disconnected and manufactured.

She seemed serene. Like the poster child for the flower-crown filter. The exact opposite of me in every way.

Reagan grasped Hannah's hand. "We were just speaking about the doctor, by the way."

Hannah nodded. "Will he be here?"

"Not sure." Reagan looked to me, arching a brow. "Charlotte?"

"Oh." I set down my crushed sandwich, figuring a white lie would be better than the truth—that Tate seemed appalled by the prospect. "I didn't get a definitive answer, but I don't think he'll show."

"Tatum isn't one for gender reveals," Hannah said as if she were an authority figure on all things Tatum Marchetti.

"Or celebrations in general," I muttered into my teacup.

"He prefers to stay pretty close to the clinic when he's on call, too."

Or maybe Tate's brother died, and he no longer sees a point to life outside of work.

At least, that was the person I saw when I looked at Tate Marchetti. Broken and functioning on autopilot.

Irene leaned forward. "It sounds like you know him well."

"We used to be engaged."

"What?" Reagan swiveled, bumping her belly into Hannah's hip. "How did I not know this?"

Hannah shrugged, the picture of nonchalance. Her voice had a musical quality to it, and it made everything she said sound like a blessing. Or lyrics to a Bonnie Tyler song. "It's all in the past."

It happened fast, the curling of her fingers.

So fast, I couldn't be sure it'd actually happened.

Did Hannah still have a thing for Tate? Or did she harbor resentment toward him? Either way, she could join the club. We could have t-shirts made in bulk.

"Well... no need to dwell on that!" Reagan decided.

"It's fine. I've moved on. He has, too. It's been four years."

I did the mental math. Kellan had mentioned the breakup junior year, which meant it'd been five years. Not four.

Did Tate and Hannah get back together after he died? Before?

The fact that I knew so little about Tate Marchetti hammered itself into me. I slumped deeper into the couch cushion, thinking about the Marchetti boys.

I wanted to grill Tate about the Harvard thing. It had nagged at me all week. I felt blindsided. Derailed. The healing I'd done in the past four years—wiped away with one fell swoop.

Frankly, I knew Kellan well enough to know he couldn't be forced to do something he didn't want. Which meant he'd applied to Harvard on his own.

Did he have a dream for the future and still choose death?

The women shifted the conversation to upcoming releases and trending nonfiction audiobooks. I downed the rest of my tea, wishing I'd gotten here earlier so I could leave now without being rude.

The regret spiked when I heard one of Reagan's cousins nearby. "Is that him? Dr. Miracle? Do you think he'll take me on if I beg?"

I snapped my head toward the door at the same time Hannah did, sucking in a breath when I saw him.

Tate.

Chapter Thirty

Tate

Let it be known that I came for my patient. At the rates Reagan paid, she deserved for her baby to pop out diamond-studded and bulletproof. The least I could do was show up at a gender reveal with a real gift and a smile that screamed THAT SIX GRAND YOUR INSURANCE PAYS PER VISIT IS WORTH IT.

At the gift table, I tossed an envelope into a basket. It contained a recommendation letter to a high-ranking preschool in the city, where a former patient held a seat on the admissions board. Probably a byproduct of my conscience working overtime. It didn't help that I felt like a piece of shit for, well, being a piece of shit. Which was why I ended up here, for the record, despite what I'd told Miss Charlotte Richards.

Snatching a pen and flashcard from a pile, I scrawled my guess of the babies' sexes and slipped it into the raffle box. Two boys, by the way. I saw the appendages myself on the last ultrasound. And yes, this was unprofessional. But I knew Reagan would get a kick out of it. Plus, the prize included noise-canceling headphones, which would come in handy whenever Terry entered my general vicinity.

A herd of women stared at me from the fireplace. Women usually stared at me for one of two reasons: 1) they wanted me in them (sexually) or 2) they wanted me in them (clinically). Either way, I wasn't interested.

I strode to Reagan, intent on spitting out a greeting and dipping as soon as possible. Then I caught sight of Charlotte Richards, followed by my ex-fiancée. They had their heads sloped forward in conversation. Charlie sported a blush the shade of baked lobster and a hemline that left ninety percent of her legs on display.

You did not come here to eye-fuck your brother's best friend.

You did not come here for Charlotte Richards at all.

I had no intention of continuing on the downward spiral where she was concerned. Consider my fixation under control. So, I had no desire to converse with her. Or worse—pull her tiny dress up and sink inside her pussy with those knee-high socks still on.

None whatsoever.

Someone clutched my shoulder. From the looks of it, Reagan's mother. "Dr. Marchetti, right?"

I stretched out my hand for a shake, wondering who invented manners and regretting that I had to abide by them to keep up my charming Doctor Miracle persona. Apparently, patients wanted Jekyll, not Hyde. Shocker.

"You can call me Tatum. I take it you're Mrs. Rothschild?"

"Jennifer." She placed a palm on either side of my hand in lieu of a shake. "Dr. Marchetti, what you've done for my daughter... I can't thank you enough for it."

Behind her, Charlie studied Hannah, who looked exactly the same as she had the day she'd moved out four years ago. Hannah's lips formed words at a measured pace. She had a tendency to think through her thoughts before she verbalized them, with the exception of all things Kellan. Which ended up being the wrecking ball to our relationship. That, and the pesky little fact that I simply didn't like her. As a human, sure. As a fiancée? Hard pass.

"I've never seen her this happy." Mrs. Rothschild's hands still grasped mine. "We're so excited for the babies to come. I've cleared out a room in my house for when they visit their grandma. How have you been lately?

Well-rested?"

1) Like I ran into my dead brother's best friend and popped a boner while consoling her.

2) Not in the fucking slightest.

But I read between the lines, knowing what Mrs. Rothschild wanted to hear. "In peak form. Ready to deliver the twins. I'll do my best," I assured her, tired.

Last night, I found Terry on my doorstep with a signed copy of *The Imperfections* and the stipulation that I give him one last chance in exchange for it. Which, in hindsight, shouldn't have surprised me, since Terrence Marchetti's true talent in life was exploiting his own flesh and blood. I carried the book inside my back pocket, curved with the shape of it, because I couldn't bring myself to treat it delicately. And after I gave it to Charlie, I would sever any ties to her.

As if she could hear me, she turned her head in my direction. Her eyes collided with mine. I figured she'd be startled at the very least. I hadn't exactly given her the impression that I would step within a one-block radius of this place. But she took my presence in stride, holding my gaze with her chin tipped up.

Reagan's mom leaned in closer. "So, tell me... the babies are girls, right?"

"I think your daughter would be upset with me if I told you before the reveal."

"She needs you too much to be upset with you."

"It's true," Reagan agreed, offering me a bottle of craft beer. "Thanks for coming, Dr. Marchetti."

I grabbed it by the neck, downing half in one gulp. "I have no doubt I'll be walking home with noise-canceling Sennheisers by the end of the night."

"You entered the raffle contest?!" She burst into laughter. "That's cheating."

I offered a lopsided grin. "You need me too much to be upset with me."

"True. Plus, I really enjoyed the bottle of Dom you gifted me," she joked, winking at me. "I'm sure even the babies got drunk." She paused.

"Oh, before I forget, I have an employee that's never been to the ob-gyn. I was hoping you'd take her on as a favor. Her name is Charlotte. You remember her, right?"

So much to unpack. For starters, it was downright irresponsible to ignore reproductive health. Which also made it seem unlike Charlie. But the last thing I needed—or wanted—was her as my patient.

Hannah darted toward us. Reagan spotted her first and tugged her mother away by the sleeve, calling out that she'd email Sylvia to coordinate the appointment details. I hadn't even agreed.

Charlie traced Hannah's movement with hawk eyes. My ex-fiancée approached me with the same hesitancy she'd displayed after Kellan's death. Like I was a grenade with a missing safety clip, and she needed to be the pin.

"Hannah." I tipped my bottle toward her in greeting.

"Tatum." She nodded toward the clear double doors that led to a small courtyard. "Can we talk?"

"Sure."

I'd planned on leaving after greeting Reagan, but I figured a five-minute conversation was the least I could do for Hannah after she'd kept me fed and sufficiently breathing in the months following Kellan's death.

Out in the courtyard, Hannah positioned herself to block me from fleeing. Couldn't blame her. The thought had crossed my mind. It'd be easy to find an excuse to slip out. Mother in labor. Emergency C-section. Potential ectopic pregnancy. I'd used all three in the past when I needed space from her.

This spot offered a clear line of sight to Charlie, which wasn't ideal, considering she looked like she had stuff she wanted to say and I found it fuck-hard to drag my eyes away. She mouthed something, but she sucked at it so bad, her tongue swiped her lips. And that got my dick's attention.

Fucking pathetic.

It was an asshole move to stare at Charlie while talking to Hannah. But yelling at me to send my brother off to military school was also an asshole move, which Kellan had apparently heard. As Terry could attest, holding grudges was a special talent of mine.

Hannah cleared her throat. "You've really moved on, haven't you?"

"There was nothing to move on from."

The words tore out of my mouth. She flinched, but I didn't regret them. I knew Hannah. If I didn't make the status of our relationship crystal clear, she'd latch onto whatever hope she could.

But also, prick was my default setting, and I found it disturbingly easy to slip into. I was Terrence Marchetti's son after all. And she was the woman who'd tried to kick my brother out of my home.

After he passed, Hannah returned and stayed around for six months, only bailing once she realized I had no plans to off myself and Kellan hadn't been the problem in our relationship. He'd been the reason for it.

My attention veered to Charlie again. She'd moved to a new strategy—repeating the same word over and over, emphasizing each syllable.

Har. Vard.

I didn't understand her fixation. In my office, I'd chalked it up to a stalling strategy. Or maybe she genuinely hadn't known about his acceptance, and it meant she wasn't as close to him as she thought she was.

Hannah pretended she didn't notice me staring. It reminded me a lot of our former relationship—pretending everything was okay when nothing had ever been. She reached for my arm, trying to draw me back into the conversation. "How have you been?"

"Is this what you wanted to talk about?"

"It's a pleasantry, Tatum," she spat out. *There you are.* "Something you say when you haven't seen someone in three years and seven months."

But who was counting, right?

"I didn't come here to fight."

Or see you. Why are you here again?

"I wanted to know why things ended, but I guess the better question is why they ever began."

"Is that important?"

"It is if I want closure, which I think I deserve."

And then it clicked. What Charlie wanted. She wanted to know The Why. Because if Kellan applied to Harvard, he wanted to get in. And if he got in, it meant he had a future. And if he had a future, it made digesting his decision to kill himself more difficult.

Closure.

The word bounced around in my head. I chewed it over, wondering if either of us deserved it.

"It's been four years, Charlie."

"Hannah," she corrected.

Shit.

"It's been four years, Hannah."

My attention drifted behind her. Charlie still had her eyes pinned on me. She could've waved a red bullfighting flag, and she'd be less obvious. Then again, I doubted I was any better. And I thought I'd escaped the spiral.

"Is she Charlie?" Hannah jerked her thumb behind her. "The girl you keep staring at."

"No." I was so comfortable lying, I did it even when I had nothing to gain at this point. After today, I wouldn't see Hannah again. It didn't matter whether she knew the truth.

I looked past her. Charlie was beelining toward me, gaining speed as the crowd thinned. If I stayed, there would be a blowup. A confrontation. It was as inevitable as death. We needed to have this conversation, but I also needed to keep my sanity intact. At least until the C-section scheduled for four in the afternoon tomorrow.

Why did Kellan kill himself? Whose fault was it? Could we have done something to prevent it? I didn't know the answers to any of these questions. I only knew two things: 1) I wasn't ready to figure anything out, and 2) Self-preservation was the first law of nature.

So, I did what assholes do.

Correction: I did what Terry always did.

I bailed.

Chapter Thirty-One

Charlotte

I came to work dressed how I felt. Chaotic. Ripped tights under a black dress littered with candy-red paint splatters. I wore a choker around my neck, fingerless gloves on my hands, and a frown on my face, which deepened when I spotted a crowd around my desk.

Irene bent forward at the waist, hands behind her back, staring at something like she was too afraid to touch it.

Abigail noticed me first. "There she is!" She stampeded toward me, looping an arm around my shoulder. "Where did you find it?"

"Find what?"

"A signed copy of *The Imperfections*. I hear Terry Marchetti hasn't done a signing since the first print, and those were eighteen-and-over events. You were a baby when it came out."

"I was thirteen."

"Yeah. A baby."

I scrunched my nose, unsure what she was talking about before I remembered my deal with Tate. "Was Dr. Marchetti here?"

"No." Her brows furrowed. "Why would he be? Is Reagan okay?"

"Yeah. Sorry, I got confused for a second."

"Wait." Abigail slanted her head. "I just realized Dr. Marchetti and

Terry Marchetti share the same last name. You don't think…" she trailed off on a laugh, shaking her head. "You don't think they're related, do you?"

God. Tate. Lately, it always came back to him, and I was starting to feel trapped. Like I'd been buried alive with him, only to learn I was claustrophobic. He was closing in on me from all angles.

I didn't know if Tate and Terry's relationship was public knowledge, so I just shrugged, mumbled an excuse, and darted to Reagan's office. She called for me to enter on the second knock.

I poked my head in first, followed by the rest of my body. Why did I feel like I was visiting the principal's office?

"I left a book on your desk." Reagan closed the manuscript perched on her keyboard. She wore a question in her eyes, but she didn't voice it.

"Thanks. Did Dr. Marchetti give it to you?"

"Yes. I thought he'd left the party, but he returned with the book." She paused, meaningfully. "He said you left it in his office when you delivered the invite."

It sounded like an excuse.

A stupid one.

Who walked around with a signed copy of *The Imperfections*? That was the type of book you kept in a glass case, framed under lock and key. And possibly insured.

I dug my heel into the carpet. Maybe the floor would get the message and swallow me whole.

Reagan was still staring at me. Waiting for an answer to the question she'd never asked. I hovered by the doorsill, unwilling to step farther inside. Insecurity churned in my stomach, making me a little nauseous. I'd risen up the ranks faster than anyone in this office, and I felt like Tate had eviscerated that progress merely by existing.

I cleared my throat, stalling. "It was actually a gift." Gift. Deal. Same thing, right? "I knew Tate's brother Kellan, but I didn't meet Tate until you asked me to set up an appointment for you in February."

"I realized after receiving the book at the party that Tate and Terry are possibly related."

I nodded. "Father and son."

In the same way Lucifer and God enjoy a father-son relationship.

"He never mentioned it."

And this was my cue to extract myself from the room. There was nowhere to go here but south if this conversation continued.

"I don't know him very well, but he doesn't strike me as the type to discuss his personal life." I planted a palm on the door handle, slowly backing up. "Speaking of dysfunctional family dynamics, I have a domestic thriller I'm dying to get back to."

Reagan dismissed me with a wave. I half-sprinted to my desk and sat, staring at the book resting against my keyboard. With its dark cover and tiny, typewritten font.

The Imperfections.

Holy shit.

An actual signed copy.

I flipped the front flap open, brushed my fingertips along Terry's signature, and turned to the dedication page, reading it for the millionth time.

> *To my son, without whom there would be no words.*

I had no doubt which son Terry was referring to. And that made me sad for Tate. But I knew what having this book meant. What Tate had said when he bailed on me at the party. What he'd told me the first day we'd met.

I don't want anything to do with you after tomorrow.

Looks like he got tired of waiting for his wish to be fulfilled. Now, one less thread connected me to him.

I didn't have Tate's number, so I wrote him a letter. A long one. Stuck it in an envelope. Scribbled the address on it. Pasted a navy Chien-Shiung Wu stamp on the upper right corner.

Then I slid it to the far edge of my desk to be shredded later.

Never to be read again.

Chapter Thirty-Two

Charlotte

I had a guilt complex. Not one I'd been born with, but one that developed after The Night Of. Now I couldn't have things others didn't. I wasn't sure if it was because I felt like I didn't deserve them or if I thought I'd get struck down by lightning as the universe's way of evening the balance.

Either way, I felt very uncomfortable in this moment, with Leah eyeballing my signed copy of *The Imperfections* every now and then. It sat on our kitchen island, awaiting the delivery of the shadow box I'd purchased online last week.

A rerun of *The Nanny* blared in the background. Neither of us paid attention to it. Leah held a beauty magazine in her hands, flipping the pages without reading them. The question sat on the tip of her tongue. She didn't need to verbalize it for me to hear it.

Where did you get it?

Leah didn't love books like I did. She just happened to love *this* one. Because everyone with a functioning brain knew about *The Imperfections*. It was *The Corrections* meets *Parasite*. Satirical commentary about the decline of the nuclear family.

It hit home every time I read it, reminding me of before. Before the fire. Before Kellan. Before life pushed me onto that roof, ready to end it all.

It was all the more impressive when I remembered that the man who'd written it had the emotional intelligence of a walnut and at least two illegitimate children (that we knew of). Granted, if the state of New York accepted common-law marriages, Kellan would be legitimate.

Point was, every major literary masterpiece that came after had a piece of *The Imperfections* inside. And everyone who'd read the book or watched the movie became obsessed, Leah included.

She used to call Terry Marchetti—the Terry Marchetti decades older than her, who dressed in cocaine chic and was once caught smoking weed through a gas mask bong in a now-viral picture—hot.

"Do you want it?" I finally asked. My heart bellowed in its cage, gaining speed with each passing second.

Please say no. Please say no. Please say no.

I already knew I would say yes, because I always said yes. Just like I knew she would ask. It was the same song and dance since that night.

A part of me—a big part—didn't want to admit what I suspected. That Leah did this on purpose to force me to make sacrifices in order to offset her big one.

I didn't mind.

Not really.

I wanted to please her.

I just wish we weren't stuck in a toxic cycle.

Leah tucked a lock of hair into her mouth, biting down. "Really?"

Her bare skin stared back at me, a symphony of pinks and purples. I found her pretty, with or without makeup. In fact, I found her so insanely beautiful, she belonged on the covers of the magazines she devoured.

But I couldn't force my opinions on her.

Only the side effects of my guilt.

"Sure." I swallowed around the huge lump in my throat. "It's not a big deal."

Lie.

"It's okay." Her eyes darted to the paperback again.

Translation: I want it, but I don't want to be the dick that asks for it.

Double translation: This doesn't absolve you of your guilt over what happened.

"Take it. I insist."

Snatching the paperback from the counter, I offered it to her. Nine years ago, I would've dumped it in her room and shouted, no take-backs!

But now, I never entered her room.

Ever.

And I never gave her things either. Not for a lack of trying. She just refused to accept anything from me. Wouldn't want to even out her big sacrifice with a bag of Skittles.

The book hovered between us. I felt like a balloon, waiting for Leah to pump me with love, appreciation, *anything* and help me float.

Her hand latched onto it.

My pulse traveled up my throat.

She opened her mouth.

The balloon grew, floating in my chest, filled with hope.

"Thanks," Leah muttered.

And then she set it on her lap and went back to half-paying attention to Fran Drescher prancing around a gazillion-dollar home.

The balloon popped.

I deflated.

Leah didn't want the book.

She wanted to hurt me.

Chapter Thirty-Three

Charlotte

The following day, I zoned out. Distracted by *The Imperfections*. Not even Reagan's weekly meeting could snap me out of it.

"Charlotte?"

I felt like I'd donated an organ, only to learn it ended up unused. And now I was missing a piece of me for no reason, trying to convince myself it would be okay with a heavy dose of delusion.

Tate will ask Terry for another signed copy for me.

Yeah, no way I believed that. He hated Terry. I assumed asking for favors fell under the hatred umbrella. He'd also made it clear he didn't want to see me again. But it would make a good opportunity to grill him about Harvard. The idea had merit.

"Charlotte?"

What to do. What to do. What to do.

"Charlotte!"

I jerked my head up, startled to find everyone staring at me. "Sorry. I didn't get much sleep last night."

Reagan shrugged. She'd reached the thirty-two-week mark of her pregnancy, a milestone she'd never hit before. I figured I could accidentally toss the next *Harry Potter* from the agency inbox, and she'd still speak to me in the sickly-sweet voice she'd been using all week. "Did you read anything promising this week?"

"Nothing popped. Are you searching for something specific?" As soon as I said it, I regretted it. Irene winced, which told me they'd just concluded the portion of the meeting that included publishing trends and submissions criteria.

There goes the promotion you wanted.

Reagan tapped her fingers on her belly as if it were a table. She had a pregnancy glow. It radiated off every inch of her body. "Young adult urban fantasy. Maybe adult UF if it's written well enough. I want the next *Hunger Games* or *Twilight*. Something that'll run up a bidding war and break Netflix."

I was in charge of the slush pile addressed to no particular agent, which meant I received manuscripts from a variety of niches and genres. Most lacked a spark to keep me hooked.

"About ninety percent of my latest reads were thrillers. Wannabe *Gone Girls* with plot twists I can spot a mile away."

Reagan nodded, and Irene took over.

This time, I paid attention.

The pregnancy glow would wear off once Reagan gave birth. My leniency period would end. I wanted to become an agent and escape the purgatory of poorly written manuscripts stapled to generic, I-sent-this-to-every-agency-in-the-country query letters.

When the meeting ended, I scrambled out of my seat.

"Charlotte?"

I paused, facing Reagan. "Yes?"

"Can you stay a moment? I need to discuss something with you."

"Sure."

The rest of the agents filed out of the room.

When the door closed behind them, Reagan leaned back in her executive chair. Her shirt lifted with the movement. The thick band of her maternity jeans peeked out a sliver.

PARKER S. HUNTINGTON

"I stopped by the clinic for an ultrasound yesterday."

"Is everything okay?"

"Yeah, great. Dr. Marchetti took a 4D ultrasound image. I got to see the faces, noses, lips, everything." She paused. "I also talked to Sylvia. She's Dr. Marchetti's receptionist. Remember our conversation last weekend?"

My stomach dropped. I knew where this was going, and I had a feeling I wouldn't like it. "Yeah..."

"Well, Sylvia mentioned an opening for a new client." The words came out slow. Stretched out. Like she was unwrapping a present one tape strip at a time. "I mentioned you might be interested, and she agreed to book the slot for you. Isn't that lucky?"

Bullshit.

I knew this was bullshit on account of the fact that:

1) If there truly was an opening, which I doubted because pregnant women wanted Dr. Marchetti more than they wanted relief from back pain and swollen cankles, Sylvia would choose literally anyone over me,

2) Sylvia knew I worked for Reagan, and

3) Sylvia—and her boss—could not stand me.

I leaned against the vegan leather chair. "Oh."

"Since it's your first Pap smear, you won't find anyone better than Dr. Miracle. Not only is he knowledgeable, but he's also the gentlest doctor I've been with."

She said it like she'd just given me a gift, and she expected me to tear it open and shower her with gratitude. Her hand made circular motions on her belly as she waited for my reaction.

The corners of my lips rose, but my body screamed for an escape. "I was planning on finding someone near my apartment."

"Dr. Marchetti is the best in the city. Probably the country." She frowned. This was probably not the thank you she'd expected. "I told Sylvia to bill it to me, since I'm pushing you into this. Aunt Jessa died of cervical cancer at only fifty-six years young. I couldn't live with myself if

160

something happened to you and I knew I had the means to prevent it."

Over her shoulder, I eyed my desk through the glass wall. Specifically, the knee-high stack of paper piled beside it. Out of the hundreds of manuscripts I'd started, I'd only finished two. The rest were DNF'd by the halfway mark. I needed a promotion so I could dump these novels and move on to queries I actually wanted to read.

Just do it. Please her. Say yes.

"If it's any consolation, I wish my first time was with Dr. Marchetti." She winced, which conjured a thousand scenarios of how this could go wrong. Not to mention the fact that this was Tate we were talking about. "The doctor stuck the speculum in too deep. Scared me away for a year."

You can do this. Reagan will be impressed. That promotion is yours.

"So, I'll tell Sylvia you want the appointment?" Reagan asked.

I found myself nodding. "Thank you."

My stomach churned.

"The appointment isn't until Friday evening, but you look tired." She scanned my body, pausing at my face. "Tell you what. Take the day off. Get some sleep."

"Thanks," I repeated, not feeling grateful in the slightest.

It'll be twenty minutes, tops.

It's no big deal.

You've got this.

Famous last words.

Chapter Thirty-Four

Charlotte

The good thing about being a virgin (and I supposed there was only one) was that I could fill out the sexually transmitted infections portion of this patient-intake form with absolute certainty. In Bernard and Marchetti's reception area, I scribbled down answers, waiting for the inevitable moment Tate and I made contact. A physician's assistant collected the paper from me and led me to Tate's office. Empty, thankfully. Once she left, I collapsed onto the seat farthest from the door.

"You can do this." I'd learned positive manifestation from a non-fiction submission I read last week. Safe to say it didn't work. But my words were true. I'd overcome far scarier things. Plus, I decided before I arrived that I wouldn't chicken out. That I had no reason to. "Reagan loves you." *She does, and she loves you most when you listen.* "You're a team player. Team players get promotions and are freed from generic slush-pile duty."

A knock rattled the door. Tate's deep voice blasted through it. "Miss Richards? Are you ready?"

Oops. Could you be any louder? Way to come off as mentally stable.

I cleared my throat, cheeks flushed. "Ready."

He walked in, looking calm, collected, and about as lively as carb-free pasta. If he was shocked to see me, it didn't show. I held my breath, waiting to see which version of Tate I'd get. Last time, he hadn't wanted to talk to me. But I figured he was professional enough to at least converse with his patient. (Low bar. I know.)

"Miss Richards." He collected a clipboard, sliding the sheets I filled earlier beneath its teeth. "I reviewed your intake form and noticed this is your first gynecological exam." He made his reluctance to treat me obvious.

I almost asked why he'd agreed in the first place, but that would require diving head-first into an awkward conversation. *Pass.*

I tipped my chin up, leg kicking back and forth. "Yep."

Eloquent, Charlotte.

I leaned back in my seat and crossed my ankles. Everything seemed okay so far. Doable. I mean, my heart was shadowboxing with my rib cage and I'd reduced myself to first-grade vocabulary, but all things considered, I appeared as if I had my shit together.

Tate leaned against his full bookshelf, clipboard tucked under his bicep. He looked professional, yet... boyish. A far cry from the man I'd met inside these walls, pounding the shit out of a blonde woman who rode a two-minute orgasm. "I could call in my colleague, Dr. Bernard." It was the white flag I needed to confirm asshole Tate would take the backseat for the day.

I considered it. "Is Dr. Bernard a man or a woman?"

"Man."

"Old or young?"

Tate cocked a brow. "Fifty-something, I believe. Do you want to see a picture?"

I tilted my head sideways, batting my lashes. "Would that be too weird to ask?"

He suppressed a grin. He reminded me so much of Kellan. Yet, they couldn't be more different if they'd tried. And that reminded me I'd liked Kellan in more ways than I'd allowed myself to admit at the time. The weird thing was, my feelings for both brothers were so strong, yet so unalike. They awoke different parts of me.

Tate's narrowed sapphire-silver eyes scanned my face. He palmed his phone, clicked away, and passed it to me. I retrieved it with shaky fingers, eyeing the picture he'd pulled up. Of a man in a blue tie, smiling at the camera. He looked like a Baldwin brother.

I handed the phone back. "I don't know about that. I've never been examined before. What do you think? Should I go with a complete stranger, or someone I know and kind of hate?" It occurred to me that I could choose neither option. If I wanted, I could leave this place. Book an appointment elsewhere. With someone who made me feel comfortable. A woman. I toed the line, knowing I'd stay and refusing to admit why.

Tate stared at me with an intensity that threatened to burn me alive, his throat rolling with a swallow. "I think," he said carefully, "I'm not the person you should be asking."

"Fair enough. Let's ask Abe Linc." I produced a penny out of my purse. I didn't feel bad about cheapening my tradition with Kellan because this was a completely different one—I was flipping a coin, not offering it to Tate. "Heads for Bernard. Tails for Marchetti. May the best man win."

I tossed the coin. Both our gazes followed its graceful somersaults in the air. It landed in my palm. I flipped it over the back of my other hand and peered down to see the verdict. My mouth went dry. I looked up at Tate.

"Well?" His voice cracked mid-word.

There were approximately a million butterflies swirling in my chest right now, kissing my heart. I felt like throwing up, but in the best possible way. I licked my lips. "Tails."

"It means nothing. I can still call Walter."

Walter Bernard. He sounded like someone they'd assign to do my taxes at H&R Block, and quite frankly, I was afraid he'd judge my vagina.

"No, it's fine. I'm sure you'll maintain professionalism."

"Of course." Tate leaned forward, pressing a button on his switchboard. "Grace, please show Miss Richards to one of the exam rooms."

A pretty girl in a gray nurse uniform materialized at the door, an iPad in hand. "Please follow me."

A deep breath heaved out of me as soon as the distance grew between me and Tate. I followed Grace to a private examination area beside the nurses' station, where she took my blood pressure, weight, and height. She asked me a series of questions about my health for the next twenty minutes, jotting notes on the tablet after each answer.

"Are you on birth control?"

"Yes. I get it prescribed by the pharmacist near my apartment."

"Any reactions to it?"

"Lighter period symptoms and a regular cycle, which are exactly why I take it."

"Are you sexually active?"

I cleared my throat, taking way too long to answer. "Not currently."

"When you were, did you use any contraception?"

"Is this..." I swallowed hard. "Is Dr. Marchetti going to read this?"

I stared at her clipboard. Her eyes dragged up from the form to mine, confusion marring her features. I couldn't blame her. What a stupid question.

"Of course." She had a soothing voice that did nothing to soothe me. "This is obligatory pre-exam information to assess the patient."

Dammit.

"Is anything wrong?" she asked gently, slanting in my direction. Her hand cupped my knee. "Do you have anything you're worried about? Have you been... assaulted in any way?"

Oh, God. She thinks I was... Jesus.

"No, no. Nothing like that. I just..." I shook my leg. "Well, I'm a virgin."

"Oh." She perked up, smiling. "Don't you worry about that at all. Many of our patients are virgins. I will make sure Dr. Marchetti is aware, so he is super careful. As it is, I can assure you he is extremely gentle and respectful."

Somehow, I doubted that based on how he'd screwed that woman in his office. Frankly, his general personality screamed callous and aggressive, but I didn't defy her.

"No need to make a note of that. I'm not attached to my hymen or anything." I paused. "I mean, spiritually. Physically, I am. Still."

God, Charlotte, shut up.

"Okay, we're ready!" she chirped, standing up and slapping the tablet on her thigh. Grace led me to an examination room with bright lights, grabbed some sort of hospital gown and a giant folded tissue sheet, and placed them both on a cushioned table adorned with flowery stirrups. "Please get completely naked and put this gown on. Dr. Marchetti will be with you shortly. I'll be outside if you need anything."

Grace left, finally giving me a second to hate myself properly for going through with Reagan's genius idea to have a man I was extremely attracted to shove his fist into my vagina. I contemplated changing my mind and switching to Dr. Bernard, but I didn't want to look like a complete wuss. Besides, getting examined by him would just present a totally different set of problems and would still be cringeworthy.

You can walk right out of here.

But then Reagan would know I didn't have that Pap smear, and she'd be disappointed, which I'd never hear the end of. I shook my head.

It's just a test. You were always an A student.

And that was the wrong thing to think, because it reminded me of the age gap between Tate and me. When was the last time he'd even been in school? Half a decade? A decade? I cleared that line of thought before it spiraled out of control.

Quickly, I removed my clothes, extremely aware that my body was far from perfect. I'd seen the woman Tate had sex with. Stick-thin with a perfect tan. I carried a little excess weight and some cellulite around my butt. Also, his job description included practically feeling up vaginas and boobs. What if mine fell short of the Manhattan elite's average? I'd shaved most of myself down there in preparation, and suddenly, I feared it might look like too much. Like I was nestling a bald eagle between my legs.

Why can't I turn off my freaking brain?

I folded my clothes, set them in a neat stack on the crème counter, then proceeded to tie the hospital gown around my neck and waist as tight as possible. Which was still not good enough, because this thing didn't have any back. My ass literally hung out there, bare and feeling the breeze. Finally, I got to the weird tissue sheet. Grace hadn't explained what to do with it, so I decided to tactfully wrap it around myself. At least my behind was now covered.

Yeah. That's much better. Now you can forget all about the fact that he's about to rummage inside your vajayjay.

In my bid for modesty, I wrapped my arms around myself to ensure I was all covered up. I sat on the edge of the exam table, literally a human toilet roll, and wondered where it had all gone wrong.

The second I saw Tate bring a woman to orgasm, I decided.

There was a rap on the door. I sucked in a breath.

Tate's low, gravelly voice rasped through the cracks. "Can I come in?"

No.

"Yes."

He opened the door and closed it behind him. This time, he wore a doctor's coat over his usual cigarette pants and tight cashmere sweater. He turned around to look at me, and his eyes widened a little. "That's an interesting take." He suppressed a smile.

I wanted to die of embarrassment. I was pretty sure my head was about to explode from all the blood rushing to my face. But I shrugged, as if it was no skin off my back. "I wasn't sure what to do with the tissue."

"Normally, you put it over your lap for modesty."

"My way seems more modest."

"Can't argue with that logic."

He took a step in, the damning clipboard in his hand. The form he'd probably already read. So, now he knew my weight, and that I took birth control, and that I'd never had sex before. He still hadn't taunted me about any of those things. Maybe he never would. Perhaps he really was a good doctor, who put our animosity aside during working hours.

Tate rested the clipboard on the counter and washed his hands, squirting soap into his palm. You could cut the tension in the room with a butter knife.

"I went through your file," he started.

Here we go.

He scrubbed his hands, his fingernails cut close to the skin, his forearms corded with muscles and veins. "Since you've never been to an ob-gyn before, would you like a general checkup?"

"What does a general checkup consist of?" I felt like an idiot. Young, and naïve, and ignorant.

"Breast exam, abdominal exam, and pelvic exam."

"Would you recommend that?" Clearly, I was fishing for some sort of confirmation he wanted to touch me.

Tate turned off the tap, plucked some paper towels, and dried his hands, slam-dunking the balled sheets into the trash. The snapping of gloves filled my ears. They were pale blue, like the ring around his gray irises.

He approached me. "I would."

"Fine. Whatever."

"I'm going to have to insist on a verbal confirmation, Miss Richards."

I inwardly rolled my eyes. "Yes, I would like a general exam. Please."

"May I untangle you from your..." He raked his eyes over the tissue paper around me. "Chastity belt?"

Heat rose up my neck and cheeks. "Whatever. I guess." I couldn't sound more juvenile if I tried. Which, as amazing as it was to comprehend, was not what I was attempting to do here.

He cleared his throat. "I will need..."

"Oh. Right. Yes. Please, *please*, untangle me from the paper."

He reached out to me, unwrapping my body from the tissue without actually touching me. This close, the scent of him—sandalwood and bonfire and heady, earthy musk of a man—made every inch of me tingle. I inched away to stop my mouth from watering.

When the tissue sat in a heap of scratchy paper beneath my body, Tate motioned for me to lie down. "I'll walk you through each step. Stop me if you have any questions or if you feel uncomfortable." His voice was casual. Taciturn.

I nodded, pushing my glasses up the bridge of my nose. He started with the abdominal exam, which consisted of him feeling my stomach through my gown. He pressed here and there, his fingers strong and expert. I suppressed a grunt, my muscles tensing. I could see why women found ob-gyns attractive. They literally dedicated their lives to learning everything there was to know about the female body. He could probably give women orgasms in his sleep. He probably gave women orgasms while *they* slept. In their dreams.

"Moving on to the breast exam." His hand drifted up to the tie protecting my chest from the A/C and mortification when Tate inevitably spotted the alert state of my nipples. "I'm going to untie the top of your gown now. Is that okay?"

"Sure."

He reached forward, tugged on the string, and... nothing. We realized at the same time that my strategy had backfired, eyes colliding in the silence. Problem was, I'd knotted the ties so tight, the neckline choked my throat. The string would take a solid few minutes to untangle.

I bit my lip when my ankle hit a stirrup too hard. "What's the protocol in situations like this?"

"There is no protocol." To his credit, he didn't laugh at me, which only made the situation tense. "This is a first for Bernard and Marchetti."

I cracked a smile. "I could skip the breast exam and take the gown as a souvenir?" He said nothing. "I'd compensate you for it, of course," I rushed out.

Oh my God, Charlotte. Make like Ariel and shut up.

Where was a fire alarm to pull when I needed one?

"Is that what you really want?"

Was he already regretting not pawning me off to Dr. Bernard? Would this become the new funny clinic story all the nurses told their nurse friends?

Shut up, brain. You're not helping.

I considered it. It was peak cowardice to show up, undress, and leave without all the standard exams. "What are the other options?"

"You can remove the gown from the back or I can untangle the knot."

Translation: You can strip or have my hands fist bump your boobs for the five minutes it takes to untangle your straight jacket.

I cleared my throat. "Let's skip the breast exam."

He quirked a brow. "Have you ever had one before?"

"No."

"I can teach you how to do a breast self-exam at home."

"What's that?"

"It's a screening tool to detect breast cancer early." He handed me a pamphlet and pivoted, opening a cabinet for something. "I'll teach you how to feel your breasts for lumps and other abnormalities—steps four and five."

I stared down at the shiny paper, which listed instructions. Step four consisted of an illustration of a woman lying down, fingers on her breast.

"And you'll teach me... over my gown?" I knew it was a stupid question as soon as he spun to face me again with a fake boob in his hand, but there were no take-backs when it came to embarrassing words. "Oh. Nifty."

For the next few minutes, he showed me how to feel for lumps, using the mock breast as an example. "This is how you do a self-exam. I recommend performing them monthly and familiarizing yourself with the landscape of your breasts, so you'll notice any potential changes later."

"Okay." I gripped the faux boob. My turn to grope it for lumps. Problem was, I couldn't feel a single one. I tried again. And again. And again. I hoped gynecologists didn't charge by the hour, because I was racking up a bill here.

"Do you feel any lumps?"

"Sure," I lied, wanting to get this over with.

He didn't seem amused. "Where?"

"Here." I pointed to a random spot.

"Try again."

"I can't feel a thing," I admitted.

His fingers descended on mine, dragging them along the breast and pressing down. "Do you feel it now?"

"No." I cleared my throat, distancing myself from him a bit. "Let's just go with option C."

"Option C?"

"The knot. Please untangle it."

"You still need to learn how to perform a breast self-exam."

I picked up the pamphlet again, waving it. "I'll YouTube it."

"Miss Richards..."

"Scout's honor."

He narrowed his eyes, but he didn't fight me on it, instead moving for the knot of doom. "I'm going to untangle this now."

"Please do."

He grasped the tie, so close to me, I could feel him everywhere. His knuckles brushed against my collarbone with each movement. I felt dizzy. Fuzzy all of a sudden. Like I was floating in a haze. I let him work in silence, counting sheep until I reached three-hundred and eighty-four sheep and he finished.

The two flaps covering my chest parted, revealing my chest to him.

Tate's hand slid up my ribcage. "I'm going to touch your breast now."

"Do you do this on dates, too? Because it sounds really awkward."

He offered me a cold, this-is-not-funny smile, all professional. *Snap.* We really had entered a different realm the minute I became his patient.

Tate's hands were on my breast now. Since I'd never been checked before, I didn't know if doctors were supposed to be this thorough, but he spent a considerable amount of time massaging my right breast, pressing down with practiced, methodical movements.

My nipples began to pucker, heat swirling under my belly button. I didn't need to look down to know both were rock hard. The two peaks stared right back at him, sensitive and begging to be touched. I peered at his face, my heartbeat skyrocketing. He wore a frown, concentrating on feeling for lumps. I felt like a pervert.

Tate moved to my left breast. His fingers slid over my skin and circled the curve of my cleavage, his thumb digging into a spot I'd never thought was sensitive. Just below my nipple. I let out a moan without meaning to, then covered it with a cough and a dumb excuse about recovering from a cold. *Oops.*

I closed my eyes, willing myself to not be wet. Too late. I knew I was. My legs were still clamped shut, and the place between my inner thighs had grown damp and warm, begging for me to rub them together for friction. He drove me crazy. I feared I'd climax before he touched me there, so staying calm when his hands traveled south was hardly an option.

"All clear," he said, somewhat hoarse. He kept such a poised façade. A passive face and relaxed shoulders.

His thumb brushed my left nipple when he moved away. It was a light, accidental touch, but I could feel it. I shuddered, my womb clenching. I let out another desperate, involuntary moan and fell into a bout of fake coughs.

No covering that up.

"Sorry," he muttered, and I opened my eyes, staring at him under hooded lids.

I licked my lips again. I needed to stop. My brain screamed at me not to check if he had an erection. He would notice.

"It's fine." It came out groggy. Like I'd been drugged.

"Now for the Pap smear. Seeing as you've never had sexual intercourse before, it is unlikely you have cervical cancer or cancerous cells. In most cases, cervical cancer is caused by a sexually transmitted infection called HPV. However, it's always good to be on the safe side. Plus, there are other factors to take in, such as a history of cancer in the family, smoking, etcetera. At any rate..." He moved toward my lower body. "I'll be very careful. The chances of your hymen being affected by this exam are absurdly low, so try to relax. Now spread your legs for me, Charlie."

It wasn't what he said but the way he said it that made my eyes snap to his in horror. He'd called me Charlie, and his voice was no longer taciturn.

It had the faintest touch of a smoky, bossy tint. One that said: This is an order, not a request.

We held each other's gazes for a second too long. Long enough to know he'd slipped up. That calling me Charlie hadn't been intentional. He was losing control, too.

Tate patted a stirrup, stepping out of our weird mutual reverie. "Need help?" His smoldering voice did things to my insides I was never going to recover from.

Say no.

"Yes, please."

He picked my feet up and placed them in the stirrups. His touch was so tender and confident, I wanted to cry. It was the first moment I let myself admit I wanted to be fucked by Dr. Tatum Marchetti. Ruthlessly hard and mercilessly filthy. I wanted us to do things that would make the pretty blonde he'd brought to orgasm in his office blush. And I was going to Hell for this, because he was my late best friend's brother.

I was wide open in front of him now. Tate placed himself on a chair between my legs. I instinctively pressed my knees together.

"Miss Richards," he said softly.

I closed my eyes, running through a series of pleas in my head, not sure which I wanted.

Please, don't make this awkward. Please, don't embarrass me. Please, don't suggest Dr. Bernard and humiliate me. Please, hurry up. Touch me already.

My nipples were so sore with need, one more flick of a thumb would undo me.

I swallowed hard. "Yes?"

"Now's a good time to open your legs."

I was sure his choice of words was not accidental, professional or not.

I'm horny, I wanted to scream.

"I'm shy," I said instead.

"You have no reason to be. Would you like to start with the pelvic exam? It may put you at ease. You might feel a bit of discomfort, but that's all it will amount to."

"Okay." I nodded, my knees still pressed together.

I thought I was feigning innocence pretty well, considering only fifteen percent of my brain was occupied by the fact that Tate was going to see my vagina up-close. The other eighty-five percent was panicking about coming on his exam table. Was that considered sexually harassing him?

Tate waited patiently. Finally, I dropped my knees apart and opened up for him. I stared at him staring at my pussy. Swallowed. A look crossed Tate's face, but I couldn't identify it. I was neither well-versed in gynecological exams nor men. But he was doing such a damn good job of staying professional that if he told me I didn't affect him, I'd believe him.

"I'm going to touch you now."

I nodded, feeling his fingers through the rubber gloves as he pried my pussy lips open. He sucked in a breath. Or maybe it was his normal breathing. Everything felt and sounded heightened right now.

I couldn't not look at him. Again, I found myself using every ounce of self-control to think about things that were not him taking me on the exam table.

"How does it feel?" he murmured.

"Good."

We both paused, letting what I'd said sink in.

I flushed, blurting out, "I mean, it doesn't hurt or anything."

His gray-blues met my greens. His throat bobbed. Goosebumps rose on my skin. I struggled to keep my eyes open. Drunk with need. I found myself raising my hips, chasing his touch.

Tate stared between my legs. "I can't perform a bimanual exam because it might damage your hymen, so I'm going to move straight to the Pap smear."

"What's a bimanual exam?"

"It's when I push two fingers inside you to check the size, shape, and position of your uterus and screen for cystic ovarian masses or tumors."

"Sounds important." My voice was thick. All I could think about was Tate sticking two of those long, strong fingers into me. I'd officially lost my mind. "Are we sure we want to skip this part?"

"I am sure I want to not-tear your hymen and get sued, yes," Tate said drily. Still the same asshole I knew and liked.

"I won't sue you."

He chuckled. "I'll need that in writing."

He was joking, but I was dead serious. I picked up my phone and shot him a quick email, confirming I'd asked for a bimanual exam and explaining I understood the consequences. Luckily, I had the clinic's email from the time I'd booked the appointment for Reagan.

"There. Check me for tumors." I dropped my phone beside me, crossing my arms over my chest.

Tate stared at me intensely. So intensely, I knew he knew what I was trying to do here. He glanced down to his phone, which lit up with the new email, then looked back at me. "No."

"Why?"

"Because you shouldn't break your hymen this way."

"That's patronizing. Don't I get to choose how to lose my virginity?"

"Break your hymen," he corrected. "I wouldn't be taking your virginity; I'd be breaking your hymen."

My lips parted. If anything, his words made me wetter. I felt like I'd just been told the special of the day at a three-Michelin-star restaurant and that I needed to beg in order to eat it.

I will if I have to, I decided. It scared me how much I wanted this. Him.

Tate blew out a breath, looking torn. "You'll regret it."

"More patronizing. Nice." I was on a roll now.

He finally snapped, his eyes lit with anger, losing his control and his professionalism. "You realize I'm about to break your hymen on the exam table, and that I won't fucking call you the next day or send you flowers?"

175

I pulled at my leg. Pushed my glasses up my nose. Probably a boatload of other compulsive bad habits he brought out of me. He tracked my hand's assault on my thigh. I scooted my butt in his direction even farther, all but offering myself up on a platter for him. "I do. And while I'm here, I really want to rule out any chance I have cancer. Do what you gotta do."

"Charlie..."

"Do it."

Tate's eyes were still on mine as he spread me with his gloved hands again, sliding his index finger inside me. Slow. Too slow. I clenched around him on instinct. My hands curled into fists, squeezing as I bit back a groan. It felt so good, I wouldn't mind dying on this exam table.

"This okay?"

"Yeah," I croaked, closing my eyes, my knees shaking. "It's fine."

He slid another finger inside me. I shuddered all over, muscles tightening. I felt the barrier he'd been trying not to poke blocking him from sliding farther, but my eyes were shut. I heard Tate take a breath.

"Breathe slow and deep into your abdomen."

He muttered something after. Under his breath. Too low to make out. Then he pushed in all the way. I lifted my ass from the exam table, my mouth falling open with pain and desire. He hadn't expected the movement, because my clit connected with his palm. My toes curled. I bit my tongue to stop myself from crying out.

When I settled back on the table, Tate hooked his fingers deep inside me, touching a sensitive spot that made me moan loud. I was on the verge of falling apart. How did women not come on his exam table on a weekly basis? If this was common practice, I was screwed.

"Does it hurt?" His voice was hoarse.

"A little." I lied to save face, pretending I was not about to come all over his fingers. I closed my eyes, trying to get through this without falling apart, trying to sear this feeling into my memory for later. I was sick. So, so sick.

"I'm going to lay my hand on your stomach and press down on your uterus now."

Tate slid the gown up until it passed my waist, exposing my entire lower half. He leaned forward and placed the fingertips of his free hand on my lower belly. Right above my uterus. He pressed them deep, digging for whatever it was he needed to dig for.

I squirmed at the touch, feeling him in me, above me, everywhere. The movement brought the heel of his palm to my clit. I fought my moan and failed. My eyes flew open, meeting his. I couldn't cough that away. Not without clenching around his fingers. My cheeks burned.

Either he had a great poker face or he didn't know where his palm was. That I was falling apart before him. The pressure between my walls grew. He pressed down on my stomach with his other hand. I clenched around his fingers, unable to help it. My eyes snapped to his. They never wavered from mine, searching my face for cues of discomfort. I didn't give him any.

I cleared my throat, trying to play it cool. "It doesn't hurt much."

"It probably hurts less than losing your hymen the traditional way."

"I'm sure. It's not that painful."

"It helps that you're lubricated," he said matter-of-factly, his palm still on my clit.

But I didn't remember him opening the tube of lube on the cart beside him. That was all natural. All me. My cheeks were on fire at this point. His fingers probed deep inside me. I'd taken health class. Seen this done in a video. This looked one-hundred percent about the exam, but it didn't feel like it. It felt like it was about getting me off.

My mouth formed an O-shape, and I knew I was coming. I'd come before, using my own fingers, but never inside myself. And it had never felt like this. Never with the sensation of my body being so full with someone else's parts, the pressure building.

My eyes rolled over in their sockets. I slammed them shut. Every muscle in my body tensed and squeezed deliciously.

"Tate," I whimpered.

"Dr. Marchetti." His professional tone snapped me back to reality. *Too late.*

"I'm... I'm..."

"Seems that way."

He slid his fingers back, slow, moving out of me, but I clenched around them. My hips thrust forward, toes curling again in their stirrups. My glutes tightened to angle myself, pushing his fingers deeper into me.

I had no control over my body. I writhed before him. There was no way I would ever be able to look him in the eye again. He'd done nothing wrong. If anything, it was me. But it was the first thing to make me feel something other than dull, static pride for doing the right thing since The Night Of. Getting the top grades. Going to a good college. Finding a suitable job.

No, this didn't feel comfortable and nice and proper. It felt real and messy and out-of-this-world. It felt like something worth fighting for.

I came down from my orgasm like I was stepping through a fog. The shudders coursing through me were like the last waves of a hurricane, washing me back to shore. When my ass finally hit the exam table, I realized Tate had withdrawn his hand from inside me and pulled his chair back, distancing himself from between my legs.

He took off his gloves with a snap. "All clear," he clipped. "On to the Pap smear."

My teeth dug into my lower lip. I watched as he turned around, washing his hands and applying a fresh set of gloves. Reality crashed in on me. *Oh, God.* What had I done? I'd come on his fingers on the exam table. And now he was acting as if nothing happened.

He'd said this would not end with him sending flowers or calling me, and I'd accepted his terms—even sent him a legally binding email about it—so why was I surprised and furious with myself when he carried on with the exam without paying any attention to what had just happened?

He had to know. I felt my wetness pooling around my thighs and the table. I'd clenched around him. He had. To. Know.

I stayed silent as he turned back to me, stepping between my legs again. I knew my face was flushed. That sweat left strands of hair clinging to my temples. That I was still wet.

As if to confirm that, he took a few tissues and wiped my sex up and down. "I'm going to put a speculum inside you. It might feel a little weird, but I'll make sure to fix the size to the narrowest setting. You're very small, which is something you may want to talk to your future ob-gyn about, if and when you decide to have children."

I was very small? That was a good thing, right? Did that mean he enjoyed fingering me? Hell, why won't he say something about what happened here two minutes ago?

And then the rest of his sentence caught up to me. My *future* ob-gyn. As in, this would be the last time this happened. The last time he saw me. Was inside me.

Tate slid in the speculum, spreading the walls of my vagina. To my horror, the sensation was still very pleasant. In fact, a suction sound came from my greedy lady part. I groaned in embarrassment, closing my eyes. If I came again, I was divorcing my body.

He swiped my insides with a gentle brush, then removed the metal contraption. I still lay on the exam table, refusing to meet his eyes. Technically, we didn't have to see each other again. He'd made it clear he wouldn't be my ob-gyn in the future, and I could drop off the donation slip in the mail.

My pride urged me to cut all contact with him, but the damn thing in my chest wouldn't let me turn my back on him. I wasn't even sure who I was trying to save at this point. Him or myself.

"All done. The results should be with you in the next forty-eight hours, a courtesy our clinic takes pride in." He spun to me, his face void of emotions.

I was eager to make him comment on what had happened, but I felt strongly that I'd reached my pathetic quota for this year on his table. "Thanks, I appreciate your time." To my surprise, it came out just as cold as his words. I grabbed for my clothes before he even left. I wanted to get out of here, block the clinic's number on my cell, and pretend like he'd never happened. Push him from my memory.

He leaned against the counter, watching me. "As for your hymen—"

"Please stop talking about my hymen."

Tate stared at me with that look that drove me mad. Like I was a first-grader who'd just learned how to wipe her ass properly. "As for your hymen..." he continued, undeterred. Bastard. "I'm not sure if you lost all or part of it, but you may experience some bleeding and discomfort. Don't hesitate to contact the clinic if this persists."

Yeah, dude. Totally. I'll call you up about the virginity you took from me using your fingers and that other metallic thing you shoved inside me.

"Sure. Yeah."

"And when you do decide to have sexual intercourse in the future, please treat it as if you are a virgin, because ultimately, you are, and your body will need to adjust accordingly."

I scowled at him, shoving my legs into my jeans. It wasn't fair. He hadn't wanted to do this. Reagan made the appointment, and I all but begged for him over Dr. Bernard. But to be honest, I was not only pissed at him for caving in to my stupid request. I was mainly pissed at myself for having zero self-control around him.

"Are you this concerned about all your patients' sex lives?" I bit out.

"Of course," he said, aloof. "I'm their ob-gyn."

"Well, don't worry about mine. This was just a one-time Pap smear. As you mentioned in your office the other day—I can't afford your clinic."

"Speaking of, Reagan requested I bill her for your appointment. Sylvia will email her the invoice." With that, the bastard left the room, without even sparing me a goodbye.

I escaped the building, relieved that at least Tate didn't know the whole story. That in his office, the penny hadn't landed on tails. It landed on heads.

Fate didn't want him to feel me up. I did.

Chapter Thirty-Five

Tate

My busy delivery schedule spared me from hours of stewing in private over Charlotte Richards' orgasm. Sometimes, patients came. It had happened in the past. Would happen again in the future. I didn't make a habit of shaming them for it. Or even thinking about it, for that matter, other than to assure them they had nothing to be ashamed about.

Yet...

Charlie had a tendency to provoke a response from me that went against the grain of normalcy. Namely, she reduced me to a low level of decision-making ability previously reserved for reality television.

Over the next few days, I shuttled from patient to patient. Even offered to take over a routine ultrasound from Walter after his gout flared up. Slathering gel onto a protruding belly failed to divert my thoughts. Didn't help that the loud squish of the transducer probe gliding across the patient's wet stomach rivaled the volume of Charlie's pussy after my fingers sank into it. (The latter required no lube, and I am not proud of how proud I am of that.)

The patient cooed over the blob on the screen, clutching her husband's bicep. I coughed up a print of the twenty-two-week-old fetus, its legs curled inward. Couldn't tell the sex for shit in that awkward position.

The parents didn't care. They fawned over the tiny photo, and I got it. With the many failed pregnancies I saw, birth had become a miracle to me, too.

After they left, I found myself with four hours to spare before a scheduled C-section. Naturally, I spent minutes one through two-hundred and forty at home, with my dick in my fist, failing to convince myself to pick up a one-night stand from the nearest bar and work out my frustration.

Not my typical MO.

Not even close.

It infuriated me that Charlotte Richards had managed to undo the control I'd built up over three and a half decades of living.

My irritation simmered, boiling over. I finished the C-section without any complications and hopped onto the subway, riding it out. I ended up at a stop I had no business being near.

Didn't take a genius to figure out why.

Charlie's office could be seen as soon as I exited the station. I hadn't expected to actually find her here—never consciously decided to come, either—but she was.

In all her Charlotte Richards glory.

Tits pushed up by a black lace corset. Neck restricted by a maroon tie connected to a fake collar. A mile of legs peeked out beneath a mini plaid kilt.

Fuck. Me.

It was time to pursue a solution that didn't involve a trip to the ER for a serious case of blue balls, the loss of my sanity, and more baggage than a St. Regis bellhop.

Chapter Thirty-Six

Charlotte

The problem was, I couldn't have sex with Tate Marchetti. For starters—he gave no real indication of it being a possibility. And second—judging by the accident on his exam table, if he really tried, I'd be done for. Ruined.

Abigail, on the other hand, had a very active sex life and wasn't afraid to share it. "Raincheck on drinks tonight? I have a date with an archeologist, and I'm hoping he'll unearth my g-spot."

I held the door to our office building open, exited after her, and shouted to her retreating back, "If the archeologist fails, you can try a private detective next. I hear they're good at finding things."

"A gynecologist might be a safer bet," a deep voice suggested from behind. "Of course, you know that from personal experience."

I swiveled to find Tate there, leaning against a concrete pillar attached to the building. He had one hand shoved in a pocket of his cigarette pants, the other toying with his phone.

Abigail had already hopped into a cab and out of sight, but like us, Reagan worked late tonight, and the last thing I needed was for her to catch me salivating over the man responsible for delivering her babies with all their limbs attached.

I pulled us into an alley, turning his body so he faced away from the street. Away from prying eyes. "What are you doing here?"

"You asked a question. I'm here to answer it."

"I don't recall asking one."

"You did. I'm no neurologist, but I hear Vitamin E may slow memory loss."

Actually, in hindsight, I might've asked something. In his office. But what? Maybe about his concern over my virginity.

My cheeks felt hot. I rummaged through my bag, pretending to search it so I didn't have to look at him. "Okay. Answer it."

"I wasn't concerned about your sex life because you were a patient," he said casually. "I'm concerned about it because I want to fuck your brains out until you lose the ability to walk straight. Unfortunately for me."

I stopped what I was doing.

Silence blanketed us.

I had half my arm shoved inside the mouth of my patchy messenger bag, the other clutching my phone. It clattered to the asphalt.

Excuse me?

Tate collected the device, offering it to me. "I didn't invoice Reagan for the exam. Consider this my official refusal to see you as an ob-gyn on the grounds that I have a personal interest in you. I'm happy to refer you to Dr. Bernard or any of my other colleagues."

"Does that mean you want to date me?" I could feel my eyes flare, but it was that damn thing in my chest that threw me into high alert.

"I don't date. I fuck. If you're happy with that arrangement, you know where to find me. I'm fond of you, Charlie, which is why I'm going to advise you, as a friend, not to take me up on that offer. I'm too old, too jaded, and too fucked-up to give you what you want outside the bedroom."

Chapter Thirty-Seven

Tate

When it came to the rise and fall of Terry Marchetti, it was always the same question—where? Where is Terry Marchetti? Where did the money go? Where did the talent go? I could answer the first two. Easy. Terry paid very little taxes on his royalties and ignored the IRS when they came knocking on his door. He blew it all on a Central Park penthouse he couldn't afford, only to learn there are some government bodies you just don't mess with. The bank took the penthouse when he stopped paying the mortgage. The IRS and DOTF garnished his quarterly royalty checks. It left him with nothing but memories of success and a chip on his shoulder the size of the *Harry Potter* franchise.

As for the talent? It'd come as a shock to us all. Whatever literary prowess he possessed used to be confined to mid-list titles that ran for one mediocre print run under a forgotten indie publisher. Enough to pay for a studio in Parkchester and a few hits of whatever drug he preferred that month. But *The Imperfections*? It was the type of release every author dreamed of. Critics raved before it reached the shelves. Shortlisted it as one of the best books in modern literature. It went on to sell millions, hitting every damn list. People studied its pages in colleges, watched the movie adaptation in hordes, and salivated over all things Terrence Marchetti, only to pick through his backlist titles like they were bowls of rotten leftover cabbage.

Which was why I hated the third question. The one I could never answer. The one everyone seemed to ask once they discovered my lineage.

"You don't have to answer if you don't want to." Reagan slid her shirt over her belly at the end of her check-up. "I was just making small talk. Plus, plenty of authors write only one hit book and disappear. I've worked with dozens of them."

I saved a copy of her ultrasound for filing and exited the browser. "I doubt he'll publish anything else in this lifetime."

"Is he writing?"

"If you consider typing and deleting writing, sure."

With the signed one-hit wonder as leverage, Terry had weaseled his way back into my house. He spent his nights typing at his typewriter and shredding the words by sunrise. Then, he slept on my couch the rest of the day, waking only to steal my food and leave a trail of messes from the bathroom to the kitchen.

"Does he still have literary representation?"

"I feel compelled to warn you—his agent dropped him after he bailed on a three-book deal and was ordered to pay back the seven-figure advance."

"Maybe he has the yips."

Or maybe The Imperfections *was a fluke.*

I'd come to terms with it long ago. So did his agent and publisher. The only one who couldn't seem to accept it was him.

"Maybe," I echoed to end the conversation.

That night, I came home after an emergency C-section to find Terry sprawled on my couch, watching a *How I Met Your Mother* rerun on a flatscreen I had installed so the place didn't feel so empty. Up until this second, I had no clue it still worked.

"Hey, son." He crammed his hand into a generic-brand bag of potato chips. "You're home?"

Like always, his use of the word "son" never failed to anger me.

"Not your son." I stabbed the kitchen light switch and swung open the fridge door, finding it empty. "Not your home."

My stomach growled. I needed two thousand calories, fifteen hours of sleep, and a time machine to rewind to a time before I propositioned Charlie, offering no-strings-attached sex like a fucking creep (she was just a kid, and we knew the same people, and it was dangerous and so unlike me). I also needed some goddamn sense, probably courtesy of a restraining order with the way things were going.

"There's some leftover pizza. A whole pie from Rubirosa," Terry called out, pausing to reword a line from the show aloud. "They should've hired me to write the damn script." He shook his head. "Thought I put the pizza in the fridge, but I might've left it in the freezer."

As far as I knew, Terry didn't have a dime to his name to pay for a stick of gum, let alone enough to cover the fare to Nolita and an entire pizza from Rubirosa. I counted down from three in my head, fighting the heat building in the back of my neck.

"Have you seen Kel's manuscript? Thought I saw it shoved beneath his bed, but you must've moved it. I've been looking around the house for it all day. Is it in your room? You didn't throw it away, did you?"

Three.

"I ate the last of your meal delivery. Hope that's okay." Chip crumbs flew out of his mouth as he spoke, landing on my rug, the couch, and his dad bod. Nothing like crumbs on a wife beater-clad belly. "Tasted like shit. Maybe find a better service? Do some research. Check that app the kids use. You know…" He snapped his fingers a few times, pointing one at me. "Yelp."

Two.

"Oh, and your housekeeper stopped by today." He munched on another fistful of high-fructose-corn-syrup-laced maltodextrin. If I didn't kill him, the chips would. "Insensitive little thing started vacuuming all over my writing space, even though she could see me typing. Hope you don't mind, but I told her to leave and come back later. I couldn't write with all the noise. Good news is, I saved you the money you left on the counter for her." He lifted a chip, waving it in the general direction of the kitchen. "Used it to stock up your pantry."

One.

I snatched the bag from his hand, returned to the kitchen, and dropped it in the trash, spinning to face him again. "This is your one and only reminder that a condition of your stay is working."

"I *am* working." He pointed to the chips. "Those were expensive!"

"Perfect. You can buy some more when you finish a book and sell it."

"I can't. Not sober." He scratched behind his ear. "I wrote *The Imperfections* drunk and on blow. I don't even remember how I did it."

"Did I chain you to the floor and lock you in the basement?" I jerked my thumb to the left. "The door's that way. No one's forcing you to stay."

He pointed to a pile of discarded paper at his feet, scrunched up in balls. "I can't finish this book."

"I suggest you figure it out ASAP, considering your agent dumped you, your publisher dumped you, and I am ten seconds and a bad day away from dumping you. If you don't want to end up on the streets, you need to write a damn book." Mostly because it would mark one step closer to kicking him out of my life. For good this time.

He planted his fists on his waist, causing crumbs to tumble from his wife beater to my floor, which already missed its weekly cleaning. "I can't!"

"Not my problem."

"What if I don't?"

I finally looked at him. I mean, *really* looked at him. A hole-ridden shirt hung loosely around his frame. The thin layer of grease coating his hair glinted in the light. Two hollowed-out bags bordered his eyes. No matter how much he slept, he would always be tired. He looked like he'd gotten in a fight with a garbage truck, and the garbage truck won.

"What if I don't?" Terry repeated, quieter now.

I couldn't pinpoint where his life had derailed. Maybe his first taste of drugs. Maybe the moment he decided to chase his career with fifty times the effort he put into his family. Maybe he was born a fuck-up. Either way, it was not my problem. He was not my father.

"Don't test my patience, Terry. You won't like what you find when I reach the end of my rope."

"I can't write another book."

"You are washed out. Bound to die an early death as irrelevant as you were the day you were born. If you don't want to do something with your life, that's not my problem. I am more than happy to see you out that door." I gave him my back. My feet slammed against the floor on my path to my room. I could hear him following me.

He cut me off before I reached the staircase, gripping the lapels of my dress shirt. "I plagiarized it! Okay? Is that what you want to hear?"

I moved my hands to pry his off me, but they stilled at his words. "Repeat that."

"I stole the damn book." He waited for me to say something, and when I didn't, he fumbled to find an excuse. "But... But... it's not like you think."

The puzzle pieces clicked into place. Memories of every goddamn time I was asked about Terry Marchetti's meteoric rise and fall slammed into me. *It's like nothing he's ever written. I didn't know he had it in him. A once-in-a-lifetime read.* I'd never read the book, but I'd read what the critics had to say about it. Thought, for a moment, that at least Terrence Marchetti wasn't a totally useless piece of shit.

"The words..." He loosened his grip on me. "The book came from someone else." He stayed silent, waiting for me to say something.

I couldn't. Couldn't fathom the possibility that the book he'd spent the past decade bragging about—the one that redeemed his existence—was a lie. "You disgust me." It came out low and heavy, clouded by rage. I pushed him aside, marching up the stairs.

"I can still stay, right?" he called out.

I slammed my door shut, ignoring the way my stomach growled and my outrage chipped at my sanity. For nearly ten years, I'd tolerated Terry Marchetti's return to my life for one reason and one reason only. Kellan idolized him for writing *The Imperfections*.

Kellan idolized him for nothing.

Chapter Thirty-Eight

Charlotte

So. About the oops-gasm. It played in my mind on a never-ending loop. A broken record stuck on the loudest part. The main problem was, I'd enjoyed it. Wanted it to happen again, even. The other problem? No way could I ever look Tate in the eyes again. Not to apologize. Not to take him up on his offer. Nope. Never.

"Charlotte?" Abigail nudged my shoulder. "You're blushing."

We were crammed in one corner of the office elevator, going down. Packed like sardines in this death trap. So close together, I couldn't make out the sign with the weight capacity past the row of bodies in front of me.

"I am?" I tried to pat my cheeks, but all I managed was a handful of someone's elbow. The doors slid open. We spilled out. Behind us, the elevator creaked its relief.

"You okay?" Abigail followed me out the building and onto the sidewalk. "You've been flushed all day. Are you coming down with a cold? I'm sure Reagan will let you sit tomorrow out."

We had several meetings scheduled over the next two weeks with some big publishers. Reagan wanted to pitch a fleet of books from authors she represented, and she'd offered to let me tag along. An opportunity I wasn't dumb enough to miss out on.

I wore Kellan's jacket over studded, high-waisted shorts and fishnet tights. He'd left it on the roof Valentine's Day junior year, and I couldn't bring myself to return it. Not after that kiss.

"I'm fine. Just hot." I shrugged out of the heavy vegan leather jacket, looped with more chains than an entire Hot Topic store. "Feels like the summer heatwave is hitting earlier this year. I plan on heading home and sleeping it off with the A/C on full-blast. I'll see you tomorrow."

I darted to the subway station, jogging down the steps and pushing my way onto the train. Kellan's books lay in the waterproof dust bag looped around my arm. I needed to part with them. It was the last thing connecting me to Tate Marchetti, aside from the mortifying memory of coming on his exam table and his shocking proposition.

The cheesy grief pamphlets St. Paul's school counselor used to force on me encouraged depressed people to seek the bright side of life. To find one single positive in the sea of negatives and latch on to it.

The bright side here, other than the fact that it was a damn-good orgasm, was that I hadn't thought about Leah and *The Imperfections* in days. Because the worst part about giving it to her—the part that really mattered—was that, in the end, the book itself meant nothing to me. It was the fact that she'd used it as a vehicle to hurt me that truly killed me. And I was. Hurt. Just when I'd thought I'd learn to live with Leah liking me significantly less than she loved me, I'd gotten my hopes up. Again.

At my stop, I hesitated before hopping off my seat. I stared at the dust bag, then the doors leading out to the platform. Great to know my cowardice didn't stop at admitting the truth to Tate. That his brother once kissed me. That I'd known his brother wanted to kill himself. That I'd been lying to him since I'd met him. And then there was the other truth. One I could never admit to myself for fear of disappointing Kellan. Loyalty is a choice, and I intended to make it.

Tate is toxic, I reminded myself, thinking of the one-eighty he'd done since I spilled my Big T to him. *He'll stab you in the heart, then ask you why it hurts so much.*

I burst through the doors at the last second, startling the couples flanked on either side. "Sorry!"

My combat boots slammed against the platform. If I didn't run to the library, I'd never gather the courage to go. My lungs fought me. Sweat trailed down my temple. By the time I reached it, my brain had become fog. Smoke where thoughts came to dissolve.

The limestone building loomed before me. I stood below the stretched awning, bracketed by thick pilasters on either side. I'd gotten as far as the front door the day after Tate passed along the books to donate, but I never made it past the balustrade. And I hadn't been there since, breaking my post-college attendance streak.

I took a deep breath and headed straight to the front desk before I could change my mind. The dust bag slapped against my thigh with each step.

"Charlotte! I haven't seen you in so long. I've been worried." Doris, the head librarian, smiled at me. "What can I do for you?"

I tapped my fingers against the countertop. Kellan's books weighed down my arm. Speaking of Kellan, would he be mad about what had happened? He hated his brother. And damn it, I needed to stop thinking about the oops-gasm. "I have—" I hesitated, hating myself for it. Tate's proposition flashed in my head. No strings attached sex. My brain didn't know what it wanted, but my body did.

If only you had a reason to see him again...

Doris frowned. "You have...?"

If you do this, you'll never see Tate.

My foot slid back a step.

You'll never get the answers you need.

Another step.

You'll never get to confront him about Kellan.

And another.

His proposition won't last forever...

"Never mind," I muttered, spinning on my heels.

Doris called out for me, along with Faye, my favorite librarian here.

I retreated through the front door, bursting outside with winded gasps. My palms fell on the balls of my knees. People spilled onto the sidewalk, parting around me like the Red Sea as I tried and failed to catch my breath. To get my shit together. I didn't know what I was doing. Or what I wanted. Or where I'd go from here.

So, I walked. I walked until my ankles hurt. Until the evening blurred into night, till the sun fell and the city glowed beneath a blanket of artificial light. Until I had nothing on my mind but Tate and Kellan Marchetti. And when I looked up and took in my surroundings, I realized where my feet had led me. The bar I'd gone to with Tate. I peered inside the windows. Just to see the place we'd once sat, exchanging stories. Probably the closest thing to healthy healing either of us would ever get. But then I saw him. The only man to ever rob me of my sanity like this. *Tate.*

He cradled an empty glass, and from the looks of it, it wasn't his first. I must have stood there for half an hour. Dazed. Staring at him through the window like something out of *Misery.* A woman sat beside him. Two, actually. Both salivating. Both interested. One of them dropped a pen back in her purse and folded up a sheet of paper, sliding it to him. Her number, maybe? He eyed it. Grabbed it. Slipped it into his pocket. I swallowed, glued to each movement of his body. Sweat crept down my neck. Bile rose to my throat. My heart did violent dives inside me.

Open the door, Charlotte. Stop this. Take him up on his offer. You know you want to.

Instead, I stayed rooted to the pavement until I couldn't watch anymore. He was drunk, and I knew I should've at least barged into the bar and offered to help him get home safe. But I couldn't bring myself to make my presence known. I fled, wondering why it mattered what Tate Marchetti did with his life. He was a stranger. Older. Someone I'd survived twenty-two years without knowing, and someone I'd survive twenty-two more years without seeing.

And then it struck me. I wasn't just *watching* Tate. I was *worrying* about him. When did I start to care? When did I stop hating him?

Chapter Thirty-Nine

Tate

Since Charlotte Richards entered my life, I'd come to the un-fucking-pleasurable realization that there was a lot about my little brother I didn't know. Kellan had a friend, and I'd never met her until now. Kellan wanted to kill himself, and I found out from a pair of cops on my doorstep.

Kellan wrote a book, and he didn't tell me.

Darling Venom remained tucked away in my nightstand. Probably the source of my recent insomnia. Not that I'd slept great the past four years. (Sleeping pills weren't an option when I needed to be on call twenty-four hours of the day.)

The bartender slid a glass of something clear my way. I lifted it to my nose, sniffing. Nothing. "What's in this?"

"Water."

"I ordered Macallan."

A whole bottle of it, in fact.

I heard the hard edge in my tone. Had the decency to be embarrassed, too. By the time I turned the legal drinking age, I'd watched Terrence Marchetti fall in love with seven different substances, bring down a tree while driving under the influence in Turtle Bay, and spend half his weekends in the drunk tanks of every precinct south of Lennox Hill.

He had one epic, life-altering, earth-shattering love. *Drugs.* Two, if you counted women. Which was why I mostly stayed away from both. But today, in the shower, I'd jerked off to the memory of Charlotte Richards coming on my fingers. I'd left the bathroom to find Terry sneaking into Kel's room to search for *Darling Venom* again, then ended the evening by delivering stillborn IVF twins at work. I needed booze, or I'd turn to something stronger.

"I'm cutting you off, man." The bartender's sad, knowing smile might've bothered me if I cared what strangers thought of me. As it was, I had other priorities. Specifically, the Macallan I'd ordered.

An argument sat at the tip of my tongue, ready to launch at the bartender until he split in two, blurring around me. I'd graduated from drunk to plastered in the past half-hour, and I could go for another round or ten. But then I spotted a flash of an oversized hair bow through the windows.

Charlie.

I blinked twice, and it was gone. Possibly never there at all. I slammed two hundred-dollar bills and the number from that woman earlier onto the counter and darted out of the bar, forgetting my coat. The night air nipped at my skin. I stumbled down the block, half-convinced I'd hallucinated spotting Charlie. Until I caught a streak of red-and-white striped boots that screamed Charlotte Richards. Definitely her.

"Charlie!"

She kept walking. I struggled to keep up, hurling a palm against a crinkle-cut roll-down for support. And why the fuck were there so many people on this sidewalk? I bumped into a group of suits, muttered a half-assed apology, and trailed Charlie across the one-way street.

"Damn it, Charlie. Stop."

She didn't. Probably couldn't hear me from this far out. But I could barely walk straight. Catching up to her seemed like a pipe dream at this point. Still, I tailed her as she veered left and jaywalked, weaving her way through a yellow sea of honking taxis.

At this point, I could admit I was out of my goddamn mind. It was late. I was drunk. Goosebumps littered my arms. Charlie hadn't taken me up on my offer. I could barely walk or see straight. The odds of catching up with her in this state were less favorable than the odds of Terry's sobriety lasting more than a month. And there were a million and one reasons not to chase after my little brother's best friend.

But I couldn't seem to conjure a single one.

She stopped at a crosswalk of a major intersection, waiting for the little red hand to switch. I closed the gap between us in uneven strides. The image of her became clearer with each step. I could make out the blurred outline of her outfit at this point. Some sort of black and silver jacket. Tiny fucking shorts that showed more than they covered. And tights tucked into chunky combat boots the pattern of candy canes.

It happened in slow motion. I reached for her arm, swaying. She spun at my touch, and we tumbled toward the ground together. I grabbed her waist to steady her but fumbled for balance.

We ended up on the hood of a parked car. Its alarm pierced my eardrums. Half Charlie's body was sprawled on top of mine, the other half between my legs.

"What the hel—" She blinked down at me. "Tate?"

I opened my mouth, aware I reeked like an eighteenth-century brothel. There were several things on the agenda for this conversation. *Darling Venom.* Terry. Kellan. Her answer to my proposition. But the only thing that came out was, "Charlie."

My lips curved up in a lopsided smile. I straightened from under her and tugged her up from the sedan, guessing we probably had thirty or so seconds before an angry owner came out to yell at us.

She shoved me off her with two hands, steadying me when I teetered. Her nose wrinkled. "You're plastered."

"Something you're well-aware of, considering you were spying on me at the bar."

"I wasn't spying." She crossed her arms. "What bar? I have no idea what you're talking about."

"You're a bad liar," I slurred. My limbs felt heavy. Weighed down by something beyond the alcohol. Which, by the way, suddenly made me feel like a Terry-shaped piece of shit. And that reminded me... "Tell me about Kellan."

We were drawing attention with all the noise. The alarm blared. People peered out of windows. A maître d stood in front of an overpriced Italian restaurant, hands planted on his hips, glaring at me.

Yeah, buddy, I disapprove of me, too.

Someone hopped onto the creaky fire escape of an apartment. "Who the fuck's car is that?! Some of us have work in the morning!"

I sloped my head skyward and yelled back, "Mind your fucking business."

Charlie pushed past me, leaving me alone to deal with the crime scene. I followed after her. "Tell me about Kellan," I demanded again, leaving no room for disagreement.

"No," she said, and apparently, there *was* room for disagreement.

I went to repeat myself about the same time I realized her jacket wasn't silver. It was all-black leather, littered with silver chains, and it was Kellan's. She was wearing Kellan's jacket. Why the hell was she wearing Kellan's jacket? I looped a finger around the thickest chain, forcing her to stop. "This is my brother's."

Charlie's cheeks flamed. She peered down at herself, brows pushed together as if she just realized what she had on. "Plenty of people own leather jackets."

"It's Kellan's." I held up another chain, fingering a charm on it. Half snake. Half compass. The implication being: Tate Marchetti is a snake without a moral compass.

Well-played, Kel.

When she didn't deny it, I pointed to the left shoulder. "There's a tear there that he covered with Sharpie. A hole in the inner lining, caused by yours truly. He also added a chain to the jacket each time I tried to toss it." There must've been at least thirty on there. "And this," I flicked a metallic snake, "is the first charm he put on it. Tell me again that it isn't Kel's. I'm waiting." Silence. "Oh, and while you're at it, tell me again how you and Kel were just friends."

Once the words met the air, once I verbalized what we both knew, the fuck-buddy offer withered to the ground and died a lonely, flaccid death.

Charlie stayed silent. She kept her eyes fixed on the sidewalk, and she'd better not be thinking of a way out of this. Spoiler alert: there wasn't one. According to Kel, persistence was my worst personality trait, and Charlotte Richards was about to get a heavy dose of it.

"Tell me about Kellan. And no bullshit this time."

"Fine. I was outside the bar, and I saw you. But Tate," she sloped her chin up, pinning me with her full attention, "you didn't turn to me once. How did you know I was there?"

I spent most of my days fielding Terry's questions regarding the whereabouts of *Darling Venom*. I didn't feel like fielding her questions, too. And yet... I tugged the oversized bow on her head. "You make it obvious."

"What does that even mean?"

"It means nothing. Tell me about Kellan."

Did it hurt that I had to resort to chasing down some girl to dig up info on my own brother? Like a fucking bullet. Everything about my interactions with Miss Richards was chaotic, painful, and a nightmare waiting to happen. Either she made an ass of herself or I did.

"All of a sudden?"

"I've only repeated the question four times now."

"I meant all of a sudden in the grand scheme of our interactions, barring our first real meeting."

"All our meetings have only ever been about Kel." I raised a brow, but everything I said sounded infinitely less serious on account of the fact that I was slurring. Heavily. "I have no reason to see you outside of him."

Lie. Our last encounter proved that.

And it was the wrong thing to say, because she took a step back, distancing herself from me. "I have to go, Tate."

I was drunk. Too drunk to be rational about this. "Fine. I'll start." I followed her down the street, struggling to catch up despite my much longer stride. "Kellan idolized Terry for nothing."

"He idolized Terry because Terry is his dad."

"He's my sperm donor, too, and I find him about as charming as a used condom. But at least one is a vehicle for pleasure."

"Terry wrote Kellan's favorite book in the world."

I snorted. "Terry is a talentless hack."

She paused at the intersection, prodding the crosswalk button. "Have you even read *The Imperfections?*"

"No, and I have no intention of doing so. Ever." I slumped against the pole. "Now tell me about Kellan."

What was that? The fifth time? I prayed to the hangover gods I'd forget this conversation ever happened by the time I woke up tomorrow. But not enough to do something logical like, you know, stop talking to Charlotte Richards and preserve whatever of my dignity remained.

"I don't have time for this." Charlie slid a hand into her pocket and pulled out a crumpled twenty, pressing it into my palm. Fuck if her touch didn't electrify me. "Call a cab, Tate. Go home."

I should tell her about it. *Darling Venom.* Kel's book. But I didn't, because if I did, she'd ask for it, and if she asked for it, I'd give it to her, and if she had it, she'd read it, and if she read it... Well, I didn't know what she would discover. I was too chicken-shit to find out. Maybe that was the part that encouraged me to move the manuscript from my nightstand to the safe in my closet.

"You don't want to talk about Kel? Fine." I folded up her twenty and tucked it into the front pocket of her shorts. "We can talk about what happened during your exam."

The crosswalk signal turned white, but she stilled, staring at me. Waiting for me to speak again.

"I *did* notice you came, and I couldn't give two shits about it. Not a big deal. And not because it happens, which it does, but because my offer

199

of no-strings-attached sex is off the table, on account of the fact that you are wearing my dead brother's jacket he was extremely and unreasonably attached to and you won't tell me how you got it." I thumbed one of the chains. The one housing the middle-finger charm. Fitting. "Pretend it never happened."

Behind her, the crosswalk signal switched to a flashing red hand.

"You're an asshole."

"Well aware of it."

I was staring at the only link I had to my little brother, and I was butchering the fuck out of our relationship. I wasn't dumb. I knew what was happening here. The more things unraveled with Terry, the more I sought out Charlotte. I knew, but I couldn't stop it. I also, apparently, couldn't control the shit that came out of my mouth, sober or drunk.

She turned to the crosswalk, saw the little red hand, and pivoted down the sidewalk instead, walking faster than normal on purpose. I followed behind her as she took the stairs into the subway station two at a time. She veered left to the nearest train, which I doubted was the one she needed.

I struggled to keep up with her, stumbling a little and cursing the bartender for not cutting me off sooner. I had such a strong grip on my life—such tight, militant control—that even the way I lost control needed to be done under my terms. The way I wanted it to happen. Under circumstances I created. And Charlotte Richards derailed it all.

She slipped onto the train as soon as a wave of people cleared it. I picked up my pace, chasing after her, fighting the dizziness rising to my head. *Jesus.* I'd reached my pathetic quota for a lifetime, and I'd like a redo on the past twenty minutes.

I got to the double doors just as they closed. My palms landed on the windows, on either side of Charlie. We stared at each other through the glass. One second stretched into ten. She turned first, cutting me off.

Overhead, the speakers warned to clear the yellow zone. I stumbled back. The metal car began to move.

And then Charlotte Richards was gone.

Chapter Forty

Charlotte

If I was a hermit with no social life, Leah Richards was a doll set that came in three models and three models only—work, sleep, and knitting. The latter of which I found her doing on the couch when I arrived home tonight from whatever that shit-show was with Tate.

Stop thinking about him. Stop worrying if he got home okay. He is not yours to care about.

I sighed, catching Leah peer up from her needles to recite a line from *The Nanny*, all of which she'd memorized at this point. Behind me, the door slammed shut, announcing my presence.

Crickets.

I didn't know what I was waiting for. For us to be close again? For her to accept my apology? For her to acknowledge my presence? I'd take any of the three, to be honest.

Unfortunately, I got none.

The television in the background drowned the sound of Leah's knitting needles clacking together. She frowned at the work in progress on her lap. The fishermen's rib stitches were uneven at best and the design almost indecipherable.

"Ugh, I love it when Maxwell puts C.C.'s reunion on hold for Fran's tonsillectomy." She finished a loop with the yarn before moving on to her back-stitch seam. "So romantic."

From the doorway, my eyes shifted to the screen, where, sure enough, seconds later, Maxwell put C.C.'s reunion on hold for Fran's tonsillectomy.

And yeah, it was romantic.

And yeah, Leah watched way too much TV if she'd memorized a show from 1993 with about a hundred and fifty episodes.

You could find your own romance, Leah. In fact, it may be down the hall.

I didn't say it, though. I never spoke my mind around Leah anymore. Not since The Night Of when she'd tossed me a penny for the last time.

I still hadn't moved from the doorway when Leah decided to shock me. "Where were you tonight?"

I pointed to myself. "Me?"

"No, the person beside you."

Even though I knew there was no one there, I turned to my left to double-check. It was that unbelievable to me that my sister would express any level of interest in my life.

My heart began to gallop, gaining speed by the second. I offered a smile and tried to play it cool. "I got off work late, walked around, and passed by a bar."

"Did you drink?"

"No."

"Hmm." She turned back to her knitting, ending the conversation.

The gallop came to a halt. I leaned against the door for support.

Hmm? That's it?

That's the thing about hope. A little of it goes a long way. Far enough to make you stupid. Far enough to make you *try.*

I kept the conversation going, not that thirty seconds qualified as conversation. "Have you eaten yet?"

It was nearly two in the morning. Of course, she'd eaten.

"Tonkotsu ramen from the place down the street." She didn't look up from her knitting needles. "Leftovers are in the fridge. The noodles are probably soggy by now."

"You dined in?" I stepped into the living room, sitting on the floor an adequate distance from her. It wasn't lost on me that I treated my sister like a homeless dog, afraid she'd flee before I could save her.

Leah sent an *are you dumb?* stare my way. "DoorDashed."

"Living the good life."

The look she gave me made me want to keel over and throw up. Of course, nothing about her life was good, and it was all my fault.

Sometimes, Leah seemed like a statue, frozen in place for the past eight years. She only ate food that came delivered, went straight from work to home, and spent any time outside of the house with animals, because at least they never judged. She'd even chosen the most silent, lonely hobby ever.

No way she enjoyed it.

I wanted to say something. To encourage her to get out of the house. Maybe even beg her to believe me when I told her I found her pretty, scars and all. That Jonah did, too. But I knew she wouldn't hear it. Worse, I knew she'd get angry.

In fact, the exact words she'd used last time were, "You don't know what it feels like to be beautiful one day and wake up the next with it stripped away. Try scarring *your* face, Charlotte. Then, get back to me. Until then, anything you say will just be seen as a selfish attempt to make yourself feel better."

I couldn't do anything, so I inched closer on the carpet until my back hit the base of the couch on the side opposite hers. Her needles paused. She reached for the remote, raised the volume of the television, and continued to knit. Message received. And ignored.

"What are you going to do with all these?" I watched the light-blue yarn transform into a blanket. I'd put money on Leah's ability to knit in front of the TV all day, if only to achieve her real goal of staying away from other people.

But she couldn't avoid me even if she wanted to.

When she didn't respond, I pressed, "Who are these for this time?" Because they were always for someone or something else.

"The cat shelter down the block."

"So, you've moved on from single-handedly making the streets of New York more hospitable for the urban coyote population to helping the cats they want to feast on. Got it."

She set her needles down. "What do you want from me, Charlotte?"

"I want to go out, and I want you to go out with me. Will you? Please?" I hopped to my feet, speaking over the obnoxious volume of the show. "Let's watch a movie. I'm sure we can find a decent flick at the twenty-four-hour theater down the block. Maybe one of the ones in that never-ending car series. We could invite Jonah. He's a mechanic. He has to like car movies."

Was that the mechanic equivalent of saying Tate was a gynecologist, so he had to like all vaginas? My cheeks flushed. One—I needed to boot Tate from my mind. And two—I was doing a horrible job of concealing my intentions, but a part of me wanted Leah to figure it out and agree to date our super-hot, super-available neighbor. Was that a crime?

"We can rent one inside."

Don't bother.

My hope became anger, and my anger became tears. I bit them back. Shoved them behind my eyes where they belonged and begged them to stay there, at least until I escaped.

"Actually..." I put my shoes back on. "I just remembered I left a manuscript at work that I need to finish tonight. Maybe some other time."

I had no right to be mad. I had no right to act on my guilt either. But I did both, moving to the front door. It slammed behind me. In the hallway, I could still hear *The Nanny* blaring at full volume. Fran Drescher's nasal tone rang in my ears.

A metal 3 and D loomed before me. It'd passed appropriate visiting hours at least four hours ago, but fuck it. This needed to stop.

My fist collided with the wood before I remembered the doorbell and stabbed it. Less than a minute later, Jonah materialized before me, bleary-eyed and squinting against the hall light.

"Can I come in?"

He stepped aside. "Is something wrong?"

"Yes."

"Leah okay?"

Of course, his first thought flew to Leah. Which was exactly why he was perfect for her. That, and the fact that he was a million times better than Phil-get-about-it.

"No, actually, she's not." I sat on one of his kitchen stools, accepting the mug of instant hot chocolate he handed me. "She's lonely. I think she knitted a stack of blankets taller than me today. She's still going at it as we speak."

"I know why you're here. You want me to ask her out again." He took his place across from me, staring directly into my eyes. "She turned me down, Charlotte. I don't want to push her and make things awkward between us."

"She's worth fighting for. She just needs a little nudge."

And it can't come from me.

"Charlotte—"

"Please." I grabbed his hand, squeezing it hard. "I'm begging you."

"I want to date her. You don't have to beg me. It's her you need to convince."

"Please, just try?" I hopped off the stool and lowered myself to my knees, pressing my palms together like a prayer.

"What are you doing?"

"Begging. Is it working?"

He took his time answering, but a smile built on his face. "Get your ass off the floor, knucklehead. I'll do it."

There was that hope again.

And I didn't care if it made me stupid.

Chapter Forty-One

Charlotte

Reagan convinced me to dress like a professional businesswoman all week. By convinced, I meant she'd flat-out told me to drop the goth-girl get-up, or she'd ditch me at the door.

In addition to the fact that I liked my job, wanted to keep it, and had my eye on a promotion, I figured it was a bad idea to get on the bad side of a very pregnant woman who couldn't seem to quit working despite the late stage of her pregnancy.

I wore a pantsuit I'd borrowed from Leah. It fit tight in all the wrong places, pushing my butt in uncomfortable directions until it resembled a pancake. I tried to ignore it. My heart struck my ribcage. Fast and hard. Its permanent state since running into Tate.

Leah's heels, a size too big, clicked on the marble floor as I walked to the meeting. My third this week. This time with Helen Moriuchi, a prominent acquisitions editor from one of the Big Five publishing companies. Also Reagan's old roommate at Columbia.

The hostess led me to a private room in the back of Toshikoshi, some upscale restaurant I'd seen on the Food Network. I smoothed out my pants before I entered, removing my shoes for her to place in the cubby at the side of the room. Reagan and Helen sat zashiki-style on tufted seat cushions scattered on the floor around the low table.

Reagan turned to me with a wave. "Charlotte, perfect timing. I was just telling Helen about the literary fiction pieces from J.T. Hawthorne. Did you bring them?"

"Yep. I emailed Helen copies, too." I produced three manuscripts from my bag and handed them to her. "Nice to meet you. I'm Charlotte."

Helen eyed me curiously. I realized I'd forgotten to smile and reminded myself to. People liked smiles. They made them feel comfortable. Told them, "Everything's okay here. Don't look too close. Don't dig too deep."

In other words, smiles were an excuse not to care.

She shook my hand, greeting me warmly.

Once the servers brought our dishes and left, we launched into the meeting, discussing market trends and what Helen wanted for the upcoming year.

She plucked a slice of A5 Wagyu, seared it on the hot stone, and dipped it into green tea salt. "I'm sure you're interested in becoming an agent yourself, Charlotte."

I twirled shirataki noodles around my chopsticks, nodding. "Any advice for me?"

"Yeah. Do the opposite of whatever Reagan does."

Reagan tapped her fingers on the table. "Funny."

"It's solid advice." Helen shrugged. "Which one of us decided a baby was a good career move?"

"Babies are fun!"

"Babies are exhausting."

"You'll regret that in forty years when you're changing your own diapers."

"Call me then when your forty-year-old sons begin to resent you for making them change your diapers. I'll be in my mansion with round-the-clock care, courtesy of the money I saved by not raising children."

They went back and forth about the merits of having kids, eventually returning to books.

Reagan pushed her bowl forward and wiped her lips with a cloth napkin. "About half the manuscripts emailed or mailed to the company are properly addressed to the appropriate agent. Charlotte is in charge of the manuscripts that aren't."

"Which means she goes through non-fiction, literary fiction, and genre fiction," Helen finished. She reached into her purse, pulling out a business card. "If you find a manuscript you're certain is a whale, you know where to find me. I'm looking for something that'll tear me to shreds. Literary fiction that can be read by the masses."

I jumped at the opportunity to prove myself to Reagan, accepting the card. "It's a big pile. I'll find you what you're looking for."

And I would.

The only thing I had to look forward to was work.

I intended to find that manuscript, even if I had to write it myself.

Chapter Forty-Two

Charlotte

It was easy to avoid Tate Marchetti. Logistically, at least. We worked in different industries, on different streets, never socialized in general, and kept to our neat, lonely bubbles without the hassle of the outside world.

Without anyone.

But if I slipped up, if I let my thoughts wander, I found myself wanting to see him. I asked Reagan about her baby checkups, probing for information about Tate's wellbeing. I even missed a subway stop last night, traveling halfway to his place before I forced myself out onto the platform and into an Uber ride-share, where I couldn't change my destination on a whim.

After our final meeting (a hotshot director interested in film rights), I hailed a cab with Reagan. We were talking about her last appointment with Tate when the yellow car pulled up.

She winced after we got in, setting a protective hand on her stomach as soon as her butt landed on the squishy leather.

I hopped inside, rattled the office's address, then turned to Reagan, meeting her scrunched nose. "Are you feeling okay?"

She clawed at her belly. "I don't know."

I'd never seen her so hesitant. So unsure of what to do.

"Do you want me to call Dr. Marchetti's office?"

"Please."

I redirected the driver to Morgan-Dunn Hospital, pulled out my phone, and scrolled through my contacts list before I remembered I didn't have Tate's number. By design. Tate's design, to be specific. So, I settled on the clinic's number.

They answered on the first ring. "Bernard and Marchetti Medical Center. This is Sylvia. How may I help you?"

"Hey, this is Charlotte. I'm calling on behalf of Reagan Rothschild."

"Dr. Marchetti is currently out of the office, but I can pass along a message."

"This is an emergency. She's in a lot of pain, and we're worried something may be wrong." I stared at Reagan's gritted teeth. "We're headed to the clinic now. Can you call Dr. Marchetti in?"

"Paging him as we speak." I heard her type on the other end and call out to someone. "When you pull up, we'll have a nurse and wheelchair ready for her."

I hung up, begged the cabbie to drive faster, and clutched Reagan's hand. It felt swollen in mine, from the hilt up to the tips of her fingers. Her face, too. It looked bad, which I chose not to disclose.

"Sylvia paged Dr. Marchetti." I kept my voice low, hoping to soothe her. "They're waiting for us."

After she passed the thirty-four-week mark, Reagan had relaxed a bit. Like she'd gotten over the hump that troubled her most and the rest would be smooth sailing. But the fear returned to her eyes.

Her face turned pale, her hands shaky.

She faced me. "Tell me this isn't a big deal."

I couldn't.

I had no clue what was happening. Which only made it scarier, because her face had ballooned, and I felt like I was holding someone else's hand, not hers.

I settled on the truth. Vague, but real.

"Dr. Marchetti is the best obstetrician in the city."

"You're right." She exhaled and nodded, pulling her shoulders back. "He is. He'll figure this out."

When we got to the hospital, two nurses helped Reagan into a wheelchair, carting her inside. I followed with our bags and sent a text to her mom, asking her to come to the eighteenth floor.

They put Reagan in a private room on an upper level of the boutique hospital, which was how we knew they were taking this seriously. I informed Reagan her mom was on the way, then stepped into the hall while a nurse and physician's aid stripped her, helped her into a backless hospital gown, and began some standard tests.

I parked myself in front of the curved reception desk, finding the nurse that wheeled Reagan up. "Is there an ETA on Dr. Marchetti?"

"He was grabbing a quick bite to eat, but he left as soon as he got the page. He should be here any moment now."

And sure enough, Tate stormed into the hall through the same door we'd entered, dressed in nice slacks and a cashmere sweater.

He settled beside me without paying me any attention, his focus on the nurse. "The patient?"

I pointed to the nearest door. "That exam room."

"The patient?" he repeated, still staring at the nurse.

He could hear me. I knew he could.

She pointed at the same door. "Exam room three."

"Thank you, Marie."

Tate gave me his back.

It struck me how much the tables had turned. He'd been the one to chase me into the subway. Now his back was a view I was quickly getting used to.

And one I didn't enjoy.

Not after the bruise to my ego left by his rejection.

Tate Marchetti was dead set on ending any possibility of us taking our attraction a step further. He went out of his way to avoid me.

211

I was literate.

I could read between the lines.

My gaze dropped lower. I noticed something tucked into his back pocket. Distinct red-and-white skull stickers peeked past the wool.

Holy crap.

My letter.

The one I'd written after receiving the signed copy of *The Imperfections.*

The one I thought I'd shredded.

The one in which I accused him of being a coward for not handing the book to me himself.

Fuck.

I jerked toward the exit, seconds from fleeing, joining witness protection, and living the rest of my life under an alias. Then I remembered Reagan's condition and stayed, dipping behind a potted plant every time I thought I spotted Tate.

An hour passed.

Tate exited Reagan's room with a clipboard and a scowl directed at the world. Reagan's mom slipped out of the room fifteen minutes later.

"Reagan's asking for you." She pulled a wallet from her pocket. "I'm grabbing some coffee. Would you like a cup?"

"No, thanks."

She placed a hand on mine, squeezing. "Thank you for getting her here and keeping her calm."

I slipped inside the room after she left for the cafeteria. Reagan lay in a hospital bed, the upper half raised. A colony of wires decorated her body, leading to a machine that monitored her vitals.

I stopped at the foot of her bed. "Are you feeling better?"

"Much. The babies are okay, too." A tired smile ghosted her lips. She reclined against the pillow. "It's preeclampsia. They're running more tests to triple-check, but that's what it looks like. Dr. Marchetti gave me treatment options, assuring me that, regardless of which I choose, he's confident about the outcome."

"Do you need anything from me? I can grab you clothes or a go-bag if you have one."

"My mom is stopping by my place to get it. She took my phone with her, since she wants me off it for the next few days." She pressed a button, elevating her bed. There was a restlessness to her, like she didn't want to sit still. Or couldn't. "I need you to let the team know I may be unreachable for the next week or two, depending on whether we decide to perform a C-section or try other options first."

"Of course."

I jotted down Reagan's instructions, including how she wanted us to divide her work for the next month. By the time I left, my legs were ready to give out, and I didn't know whether I craved sleep or food more.

A cab pulled up in front of the hospital. I scanned the street one last time for signs of Tate before sliding into the car and rattling off my address. Tate hadn't seemed mad, just... I don't know.

Rigid?

Strained?

I racked my brain, trying to remember the exact words I'd written in the letter. The dirty, cruel, scandalous things I'd only written because I thought he'd never read it. And that was before the oops-gasm.

Before he offered no-strings-attached sex.

A few phrases bounced around in my head.

I settled on the last one.

The most horrifying one.

It seems you're incapable of growing a pair and acting on your desires. So, I'll be the bold one and tell you what I'm thinking. Last night, when I touched myself, I imagined it was me you fucked on your desk. I think you did, too, that day, because you couldn't keep your eyes off me while you were inside her. Face it, Dr. Tatum Marchetti, I am in front of you, around you, in your head.

And I'm here to stay.

Chapter Forty-Three

Charlotte

I climbed the stairs to my apartment. The hall light flickered on and off. Contrary to his promise, our landlord had not changed the bulb. Before me, a large shadow cast over the carpet. Still. Unmoving. *Waiting*.

Dread slithered up my spine. My heart bottomed out, sinking further by the second. I clutched my phone and jabbed nine-one-one just in case, angling the device forward like a weapon. The light died. Shoe squeaks echoed down the corridor. A flashlight turned on. Inches away from me. I screamed, charged forward with a battle cry, and thrust my phone into something hard. Above us, the light came to life again. I found Jonah against the wall, clawing his stomach.

"Jesus, Jonah." I helped him up. "You scared me. Why were you standing in the dark in the middle of the night?"

"I was waiting for you."

That dread returned, nipping at my gut. "Did something happen?"

"I asked Leah out."

My whole body sighed. "She turned you down."

"Told me if I asked her again, she'd move."

Oh, boy. I knew it was bad, but I didn't know it was *this* bad. That she'd uproot us just to escape a crush. We weren't suffering financially compared to eight years ago, but I didn't think we could afford anywhere else. At least not without trading our perfectly safe, albeit small, two-bedroom for a cockroach-infested Petrie dish on the bad side of town.

"Leah and I are not moving," I promised.

"She sounded serious."

"She was scared."

That was Leah. Scared of her own shadow. Or, more specifically, people seeing anything but her shadow. I was convinced that, despite the burns, if Phil had stayed, she would've made it out with her confidence intact. *That fucking asshole.*

"Tell you what." I patted Jonah's arm. "I'll talk to her and sort it out."

"I don't think it will help. Not tonight, at least. There was a moment after I asked that I really thought she would say yes. She looked so damn happy, Charlotte. And then a kid stared at her face too long, and something switched." He straightened, so huge, yet gentle. "Until she learns to see herself as we do, there's no chance she'll say yes. You can't love someone who doesn't love herself." He was right. Of course, he was right.

I felt helpless. Without answers. The weight of too many lives overloaded my shoulders. I waited a few minutes after Jonah retreated to enter my apartment. The door creaked open. I poked my head inside. All the lights were off, but Leah usually stayed up at this hour. Then I noticed her. In the dark. A glass of wine cradled in her hand. Filled to the brim.

I flicked on the lamp beside the couch. "If our utility bill seems low this month, I know why. You are single-handedly saving the environment. One bulb at a time."

"Phil's engaged." It came out low. Detached. Like she was informing me it'd rain tomorrow.

I winced. "To Natalie?"

She didn't answer. I watched her sip the wine, continuing even when I thought she'd stop. Once she emptied it, she set the glass on the carpet at her feet, staring straight ahead. Streaks of black stretched down her cheeks. Dry. The tears must have stopped a while ago.

Oh, Leah. How long have you been sitting here?

"Do you think they were together while we were together?"

Honestly, I wouldn't put it past Phil. But that had nothing to do with Leah's worth and everything to do with Phil being worthless.

"Does it matter?" I sat on the opposite end of the couch. My hand itched to touch her. Comfort her. Give her a sister to rely on. "He's a jackass, and you deserve way better than him."

"Do I?"

My heart broke. Shattered right there on the cheap carpet for both of us to see. Only, she wasn't looking. She never did. Leah couldn't see past her own despair. If only I could shake her and beg her to open her eyes. But the last time I'd done that, the last time I'd offered a list of everything I loved about her, she'd only become *more* self-conscious.

So, I settled for: "I'm not even gonna dignify that with a response."

"Which is a response itself," she pointed out. "Don't worry. I don't blame you. For not wanting to reply to that, at least." But she blamed me for the fire. For ruining her life. If I knew what to do to make this better, I would do it in a heartbeat. No matter how much it hurt. No matter how much I suffered. She finally turned to face me, gifting me a glimpse of how many tears she'd shed tonight. A lot. Enough to leave her eyes swollen and her cheeks dotted with mascara clumps. "Did you tell Jonah to ask me out?"

"He wanted to ask you out on his own." I reached for her hand. She pulled it back so fast, her nails scratched my skin. I forced myself not to wince. "He asked you out that first time—"

"I'm not talking about the first time. I'm talking about today."

"Let's calm down and talk about this over a cup of hot cocoa."

"We're not five, Charlotte. Our parents are not alive to mediate our fights. They're dead, in case you've forgotten." Wow. She was intent on hurting me today. More so than usual. She gained volume, transforming into something I didn't recognize and, frankly, didn't want to. "We don't need chocolate and a hug to handle our problems anymore." Her voice turned hard, lashing. It whipped my skin and left it raised. "Did you or did you not tell Jonah to ask me out? I heard you talking with him in the hall, so don't even think about lying."

I launched myself onto my knees before her, unable to hold it in anymore. "Yes, Leah. I did. I want my sister to be happy. To find love. To move on from fucking Phil. Is that a crime?!"

"Do you want to know how I felt after he took me to see the Berlin Wall, brought me to a restaurant, and asked me to be his girlfriend? Like... like I'm not *this*." She gestured to her face, lips curling up in disgust. "Like I'm special. Like I'm *beautiful*. I can't believe I was dumb enough to even consider saying yes."

"He took you to see the Berlin Wall?" My heart did a dance in my chest. I just wanted Leah to live. *Really* live.

She stared at something behind me. Maybe nothing. "He brought me to the piece of the Berlin Wall in the United Nations Sculpture Garden and centered me before the mural on it."

I knew the one. Of a man and woman embracing over a wall. I knew in my gut why Jonah had taken her there. "He wanted you to see the aftermath of tragedy. That it can still be beautiful and celebrated."

"Pain and scars are the armor beauty wears. That's what he said." She scoffed. "What a load of bull."

"He's right. And he obviously put a lot of thought into today. You should give him a chance."

"You took the choice away from me. By running to Jonah and asking him to pity date me, you took away my opportunity to date him on my own."

"He already wanted to date you."

"Yeah? Well, *I* already gave up my face for you. I won't give up my freedom, too." She stormed to her room, stopping just at the threshold to add, "I'm not your friend, Charlotte. I didn't choose to have you in my life. At least let me choose the other people in my life."

Fucking ouch. It stung. But she was right. We *weren't* friends. We were sisters. Connected by a stroke of fate. Of misfortune. A red thread tying me to her. We didn't choose to share the same blood, just as I never asked her to run through fire to save me and she never asked to be placed in a position where she had to make the choice. Sometimes, her words hit so low, I wanted to leave her. Permanently. And then I remembered why she hated me.

Leah slammed the door behind her, knowing I wouldn't follow her in there. I'd never been inside Leah's room following The Night Of. Not after we moved to the Bronx. Not when we moved away. Since the fire, I made it a point to never invade Leah's space again.

Well, not this time.

My hand hit the doorknob. I twisted it, heart ratcheting in my chest like a jackhammer. I could've died then of a heart attack. But I took a step inside. Stunned silence met me. In fact, I think we were *both* shocked silent. I didn't even remember what I'd wanted to say anymore.

"You're in my room," Leah whispered.

I closed my eyes, inhaling the familiar scent of citronella oil and laundry. It smelled like her room nine years ago. Different place. Same person. *She's still in there. She's worth fighting for.*

"I love you, Leah." My eyes shot open, zeroing in on her. Perched on the edge of her bed as if she wanted to make her existence as small as humanly possible. "And because I love you, you can say all the mean shit you want, and I will always be here for you. Always."

Was this what it was like between Tate and Kellan? Good intentions and poor delivery. Tragedy and heartbreak. Love and hate. A tear slipped past my cheek. I let it fall to the carpet before I wiped away its trail.

"Butt out of my life, Charlotte." But the words didn't hold heat. They were just tired. So damn tired of it all.

I sighed, turning to leave, when my eyes caught sight of it. Grand loops and tight lines. The familiar swirls of Kellan's cursive. Inked on an envelope tucked between the end of Leah's bookshelf and a beauty manual on covering scars. I dove forward. Snatched up the letter. Bit my tongue at the sight of a surviving piece of Kellan, swallowing the bitter blood.

"Where did you get this?"

Leah shifted on her bed, almost falling. "It's old."

218

"Leah, where the hell did you get this?"

"Some kid stopped by with it a long time ago. On Valentine's Day, your senior year." She lifted a shoulder. "He wanted me to give it to you. I figured it was just a birthday card."

I strode to the bed, shaking her shoulders. "Tell me exactly what happened."

"What's the big deal?" She jerked her body away from me, scooting back on the mattress to gain distance. "It's just a letter from a high school boy."

"Kellan."

"What?"

"The boy who gave you the letter. His name was Kellan, and he killed himself. That night."

I'd never told her. Never wanted her to feel like I was threatening her ownership on tragedy. That was my fault, but it was also hers for making me believe I was a regret. That saving me ruined her life. That I couldn't talk to her about the hardships I faced for fear of overshadowing hers.

Not only did Kellan kill himself after delivering the letter to Leah, but it also could have been the last thing he'd done before he took his own life. I kept this from her. She didn't need to know the pain of trying to save someone and *failing*. It was painful enough to have succeeded. I saw that every time she looked at me.

Tate's words from the day I confessed my Big T echoed inside my head. He was right. For the first time, I acknowledged the fact that there was a worse possibility than Leah saving me.

"Charlotte..." Her voice was soft. As if she thought she would shatter me if she raised it just a notch higher. I think something she saw when she looked at me scared her, because for once, it was her turn to act like she had something to lose between us. She stood, slowly, as if she were corralling a cornered animal. "Charlotte," she repeated.

I didn't answer. I turned and walked away. That red thread of fate connecting us unraveled, freeing me.

Somehow, I only felt more trapped.

Chapter Forty-Four

Charlotte

If I fall, will I regret it?

The thought occupied precious real estate in my head. I ended up on the roof for the first time since Kellan's death, hovering over the ledge, wondering how lonely it felt to fall with no one to catch him.

How scared he must've been.

The letter was hidden safely in the pouch of my hoodie. I'd opened it on the cab ride here, read the first line, and slipped it back inside its envelope.

Too scared of what I'd find.

Which was a given, considering 1) it was Kellan we were talking about (the boy was a master at pushing every button of mine) and 2) the first sentence consisted of a threat.

St. Paul's still hadn't walled off rooftop access beyond that ridiculous rusted chain and a DO NOT ENTER sign situated above a contradictory set of emergency instructions to climb it in case of a flood.

To be fair, whoever maintained this place had done their damnedest to make the roof tiles as inhospitable as possible. It was the same and different. Unsettling and cold, yet full of memories that were warm.

Bird poop, crow spikes, cigarette butts, and distant echoes of drinking beer and talking books—and that was just what I could see.

It was dark out. I crept back a few steps, barefoot, because I'd darted out of the apartment without stopping to grab my shoes. My toes curled inward from the cold.

"Do it, Charlotte. Open it. Stop being such a chicken."

I sucked in a breath and flashed my phone's light, staring down at the envelope. It bore a wax seal with the Circle-A symbol. Cracked in half by me. I couldn't help myself in the cab. But it was a sign Leah had never read it.

Maybe she really did think it was a birthday card.

I flipped open the flap.

Two keys tumbled onto my lap. The heavy, vintage type. Forged by hand. I tucked them into my pocket to study later.

Then, I unraveled Kellan's letter, smoothing out the edges that had curled inward with age.

I read.

I cried.

I broke.

Chapter Forty-Five

My darling Venom,

Let me preface this by saying, if you cry, I'm going to disown your ass all the way from Hell. Not that I believe in Hell. And not that I particularly believe you'll cry. Just covering my bases here.

Here goes nothing.

Let it be known that this is not a suicide letter. It's a letter that happens to be the last one I'll ever write. I'm telling you now not to blame yourself for anything that happened. In fact, you were the only reason I lasted these four years.

I'm not going to get into the whole why-I-did-this part. We both know why I offed myself. It's been a long time coming, and even though I know your heart was in the right place, you and me aren't made of the same stuff. The black slug. I know you'd like to think we are, but trust me, there's something sturdy beneath your exterior. Inside, I'm all bled out. Empty and gone. I'm a walking corpse, and my existence stinks.

I know you said I might regret it mid-fall, but let me tell you, sweets: I've flirted with cutting all year, and I only feel regret when I withdraw the blade from my skin.

I'm ready.

Now that I've gotten that out of the way, I have a favor to ask you. Before you say anything, remember—my funeral, my rules.

I left something for you. Actually, I left several things for you. They're in the two desk drawers in my room at that asshole's place. Tate. The keys are in this envelope. The first is a manuscript I wrote (officially, anyway).

Since Tate thinks Dostoyevsky is Dad's favorite brand of liquor and is a world-class douchebag, and Dad can't be trusted with a fucking tissue paper, I am leaving this to you.

I couldn't finish the book, Dicks. No matter how much I tried, I always felt like I'd only ever get half of it. Until I realized you were the missing piece.

I got the death part right. The despair. The darkness. The bleakness of existence. Now I need you to color in the shades, and if the final product doesn't suck, release it into the wild. Maybe it's the next The Imperfections. I dunno.

I'm passing the torch to you. It's a torch you never asked for, but I know your ass has never shied away from a challenge before and you'll be damned if you let this one slip.

I dare you to finish it, Venom.

I dare you to look inside yourself.

This book is my final penny to you.

I saved yours.

Will you save mine?

Yours,
Kellan

Chapter Forty-Six

Charlotte

A wail ripped up my throat.

I stumbled. Right where Kellan once saved me from plummeting to my death. At the last second, my fingers reached out, grasping for something, anything, to hold on to. They met the chimney. I curled around its mouth in a death grip, ignoring the pull of my nails lifting a bit at the tightness.

Goosebumps rose along my arms. I shivered, not from the cold. If I didn't sit, I'd keel over. Part of me wanted to. Welcomed the idea of falling, just to feel what Kellan did before he left.

Instead, I collapsed onto the shingles and plucked at my leg. I pulled them both to my chest and wrapped my arms around my knees to stop the shaking. It wouldn't stop.

I screamed his name. Over and over again.

"Kellan! Kellan! Kellan!"

It became a chant, dipping into a whisper. My throat ached.

I rarely contemplated the existence of an afterlife, but today, I wondered if one existed. And if it did, was Kellan there, watching tears flood my cheeks, and disappointed in me? Had he disowned me already?

"You're wrong, Kellan." I forced the tears to slow, folded the letter in thirds, and tucked it into its envelope, carefully sliding the cardstock into my hoodie pocket.

"I *don't* know why you did it. You had me. You had Harvard. And even though you didn't think it, you had Tate. Hell..." I wiped my face with the back of my hand. "I think, in a weird, fucked-up way, you even had Terry."

I stared up at the sky. Even if he thought he was Hell bound, I didn't. I believed a special place existed somewhere for people who were so tortured on Earth, they felt the only way out was to end it all.

A place where they got to experience everything they missed out on in this plane.

Love. Happiness. Relief.

"You're a real asshole. You know that, Kellan?"

The wind picked up. I placed a hand against the chimney to steady myself.

"I guess you do."

I laughed, unsure what hurt worse—his presence in his absence or when he disappeared completely.

"I can't believe I've been so scared to come to the roof. The happy memories are still here. I feel them."

If I closed my eyes and cleared my mind of the past four years, I could almost see us up here again, stealing glances and laughing about some dumb thing one of us said.

"There's something I've been wondering..." I leaned against the column, enjoying the wind. Drunk off pain, I could almost convince myself it was Kellan. "Why would you even apply to Harvard if you didn't intend on going there?"

The wind slowed.

I waited for an answer, but none came.

After a while, the wind stopped lapping at my cheeks. The level of my loneliness sank in. I didn't have anyone to talk to about Kellan's death. Anyone to yell at. Rage to. I didn't even have the guts to visit Tate and vent my anger at him, his father, Hannah. It was just... me. That was the thing about loneliness. Once it entered, it didn't leave.

"The loneliness is a prelude, isn't it? A taste of the days to come."

I still had a sister. I still had a future. And I lived in the most populous city in the country. If I couldn't find a single friend out of the nine million people who lived in New York City, I had no one to blame but myself.

It's not that you can't. You don't want to. No one can compare.

"If she gave me the letter on time, if she hadn't asked for those fucking cigarettes that night, would you still be alive?"

No answer.

"How can I forgive Leah?"

Again, no answer.

But I'd already come to the conclusion myself. My heart had finally caught up with my head. There would be no forgiveness. No future between us. No confrontation.

There was nothing to say.

The final crack to the mirror had been dealt.

We couldn't fix it.

We were irreparably damaged.

The intent didn't matter.

It just didn't.

All I could focus on was the outcome. Kellan died, and I could've prevented it. No wonder Leah ran into the burning house that day. Because the alternative—*this*—felt like shit. Like failure. One I was forced to remember every single day I spent breathing while he couldn't.

I stared at the letter as if it were my lifeline to Kellan. "This time, I won't fail you."

I had nothing to say to Leah.

But I had plenty to say to Tate.

Starting with the manuscript.

Chapter Forty-Seven

Tate

Terrence Marchetti never failed to invent new ways for me to hate him. I woke at three in the morning to the doorbell ringing nonstop without any pauses. Like a child would do.

In other words, Terry. And probably the seventh time this month he'd forgotten his keys and made a ruckus in the middle of the night.

Goddammit.

For once, I'd like to know what a normal family dynamic felt like. Instead, I smashed my face into my pillow, gunning for a few more minutes of sleep.

No such luck.

Terry graduated from stabbing the bell to punching the door.

The fuck?

I stormed down the stairs, taking them two at a time despite my bleary vision. If I ended up in the hospital with a broken neck, Terry would probably find a way to sue *me*.

I white-knuckled the knob and yanked it open, sucking in cold air. "New house rule: if you forget your key, don't come hom—"

I came face to face with the bane of my existence. She wore the same thing she'd worn at the hospital earlier today. An unimpressive skirt suit that reached her calves and drowned her curves in an excess of cheap cotton. An oversized hoodie covered her torso.

Only this time, she was barefoot. Red-eyed and clutching onto each arm to hold herself together. Her teeth chattered. She looked like she could use a hot bath, a brush, and a Xanax.

"Charlie?"

It's Miss Charlotte Richards to you, asshole.

"I'm here for Kellan's manuscript," she said flatly. Blood dripped from her knuckles, splashing onto the draft stop.

"Jesus. What the hell happened to your hand?"

"You weren't answering your door."

"So, you punched it? Do you get how wild that sounds?" I reached for her fist. "I have a first-aid kit."

She shook her head, jerking it out of reach. "It's just a scratch. It'll heal. Don't change the subject."

What the hell was the subject again? Her fist distracted me. I racked my brain, trying to remember what she'd said.

Something about Kellan.

"The manuscript," she provided.

I shook my head. Raised my palm. Realized I had nothing to grasp and fisted the damn thing, holding onto myself like she was doing.

She knows about the manuscript.

Naturally, it came as a surprise to fucking nobody that I was the only one clueless when it came to Kel. Pathetic, if you considered the fact that I spent half my weekends ransacking his room for drugs and the other half stalking his ass on that kiddie-tracking app advertised by a shit ton of celebrities with live-in nannies. Not that I had a right to judge.

You were never home.

"It's three in the morning, Charlie." The softness in my voice almost gave me pause.

Meanwhile, hers carried an edge of determination. "I need the manuscript."

If I budged an inch, I bet she'd barrel her way past me. The right thing to do would be to let her inside, help her escape the cold, and wrap up her knuckles. Anything but staying rooted to the spot. Which—surprise, surprise—I did. A physical barrier between the outside world and my personal space.

Truth was, I wasn't ready to give up *Darling Venom*. I hadn't read it. Didn't plan on it, either. Emotional torture wasn't my kink. I preferred the blood-pumping organ in my chest intact, thank you very much.

Fiery resolve slashed across her face. She fished out two tiny keys from her pocket, dangling them by a loop. "I have the keys to his drawers."

"All of a sudden?" I narrowed my eyes. "You didn't have them a month ago when we cleared his room, but you have them now..."

"The circumstances have changed."

"Explain." I lowered my voice, aware I had neighbors, Charlie possessed that look that could pass as eighteen or twenty-six, and the last thing I needed was rumors of Dr. Miracle entertaining late-night visits from a minor. "It's not like I have anything better to do at three in the goddamn morning."

"It's not my place to."

She didn't have the decency to look guilty. Instead, she clocked the gap between me and the door, as if debating whether she could make it through.

Answer: she could.

But only because I'd get out of the way. I didn't trust myself to touch her right now. Or ever.

"Considering you're on my front step at three in the morning, demanding to see *Darling Venom*, I think an explanation is warranted."

"*Darling Venom?*"

Fuck me.

So much for neither confirming nor denying the manuscript's existence. Remind me to never apply for a job at the CIA.

She swayed on the top step. I moved to catch her and stopped myself.

Charlotte Richards was nothing but my former patient.

Not my girl.

Not my problem.

I watched her shut her eyes and take two deep breaths. To steady herself, maybe.

Then her gaze shot to mine, pinning me with its intensity. "Is that its name?"

Did it surprise me that Kellan told her he'd written a book? Not the slightest. She was his friend. His only friend. Which, technically, made her his best friend. But something seemed off. Like, as off-balance as she'd thrown me, she was even more so. Teetering on a ledge she couldn't quite save herself from.

That didn't mean I would be her knight in shining armor. And it certainly didn't mean I would be giving up the only thing left of my little brother.

"You're not getting the book, Charlie. Don't bother trying."

At this point, I couldn't make it clearer if I mailed her a postcard and took out a Times Square billboard with the words printed on them.

Still, she persisted. And goddamnit, she had a trump card.

"Kellan gave me a letter that night."

I scoffed, but something prodded the back of my mind. The possibility, even if slight, riled me up. Drove me fucking crazy. I kept my voice level. "And you've just remembered it tonight? That's convenient."

"Don't. Don't you dare hit me with this bullshit, Tate. He *did*. And in it, he told me that the manuscript is mine and he'd like me to finish it. Actually, he *challenged* me to finish it."

"That's a cute story you've concocted, but it's time for bed." I lifted my bare wrist, pretending to check the time. "I'm sure curfew's almost up. Run along now."

The look she shot me, of disappointment and something else, something more ferocious, rocked me. Not enough to make me relent. But enough to make me reconsider her words as truth. Actually, at this point, I was sure she was telling the truth. I just didn't want to accept it.

I watched her pull something out of her pocket like you'd watch a car crash replay in slow motion. Eyes transfixed. Heart putting in overtime. Adrenaline crackling. My pulse ratcheted. Something like a giant boulder lodged itself in my throat. I couldn't swallow it. Couldn't do anything but stare at the envelope in her hand, inked with messy, bold, Kellan-shaped scribbles I instantly recognized. After all, I'd spent half my weekends going through his shit. Including the drawers that, up until his death, he'd never kept locked.

She parted her lips. I didn't want her to say a single thing; I wanted her to say everything. Strung out, I could only watch her lips move.

"It was his dying wish, Tate."

Car, meet crash.

I must have staggered back because she was past the threshold in a flash, shutting the door behind us and locking it. I kept my eyes fixed on that thing in her tiny fist. She yanked the letter back when I reached for it.

I eyed it. Then her. Then it again.

"Tell you what," I began, like a sleazy used car salesman about to offer her the deal of a lifetime. "Let's do a little trade-off. I'll give you the manuscript if you give me the letter."

"No."

I raised a brow. "No?"

This is so not the time to realize you've never heard that word from a woman, asshole.

"No." She had a voice of steel and the spine to match it. "Here's how this is gonna go. You'll give me the manuscript because it's what Kellan wanted. And I *won't* be giving you this letter because Kellan wouldn't have wanted me to."

She said it as if she had some ownership over Kel that I didn't. It struck something fiercely protective inside me. Or perhaps plain stubborn. This wasn't only about refusing to relinquish power to Charlie. It was about refusing to relinquish power over my brother.

"It's a little bold to be making claims about what Kellan would have wanted." Strong words, considering my resolve dissolved by the second. Thread by fucking thread. "For someone who was 'just friends' with him, you sure seem to know a lot about him that his own family doesn't."

I set myself up. Felt it as soon as I said it. Kellan's family didn't know a thing about him because we were an awful family. Trapped in our own self-absorbed bubbles. Incapable of making time for him. In fact, it said more about Terry and me than it did about Kel and Charlie.

I knew why I said it. I hated myself for being unable to let it go. Because, in the end, no matter the fuss I put up about not giving a damn about her, it mattered to me what Charlotte Richards had been to Kel.

Charlie could have taken my sentence and run with it, but she had the decency not to. Instead, she produced a letter from an envelope.

I stilled, unmoving, watching her as she carefully unfolded it and brought it to my face. Her fingers splayed out, stretching in a way that covered most of the lines. She wanted me to see as little of it as possible. Message received.

I read the snippets that I could.

My darling Venom,
I left something for you.
I couldn't finish the book.
I'm passing the torch to you.
I dare you to finish it…

She wasn't lying. Kellan called her his Venom. Wanted her to have the book. Maybe he'd even written it for her. *About* her.

The silence expanded, filling the empty crevices of my home with more emptiness. I had nothing to say. By the end of the night, she would own the only thing I had left of Kel.

Charlie planted a fist on her waist. The other still carried the letter. "Before you say no again, consider this. There are two sides to every story, and Kellan's is that you were unsupportive, always busy, and never willing to give him what he wanted."

"What he wanted was to live with an addict who had no business raising a teenager," I seethed. Not to mention, I never had a choice. Once Terry dumped Kel on my doorstep with hardly a second glance at the kid, his options became me or the streets, and I wasn't a big enough asshole to let Kel fend for himself.

"I'm not saying you didn't have good reasons." She edged forward, toes bumping mine. This marked the first time I had her this close without wanting to touch her. "I'm saying Kellan had wants, and needs, and desires, and you said no to them. This time, you have the opportunity to grant his wish. He wants me to finish this book, so I will. If you don't give *Darling Venom* to me, you're going against his wishes." She rested a hand on my chest. The bloody one. My heart threatened to bruise her palm, the way it raced. "Pick Kellan's side this time, Tate."

I knew how this night would end. Her, in possession of the manuscript; me, in possession of an empty home and an emptier heart. My silence only prolonged the inevitable.

Her hand dropped. She stepped back. A spark fizzled out in her, as if I'd disappointed her somehow. "It's about Kellan, not you."

My fists burrowed in my pockets, so I wouldn't be tempted to do something stupid like grab the letter and hightail it to the Canadian border. "It's in my closet safe. 02-28."

"Kellan's birthday."

I didn't answer. Just moved aside.

She slinked up the stairs, making as little noise as possible. Something about her movements told me she was used to being unseen, and that disappointed me.

When she returned, she carried the thick bundle in her hands, cradling it as if it were one of my newborns.

She stood on my front step. "I'm going to make Kellan proud, Tate."

I shut the door in her face, severing our ties. Forever.

Seemed like Kellan Marchetti had three big secrets: suicidal ideation, *Darling Venom*, and Charlotte Richards.

Chapter Forty-Eight

Tate

Back in a bed that didn't feel like mine, in a house that never felt like a home, I stared at the ceiling, wondering if Charlie made it home safe.

I replayed the way she moved up the stairs. With dignified silence. Like she was so used to being invisible, she didn't have to worry about making a sound. She knew she wouldn't.

Then I thought about *Darling Venom*.

How many words were in the manuscript? How many words were in a book in general?

I knew nothing about books. Kel took after our sperm donor—all bursting creativity and written words. I took after my mother, excelling at math, biology, and chemistry.

Would she know what to write? Would it make her miss him? Would it bring back old memories? More things I could find out about him, but never would, because I was being a horrible bastard to her.

I tossed and turned. Moved to the right side of the bed. Glared at the red digital numbers on my alarm clock.

I kept checking my arms and legs for missing parts.

None.

But it felt like something was missing.

If I were being honest, I couldn't blame Charlie. She didn't need to follow through on Kel's wishes. She did it because she was a good person. It was, perhaps, my favorite thing about her.

Here was the ugly truth.

I didn't want tonight to be the last time I saw Charlotte Richards. Her presence soothed me where I normally burned. In a lot of ways, she was my last hope. My only connection left to Kellan.

But *Darling Venom* was the last possession I had of his. Without it, she and I had no reason to see each other again.

You could pick up the phone and ask to meet her. To hear more about Kel.

But what was the point?

Every time we stood in the same room, there was confusion, anger, and tension. I couldn't stand her, yet I couldn't keep her away either. She couldn't stop looking at me, yet she wouldn't budge when it came to doing justice for Kel.

That was another thing.

Charlie's loyalty was with Kellan.

Not me.

Never me.

Kellan.

Why did you do this, Kellan?

But I already knew why.

Part of it was because of me. Because I was so busy pretending to be a grownup, I forgot to check on him.

Kellan never forgave me for that mistake.

And I very much doubted Charlie would, either.

Chapter Forty-Nine

Charlotte

I ran my fingers along the spines of old hardcovers as I walked along an aisle, breathing in the earthy, musky scent of aged paper, dust, and cherished ink. An entire week had passed since I'd bid Tate goodbye, and today I finally mustered the courage to let go of the one thing that still bound us together. Kellan's books.

I didn't go to the New York Public Library in Midtown West to dispose of the precious, pricey paperbacks. No. That was the touristy, well-loved, wealthy library everyone knew and cared about. Kellan would have hated knowing his books had ended up there.

I went to the one I'd frequented every week since I was a kid. The New York Society Library. I'd already deposited the precious *Wizard of Oz* first editions with three trusty librarians I knew—Doris, Henry, and Faye. They'd fawned and patted them like they were newly born unicorns. Not that it did anything to dull the *what the heck?* feeling I'd left Tate's house with that night. But unlike Kellan, I excelled at pretending everything was okay.

I glanced at the time on my phone. Forty minutes until my lunch break ended. The rows upon rows of novels relaxed me. Between the heavy, dark oak and the thick tomes, I felt at home. Warm and safe.

I slung my courier bag over my shoulder and relished the silence, fingering a novel—*Jane Eyre*—at the same time someone from the aisle in front of me touched it. I withdrew quickly. So did the person behind the screen of books.

I watched the book intently to see if they'd take it. They didn't. I smiled to myself and proceeded along the aisle, my eyes gliding over the stack of hardbacks.

The person ambled along at the exact same pace, a big shadow I could see through the cracks of neatly lined-up books. Whoever it was, they were tall. At least a head and a half taller than me, anyway. A man, probably.

I told myself not to panic and willed my heart to chill out. But the slower I walked, the slower the person walked.

I decided to test him. I stopped again, pawing a volume of *The Green Dwarf* that sat beside eight identical copies. The person behind the curtain of books stopped, too.

My mouth hung open, my pulse skyrocketing into oblivion.

Boom, boom.

Boom.

I touched the novel, placing my index finger on the top of its spine. The person from the other side did the same, touching the back cover. It occurred to me that he was seeing completely different spines, and he'd picked *Jane Eyre* because I'd touched it, not because he'd wanted to read it. He probably couldn't even pull it out all the way.

I swallowed hard.

I should turn around and leave. It was exactly my luck to fall prey to a serial library masturbator.

Glancing around, I confirmed there was no one here. Just me and this person.

Jesus.

I stepped back, withdrawing my hand from the book. Invisible ants ran up and down my limbs.

Get out of here, Charlie.

I turned around, about to race down the aisle.

Finally, the person on the other side opened their mouth. "I have a confession to make."

And just like that, the air stuck in my lungs escaped in a rush. I recognized the low, gravelly voice immediately.

Tate.

With the transfer of *Darling Venom* into my care and the *Wizard of Oz* editions into the library's, we were officially done. Finished. No reason to see each other or talk to one another ever again. So, what was he doing here? And how did he know I'd be here?

I didn't ask any of those questions. Butterflies filled my chest up to my neck, flipping ferociously. I reclined against the shelf opposite from the one we shared, tucking my hands behind my back.

"This is not a confession booth." It came out shakier than I would've liked. I swallowed, scratching the scar at my wrist.

"Could've fooled me."

I heard the smirk in his voice, and I was done for. Every single effort I'd made not to think about him evaporated. The line between wanting to save him and wanting to kiss him—and yes, I realized bitterly, I did very much want to kiss him right now—blurred.

He was right. It did feel like a confession booth with the divider between us, of books that were going to hold this conversation secret forever. My fingertips tingled.

"Let's hear it then," I whispered.

"I hate reading."

His words jarred me.

My eyes widened. "You mean... like, in general, or...?"

"Books. Poems. Songs. Fucking IKEA manuals. Reading's not my jam. Never was. I think I'm allergic, thanks to Sperm Donor dearest."

I wished he'd stop calling Terry that.

I wished he'd just be grateful his dad was still alive.

He continued, relentless. "It's the William Ford effect. Why the hell would I try my luck at something my father mastered in a way the entire world is going to remember? So just in case, I never read for fun. To extinguish the risk of wanting to write myself."

I started walking along the aisle again once my heartbeat resembled its normal pace. So did Tate. I tested the waters, running my fingers through the books between us as I passed them.

He did the same.

"Why are you telling me this?" My voice was thick and cracked and not mine.

"Kellan hated that I wasn't #TeamTerry. He adored his father so much, the fact that I wasn't on board made him resent me. The more I tried to separate them to save Kellan, the more he loathed me, and the more Terry did, too. By the time Kellan took matters into his own hands, no one in the Marchetti family could stand my face."

His fingers brushed mine suddenly. I sucked in a breath.

Whoa.

Was I supposed to feel this way? Like I'd walked into a sedative, silver fog? I fumbled to keep the conversation thread.

Tate proceeded. "I've been on the defense for so long, with so many people, it's hard to accept your good deeds. Especially when they are dipped in a reminder that I failed Kellan."

"I understand." Surprisingly, I did. "Is this an apology?"

"Do you want it to be?"

"Kind of."

"Then it is."

"Tate..." I paused, unsure how to say the next part. "It's okay that you fucked up. Everyone does, sometimes." I thought about me and Leah. About how I failed her. "And it's okay to forgive yourself, too."

"Say that to yourself, Charlie. Often. And loud."

His fingers touched mine again. It felt like a row of books falling with a loud thump in my chest. We exhaled together. Inhaled together.

I stopped walking when we reached the end of the aisle. One more step, and we'd be facing each other, and I wasn't ready for this moment to end.

Tate mimicked me. I turned around fully to the aisle. Our eyes met behind the row of books on the top shelf. He watched me in silence for what seemed like forever. This felt monumental in ways I wasn't equipped to deal with.

"Truce?" he asked.

"Truce."

"I'm tired of war."

"I know." I choked on my words. "Nobody wins it, anyway."

His eyes told me he knew pain, and pain knew him, and they were in a committed, unbreakable relationship. I opened my mouth to say something because I thought I should, but nothing came out.

His hand gripped mine under the shelf. He yanked me forward. Our faces were inches from one another. My breathing became labored. This was the second indication I'd ever received that Tate saw me. Really saw me. As a woman, not just a mason jar full of painful memories.

"Tate."

"Charlie."

"I don't hate you," I admitted.

"I know." He curled his lower lip. "Poor Charlie." Every bone in my body shook. "Now's a good time to run," he said in his sad, silky voice, his eyes still hard on mine. "Because if you don't, I am liable to kiss you."

I'd sunk into that silver, drug-scented fog again. My knees grew weak. My bones melted. Somewhere in the back of my head, I knew this was not a good idea.

"I have a confession to make, too." Kinetic energy sizzled between us. He didn't interrupt my flow of words. I wished he would. "I want you to," I whispered.

All it would take was one step, and everything would change. We both knew that, so neither of us took it. We just stood there, entranced. I'd started to think the kiss would never happen when Tate finally took a step forward to the corner of the room. Out of the aisle.

I still didn't move. He rounded the shelf, standing in front of me. He wore a full-blown gray suit.

"One last chance to run," he hissed, his blue eyes darkening.

I made a point of not moving an inch here or there. He picked a book off of the shelf—*The Merchants of Souls*—and used it to cover both our faces as he yanked me to his hard body, pressing my waist against his. He grabbed the front of my neck almost punishingly, possessively, then his lips crashed down on mine like a thunderstorm.

It felt like my body was about to burst with adrenaline as his hot, expert lips closed in on mine, greedily. He sucked my tongue into his mouth, releasing a feral groan that bounced on the mosaic ceiling.

I grabbed his face with both my hands, desperate to get closer. The book dropped on the floor. He backed me against the shelf that served as our confession booth, pinning me between his arms as he grabbed my jaw and deepened our kiss.

His tongue stroked mine with intent, and he pressed himself to me. He was hard. So hard, my mouth watered and my body arched, begging for more. I should be running to the office before my lunch break ended, but I couldn't, for the life of me, snap out of this moment.

It was angry, and frantic, and everything. I pushed eight years of frustration into him, and he delivered it back, tenfold.

"Sugar, cookies, cypress," he talked into our kiss. I knew exactly what he was listing.

I smiled, tugging at his lower lip. "Sandalwood, bonfire, citrus… sex."

"Sex, huh?" His voice was husky and groggy. "I'll show you sex."

He grabbed the back of my thighs and pulled me up, trying to get me to wrap my legs around his narrow waist. I was sure I was too heavy for him. I attempted to plant my feet on the carpeted floor, but he just yanked more forcefully and wrapped me around him.

"I'm heavy," I whimpered.

"You're perfect." He shut me up with a kiss as he rolled his hips between my legs. I let out an involuntary groan. "When's your lunch break over?" he asked.

What?

I pulled away, tilting my head. "How do you know?"

"I asked Reagan when I stopped by her exam room."

This was why he came here. *Duh.*

"Why did she tell you?"

"Because she worships the ground I walk upon. And because she thinks I'm supposed to give you something personal I made up months ago. So? What time?"

I barely suppressed my laugh. This man was unbelievable.

I shook my head. "Probably in ten minutes or so. Two-ish."

"Fuck." His forehead dropped to mine. He stole another kiss. He really did drop the F-bomb way more than any other doctor I knew did. "You should go before I fuck you between science and fiction."

I nodded. I didn't ask for his number. Not this time. I was actually proud of myself as he lowered me to my feet, and I collected the courier bag I'd dropped sometime during us exploding on one another like two shooting stars.

"You should ask them for that donation certificate." I didn't dare rub my lips, even though they felt all tender, swollen, and tingly from our kisses. His taste was still in my mouth, and I doubted I'd eat anything today.

He bit his inner cheek, nodding. I noticed he still didn't look ruffled. Just like with the blonde in his office. He was basically incapable of letting go.

I turned around and started walking away.

Ask for my number.

Ask for my number.

Ask for my number.

With each step I took, a heavy stone settled in my stomach.

One stone.

Two.

Three.

Four...

By the time I got down the stairs and through the entrance, there were maybe eighteen of them.

No phone number. No continuation.

I'd just let him kiss me stupid because he wanted to. Because *I'd* wanted him to.

Stupid me.

My phone buzzed with a call. Shit, it must be Abigail. I was so late.

I tore it from my courier bag and answered before checking the caller ID. "Hello?"

There was silence from the other line.

"Hello?"

Nothing.

I was about to hang up when he finally spoke. "This okay?" His voice sounded strained. Almost tender.

I was close to falling down on my knees in the middle of the street. I closed my eyes, taking a deep breath. "Yes. How did you get my number?" I'd left that section blank on his patient intake form on purpose.

"That class contact sheet. I found it after you left."

He was lying. There was no such thing. However Tate had gotten my number, he'd had to work for it. This made me smile. Along with the fact that he remembered my words from the day we'd cleared Kellan's room.

"A penny for your thoughts," I whispered to him, my voice still smoky.

"I would like to see more of you and less of your clothes. A penny for yours."

I want to kiss you hard. To let you rip me to shreds with your hands and tongue and words. I want to tell you the whole entire truth and hold you while you come to terms with it.

Instead, I let my right leg rock as I sighed. "I'm thinking I should move before I get in trouble for being late. Goodbye, Tate."

Chapter Fifty

Tate

I felt like a criminal who had committed the deed after weeks of preparation.

From the moment I first saw Charlotte Richards, I'd wanted to kiss her. I finally had, and the world didn't end. The NYPD didn't come knocking on my door with an arrest warrant for stalking. Satan didn't take the elevator up to Earth and hand me my passport to Hell.

I kissed her, and the world didn't end.

I kissed her, and I didn't even feel half as guilty as I should.

I kissed her, and soon, if it were up to me, I would do much more than kiss her.

Chapter Fifty-One

Charlotte

If books were men, they would be the player who dated all the Jessicas in the tri-state area, cheated on you with your best friend, and dumped you for your sister through a text message.

I knew myself well enough to know I didn't survive books. They tore me to shreds. I'd never met an inanimate object as talented at breaking hearts as a book. Which was why I delayed starting *Darling Venom* until Friday night, knowing full-well I'd be a mess of tears and snot by the end of it.

I waited for Leah to leave to her supplemental night class on microblading—not that we were acknowledging each other's existence at the moment—before I locked myself in my room, blasted a playlist filled with Kellan's favorite bands (Anti-Flag, Antischism, Anti System, and well, there was a pattern here), and pulled out the manuscript from its hidden spot beneath my bed.

It was thick. Thicker than the page count implied, layered with Post-its in five different colors, time-stamped comments inked beside the text, and so many dog-eared pages, it rendered them useless.

I opened it to a random page. Notes littered the column, addressed to me by name. As if Kellan had gone through the entire manuscript, knowing I would be the one finishing it.

He planned on leaving this to you.

He planned on dying.

From the beginning.

The literal beginning, too, seeing as the first time-stamped comment was dated the day after we met. He'd started this in eighth grade. He might not have finished it then, but the fact that he'd started it so young...

I could only think of a handful of authors I loved who'd written their first books around that age.

S. E. Hinton and *The Outsiders*.

Matthew Gregory Lewis and *The Monk*.

Christopher Paolini and *Eragon*.

Mary Shelley and *Frankenstein*.

Kellan Marchetti was prodigal, and he'd never let himself shine.

I swallowed thickly, refusing to let what that meant sink in. I needed to be pragmatic about this. To treat it as if I were an agent, and it was a book from an author I represented.

The good news was, it looked fully finished. Three-hundred and forty-six pages, single-spaced. Ready to be edited. The bad news was, I was familiar with the editing process, but I'd never done it myself.

I flipped to the first page and spotted a note in the margin that said: DICKS, READ THIS FIRST! So, I did.

Dicks,

Most of the notes are from me. The rest are from a pretentious Ivy League dickwad with too much time on his hands and an overly high opinion of himself (read: my future, if I didn't off myself, so the world dodged a bullet there). Basically, I spent a shit ton of time and effort applying to Harvard on special concentrations, designing a creative writing curriculum I knew I'd never follow through with, all to get Professor Dickwad to read Darling Venom and tell me I don't understand loss. Take from that what you will.

— K

P.S. That Asshole found out I got into Harvard and is ten seconds from buying me a brand-new car (probably a Prius because he relishes in my eternal suffering) to make the commute.

The puzzle pieces clicked into place. Kellan needed feedback on his book. He never actually wanted to attend Harvard. Knew he wouldn't make it that far.

I wondered if Tate had any clue what he'd been up to, but it seemed unlikely.

It took me one chapter to realize the book was good.

And I mean *The Imperfections* good.

Just... *Wow.*

Another four chapters for the book's purpose to sink in. Two more chapters to accept I couldn't finish it.

Not today, at least.

Not with my sanity intact.

And another chapter to grasp just how screwed I was.

Kellan—punk-loving, kilt-wearing, forever-rebellious, too-cool-for-school Kellan—had written a love story.

A love story between me and him.

A love story that never happened.

A love story that never would.

And within the confession, he'd laced an apology for everything he put me through.

I reread a line, touching it reverently, as if it would come to life and bring Kellan back with it.

I realized, with depressing clarity, that she wasn't the venom at all. She was the antidote. But the quantities were all off.

My fingertips grazed my lips. The same lips Tate had devoured. I remembered when Kellan first called me Venom. He'd kissed me, shoved a penny into my pocket, and offered me a carefree smile, promising to see me again next year.

It got hard to breathe. I wiped my face with my sleeves, forcing away the tears that burned the back of my eyes, and continued reading, pausing when a line hit me so hard, my teeth chattered.

Suicide is a war of two fears—fear of death and fear of the thing that pushes you toward it. The stronger side always wins. And if you lose, the penalty is death.

I slammed the manuscript shut. Shoved it back beneath my bed. Curled into a ball on my carpet. I bawled. My shoulders shook with the effort to not fall apart. Shudders racked out of my body. It felt like my organs would fall out one by one if I didn't keep myself together.

The carpet burned my cheek. Its scent, of old age and overuse, barreled into me. It would be so easy to fall into nothingness. Afterall, we were well acquainted.

Tears soaked my sweater sleeve. I wiped my eyes again, streaking mascara everywhere.

A shoe slammed against the rack outside, marking Leah's arrival, but I couldn't stop the flood. Footsteps thudded. They paused in front of my door. I stared at the shadow beneath, waiting to see what she'd do.

She must've stood there for a few minutes as I sniffled-cried-bawled before she continued to her room. I heard the door swing shut a moment later.

Turning over onto my back, I repeated a line from *Darling Venom* in my head. A line that gutted me.

Once a year, for a stolen hour, I let myself be the venom. The toxin. The thing that poisoned her. But with one momentary lapse in selfishness, I pushed her away. I've regretted it every day since.

For the first time, I saw Kellan.

The thing that made him breathe and bleed.

Me.

Chapter Fifty-Two

Tate

So, this was what they called a spiral.

Step One: Snap at your receptionist all day, to the point where you catch her in the break room in tears, shoveling a Snickers bar down her throat while angry-texting her friends to tell them what a dickbag her boss is. The first time you've ever witnessed her consume a single carb, by the way. Even then, you ignore it because the alternative—compassion—is beyond your realm of capabilities today.

Step Two: Reveal the baby's sex to a couple who wanted to keep it a surprise because you cannot keep your shit together. A couple who spent over a decade and several rounds of IVF conceiving. When they collapse into tears but decide to keep you as their doctor because no one else can do what you do, offer them a voucher for a free visit as if their designer everything and straight-off-the-Mayflower last name indicate they'd ever use it.

Step Three: Arrive late to a C-section, call the nurses you've known for years by the wrong name, and leave as soon as the surgery is done with barely a congratulations to the new parents. Demand your practice partner supervise the rest of the patient's care for the day because you don't trust yourself not to make a mistake.

Check, check, fucking check.

The reality of Kel's note sank in as soon as Charlie arrived at my place. But I'd pushed it aside, forcing myself not to process it. Which backfired in spectacular fashion.

Specifically, it bit me in the ass exactly two days after I kissed Charlotte in a library, hitting me during my morning coffee on my way to work. I spilled it in the elevator and walked around the rest of the day with a shit-colored stain and the fact that my little brother had written what had to be a suicide letter ramping up the pressure in my brain.

By noon, a headache threatened to crack my skull in two, and I'd made more poor decisions in one morning than I had all my life. But these were reversible poor decisions. They were not of the un-doable magnitude that would haunt me for the rest of my life, of which I only had one.

Not catching the signs with Kellan.

So, I told myself it wasn't a big deal and went on with the day, being a huge, distracted, and absolutely fireable dick. Good thing I was self-employed, or I'd be out of a paycheck. Though, at this rate, my reputation had taken a nosedive, and no one wanted to share a room with me.

Didn't blame them.

When I asked Sylvia to clear the rest of my schedule, she leapt to her keyboard, relief clear as the August Hawaiian sky.

Terry wasn't home when I arrived at my brownstone. Come to think of it, he hadn't been around in days. But I couldn't bring myself to give half a shit.

In fact, I relished the silence.

Needed it to hate myself in peace.

I sat on my bed. Stared at the ceiling. Debated whether to enter Kel's room and decided against it.

After an hour or so of being generally useless, I called Charlotte Richards for the second time ever and not in the way I'd intended on using her number when I'd lied my way into getting it from Reagan.

She answered on the absolute last ring, saying nothing.

I said nothing, too.

So, we sat there, listening to one another breathe, neither of us budging. It made me feel dirty. Like a sick bastard.

It was clear from the fact that she'd received a final letter from Kellan while Terry and I hadn't that he'd had a crush on her. Not to mention he'd referred to Charlie by the same name he'd given the book.

I kissed your high school crush, Kel.

I want to do it again.

I want to do more.

Fuck, I suck. I suck so hard. I deserve every single bad thing you've ever said and felt about me.

Now I knew what it was like to be a thief, and it didn't feel nice. I didn't feel as if I'd gained something at all. But I knew why I was quiet. Her reason for silence, however, eluded me. Especially with the way we'd left things in the library.

I broke first. "I have a question, Miss Richards."

"I—" Her voice cracked. It sounded like she'd been crying, and she didn't strike me as a crier. "I can't guarantee an answer, Dr. Marchetti."

"It's about the suicide letter."

"Then I definitely can't guarantee an answer."

"So, it is a suicide letter."

"I never said that." She cleared her throat, and I heard the shuffling of paper. A lot of it, judging by how long it took her to settle. "Don't take my word for it. Take his. Kellan said in the letter that it's not a suicide letter."

I ran a knuckle down the column of my throat, feeling like I had something stuck in there. "So, it just happens to be the last letter he wrote?"

"Yes." She laughed. The morose kind people used when they didn't actually find anything funny. "That is nearly verbatim what he says in the letter, actually."

Says.

I never understood why people talked about the written word in the present tense as if it were still happening. The author could be dead, and the readers would still say, "Ray Bradbury *writes* about censorship. Harper Lee *tackles* racism. F. Scott Fitzgerald *brings* us back to the Jazz Age." It was so Kellan Marchetti to be both his own killer and immortalizer.

I said this aloud, and Charlie laughed.

A genuine one, this time.

"He had a talent for getting what he wanted," she whispered, like she was letting me in on a secret.

"Except when I stood in the way."

"What are you doing, Tate?"

"Talking to you."

"I meant emotionally." Her voice gained volume. I could picture her nose scrunched up like it did whenever we argued. "I didn't go over to your home to make you fall apart again."

"I was never together in the first place, Charlie."

"Maybe not, but you learned to live with the grief." She paused. "I didn't mean to unravel you."

I had nothing to say to that, so I didn't reply. We were going on our twentieth minute now, and I still felt like the gum beneath a shoe. Charlie was Kel's. I couldn't even leave that untainted.

"After Kellan died, I confronted St. Paul's principal," she admitted.

"You did?"

She was just a baby at the time. But something told me Charlie did a lot of grownup things for the people she loved.

"Yeah."

"What did you say?"

"I blamed her for not protecting Kellan better. He was getting bullied on a regular basis. I'm talking physically, too, Tate."

I shook my head, trying to recall if I'd ever seen bruises on Kel. "How bad?"

"Bad. So bad." She gave me time to digest her words. "The teachers knew. The whole school did. But these kids pay an enormous annual fee.

Their parents are all in powerful positions in the city. Country, even. Nobody wanted to touch that explosive situation with a ten-foot pole. No amount of fuss a scholarship kid with dead parents and a broke sister could kick up worked."

The last sentence sounded like it was meant for her. Like she was trying to reassure herself that she'd tried. It served to remind me how much more I could've done.

"The principal did nothing." A hard edge entered her voice. "*Kellan* did nothing. I tried to talk to him during lunch once. It didn't go well. So, I dropped off a letter in Principal Brooks' office. Kellan found out and got mad at me for narcing. In the end, nothing happened. The bullying didn't stop. For a while, I searched for someone to blame, and she was the easiest target."

"What did she say when you came to her?"

"She told me not to spread rumors. I think she was covering her ass."

"Definitely covering her ass. At Kel's funeral, she told me she had no clue what was going on. As if 1) I believed her and 2) not knowing absolved her of any responsibility regarding what went on within her campus."

She hummed her agreement. It might've been the first time I let myself release my rage over what happened to Kellan to someone who felt the same way.

"She also sent me to the student counselor after I confronted her."

"What did the counselor do?"

"He gave me a pamphlet on grief. It was the same one he gave me after my parents died, but I don't think he remembered that. I read the thing again. It told me to find someone to make me feel better." She snorted, getting more worked up. "How idiotic. It's like the dude who made the pamphlet never lost anyone. It's grief! The only person who can make you feel better is gone. That's why it hurts so damn much."

She grew silent.

I didn't say anything. I didn't want her to stop talking. In fact, I clung to her words, hungry for anything she could tell me about my brother. It felt like I was meeting Kel for the first time through Charlie.

"I turned to books after that," she said on the fortieth minute of our call. On the dot. Almost as if she'd been staring at the timer counting up.

I wondered if she'd decided ahead of time how long she'd let this conversation go on. After all, it was dangerous.

I wanted her.

She, in a fucked-up way, wanted me, too.

We were grieving Kellan and betraying him at the same time.

"I've always loved them, of course," she continued. "It's how Kellan and I connected. We loved the same books. We shared recommendations. He'd send me some stories he wrote, and I would beg for more. Some people don't want any reminders of the person they're grieving, but I crave them. I see Kellan in every word I read, and it keeps me going. I wish I could find that thing for you, Tate. The thing that keeps you going."

"You should hate me."

"I don't hate you." I heard her get up and grab things. "I resent you. There's a difference."

"Not a big one."

Sudden noise came through her end. Cars honked. People buzzed around her. A dog barked. She was outside. Somewhere crowded.

Charlie didn't disagree with me, instead switching topics. "You're a doctor."

"Last I checked."

The background noise faded. She said something to someone, but it came out muffled, like she had her hand covering the phone's mic.

She returned to our conversation. "What's a side effect?"

"Are you sick?"

"Not in the way you're thinking."

"Do you have a specific side effect in mind?"

"No. I meant in the context of an illness or disease or cure. In the general sense. Like how you would use the term at work."

"It's a physical or mental feature indicating a condition of disease."

"I think that's what we're suffering from. The side effects."

"Of?"

"Of love. Grief is a side effect of love. It lasts as long as the love lasts. You get used to the pain until you're reminded it's there. That's how it always works. What you need is a distraction."

"What I need is a cure."

"Cures have side effects, too, doc. And some conditions? Well... they're incurable."

And then she hung up.

I didn't have time to let her words sink in before the doorbell went off. I stomped down the stairs, hoping to God it wasn't Terry, or I didn't know what I'd do.

It rang again, followed by a rough knock. I swung the door open, meeting Charlie's doe eyes.

"I'm going to do something you're not going to like," she warned, stepping past me.

"Then don't do it."

"You said you need a cure. I'll do you one better." For a second, I thought she'd kiss me. Instead, she pulled the manuscript out of her bag, raised it beside her head, and declared, "I have a distraction."

"I'm not reading it."

She nodded, as if she'd expected as much. "I figured you hadn't and wouldn't." That only made me more curious about the contents. "I'm commandeering your place."

"The hell you are."

"I am," she repeated, and I had a sick feeling that this would end like last time—with her getting her way. A trait she shared with Kel. "I need to be here to finish *Darling Venom*."

I opened the door again, gesturing to the cavity. "Consider this me politely declining on account of the fact that we cleared Kellan's room, and there is nothing you will find up there that you cannot find elsewhere."

"*The house remained empty most days, my room perfectly situated to bear the bulk of the winter wind. I let thoughts of her thaw the bone-chill. Of laughing with her. Of kissing her. Of the things I wanted to do with her but never would. And even with my brother gone and my dad hidden away from me like a fugitive, the emptiness fled. Venom was here.*"

She was panting by the time she finished, staring at me with wild eyes, chest ballooning and collapsing with each breath.

"It's a passage from *Darling Venom*," she explained. "And if I want to continue Kellan's book, I need to experience what he did. I can't do this without walking in his shoes. There is no point in giving me this manuscript if you're not going to help me finish it like he wanted me to. And my gut tells me you don't actually want this book back."

"Fine," I bit out, hating her for being right.

I didn't have a choice.

It was Kel's last wish.

Even in his grave, he managed to uproot my life. Create chaos in his wake.

She gave me her back, barreling up the stairs without further invitation.

I confirmed three things at once.

1) Charlie was Venom,

2) Kellan Marchetti had been deeply, madly, infuriatingly in love with Charlotte Richards, and

3) He wasn't the only one who had a weakness for the odd, eccentric beauty.

Chapter Fifty-Three

Tate

I remembered the night Kellan died, exactly as ordered:

8:15 p.m.—I leave work early to meet Kel at a diner. Odd that he'd want to eat with me, in public no less, but I'm excited. Hopeful, even, the optimistic idiot that I am. That morning, I told him I'd lay off and give him unsupervised visitation with Terry (which will require me convincing the useless bastard to actually meet with his son, but one hurdle at a time). After that, Kel seemed... different. A good different, I think, because as mentioned, he invited me to dinner tonight right after.

8:33 p.m.—Receive an emergency page about a patient and her triplets. Rush to the ER. In my haste, I forget to shoot Kel a quick text, explaining the situation. (Why the fuck did I prioritize someone else's kids over my own fucking brother to the point that I couldn't take just two seconds to text him that I'd see him later tonight? Why the fuck is time irreversible? They say you learn from your mistakes, but it's pointless if you'll never be in a position to apply that lesson again. What a goddamn lie.)

8:45 p.m.—Kel shows up to the diner, doesn't see me, and thinks I ditched him. He sends me a text, which I miss, because I'm prepping for an emergency C-section.

9:00 p.m.—Start the surgery, three crying terrors enter this world,

Sienna Omri names one after Kel. Which reminds me, I stood him up without a word. But fuck, I'm excited to tell him he has a legacy. A human named after him. He'd think it's cool, yeah?

10:45 p.m.—*Check my texts to see one from Kel. It reads:* I ordered you a chicken parm. It's in the fridge, Dr. Miracle. Don't say I never did anything for you. *Unsure about the tone of said text—is he pissed or genuine? Nevertheless, I'm excited to tell him the news. And that he needs to get his shit together before the baby grows up and realizes he was named after the lamest person ever.*

11:05 p.m.—*Arrive home. There are cops. Two of them. From the looks of it, it's not pretty. My first thought is Kel got busted for drugs, and I'll have to spend my night bailing his ass out. I'm wrong. And a bastard for even thinking it. They tell me my little brother no longer exists on this Earth. They tell me he's in a better place. If (and only if) he's really dead, I believe them, seeing as anything is better than this hellscape.*

11:16 p.m.—*End up at St. Paul. No memory of how I got here, but I'm in my Lexus. I stop the car just before the bend. Kellan's not dead. I don't believe it. And if I don't see another cop, the crime-scene tape, the aftermath, he is alive. I leave. I tell myself that when I return home, Kel will be there, his heart still beating and a half-assed excuse for being out past curfew.*

11:32 p.m.—*Kel isn't home.*

11:49 p.m.—*Try to eat the chicken parm in the fridge because it's the last gift Kel gave me. I get as far as swallowing before I throw it up. It's no longer my favorite food. Haven't stepped foot in Pauli's Kitchen since.*

11:50 p.m.—*Hannah comes over after a call from Walter and forces me to sleep. I agree because I don't want to look at her face. It's a reminder of a bad decision in a long line of bad decisions.*

12:01 a.m.—*Regret trying to sleep. All I see is Kellan when I close my eyes. Falling from the rooftop. In slow-motion. Fast-forward. Real time. It hurts every way. By the fourth replay, I am convinced he regrets it. I'll never know.*

2:30 a.m.—Wake up. Slept like shit and barely functioning. Email my receptionist, asking her to cancel all my appointments for the year. Don't care how she'll manage that. I try to eat, puke it up, and discover a voicemail from Kel. Later, I learn he sent it an hour before his death. Still haven't listened to it.

Kellan's death had coincided with my malpractice insurance renewal. It required a psych eval with a shrink who'd decided it would be a good idea to force me to relive the day my brother died. He'd forced me to jot down what I remembered from that night on a list, so we could tackle each timestamp. Something about reliving history in order to let it go. As if I'd ever let go of my share of the blame in my little brother's death. As if I'd ever be able to.

I sat in the dark, legs tucked beneath my desk, reading the notebook I still kept from my days meeting Dr. Felton. The existence of Kel's letter upended my timeline.

When did he write it? When did he drop it off? Did he give it directly to Charlie? Did that happen on his Death Day?

The one thing I knew, without a doubt, was that it was a suicide letter. If Charlie didn't want me to see it, it meant she—*they*—had something to hide. The ugliness of my relationship with Kel pretty much inked into my brain what that something was. I wouldn't be shocked to learn the letter he'd produced before his death consisted of a five-thousand-word Tate Marchetti hatefest.

But that only posed more questions. Namely, why didn't Terry receive one? Kel worshipped his father more than any god known to man. Seemed odd he wouldn't write him one. Unless there was more to their story than I knew. A question I would never ask Terry, because... well, fuck him.

The intercom went off. I pressed a button, accepting the live feed.

Sylvia's voice echoed in my office. "Dr. Marchetti, I've canceled your appointments for the day as you requested. Dr. Bernard agreed to cover your three o'clock, though he seemed unhappy about it being a routine checkup and—"

I released the button. Didn't care to hear the rest. All I cared about was figuring out where Charlie's letter fit into the timeline. I spent the next two hours trying to piece together the puzzle, knowing the only way I'd ever get answers was to actually ask her.

But that required picking up the phone and calling her. The last time I did that, I'd ended up with her in my house, invading my space.

The door creaked open. I saw a leather, memory-foam loafer step into my office and followed it up to the Baldwin-brother knockoff it belonged to.

Walter flicked on the light switch, eyeing me with suspicion. "I heard a rumor I hope isn't true."

That one of my patients came on my exam table, and I'd like her to do it again?

I arched a brow. "Do tell. You know I love gossip."

He disregarded my sarcasm, though this felt a little sharper than our usual heavy banter. "You arrived late to Isabella Romero's appointment."

"I've arrived late to several appointments in the past, such is the nature of our profession, but they've never warranted an in-person visit from the great Dr. Walter Bernard."

He shrugged. "You've never arrived late for an ultrasound with the daughter of a doctor who happens to sit on the New York State Medical Board before."

"I don't do preferential treatment."

"You also don't clear your schedule with no notice and pass routine check-ups on to me while you sit in the dark in your office doing God knows what, but here we are."

"Is this an intervention?"

"Do you *need* an intervention?"

"No, but I need this conversation to end."

"I'm not just worried about you. I'm worried about your patients. You know what happens if you take your eye off the ball."

"It hits you in the face," I finished, letting that familiar ice expand in my lungs. Until I transformed into cold, clinical Tate again. My only defense against the world. "Concern noted. You may continue with your day."

After he left, I returned to my staring contest with the ceiling, notepad flipped open on my lap. A position I maintained until it was reasonably late enough to leave the office and I was sure Charlie had left my house.

She'd stolen a key from my key chain. For the past week, she entered and exited at her will, turning it into a minefield I was determined to avoid. Which meant late nights in my office. Alone with my thoughts. Not doing actual work.

It confused the hell out of my staff, who didn't like to leave until I did.

Terry was gone when I arrived home, thank fuck. He'd returned a few days ago. Apparently, from a gambling trip in Atlantic City, which I had no clue how he funded.

(Note to self: make sure all the furniture is in place.)

Now his daily routine consisted of leaving for several hours at a time and returning sober, so I couldn't kick him out on the grounds of a rule break. Then he'd beg me to cough up *Darling Venom* until I was damn near close to booting him on the street.

A box sat on my front porch. The meal-prep delivery. I'd meant to take it in a few days ago, but I'd forgotten. I set it on the kitchen island and opened it, turning my nose away at the rotten stench.

There were a lot of things I should be doing, one of which included tossing it in the garbage outside, but I couldn't conjure the motivation. I shoved a granola bar down my throat, barely taking the time to chew. Then I trudged my way up the stairs and collapsed on my bed with my shoes still on.

Did I need to get my shit together?

Yes. Lives were on the line.

But it could wait one more day.

Chapter Fifty-Four

Tate

It was the same dream. Kellan falling from that roof, arms dangling, feet fluttering. Regret filled his wide, surprised eyes. Only this time, I was there to catch him. I held the letter in my hand. A full-page manifesto on all the things Kel hated about me. All the reasons I made him want to die.

I positioned myself in his trajectory.

Reached out to catch him.

And woke up.

My hand slammed on the nightstand, silencing the alarm. That organ in my chest threatened to burst. I felt like I'd run a marathon. In reality, I'd slept a cool seven hours. I preferred the rotating dreams of my mistakes to this one. The undoable mistake. It was the one that turned me into an insufferable ass all day, but since that seemed to be my default lately, I doubted anyone would notice at work.

When I got out of bed, I felt just as shitty as I had the past couple of weeks. Maybe even shittier. I washed up, tossed on enough clothes to make myself look mildly presentable, and bounded down the steps.

A melodic hum traveled up the staircase, reaching me. *Charlie.* I checked my phone, realizing it was a Saturday, and she didn't have work. Usually, I woke early and snuck out before she arrived. Her questions about the manuscript formed a constant assault. I didn't want to know a single thing about *Darling Venom*. But we'd started a cat-and-mouse game. I left earlier and earlier; she arrived ahead of schedule to match it. Today, she won.

I entered the kitchen. A citrusy scent invaded my nostrils, followed by the faint smell of something dying. Which reminded me. *The delivery food.* I scanned the kitchen island for the package and failed to find it.

Charlie followed my line of sight. "I tossed it. All the meat went bad. I tried to keep the veggies, but they smelled like rotting flesh. I opened up a new bottle of air freshener. I'd say I hope you don't mind, but I doubt you would've realized if I hadn't told you."

I wouldn't have.

She ran a rag over the counters. They looked clean. Cleaner than this place had been since Terry gave my housekeeper Hilda the boot and she decided she didn't want to return. *Note to self: figure out what Terry did and said to make poor ol' Hildy run for the hills.*

Charlie gnawed her lower lip. "Your fridge is empty. When was the last time you grocery shopped?"

I did what I often did when Charlie showed up before I managed to escape. I ignored her. Pretended she wasn't here, and I didn't want her. This was my best defense against the fact that I was at risk of kissing the shit out of her.

In my periphery, I saw her lift a frame, waving the gold clunker. It held a picture of me and Kel on the day we met. The only photo we had together. Growing up with paparazzi did a number on him. Didn't help that he hated me.

Without the senior yearbook photo of him (where he looked ten seconds from taking a machete to the photographer, turning to witchcraft to unleash a tsunami on all of New York City, and finding refuge in a Hot Topic), I wouldn't own a single image of Kel in his final year alive.

"I found this while cleaning the mantel. It was facedown."

Another note to self: move the frame to my nightstand, where Charlie can't see it.

And why the hell was she still cleaning? A few days ago, I'd thought my housekeeper had returned, but this made more sense.

"I noticed there aren't any other pictures of Kellan in here. I have some..." She bit her lip. "If you want to see them."

I froze, tempted for one foolish moment. Not enough to break my silence.

"Are you ignoring me because you're mad I barged in here?"

I'm ignoring you because I shouldn't want you, but I do.

I grabbed a bar from the cabinet, read the expiration date, and figured I wouldn't lose an organ over something three months too old.

"It won't last long. I'll finish the book soon, and I'll be gone. Out of your hair." She paused. "Out of your life." I turned, and she was there. In my space again. She blinked up at me, eyes lowering to the headphones looped around my neck. "Those were the prize for guessing the sex of Reagan's twins."

I clocked the small gap between us and the counter. I could push past her, but then I'd have to touch her. I settled for a, "Yes."

"But you're her doctor. You already knew the babies' sex."

"Yes. But I doubt you're here to discuss the ethics of gender-reveal participation. What do you want, Charlie?"

Don't ask me about the scenes. Don't ask me about the scenes.

"I'm worried about you."

That was almost as bad as asking about the scenes.

"Really? You shouldn't be," I said conversationally. "I'm not your problem to worry about."

"I shouldn't have told you about the letter."

"While you're out there gatekeeping what I should and should not know about my own brother, feel free to walk through the iron bars and lock yourself out."

"You're spiraling, Tate." She looked concerned. Genuinely so. If I had a heart, it'd be racing. "I barely even know you, and I can see that. Aren't you scared to fall?"

Like Kellan did?

It was a poor choice of words, and we both knew that. I watched her wince, gears churning in her head.

"Do you take Visa?" I deadpanned. "This isn't therapy. Lose the questions, *Lottie*."

She didn't even react to the nickname. Guess today we were focusing on my demons and my demons only.

"The question stands."

"My answer is the same: none of your business."

"I've lost one Marchetti brother. I'll be damned if I lose the other. You are falling, and you're about to hit rock bottom. That organ in your chest is barely beating, pumped full of bitter blood, and fear, and regret."

I felt very much like Terrence Marchetti's son in that moment. An asshole. A mess. Unworthy of my breaths. I risked her touch, brushing past her on my way to the door. "This isn't working."

She trailed after me. "My questions?"

"You being here."

"I need to finish the manuscript."

"It's been two weeks." I slid my feet into a pair of Italian oxfords, kneeling to lace them up. "You said Kel finished it, and it just needs editing."

"*Heavy* editing." She followed me to the doorway, and this was starting to feel too domestic for me. I needed to get the hell out of here. "Full passage rewrites. Plot edits. Even some dialogue changes."

"People write full-length novels in two weeks."

"I'm not an experienced novelist."

"Perhaps Kel should have asked someone else."

"There was no one else," she snapped. I'd poked the right button. Gotten her so mad, I knew she didn't want to see my face.

Good. Maybe you'll leave me alone to be miserable in peace.

My hand hit the doorknob. I swung it open. "Mind your own business, Charlie, and hurry the hell up. When I return from my delivery, I expect you to be gone."

Chapter Fifty-Five

Tate

Contrary to my wishes, I returned home to find Charlie there. Deep at work. A notepad in hand, the manuscript perched on the edge of the island.

From the doorway, I watched as she walked around my place like she owned it, taking notes, consuming the space. It felt fuller. Fuller than I ever remembered it. Not with Terry. Not with Hannah. Not with Kellan.

She spotted me after a minute or two, lowering the notepad and picking up *Darling Venom*. "I photocopied the manuscript. The original is in a fireproof safe at home. I can make you a copy if you'd like." *No, thanks.* "I have a question," she said after it became clear I wouldn't be using my mouth. "It's about a passage where Kel—"

I slipped the noise-canceling headphones on, muffling her voice. She cut into my path. I stood there, watching her lips move, pretending the cancelation feature worked better than it did. This was not the first time we'd done this song and dance.

Here's how it normally went: Charlotte opened her mouth, I caught sight of the determination sprawled across her face, and I dipped. If that didn't work, I found a way to tune her out. Once she realized I wasn't listening, she left. Only this time, she wasn't leaving.

My feet brought me to the living room, where I plopped on the couch and flipped on the television for the first time ever. I still wore my headphones. Couldn't hear her or the TV, but I did succeed at feeling a helluva lot like my deadbeat father. Speaking of whom, all Terry did these days was eat, sleep, and disappear. I recognized the signs of depression. Now, at least. Couldn't bring myself to help him, though.

Charlie settled beside me. We watched a documentary about lions in the wild on the Discovery Channel while a birthing podcast played in my ears. The obstetrician, who sounded like he'd gotten his medical degree in the basement of his mother's home, droned on about the beauty of the birth canal's ability to adapt. The vagina. He was talking about the vagina. Only, he couldn't bring himself to say the v-word.

I switched the podcast off. Charlie had stopped talking, who knew how long ago. I slid my headphones into my pocket, waiting for her to pick up where she'd left off. She didn't. I don't know why I did it—maybe sleep deprivation, maybe insanity—but I offered an olive branch.

"You don't get it." I stared straight ahead, at lions eating zebras. "It makes me physically ill to think about this book and what could be in it."

"You just need to read it once, and you'll know." But the way she said it, like even she didn't want me to read it, spoke volumes.

We finished the documentary together. This time, I didn't wear the headphones. This time, she didn't talk. When the end credits materialized, her stomach growled.

She winced. "I didn't have time for a meal, and your place is a food desert."

It was nearing midnight. Having her here was already dangerous. Having her here, late and alone and beside me? Absolutely lethal.

I sighed, strode to the kitchen, and tossed a pile of takeout menus on the island. "Pick one."

A grin lit up her face. She fanned out the menus, taking her time to choose. The logo for Pauli's Kitchen glared up at me. *Don't pick it. Don't pick it. Don't pick it.* Of course, she picked it. She had a knack for making me fall apart. It was a marketable talent at this point.

She lifted her phone and dialed the number, covering the mouth of her phone. "Do you want anything?"

"No."

"The chicken parm looks good."

I froze, biting out another no. She gave me an odd look, placed her order, and hung up. While we waited for the food, my eyes darted around the kitchen, searching for a distraction. They fixed on the scar on Charlie's wrist. "What's that from?"

She cradled it. "I wanted to die with a scar on my wrist."

Like her sister. I read the subtext. She'd done it to herself.

"How does it feel?" I lifted her wrist, bringing the scar to my face. It was red, raised, and angry. Something that must've grown for months if not years. "I'm no dermatologist, but it looks like a keloid. They can get tender. Sometimes painful."

"Nothing I can't handle."

"Did you get it checked?"

"No."

The food arrived before I could press her to visit a specialist. I paid for the takeout while Charlie produced a pasta dish and the same chicken parm Kel bought me the day he died from the bag. They still used identical packaging. I was going to throw up if I didn't get out of here soon.

"Where's Terry?" Charlie swirled tagliatelle noodles with her fork.

"Who cares?"

"He's your father."

"He's my sperm donor."

"So you keep saying. He also happens to be your father."

"And as reliable as a flat tire, which revokes any claim he has on parenthood."

She cut into the chicken. I watched it bleed juices onto her plate, diluting the blood-red sauce. She shoved a forkful into her mouth, sighing. "This is sooo good. Are you sure you don't want any?"

"Certain." I needed her to finish the food and leave. Get out of my space. Out of my head.

"Kellan used to watch me eat. We met on my birthday each year, and he'd bring me something sweet to eat each time. Even when it was gross, I loved it. I think I liked his eyes on me. No one else paid me any attention."

The way she said it—the way her eyes dipped down after—made it seem like things hadn't changed. Her situation at home still hurt.

"Did he ever tell you about the first time I met him?" I remembered the weekend with perfect clarity. I'd returned home from college for Spring Break, just in time to see a brother I'd never met thrust upon me like one of his mom's out-of-season designer dresses.

"No. What happened?"

"Are you okay with losing your appetite?"

She pushed her plate away. "If this turns out to be some groundbreaking diet method, I'm telling you right now, I'm patenting." I was going to miss her when she finished her project, that was for damn sure.

"His mom was God knows where. Same for Terry. My mom showed up with Kel one day and said, 'This is your brother. We're taking care of him today.' It was the first and only time I met him until Terry showed up on my doorstep with Kel in tow."

She clung to my every word. As if they were precious crumbs to savor. "How old was he when you met?"

"Eight. Old enough to remember what happened."

"What happened?"

"We were out at a restaurant for lunch. He was crying because he wanted to know where his mom went, so I distracted him with that pull-my-finger joke."

"The one where you pull and fart?"

I matched her smile. "I made the sound with my mouth, but yeah."

"Let me guess." She leaned closer as if we were sharing a secret. "Kellan wanted to try?"

"Yeah. So, I pulled his finger, and he farted. But that wasn't all he did."

"No." Her jaw dropped. She fell back against her seat. "No way. In the middle of a restaurant?"

"He started crying. Mom let him tie her sweater around his waist, and we left so fast, I don't think the staff understood what had happened. Kel couldn't look me in the eye for a solid week when I saw him the next time, which was a feat, considering he was living with me. He bought my mom a sweater every year for Christmas after that." I snorted. "I think he took some of them from his mom because they were used and smelled of perfume half the time."

Charlie threw her head back and laughed. I could see why Kel loved her. She was edgy yet sweet. Somehow able to sink under your skin in such a short amount of time. She was lethal. She was Venom. *His* venom.

My smile dropped when I realized what we were doing. Smiling. Laughing. It seemed eerily close to happiness, and I'd never earned that right. I was destined to die a miserable fuck. And I deserved it.

I cleared my throat. "How often did you spend time with him?"

"Not often enough. Our meetings were always on his terms, and for the most part, I was too much of a coward to fight that. I eventually sought Kellan out, but he declined." She shrugged, rearranging the noodles on her plate in the shape of a circle. "I think he was saving me from his bad reputation rubbing off on mine."

"He had a hero complex?"

"With me, at least."

"I never knew."

The words were spoken under my breath, but she heard them.

"It must be painful sharing a heart with all that grief."

I swallowed. Looked away. At the clock. Back again. "It's getting late."

"I'm not done eating."

I called bull, but it didn't stop her from sinking her fork into a piece of chicken parm and shoving it past her lips. She took her time chewing. When she opened her mouth again, I braced for her words.

"He once wrote a short story about two children who sought a witch to grant them wishes. Do you want to hear it?"

I knew I should stop this if I wanted to survive, yet I found myself nodding.

"The girl and boy lost their parents." She swallowed, averting her eyes. I wondered if Kel had written this story for her. And for himself. An orphaned girl and the boy who found his mother dead. "She feared the loneliness. He loathed the pain." Charlie's eyes fluttered shut, brows meeting in the middle as if she were imagining the scene as she narrated it. "Together, they found a witch who granted wishes that lasted forever."

My eyes pinned on her like I was the arrow and she was the target. For one startling moment, I wondered what it was like to read for pleasure. What she enjoyed about it.

"The girl wished to live without fear, while the boy wished to live without pain. The witch granted these wishes. Years passed, and the girl no longer felt fear, and the boy no longer felt pain. Still, neither of them smiled. They returned to the witch and begged her to grant them another wish—happiness. The witch told them she couldn't, because their previous wishes were permanent and you can't experience happiness without knowing fear and pain." Charlie reached forward, grabbing my hand. "Pain is growth. Fear is risk. You can't be happy if you're not growing and taking risks."

I heard the words she didn't say: *Read the manuscript, Tate.*

I slipped my hand from hers. "Kellan wrote fairytales." I sounded skeptical, but I wasn't. Not really.

"Yes."

"Did he actually write that? Or are you trying to tell me something?"

"Both." She idled, resting her fork on the counter, marking it with marinara sauce. "Just so we're clear, I'm only concerned about your well-being because you are scheduled to deliver my boss' babies this coming week."

"Crystal clear." *Not.* I didn't think for a second this had anything to do with Reagan's upcoming induced labor.

Charlotte Richards was right. I was falling.

But so was she.

Chapter Fifty-Six

Tate

> Terry: I need Darling Venom.
>
> Me: 09609999 Error invalid number. Please re-send using a valid 10-digit mobile number or valid short code.
>
> Terry: Har. Har.

I entered a consultation with a forty-two-year-old patient who wanted to try another round of IVF. When I finished the meeting, I found three too many texts from Sperm Donor Dearest.

> Terry: Not funny.
>
> Terry: I'm serious.
>
> Terry: I need to see the manuscript.
>
> Me: The closest you are getting to Kellan's book is in a courtroom when I file a restraining order on your ass.

He called me immediately. I pressed ignore. Part of me wanted to block him entirely, but I figured I'd do the NYPD a favor when he inevitably OD'd and ended up on a slab in their morgue and they needed to ID him.

> Terry: It's important.
>
> Me: You survived eighty years without it. You'll survive more.
>
> Terry: I'm sixty-three.
>
> Me: May I suggest Botox?

I turned my phone off the remainder of the day, returning home after a long delivery exhausted, hungry, and grouchy, only to find Terry asleep on the couch. His current favorite way to pass time after I'd forced drugs off the table. Nowadays, he didn't possess a personality beyond necessary bodily functions and begging for *Darling Venom*.

After Kel passed and I decided torture would become my newest hobby, I'd searched the signs of depression. There were eight key things to look out for: hopelessness, loss of interest, fatigue and changes in sleep patterns, anxiety, irritability, changes in appetite and weight, uncontrollable emotions, and suicidal ideation.

Terry checked off almost all the boxes. So did I, for that matter. But I couldn't bring myself to care. Or decide either of us was worth saving.

I left him to sleep and debated whether I should give him the boot come sunrise, citing his lack of progress on his manuscript as a breach in our agreement. I'd decide in the morning.

I swung open the fridge door, expecting to find nothing. Instead, I came face-to-face with a fully stocked vessel. Tidy columns of electrolyte drinks, bottled coffee, and pressed juices. Some poultry and protein organized in a dedicated row. The crisper held lettuce, vegetables, and fruits—washed and stored in separate glass containers.

Charlie.

Only person who would do this for me. Terry sure as shit wouldn't (and didn't know a cucumber from a zucchini), Hilda quit, and no one else had a key. I made myself a sandwich, swallowed it in fewer bites than was civil, and pounded up the stairs, eager to escape a hundred-foot radius of the sloth glued to my sofa cushions.

I found Kel's door cracked open, sound drifting past the barrier. Charlie's voice, to be exact. I peeked inside, hovering in front of the gap like a goddamn creep.

She was sprawled across the floor, hair fanned out in a halo, staring at the ceiling. Talking to herself. Or maybe to Kellan. I don't know. We all did weird things when it came to Kel.

"Remember when I waited in front of your house?"

For a moment, I thought she was talking to me.

But then she continued, "I waited all day for Tate to come home, building up the courage to yell at him for not treating you right, but he never showed. And you called the cops on me. I was embarrassed when they kicked me out. And mad. God, I was so mad."

Her hand met the hardwood. She traced a pattern I couldn't make out, sighing. "I sometimes wonder what would've happened if you hadn't called the cops when I showed up, if Tate had arrived, if I had the opportunity to talk to him. Would it have made a difference? Would you be alive?"

A single tear trailed down her cheek.

"I'm so sorry, Kellan. I'm so sorry I didn't try harder. I'm so sorry we all failed you." She turned on her side, curling into a ball. "I think about our pact a lot. About the fact that you broke it. About the fact that I broke a rule first. But you were supposed to meet me on the roof every year until senior year. You robbed me of a meeting, Kellan."

I wanted to hold her. To hide her inside me and protect her from the world. A pipe dream. But I found myself gripping the doorknob.

She spoke again. "The unknowns haunt me. I thought I would figure them out if I read *Darling Venom*, but your words left more questions than they did answers. If you knew you were going to kill yourself, why would you agree to the damn pact? Why would you agree to check in on each other every year? Why did you stop yourself from committing suicide the first time we tried?"

We.

I froze. They weren't just suspicions. She full-on knew Kel wanted to commit suicide, and she did nothing. She. Knew. My hand gripped the doorknob so hard, I almost broke it. There would be no going back from this. No looking Charlotte in the eyes and wanting her. I hated myself for craving this.

I turned without confronting her. There was nothing to say.

Kellan knew her best.

Charlotte Richards is Venom.

Chapter Fifty-Seven

Charlotte

I finished editing *Darling Venom* last night.

Three rounds, multiple proofs, and a ton of all-nighters. I'd never felt more accomplished in my life.

Never felt more tired either.

"You okay?" Abigail stopped by my desk with a mug of hot tea. She set it down, careful to avoid nearing a stack of paper. "You look exhausted."

"I've been having trouble sleeping. Passion project."

"Dayum. A manuscript?"

I nodded but didn't elaborate.

She took the hint, returning to her office.

To be honest, it wasn't just *Darling Venom* that consumed me. Tate ignored me now, and I couldn't pinpoint why. I'd thought we'd come to a truce over dinner, but his behavior had become... different.

Was it the letter?

It always seemed to come back to that.

I couldn't give it to him.

What could I tell him? That his brother wrote me a goodbye letter and didn't mention him at all except to call him "that asshole"? It was such a Kellan thing to do, I didn't know whether to get angry or cry.

I did neither, pulling out my wallet and retrieving what I needed.

A business card.

I fingered it, staring at the gold foil like I expected it to bite me. The light glinted off Helen Moriuchi's name. For all I knew, her invitation to cough up a manuscript had been a nicety. Like a "see you again" you threw to a distant acquaintance, knowing you had no intention of ever seeing them again.

My pulse thrummed against my neck. I picked up the phone, entered her number, and stopped myself from pressing call. If I did this, it cemented my commitment to completing Kellan's manuscript.

There was no going back.

I would be locked in.

Revoked of my ability to step down.

I pressed call.

Helen answered in two rings. "Helen Moriuchi speaking."

"Hi, Helen." I cleared my throat. The phone slipped a bit. I gripped it again in my clammy palm. "It's Charlotte Richards... from Rothschild Literary and Management."

"Charlotte." Her voice was welcoming, which helped. "I hear Reagan gave birth last night."

"She did. She'll be able to accept visitors soon."

"I've already put it in my planner. So, how can I help you? I'm sure you didn't call just to talk about Reagan. Do you have a manuscript for me?"

"Actually, I do." I released a breath, almost forgetting to inhale. "I think it's the one you've been hunting for. The big one. The game changer."

"I'm intrigued. Does this manuscript have a name?"

"*Darling Venom.* I can't adequately describe it in words. It's a love story that never happened. Social commentary on life and human decency and survival. The readability is up there. The author is sharp-witted, quick, and easy to follow. I think you'll fall in love with the manuscript like I did."

"Anything of the author's I can look up?"

"He's a debut."

"Hmm..." I heard her chair creak. "I like physical copies. They let me feel the power of a highlighter in my hand. So, how about you send the manuscript to my office? The location and suite number are on the business card I gave you. Address it to me, and I'll read it as soon as I can."

"Thank you."

Something like hope bubbled inside me.

I hung up after she did.

A big, goofy smile consumed my face. I slid a newly printed copy of *Darling Venom* into a padded Manila envelope, taking extra care to keep the edges nice and crisp.

I'd left Kellan's name off the manuscript, needing to make sure she liked it for its merit and not the commercial aspect of a hit novel from Terry Marchetti's son.

When the courier picked it up, the weight anchoring my body lifted. I felt light.

Lighter than I had in over four years.

Chapter Fifty-Eight

Charlotte

Reagan wore the proud smile of a new mother. But it wasn't directed at her twins. She'd given birth to two beautiful, healthy boys three days ago. Noah and Ethan Rothschild. I had one in my arms while she held the other to her chest, breastfeeding him.

"Helen visited yesterday."

"She did?" I tried to appear casual. "What did she say?"

"She said you couriered a manuscript to her office."

"Did she read it?"

"Not yet."

"Oh." I deflated. "I'm sure she's busy."

"She wanted to know if it was okay that she got it from you. I told her of course it was, considering my agency gets a nice cut of whatever you sell." She winked at me. "I also let her know I gave everyone in the office free rein to make their own decisions until I return."

"How generous of you," I teased, swapping Noah for Ethan so she could feed him next.

"Didn't think you'd go and find your first big manuscript in that time," she joked back.

We chattered for another hour, talking about everything from the babies, to the painful labor, to life in the office without her. When the evening ended, I returned home in a good mood, which vanished the moment I found Leah on the couch, knitting again.

Sweaters this time.

So small, they'd fit a monkey.

She said nothing when I entered the apartment, strode to the kitchen, and made myself a bowl of instant noodles; I said nothing when she finished her sweater/monkey outfit and added it to a pile of similarly atrocious knit goods, standing to stretch.

She passed me on her way to grab water.

I downed my glass.

Her leg accidentally clipped mine.

Both of us pretended it never happened.

She sighed.

I sighed, too.

And then she shoved her needles in the drawer beside her, gathered her knitted knickknacks, and entered her room, shutting the door behind her.

I exhaled as soon as she left, able to breathe again.

I was resigned to what we were.

Two ghosts haunting the same space.

Chapter Fifty-Nine

Charlotte

A week later, Helen invited me to eat in the same private room at Toshikoshi.

I couldn't gauge her state of mind from the call, but if she had any taste, she loved Kellan's words. Anyone worth their salt in the literary business would foam over the goldmine that was his writing.

And me?

I was this manuscript's protector. The second I decided to accept Kellan's challenge, I vowed to shield his story. *Darling Venom* would not be butchered. Warped by outside minds who'd never met, known, and loved him. Turned into commercial fodder to feed the masses.

Last time I'd dined with Helen, Reagan forced me into business attire. This time, I reconsidered. If Helen couldn't accept me the way Kellan wrote me, I couldn't trust her to handle his manuscript without changing its fabric.

So, I decided last minute to ditch the business outfit I'd laid out, arriving in boots that laced up all the way to my thighs beneath my favorite pleated plaid skirt, a top with oversized sleeves, and a neckerchief. In other words, Dead Master's answer to Sailor Moon. Just like Venom would wear.

Helen's brow popped up at the sight of me. I hadn't exactly considered the dining situation when I picked these shoes. Unfortunately for her, she boasted a front-row seat to me untying the knee highs and shoving them as gracefully down my legs as I could manage.

I wobbled like I was on a speedboat, hopping on one shoed foot. The poor waitress stood off to the side, waiting for me to hand her the boots so she could tuck them into a cubby and give us time to browse the menu.

"Killer shoes," Helen commented when the waitress left us alone.

"Literally." I plopped onto the floor across from her, picked up the menu, and squeezed my hand around the edge when the urge to rock my leg reared its ugly head. "I was two seconds away from breaking my neck."

Nice, Charlotte. Real nice. God, if you're up there, if you can help me manage this without fucking up, I will donate my brain to science and maybe they'll find the cure for idiocy.

It felt like one of those jokes. A literary agent assistant and a top acquisitions editor walk into a bar... Only, it was a private room at an exclusive restaurant with zashiki seating. No debut author got this kind of treatment. Especially one repped by someone who'd yet to receive a promotion to agent.

"Before we begin, can I ask why you sent this to me?" Helen's menu remained flat on the table in front of her. There was something in her unwavering gaze. Something... peculiar. "While I'm not well-acquainted with you, Reagan is one of my oldest friends. I'm sure you're aware it's a risk to negotiate with someone you have a personal relationship with. Because equitable deals are rare, there's a chance one of us will edge ahead of the other."

"I couldn't give the manuscript to Reagan. With the preeclampsia and the birth, it wouldn't be right to put another load on her." My leg shook. Just the one. "I sent this to you first before shopping it around because I need this book in the hands of someone I trust. Since you're one of Reagan's oldest friends, I believe that's you."

"And this is the manuscript you selected as your hill to die on?"

Nerves rattled my hands. I fisted the menu tighter to settle them. But

I didn't think I seemed on edge, and that mattered to me. I needed her to know how confident I was in Kellan's work.

"If it's the hill I'm going to die on, it's a damn good hill." I set my menu down, resting my palms flat on the table. They were steady now. I had this. "I've read hundreds of manuscripts in the past year, and none of them came close to the one I gave you. It's magic. I know you agree, because magic is the thing we look for in this business. This evasive, never-quite-there thing we chase."

She nodded. "You're right."

The beginnings of a smile curved one side of her lips. Amusement hadn't been on my bingo card for the meeting, but I'd take it. I waited for her to continue. At this point, she seemed to drag this out on purpose, either to haze me or for theatrics.

"I loved it," she finally said, brown eyes glinting. "In fact, it was so compelling, I forgot to jot down notes the first time I read it."

"You read it more than once?"

"Several passes, actually."

"Seven." I tipped a shoulder up, unashamed. "That's my count."

She fished the manuscript out of her messenger bag, set it on the table, and stroked the title page, which notably lacked the author credits. Her fingers tapped on the empty space. "Where did you find the author?"

This was where it got tricky.

"It's a posthumous manuscript." That meant no existing backlist to boost sales. No future books to purchase. The transactions began and ended with this book. I held my breath.

Helen's fingers halted. "Do you have full rights?"

"The manuscript was bequeathed to me, yes."

Bequeathed. Such a strong word, considering the gray area of *Darling Venom*'s ownership. But Kellan had made it clear in his letter that he wanted it in my hands. Though I hadn't consulted Tate, I suspected he wouldn't fight me on this. For once.

As for Terry... Well, Tate's opinion mattered to me more.

I considered my next words. "I'd like the proceeds to be donated under the author's name to the New York Society Library."

"It will be a windfall." Helen's brows shot up.

"I hope so." I paused. "I also hope, regardless of whoever's hands *Darling Venom* ends up in, it's well taken care of. The integrity of the manuscript needs to remain intact."

"A debut author with no backlist is a gamble for the publisher, but this... It's the type of book that is studied, ad nauseam, in literature courses."

"The type that gets fast-tracked to all major book clubs. Reese's. Oprah's. *The Times'*."

"I'll be honest with you because you're Reagan's, and she told me to tone down the shark and act like a mentor today."

"She did?"

Helen nodded. "I'm interested in the manuscript. In being the editor for it. In offering a pre-empt before it goes to auction. In a negotiation with very favorable terms for you. In taking part in *Darling Venom*'s journey, no matter the manner."

"Wow." *Oops.* I hadn't meant to say that out loud, but the word still stood. *Wow.*

"Normally, I wouldn't show my enthusiasm like this. It shifts the tides of negotiation in your favor. But we both know, whatever the advance ends up being, this book will earn out fast and move on to several print runs, adaptations, and translations. So, what's the point of hiding my excitement for the project? But there is one thing I'm curious about."

"Oh?"

She lifted the manuscript, flipping the first page and skimming its empty backside. "I noticed you left the writer's name off the title page and headers." She narrowed her eyes. "And that you often refer to him as 'the author.' Don't tell me you got this off a prolific serial killer." Her head slanted. "Actually, that would be quite a marketing goldmine. The next *The Imperfections*, written by Ted Bundy's protégé."

I swallowed. Of course, she'd noticed.

I took my sweet time answering. "The author's name is Kellan Marchetti, and he's not a serial killer."

"Marchetti..." And the shock just kept coming. She shook her head. "As in, Terry Marchetti? Any relation?"

"Kellan is... *was* his son." The words came out slow. Reluctant.

She must've sensed my discomfort because she hid her reaction, pasting a neutral expression onto her face. Still, I caught her vibrating palms and flushed cheeks. "It makes sense now that you say it."

Her fingertips met the manuscript again, grazing the title so gently, I doubted she'd handle Reagan's babies with more care. I understood the reaction. What this meant for the book world. It was why I'd waited until after I knew she adored the book to tell her.

She caught herself in another caress, returning her hands to her side. "The talent must be hereditary."

"I think so, too. I see a lot of Terry in his writing, though they have their differences."

The same tortured outlook. Two very different circumstances.

"Not that I'm keeping Kellan's identity from Reagan," I added, "but can you let me be the one to break it to her? I want to explain how I came to acquire the manuscript myself."

"Of course. She told me to take care of you when I visited her at Morgan-Dunn. Also said she had high hopes for your future. I can see why. Frankly, I don't think you need any preferential care. You're bolder than I expected."

Because I have something to fight for.

"Thank you."

"I do have notes on the manuscript for the author. If you decide to sell it to us, I'll expect them to be addressed. Now that I know it's a posthumous novel, the problem becomes *who* will do the rewrites. Is this the raw manuscript you received or did you do any passes through it?"

"I did three passes and two rounds of proofing. It's very similar to the original manuscript with a few tweaks here and there, particularly the woman's reaction to the hero."

"Hmm... I actually found an issue with that area of the piece. Venom's reaction to the unnamed hero lacks consistency. In most areas, it's raw, guttural, real. Chock-full of insecurities that make my heart ache for the hero."

I waited for the but, and damn, Helen delivered. "But the book is first-person, past tense, single point of view. Venom's reactions need to be shown through the hero's lens. If he's anxious and tortured, he won't notice that Venom loves him. He'll notice the bad things—her hands fiddling, skittishness, etcetera—and assume she dislikes him. When he sees her and becomes hyper-aware, it's sometimes about the wrong things. Those passages don't land."

She flipped to a tabbed page of the manuscript and slid it to me, pointing at the passage. I read it.

Venom splayed out on the rooftop before me, body resting on the panels, back arched to admire the stars. The look she wore matched the one she sent my way between classes. Longing. Hunger. Tangled with something fiercer. When I saw her like this, words shotgunned to my head, demanding to be heard. Mom and Dad were toxic together, and they called that love. I think true love is an uncontrollable habit, like breathing. We are born with the capacity for it, so when it happens, it's easy. It's me and Venom. On the roof. The only people in the world. Us and the stars.

It was a scene I'd revised. In the original version, Kellan saw the way I turned away from him as he spoke and assumed I didn't want to hear him. That I was there for the thrill and not for the company. After I left, he considered catapulting himself off the building, brought himself as close as dancing at the very tip of the ledge, and stopped when his half-brother's mom sent a thank-you text with a photo of herself in the sweater he'd gifted her for Christmas. I couldn't stomach the scene. It didn't feel real. As if he'd embellished it for the dramatic flair. But I knew Kellan enough to know he'd meant every word. Worse, he knew I'd see the manuscript, and he'd still written it. I could never bare my soul like that, for the world to see my biggest mistakes, deepest fears, and failure to love. In fact, I couldn't even tell the one person that mattered. Kellan.

I plucked at my leg, shaking it. The room felt hot. I hunched forward, lost in my reverie, until Helen snapped me out of it in the worst way possible.

"Do you think Terry Marchetti would be interested in completing the edits?" She collected the manuscript, flipping through it absentmindedly.

I don't think he deserves to.

An anchor settled at the bottom of my stomach. I felt the rest of my body plummeting with it, starting with my heart and lungs. It was hard to breathe all of a sudden. It must've looked like I was gaping.

Helen read my hesitation. "Before you say anything, this is not a ploy to get Mr. Marchetti's name tied to this project. It already is by default. I see strong seeds of *The Imperfections* in the book, maybe because of their relation, and I think Terry Marchetti would be a great match. It is obvious Kellan has taken a lot of inspiration from his father."

"I'll discuss it with him."

Unlikely.

"Please, do. Actually, I don't often do this on a book I haven't inked a deal for, but these are my notes on the manuscript—line, copy, and developmental." She returned the manuscript to me. "It's yours. Even if you don't sell the book to me. Even if you sell it to Loran Greene from Hatch Press, that asshole."

I picked up *Darling Venom* and dropped it into my bag as fast as I could, scared it would burn me. "Thank you."

"How about you make these edits—yourself or with Mr. Marchetti's help—and get back to me about the pre-empt? Then we can go from there, or you can shop it elsewhere or take it to auction." Helen leaned forward, her body language at odds with her words. She wanted the book, and she wanted it bad. So, the fact that she didn't sell herself on it, that she'd committed to doing the right thing, made me want her as the editor more. "No hard feelings," she promised, "though I'll definitely be jealous of whoever lands it." She flashed me a smile.

I knew I should express my gratitude, but it was hard to speak around the ball of emotions lodged in my throat. Instead, I stood with her, gathering my boots from the cubby and trying to lace them on as fast as I could without appearing rushed.

"And Charlotte?" Helen asked when my hand hit the door.

I turned back. "Yes?"

Her eyes gravitated to the bag slung over my shoulder, which held the manuscript and nothing else. She wore a look full of questions. Ones I couldn't decipher. But then her shoulders dropped, and she offered a soft grin. "Great job today."

But not great enough.

I skimmed Helen's notes on the subway ride home. They filled the margins, written in militant script. She had big critiques for the parts I paid the most attention to, loving the passages I kept despite everything in my body protesting the way Kellan portrayed himself—scared, alone, broken. Hopeless.

What if you can't do the book justice?

The question haunted me until my boots hit the familiar carpet of my complex's hallway, and I forced myself to admit the answer. "Then you'll have to ask Terry."

I entered the living room to find Leah making a graveyard of mismatched knit scarves. The television blared before her. A *Fear Factor* rerun where bikini-clad women take turns lying in a bathtub with a gazillion leeches. Her favorite show. Meanwhile, for the past eight and a half years, Leah had never once faced her fear. Textbook irony.

She paused mid-loop, knitting needles suspended in the air. I held my breath and waited for her to say something. She didn't. My shoulders dropped. I grabbed a glass of water just to be near her, in case she decided I was worth talking to.

Nope.

After an hour of force-feeding myself a second meal to be near my sister, I retreated to my room. Sharing a roof with a perfect stranger I couldn't help but miss terribly.

Chapter Sixty

Tate

Charlotte Richards unsettled me. I spent the past several months convincing myself that if we swapped Kellan stories, if we cleared his room, if I gave her his *Wizard of Oz* books, if I passed on *Darling Venom*—if, if, fucking *if*—I could sever ties with her once and for all.

I was wrong. Full stop.

How wrong? She still bombarded my place every day, ignoring me when I asked whether she'd finished the manuscript. The food in my fridge? Hers. The perfume in the air? Hers. The corpse-sized duffel bag I discovered in my hallway this morning? *Ding, ding, ding.* Hers.

At least, I was ninety-nine percent certain it wasn't mine. I stared at the offending object, wondering if I'd bought it. Or worse, Terry. But when I bent and dug through it, ready to chuck its contents into one of the city's brand-new electric collection trucks, I found a corset. Black lace paired with an oversized red bow I couldn't *not* picture on Charlie.

I thundered down the stairs and dumped the bag onto the kitchen island beside its owner, not buying it when she pretended not to see me. She held a rag in one hand and an eco-friendly cleaning solution in the other. Her finger pulled the trigger. Half of it diluted in the air. The other half landed on my shirt.

She leaned forward and wiped the counter, humming. I rounded on her, forcing myself into her line of sight. It was not lost on me that I often bent my existence into shape to fit hers. In essence, she stripped away my will, and it was easy to hate her for it. In my eight years of knowing her, Hannah never once made me feel like I'd lost control of myself. Like I needed to be elastic, and adaptable, and growing.

But Charlie... *Goddammit. She should've warned me Kellan had suicidal thoughts. She also shouldn't have lied about it when she finally met me. What else did she know?* The prospect alone made my anger grow hotter. I let it simmer. Something crackled between us. Dense and foreboding. Her attention jerked to me. First my feet. Then my legs. Then my chest. My pulse spiked with each progression like a feverish outbreak that wouldn't stop growing.

"This is not the Four Seasons, Miss Richards. Leave your luggage at home. Better yet, stay there while you're at it." I jerked a thumb at the duffel, speaking once she finally raised her eyes to meet mine.

"Hello to you, too, Dr. Marchetti." She set the spray bottle onto the countertop and crossed her arms. The rag brushed her bicep, and why the fuck was she always cleaning? I had to admit, since she'd arrived, my place was the cleanest it'd ever been. "Odd weather we're having," she noted. "It went from sunny to cloudy real fast."

"Perhaps you irritate nature, too."

"I'm not talking about the actual weather, Tate."

I arched a single brow. "I'm not talking about nature, either, *Lottie*."

She recoiled at the nickname, cutting off the conversation with her back. I considered kicking her out but swung open the fridge instead, jerking at the collar of my Tom Ford button-down. She was right. The weather seemed to change at wild speeds. I was hot all of a sudden. Desperate to get out of here.

I grabbed a bottle of electrolytes and downed half in one gulp. By the time I turned, she'd continued cleaning on the opposite end of the island. I told my feet to get me the hell out of here. They didn't budge. It was a great metaphor for what we were. Me, the shadow. Her, the body.

The fuck am I still doing near her? Get me the hell out of here, feet.

Again, those assholes didn't listen.

I sat on an island stool, not bothering to hide the fact that I was watching her. "I did some research last night."

She didn't reply.

"On the amount of time required to edit a full-length novel, such as Kel's."

Still nothing.

"Found some interesting stuff."

Nada.

I tried another angle. "I found termites this morning. A full-blown infestation. I'm having my house fumigated. You'll need to leave. I'm sure by the time it's done, you'll also be finished with the manuscript, so no need to return."

Bullshit and a half. The termites. The infestation. The fumigation. All of it. I didn't expect any of it to work. Our lives were a carefully crafted web of calamity. A thread could snap, but there would always be more standing. In this case, the threads that snapped were trust and betrayal. I would never forgive her for keeping secrets from me. I'd never trust her again, either.

"The fumigation is set for a few hours from now. I expect you to clear out by then."

Silence.

Charlie seemed distracted. Consumed by her own thoughts.

Her well-being is not your concern, Tate.

I needed to let it go on account of the fact that she knew Kellan wanted to kill himself and never said a thing. My feet finally took the hint and moved. I walked past her and made it halfway up the stairs before I paused.

Don't take a fucking step toward her. It's none of your business. You can't stand her.

I took the damn step. Then another. And another. Until I stood in front of Charlotte Richards, who was *still* cleaning my counters. Counters that, for all intents and purposes, could be an advertisement for Clorox in this state. Or whatever bullshit organic brand she had in her hand.

"Charlie."

"Mmhmm," she mumbled, eyes pinned on nothing. Just blank.

"Have you finished the manuscript?"

"Mmm."

"Do you have any intention of leaving my house in the next century?"

"*Century?*" She yawned, blinking slowly. "Sure. Yeah. I can commit to that."

My eyes narrowed. "I ate my foot today."

"Sounds yummy."

"It tasted a little too funky, but I guess that's what ketchup is for."

"Sriracha, too. Don't forget Sriracha." She wasn't paying the faintest of attention.

"I think next time, I'll try barbecue sauce."

"Hmm. Let me know how it goes."

"Or maybe your foot would taste better."

"Uh-huh."

"Charlie."

"Yeah?"

"Charlie."

"Totally."

"Charlotte Richards!"

Her head snapped up. "Huh?"

"Unless you've developed a taste for cannibalism or a very peculiar variety of foot fetish, you haven't been paying attention to a thing I've said."

"Foot fetish?"

"What's up with you?"

She sighed.

I shook my head. "And before you deny it, remember it would be hypocritical of you to lie, considering how hard you've been pressing me for the past several months."

"It's noth—" She clocked my cut-the-bullshit expression. "Fine. Whatever. It's Leah. We aren't talking."

"Aren't talking... as in, at all, or less than usual?"

"As in... legit beefing. I'm not talking about our usual Cold War."

"When did this begin?"

Why do you care?

"Maybe a month ago. Could be more."

"What started it?"

Again, asswipe—You. Don't. Care.

"Kellan's letter."

"Elaborate."

There went another thread. Patience. It was, admittedly, the smallest thread in the first place. And only reserved for moments like this, to remind me I spun wildly out of control when it came to Charlotte Richards.

"I never go into her room." Charlie set aside the rag and spray bottle, resting her hip against the island. "Not after the night of the fire when I stole her cigarettes and her space became ground zero to our suffering. But we fought last month, I barged inside, and I spotted the letter."

I swallowed. "For the first time?"

"Yes. I recognized the handwriting immediately and snatched it up. Leah told me Kellan handed it to her the night he died and asked her to give it to me, but she never did. Instead, she sent me out for a pack of cigarettes, and I arrived late to my meeting with Kellan."

On the roof, I thought, remembering what she'd whispered in Kel's room. They met on the roof at St. Paul's. Every year. To check up on each other.

She needed to be checked up on.

It didn't surprise me. She considered her parents' deaths her fault. It didn't help that Leah blamed her for the state of her face, instead of simply being grateful she had a sister that was alive. I would give fucking anything to have Kellan back. Any. Thing.

"She was the last person he saw?" I stopped myself from pushing her about her arrangement with Kel.

Charlie eyed me warily, rushing out, "Before you get mad, and you have every right to be, understand that she didn't know Kellan would kill himself. I also never told her after he did. So, the letter just sat in her room. Untouched." She jutted her chin out. "But she took it with her when we moved, and I'd like to think that means something. Or maybe I'm making excuses for her. Either way, for the first time since the fire, I'm mad at her, and I feel like I have every right to be."

"But you still feel guilty."

Charlotte Richards: the martyr.

She could be so damn stupid sometimes.

"She sacrificed so much for me." She jerked a finger at her chest, nailing herself right over the heart. "I'm the reason she lost her parents, hates her own face, and dropped out of college." *Jab. Jab. Jab.*

"Those were her decisions to make."

"The fire—"

"Was started by cigarettes *she* left out before *she* snuck out of her home past curfew."

"I'm not looking to blame her."

"No." I stalked forward, caging her against the island so she had no choice but to be surrounded by me and my words. Consumed. "You're looking to blame yourself. Newsflash, Charlie, it helps no one. Least of all her."

"I've tried everything. I've extended an olive branch again and again and again. The whole goddamn tree. She doesn't budge."

"Then extend another fucking olive tree. Hate to break it to you, but it won't kill you." I backed off, physically at least, edging my foot toward the row of cabinets behind me.

It occurred to me how fiercely wrong I was to broach this subject. How hypocritical it made me. How fragile she was when it came to her sister.

I softened my voice. "Make up with Leah. I don't care how or what you have to do for it to happen or who has to reach out first. I will die with my shitty relationship with my brother as my biggest regret. You have the chance to salvage yours."

She averted her eyes, crossing her arms. "That's rich coming from you." Our gazes locked. "Ever consider reconciling with Terry? He's been sober for months, Tate."

"He lives in my home," I said as if it were enough. And it was. Too much, actually.

"Wow. How generous of you." She did a slow clap, golf-style. "You should be canonized into the sainthood."

"Difference is, Terry is a useless piece of shit."

"He's your dad."

"That's a cop-out. There are some people you don't need in your life. There are things no one should ever have to put up with. Haven't you been on a plane?"

"Yes. What does that have to do with this?"

"And you've heard the safety spiel?"

"Of course."

"Then you know how it goes. You're supposed to put the oxygen mask on yourself before you help the passenger sitting next to you. It's okay to choose yourself first. In fact, you should. Remember that, Charlie. Let it sink inside that stubborn skull of yours."

She threw both hands up, switching topics. "I sent Kellan's book to an editor. A big one. One of the biggest in the country."

I drew in a breath. "And?"

"And she loved it." Charlie gnawed at her lip, dipping her chin into her chest. "She also gave me feedback. I went through the notes and tried to fix the things that need fixing, but... I'm having trouble. I can pinpoint issues better than I can fix them. I'm not a writer. I'm beyond my depths. I think... I think I need Terry's help with this. Would he agree to it?"

"Don't bother."

"He's the only one who can do this."

"Terry is a talentless hack."

"He's one of the most celebrated authors alive."

"He's a fraud."

"You haven't even read *The Imperfections*. You said it yourself."

"I don't need to read *The Imperfections* to know he's a talentless hack. He's the last person you should ask for help."

"Oh? And why is that?" Her arms crossed. She tapped her feet against the hardwood. "I'm waiting."

"Because he plagiarized *The Imperfections*!" I jerked forward, my movement erratic.

Her arms dropped to her sides. Her feet stilled. "Excuse me?"

"He admitted it himself."

"Impossible."

"Did you know Terry asks about *Darling Venom* every goddamn day?"

As soon as she averted her eyes, I knew he'd asked her about it, too. So predictable. Some people never changed.

"Of course, he asks about it. It's his son's book."

"Terry has never met a temptation he hasn't given in to. It's who he is. It's who he's always been. I doubt he's asking for *Darling Venom* out of the goodness of his own heart."

She wrapped her arms around her stomach. "Give him a chance, Tate. Everyone deserves a second chance."

"Like you're giving Leah?" I shook my head. "Terry's had a second chance. And a third, and a fourth, and a fifth. So many chances, I've run out of fingers to count them." I released a laugh, drier than Mother Teresa's dry spell. "Kellan didn't know Terry plagiarized *The Imperfections*, and he wasted his life idolizing his dad for nothing. Look where that got him, Charlie."

"But—"

"Don't go to Terry. It won't end well. It never does."

Chapter Sixty-One

Tate

Iknew it was a bad idea as soon as it went through my head. But my impulse control was shot these days. Ran in my DNA, I supposed. I was Terrence Marchetti's son, after all. Which was the excuse I went with as I slid into my Lexus for the first time in a while and cruised to an area of the city farther north than I ever frequented.

Morris Heights consisted of multi-unit townhomes and apartment complexes, built after a wave of arson in the seventies. They lined the streets, dominated by mid-height tenements, vacant lots, and steep stairs that explained the shape of Charlotte Richards' buns of steel.

I parked in the only spot I could find and bore the unusual heat, cursing the hills with each step. At this point, I was actively ignoring all the signs I shouldn't have come. I needed one I couldn't brush off. Lightning strike. Heart attack. Stroke.

You there, God? Take your pick.

I passed a few mom-and-pop restaurants. A shit ton more stairs. And finally, I found myself in front of Charlie's apartment complex, waiting for someone to buzz in so I could slip through like a stalker.

I'd reached the criteria for unhealthy fixation about thirty mistakes ago, and I wondered if I could ever go back. Rewind time. Undo this level of foolishness typically reserved for prepubescent boys with underdeveloped brains.

Nope. I slipped through the door right after a family of four, and that pretty much sealed the deal on the is-my-soul-salvageable debate. I reached 3C. Charlie's apartment. Which I had no good excuse for knowing... other than the fact that I never asked her to choose me as her gynecologist, I couldn't be blamed for having access to her patient records, and it wasn't my fault she'd left her wallet flipped open on my counter one day. No one invited her into my home. Certainly not me. If anything, I could place the blame on her for doing useless things.

Reach any further, asswipe, and you could join the NBA with that wingspan.

I pounded my fist on the door. Charlie was still at my place when I'd left, which made this a good time for confrontation. The door swung open. I offered my best trust-me smile, aware I was a strange man showing up on her doorstep and, according to her sister, Leah had an issue with people in general.

"Hello." I stuck my hand out. "My name is Tatum Marchetti. Nice to meet you. We need to talk."

"Marchetti," she repeated under her breath. "Where have I heard that? Can't be the letter—" Her eyes widened. She ignored my outstretched hand, recoiling from it. "Kellan's brother?" I nodded. My smile slipped. As if I needed the reminder of how she knew Kel. She stepped into the hallway and began to close the door behind her, but her eyes caught on the unit across from us. 3D. Her feet drifted back into the apartment. She moved to the side, letting me in. "Is this about the letter?"

"No."

Leah fidgeted. Seemed to do it a lot, too. Her fingertips reached up to brush her face, but she lowered them before they made contact with the thick layer of makeup. It was her own version of Charlie's leg tick. The Richards sisters were damaged, and they had the power to heal each other.

She redirected her hand to her opposite arm, rubbing it at the crook.

"What's this about?"

"Charlie."

For the record, this wasn't actually about Charlie. I saw myself in Leah. I saw every single opportunity I missed with Kel. The holidays. The birthdays. The banter. The aging. The future he could have had if I'd gotten my shit together sooner and paid attention. And this was why I couldn't help myself, no matter how often I'd pulled over and made a case for why I should flip a U-ie and head back home. I saw all the mistakes I made in Leah Richards, and it made me furious. This was not about Charlie. It was about me.

Sure.

"Charlie..." Leah quirked a brow, reevaluating me. Her hands moved to her hips. The hesitance faded. "You mean Charlotte?"

"I mean the woman who can't focus on anything for longer than thirty seconds because of you."

"Excuse me?" Fire lit up her eyes. The same shade as her sister's. "Listen, bud, who the hell are you to barge into my house and talk to me about my own sister?"

"You opened the door for me and stepped aside." I leaned against the wall, offering her distance. "I would hardly categorize that as barging."

"It's whatever I say it is. My house. My rules."

"Interesting," I muttered, more to myself.

And it was. Leah sounded just like me. In fact, I might've said that verbatim to Terry a few dozen times. In the last week alone.

"Interesting?" She wrinkled her nose. "I don't know you. It's not your place to intervene in my life."

"I know Charlie. It is my business." I kicked off the wall, straightening. "Let's be real here. Even if I paid attention to her for half a second, it'd be light years more attention than she receives in here."

"She started a fire in our childhood home," Leah spat.

"Well aware."

"Then, I'm sure you're also 'well aware' that, in doing so, she killed our parents."

"Yes, but I'm not going to hold an accident that happened when she was thirteen over her head."

I'd flipped that switch. Everyone had one. The thing that could single-handedly make them self-destruct.

Leah tossed her hands in the air. "It's not your place to decide whether it matters that the fire was an accident!" She stepped toward me, getting more riled up by the second. "I ran into that house. I saw the flames consuming their bedroom door. And I didn't even have time to let their deaths sink in before I ran to save my sister. So, excuse me if I don't give a damn what a complete stranger has to say to me about a sister I saved."

Her chest rose and fell in wild jerks, and it occurred to me that I would never, under any circumstances, air my 'Big T' out to a total stranger. But she was a kettle, steam escaping her in loud hisses, ten seconds from spilling everything. This might've been the first time she'd ever spoken about this, with the way her words poured out.

"You're angry."

"Of course, I'm angry. She robbed me of everything." Her finger met the center of my chest, jabbing it with each sentence. "My future. My boyfriend. My *face*." *Stab. Stab. Stab.* "Until you know what that's like, feel free to walk out that door and never come back."

"Your boyfriend was a dick for leaving. You're better off without him." I ticked my fingers with each rebuttal. "Your future is still here. Ripe for you to take. It's never too late." Another finger. "And your face? It's not the same face you had before that night, but it's beautiful, nevertheless. It's also a reminder that your sister is alive." I peered down at her, seeing Leah but also seeing myself. "I would give anything to say the same."

"I am ugly," she said, as if it explained anything.

She wasn't ugly. Not even close.

"Your self-esteem took a hit. But so did Charlie's. Have you ever noticed that thing she does with her leg? Yanking it like she wants it off her body?" I studied Leah. From the looks of it, she'd never noticed.

Almost nine years, and she'd never fucking noticed. God, what else hadn't I noticed about Kel? I swallowed, forcing myself to continue, "Or when Charlie realizes she's shining brightly and recedes into herself, not because she wants to stay hidden but because she's conditioned herself to believe she doesn't deserve attention. Charlie is hurting. Bad. Not everything is about you, Leah."

"Finally, you're right about something. Nothing is about me. Absolutely nothing."

She wore a look on her face. One that said she needed to prove something. To me? To Charlie? To herself? I needed to provoke her. Get her to release it all until nothing remained. With Charlie's luck, chances were, her sister's anger was a bottomless abyss she could pull from, and Leah would always have Charlie in her sight. But fuck, I had to try.

"Grow up, Leah. That's life."

"Grow up?! Grow up?!" she spat the words out. "You're a real peach."

"And you're out of touch." I shook my head, not believing the card I was about to pull. Of shit I heard from a grief podcast Hannah used to play. "Some people are so afraid of love, they only know how to hate."

"And you think that's me?"

"I think you lost your parents, and you're afraid of letting anyone else in—including your sister—because you might lose them. So, you act like this instead."

"Or maybe I have every reason to hate my sister." She gestured to her face. "Because of her, I don't go out. I have no one in my life. I am alone. Withering as life passes me by. I look out the window every day, staring down at my neighbors, knowing I will never have what they have. It was stolen from me by Charlotte."

"Lottie. Your nickname for her is Lottie. I think she'd like it if you called her that again."

"That's not for you to decide."

We were going in circles, and the scenery sucked. I didn't need a PhD in psychology to know this wasn't working.

I decided to lay myself bare, swallowing back the bile. "I'm sure you know by now that my brother died."

"Yes." She nodded, turning her head away. When she met my gaze again, the anger had faded from her eyes. "I'm sorry for your loss. I'm sorry for not giving Charlotte the letter. If I'd known, I would have."

And if Charlie had known she'd start a fire, she wouldn't have smoked that night.

"What Charlie probably left out was that I had the chance to save my brother, and I didn't know it. There was no fire for us. I didn't come home to a burning building and see the obvious options in front of me—save Kellan or let him die. His death began way before he stopped breathing. Suicide is a long road with a dead-end. It isn't instant. There are pit stops along the way. I could've saved him at any one of those, but I didn't. I have to live with that. Have you ever stopped to be grateful Charlie is alive? Have you ever told her you're glad she made it out of the fire?"

"Of course, I'm grateful. Did she tell you I'm not?"

Charlie didn't need to tell me. I saw it every day. She genuinely believed Leah didn't want her in her life.

"Have you ever asked her if she's okay? How she's shouldering the blame?" I paused. "Have you ever wondered if she's ever been on that one-way road?"

Leah staggered back like I'd shot her. "No." She clawed at her chest, pressing down. "She's never—"

"Try asking her how she met Kellan."

As I said it, I knew it to be true. There was no other reason for them to make a pact to meet on a cordoned-off rooftop at St. Paul's. I also considered the fact that I'd crossed a line, but it was the same line Charlie had been willing to cross.

I sometimes wonder what would've happened if you didn't call the cops when I showed up at your home, if Tate arrived, if I had the opportunity to talk to him...

I remembered her words. They brushed off any guilt that bounced around inside me. I intended to make my point so well, it never needed to be made again.

"I..." Leah's head hung. She couldn't finish her sentence. Imagine how Charlie felt. Silenced for nearly nine years.

Any empathy I had dried. I was admonishing Leah, but I was also condemning myself. And it was savage, and brutal, and ugly. The only way I knew to be.

"Give your sister a break. She is ruining herself trying to please you. Stop acting like she owes you jack-shit," I spat out. There would be no misconstruing my words. No more excuses after this. "*You* left a pack of cigarettes for a thirteen-year-old to touch. *You* left flammable shit in your trashcan. *You* left the lighter. *You* were the one who broke her fucking heart that night. It is time to take responsibility for your own actions. I've been in your shoes, Leah. I tried pinning the blame on my little brother for a while. And it got me exactly where it got you—fucking nowhere."

I didn't wait for her to respond. There was nothing to be said. I knew my words had reached their target, settling somewhere deep. A tear dropped down her cheek. She hiccupped. I shook my head and turned to leave, closing the door quietly behind me.

A man stood in the hall—tall, tatted, and covered in motor oil. He stared me down but let me pass, giving me one tiny nod to let me know he'd heard everything. "I'll take care of Leah." He paused. "I don't know who the hell you are, but I do know Charlotte's gonna hate that you went to see her sister."

"Yep," I muttered as I pushed past him. I barreled down the staircase, knowing Charlie would kill me if she found out what I'd just done and not regretting a second of it.

You're supposed to hate her.

But deep down, I knew I didn't.

I also knew I was a hypocrite.

Because Terrence Marchetti would never get another chance from me.

Chapter Sixty-Two

Charlotte

I staked out Tate's home, dumping an unholy amount of ketchup onto a leftover Petrie dish hot dog I bought from a stand earlier. I stood just around the block. Waiting. Three hours and forty-two minutes and counting. My head poked out past the corner. Still no sign of Tate.

Terry had entered through the front door half an hour ago, but I needed Tate to leave before I could let myself in. He didn't want me to involve his father in *Darling Venom*, but: 1) Tate's hatred for Terry didn't change the fact that Kellan worshipped his father, and: 2) I couldn't do this without Terry's help. I accepted the fact soon after my meeting with Helen and developed a game plan to tackle the next round of edits. Stage one? Ambush Terrence Marchetti behind his son's back.

Finally—*finally*—the door swung open. Tate stepped out, turning to lock it. He wore a three-piece navy suit, tailored to hug every inch of him, and a giant frown I could make out from here. A clear sign he'd shared an interaction with his father. I popped the rest of the hot dog into my mouth and glued myself to the exterior of the brownstone I stood beside. My heart ran laps inside its cage. My arms hugged the wall. Literally.

Tate slipped into his Lexus, not even warming the engine before he sped down the street and out of sight. My shoulders dropped. I sagged against the brick siding and waited a full ten minutes to make sure he didn't return, baking in the sun. It had decided today would be a good day to challenge me with ninety-seven-degree weather.

"Um. Hello?"

I turned to the owner of the voice. A kid stood there. I peeled myself from what must have been his house and waved before darting across the street. The last thing I needed was a cop showing up to stop me from getting into Tate's home. Again. His front door loomed before me. A shot of nerves struck my stomach. I'd done this nearly every day for the past couple months, but there were warning bells in my head today, courtesy of the constant tension between us lately. Maybe I shouldn't...

I stuck the key into the slot. Turned the knob. Strode into Tate's home like I wasn't certain I was making a huge mistake. A symphony of voices greeted me. I followed the noise to the living room, where Terry sat in front of the television, dressed in a uniform of oversized boxers and a torn wife beater. *Charming.* He kept his attention fixed on the show. *Fresh Prince of Bel-Air.* The theme song kicked in. A laugh track blared from the speakers. Uncle Phil yelled at Aunt Viv. Hilary entered the McMansion with shopping bags. Ashley battered a drum set while Geoffrey slipped on earplugs. By the time I realized Terry had no intention of acknowledging my presence, over five minutes had passed.

This is such a bad idea. You can't even talk to him. How are you going to edit an entire manuscript with him?

"Hi." I cleared my throat, hovering between the kitchen and living room. "We haven't had the opportunity to... um, talk."

Will took a dig at Carlton. And another.

Terry threw his head back and cackled. He lowered the volume, shaking his head. "They don't make shows like this anymore."

Well, actually, they do. It's called a reboot.

But I doubted pointing that out would help my cause, so I kept my mouth shut, waiting for him to deem me worthy of his attention.

"Charlotte," he finally declared, looking way too amused for a simple greeting, and I realized instantly that I needed to treat him roughly or he'd stomp all over me. "You here for a good time?"

It took everything in me not to vomit. *"No."*

"I get it. No one wants a used car nowadays. Not when they can afford the brand-new one." He belched, waving a hand at the stench, and I think he meant Tate. Somehow, he managed to make the enticing prospect of sleeping with Tate... dirty. He added, "Well? Are you here for my son?"

"Yes."

"He left." Terry didn't budge from his position on the couch, sprawled lengthwise like a Greek goddess expecting to be fed grapes. "Tried to kick me out, too. Says I'm drunk. That I broke our sobriety agreement. I told him to prove it. He's probably out stealing a breathalyzer from a police cruiser as we speak." He winked at me. "The trick is to hold your breath before you blow."

"I'm talking about your other son."

The one you probably miss terribly.

His brows shot up. "Kellan?"

Unless you have a third Marchetti Jr. wreaking havoc in the city. Which, to be honest, wouldn't surprise me. What did surprise me, however, was how much animosity I harbored toward Terry. I hadn't realized it until now, but I placed a huge chunk of the blame for Kellan's death on him.

"Yeah." I stepped deeper into the room, perching on the arm of the recliner beside the couch. "It's about *Darling Venom*, actually."

Terry's entire body perked up. I could almost see the interest ballooning inside him. He went from haggard to glowing within four words. A million alarms sounded in my head. Tate's warning echoed.

"Really?" Terry sat up, leaning toward me. He pressed his palms together, rubbing. "Have you seen it?"

"I've read it."

"Is it... I mean, how is it?" He was almost bursting at the seams.

I regarded him with interest. Okay. I wasn't expecting that reaction.

"Is it any good?" He shook his head, his shoulders quaking with something between a chuckle and a barely contained sob. "Never mind. Of course, it's good. Kellan wrote it." He paused as if realizing he sounded like a proud father for the first time, then pivoted, clearing his throat. "But is it sellable? He wrote some weird shit sometimes."

The spider story shot to the forefront of my mind. Weird, but beautiful. Pure, authentic Kellan. As the first thing I ever read of his, it held a special place in my heart. I still had a copy of it tucked in a box on my bookshelf.

"You've read his stories?"

It surprised me. He struck me as someone incapable of paternal love. Reading his teen son's writing seemed too fatherly for him.

"'Course I have. The kid snuck into my office and planted them on my desk whenever he could." Terry shook his head, but he sounded amused. Maybe even nostalgic. "Always been desperate for feedback and acknowledgment, that one."

"And *Darling Venom?*"

"Tate's got me punching out a manuscript like a war-era dictator. I'm beat. Got to the end of the first chapter of Kellan's book before the back-to-back all-nighters hit me hard. Had to take a nap. Didn't expect the buzzkill to show up before I woke, or I would have hidden it."

"What if I told you I have a copy?"

He eyed me skeptically. "You steal it from Tate?"

"Kellan left the book to me." I sounded defensive, which I hated.

Terry possessed two modes—brash and persistent. I didn't trust him enough to give him any leeway, which meant I needed to be tougher. To win, I needed to meet his brashness with my own. To be the meaner one.

"I'm gonna have to see proof." He slammed his palm down on his knee like he was a judge and it was a gavel.

"He left it for me in a letter." I kept my tone light. Casual, even when my pulse kicked up a fuss. "I can make a redacted copy of that for you."

"Redacted?"

"The rest is personal."

"What's more personal than my relationship with my son?"

You'd be surprised. I shrugged, feeling oddly protective toward Kellan from his own father he loved.

Terry snorted. "You and my son bumped uglies?"

Wow. What a piece of work. Déjà vu hit me hard. I recalled Tate saying something similar. Guess I figured out where he got it from.

"Not that it's any of your business, but no."

"Why else would he leave it to you?"

"Because the book is also about me." I exhaled. I'd have to tell him sooner or later if I expected him to edit *Darling Venom* and keep the text authentic.

But I'd shocked Terry silent. He scanned me again, as if finding me worthy of taking inventory for the first time. "He wrote you a book, huh?"

It sounded as if he believed me. Or was starting to, at least.

"Maybe." I circled my toes over the floor. "I'm not sure what went through his mind when he wrote it."

Lie. It was obvious. I just had a hard time swallowing the truth. And if Terry agreed, he would read it, and he would see me as Kellan saw me. The prospect churned my stomach.

He steepled his fingers, tucking them beneath his chin. "If the book is indeed in your care, why would you let me read it?"

"Why wouldn't I let you read it? You're his father."

He howled with laughter, smacking his hand against his thigh. "Sorry. It's been a while since I was called anything but Sperm Donor and Sperm Donor Dearest."

"Tate's manners leave a lot to be desired." *And I don't blame him.* "But Kellan never called you that."

Something like guilt rippled across Terry's face. He sobered in an instant. "Kellan was a decent kid. Too naïve for his own good."

"He looked up to you."

"Like I said. Too naïve for his own good."

"Naïve or not, he admired you. Which is why I'm here."

He patted his boxers and pulled out a soft pack of Winstons from the waistband. I stilled. I hated cigarettes for obvious reasons. He held a match between his fingertips, but he didn't light it. It seemed like he was waiting for the worst, and it suddenly shifted the tides in my favor.

Terry nodded for me to continue.

"Kellan asked me to complete his book. Actually, he challenged me to. I made a few passes of edits and received positive feedback from an acquisitions editor."

"You shopped it around?" He sounded disappointed. I tried to ignore yet another sign that loomed over me like a harbinger and named the publisher Helen worked for. Terry whistled, plucking the cigarette from his lips. "How'd you pull that off?"

"I work for Rothschild Literary and Management."

"And this editor... He wants to buy it?" He hiccupped. *Is he trashed?*

I stilled, then shook my head. I'd told Tate his father had been sober for months. Surely, Terry wouldn't break that sobriety just to lounge around and watch *Fresh Prince* in his underwear.

"*She* is interested. Very interested. She handed me notes and told me to get back to her once I complete the edits. Which is where you come in."

He plucked the cigarette from his mouth, pointing it at me. "You need my help."

"I do."

"What's in it for me?" The words spat out of him in a flash. Like a reflex. Was he serious? No wonder Tate loathed him.

"Other than the joy, privilege, and honor of helping your son's book get published?"

"I'm broke," he explained. "And I haven't been sober for about two and a half decades."

I felt duped. Like an idiot. Falling for the sobriety act when Terrence Marchetti's entire history suggested otherwise.

I shook my head, part of me wanting to back out the door, but I stayed for Kellan. "If you're seeking financial incentive, I already told the acquisitions editor the proceeds will be donated."

"*Donated?*" he parroted.

I waited for him to kick up a fuss. To threaten to take me to court, where we'd have to battle over the book rights. But this conversation didn't seem headed that way. If he'd plagiarized *The Imperfections*, as Tate suggested, he wouldn't want to draw attention to himself like that. Well, assuming he'd plagiarized. I believed Tate because I knew he wouldn't lie to me about this. But it was unbelievable in the same way tragedies were. They took time to sink in.

"You really think you can sell it to her? Kellan's finite. A debut with no backlist and no future manuscripts to build on."

I couldn't hide my flinch. He was so callous when he spoke of his son, it was hard to believe he ever loved him. I edged closer, sniffing for alcohol. He had to be drunk. His eyes shined like the top of a glazed donut.

"I won't stop until the book is sold," I vowed.

He stayed silent for a moment. I waited, holding in a breath. One second stretched into ten. Then twenty. I exhaled at the same time he spoke again. "No."

"No?"

"You need a Q-Tip? I steal 'em from Tate's room all the time."

"Why?"

"Because they're free, I'm broke, and the ungrateful shit won't spare me a damn dollar." He tsked. "You'd think with the way I birthed the fucker, he'd be more grateful."

"Pretty sure babies come out of vaginas, but you can ask Tate. I'm not the obstetrician."

He waved his hand. "Same shit."

I crossed my arms. "And I meant, why won't you help edit Kellan's book?" I raised a single brow. "But we both know that's what I meant."

He rolled his eyes, slurring out, "Because there's nothing in it for me." His brows waggled. He scraped his eyes down my frame suggestively, and this had to be a record for the lowest rock bottom. Mariana Trench-low.

"Unless you wanna sweeten the pot."

I didn't believe him. I didn't believe he could be this selfish (or disgusting). No way. There had to be something else holding him back. I pulled a page of *Darling Venom* out of my bag, then smoothed it over. My heart kicked up a gear, like it always did whenever I saw the words. I'd prepared the passage in case the negotiations reached DEFCON 1. Terry stared at it like it was a contagious disease he didn't want to catch.

He knows.

The same way I knew there was something else keeping him from helping me.

I cleared my throat and read, *"What's there to say about a man with a shadow bigger than his body? My father chased attention and realized quick that the only way he got it was through books. It worked out fine for a while until reality hit him like Miley Cyrus' wrecking ball. Turns out, when you chase attention, it bites you in the ass. This time, in the form of a heavily mustached paparazzo. Which brought me to today."*

"Enough," Terry barked.

I persisted. *"I cut class when I knew That Asshole had a C-section scheduled for the morning and wouldn't be there to field calls from St. Puke's administration. Dad seemed hell-bent on drinking himself to death these days, bringing a whole new twist to Bruce Lee's 'be water.' The dive bar down the street from his place sold drinks for a buck-fifty on Titty Tuesdays. Since Dad began to show signs of coming to terms with the fact that he was David in this battle with the IRS, it became his new go-to place."*

Terry clutched his knees, turning a shade of purple I didn't think was humanly possible.

"Once I arrived, I selected a seat in the back. Somewhere with a view of the entire room. My hoodie hid the important parts of my face. Dad stumbled past the rickety door, looking like he'd spent the past three days pre-gaming for this moment. Even if he could see me, he wouldn't recognize me. Not in this state."

Terry collapsed against the sofa, staring at the ceiling. He looked like he'd checked out. Like he knew what came next and thought he deserved the pain of hearing it.

"The bartender watered down a shot of cheap vodka and slid it his way. He downed it like it was God's nectar. I came from this man. Shared DNA with him. Maybe that was how my life had spiraled into this raging fuck-fest. I almost didn't confront him. Almost let it slide, he was that pathetic. You know the saying. Pathetic lives create pathetic lies. Well, he made a big, fat lie. So, what did that make him?"

A choking sound croaked out of Terry's mouth.

"I learned the truth from a reporter Dad paid off. He thought he was doing me a favor by shattering the life I'd barely managed to stitch together with duct tape and Venom. This is the truth in all its ugly, fucked-up, life-shattering glory: Dad gave Mom the drugs that killed her. He found her dead first. He left, knowing I would be the next to discover her. Knowing if I did, he wouldn't have to deal with paparazzi camped outside while the M.E. wheeled Mom out in a body bag. Here's the thing about disappointment. It means you expected something. My bad. Lesson learned. Mistake, never to be repeated again."

"Stop."

"I stepped forward, planted a hand on Dad's shoulder—"

"Enough!" Terry kicked the coffee table forward. It shot to the wall and left a dent.

I startled, lowering the page. If this rattled his cage, the manuscript would break the entire thing, releasing his demons to roam free. This scene was tame in comparison to the rest.

He needs this. So does Tate.

"Okay," he muttered.

"Is that a yes?" I crossed my fingers behind my back, praying.

"Fine, fine. Yes."

I pulled a document and pen from my messenger bag, shoving it toward Terry. "I need you to sign this."

"What is it?"

"It's a contract giving up any claim you have to *Darling Venom*, including after you contribute to the editing process."

He waved the paper, wrinkling it. "You expect me to sign this?"

"It's the only way you're getting the book."

"Maybe I don't need to—" he started playing hardball.

I raised a hand, shaking my head. "No. We both know you owe it to him."

"Smart girl," he grunted, scribbling his signature onto the paper, using his scrawny thigh as a table. "Tougher than you look. Sadistic, too."

I collected the contract from him, snapped a picture on my phone just in case, and tucked it safely into a thick padded envelope, returning it to my bag. "Before we begin..." I trailed off.

This was where it got tricky. I tucked my lower lip into my mouth.

"You want something else from me? Seems like I'm doing a lot of giving and getting jack-shit."

"I need you to understand that I plan on supervising any time you have with the manuscript. I won't leave you alone with it. Treat it like it's my baby. Actually, I'll give it to you one chapter at a time and take that chapter when you need a new one or when I leave."

My words were met by silence. Terry burst out in sudden, manic laughter, adding conversationally, "Tate told you about the plagiarism."

About the plagiarism. So matter of fact.

"Yes."

"I was young and dumb." He waved it off with a hand, like he was swatting away a fly.

"Not that young," I pointed out.

"Whatever. No big deal. Won't happen again."

He admitted it. The great Terrence Marchetti just admitted to plagiarism. Staring at him was like staring at the ruins of a once-great building. I didn't know how to navigate the rubble without cutting myself.

"He thought you were the best thing that happened to Planet Earth," I mouthed, finally.

Terry chuckled bitterly. "Yeah. At some point, I thought that, too."

Chapter Sixty-Three

Tate

It finally sank in that my problem with Charlotte Richards was here to stay.

I couldn't pinpoint a word to describe us, but it sure as hell didn't qualify as friendship.

A friend would not stalk her to a library and kiss the shit out of her.

A friend would not allow her to enter and exit his home as she pleased.

A friend would not visit her sister and bark some sense into her, because the idea of having Charlie unhappy at the hands of someone else made my skin crawl. Even if I, myself, did the same thing.

I was in deep shit, and I knew it.

Charlie stood before me in my entryway, tucking her key into her pocket. She strode to the kitchen, entered the pantry, and exited with coffee grounds I didn't know I owned.

From my perch on the stool, I watched her scoop Vietnamese condensed milk into a tall glass (something I'd never tried) and stick a French press over it (something that also never existed here pre-Charlie).

She caught me staring and quirked a brow. "Coffee?"

If she knew about my little visit with her sister, she showed no signs of it.

Good, Leah. For once, you did something right and didn't rat me out.

"I handed you the manuscript months ago, and you have yet to complete it." Surprisingly, my voice lacked any real venom. I shoveled cereal into my mouth, not really tasting it. "Is Reagan aware of what an unproductive worker you are?"

"I'll let you in on a little secret." She grabbed a drink shaker from a cabinet, and at this point, I was convinced she was doing this on purpose. Piling up dishes in a home so old, dishwasher was nowhere near its vocabulary. "I'm Reagan's favorite employee."

"How do you figure?"

Stop entertaining her, dammit.

"She promoted me when she came back to work this week. Said she needs to reduce her workload, and she values my contributions." A cheeky smile spread across her face. "You're looking at Rothschild Literary & Management's newest associate agent." She took my silence as an invitation to go on. "Basically, I'm a newbie agent that'll receive mentorship from the principal agents. Associate agents actively seek new clients and work more often with debut writers, which is perfect for where I'm at right now."

I frowned. "Reagan shouldn't be back at work."

"She's taking it easy." Charlie sounded defensive.

"Have you ever known Reagan to take it easy? She walked herself out of Morgan-Dunn, ignoring Nurse Kelley when she offered a wheelchair."

"She stays glued to her desk." She filled the coffee glass with ice, added a dash of salt, and covered the opening with the shaker. "I promise."

"Sure," I deadpanned, watching her mix the drink. "Because I trust you to narc on your boss. She's a single mom and too controlling to let someone babysit her kids so soon."

"The babies come with her to work in this giant stroller contraption that must have cost a fortune. She has this whole nursery setup in her office, and we have a tiny lactation room next to the break room from when one of the sub-rights agents gave birth."

"It's a bad idea."

"She seems happy. Happy enough to promote me." She winked. "I'm moving up in the world."

"Speaking of moving, when will you move on from my home and out of my life?" Again, there was no real poison left in me. I was actually pretty sad about it.

I needed her to leave ASAP, because I was liable to kiss her again. Lately, it was all I could think about, and I hated myself for it. She knew about Kellan's suicidal ideation and said nothing. It should've been a deal breaker.

"Soon. Maybe," she said in a way that was about as reassuring as getting held at gunpoint and being told the survival rate of a bullet wound was five percent. "I've got a helping hand now. I asked Terry to help me with the manuscript."

"He wouldn't say yes."

"He did."

I narrowed my eyes. "What do you have on him?"

"Is it that hard to believe he did it out of the goodness of his heart?"

"Yes. Impossible, actually, on account of the fact that he has no heart."

"And yet, he's alive and breathing. Impressive stuff. Someone should call God. I think we have a miracle on our hands."

"What did you have to give him to do this?"

"Nothing. Absolutely nothing."

"I don't believe you."

She shrugged. "Maybe he's changed."

"People like him don't change."

"Maybe you don't know everything, Tate."

"I know Terry."

"Do you? How often do you talk to him these days? When was the last time you had an actual conversation with him? You know, what you told me to do with Leah despite refusing to do so yourself? There's a word for that." She tapped her chin with her pointer finger, looking up as she made a show of pretending to think. "Absurd? Illogical? No, that's not right." She snapped her fingers. "Oh, I know! Hypocrite!"

"He'll disappoint you," I warned, ignoring her theatrics. Again, my heart sank for her. Why did I care so much about her feelings? "He always does."

"I'm prepared to be disappointed. But on the off chance he doesn't, the manuscript will be better for it. That's all that matters."

"Did you forget the part where he's a fraud?"

"He's still talented. We already went through the first twenty-thousand words. It's good stuff. His insight is spot-on. The wit and humor he adds complements Kellan's manuscript well, especially when it veers too dark."

Leave it to my brother to write a manuscript so dark, Terrence Marchetti's contributions were considered light.

"I trust him with this, Tate."

Either Charlie was more naïve than I'd thought or she knew something I didn't. Both options displeased me.

"Don't tell me I didn't warn you when he stabs you in the back with his fountain pen."

She rolled her eyes. "First—no one writes in pen anymore. And second—you're the last person I'd go to if I had a problem."

"Interesting. Yet, you received my help so well on my exam table."

Yeah. I went there. It was the wrong thing to say on so many levels. Unprofessional. Low. Inappropriate. But also true. So fucking true, it was seared into my goddamn brain.

Her cheeks flushed, throat bobbing. She averted her eyes. When they returned to mine, she licked her lips. "Let's make a bet."

"Gambling is a vice, Charlie."

She mimicked my didactic delivery. "Everything is a vice, Tate. Gambling." She lifted her cup. "Coffee." A beat. "*Lust.*"

I swallowed hard. We were treading in dangerous waters. I pinned her with my undivided attention as she set the glass down, rounded the island, and stood in front of me, swiveling my round stool to face her. She fit between my legs perfectly, lips level with mine. I felt her sweet coffee breath fan me as she spoke.

"Living is an addiction, and it's better to crave it than hate it."

My hand met the outside of her thigh before I could stop it. I palmed her smooth skin, sliding up, relishing in the surprised intake of her breath.

"I don't do addictions, Miss Richards." I used my hand on her thighs to nudge her away from me and abandoned the seat for the door.

"It's Charlie," she breathed, following me. "To you, I'm Charlie."

I shoved my feet into the first pair of shoes I could find. I needed to get out of here before I did something I wasn't sure I'd regret, but definitely knew I shouldn't do.

She knew about Kel, I reminded myself. *She knew, and she lied.*

The words did nothing to reduce the temptation.

"Talk to me, Tate." She worried her bottom lip. The squeaks of her shoes as she shifted from foot to foot filled the silence while I scoured the area for a raincoat to protect me from the shower. Her feet settled. She approached me, not giving up. "I haven't asked because I didn't want to push you, but you've been off lately. Why? You can talk to me."

Fuck it.

I gave up on finding a coat, doing my damnedest to ignore her. My fingertips met the knob. They settled there a second too long, and even my body wasn't agreeing with my brain. The traitor.

I turned to her, keeping my fist around the metal sphere behind me. "Miss Richards?"

Hope bloomed on her face. "Yes?"

Tell me you didn't know. Tell me you had no idea Kellan wanted to kill himself years before it happened. Tell me you weren't careless enough to say nothing.

Something in me couldn't chance unearthing the truth.

I swung the door open. "Congrats on the promotion, Charlie."

I left, slamming it shut behind me. It was pouring. One of those hot, sticky summer rains that wet everything from head-to-toe, outside-in.

I looked down at my feet. At the pair of shoes I'd grabbed in my rush. Slides. And now my socks were soaked on top of the shit show that was today.

I sat on my front porch once I realized I hadn't grabbed my car keys in my rush out of the house. Walking in this weather, even a block away to a busier area to hail a cab, would be asking to slip and crack my head open. A lovely prospect, but I needed to be on call for two of my patients in the last stretch of their pregnancies.

My mind drifted to Kellan. The first time I realized my brother had a serious problem, it'd manifested in a blowout fight. I filled the toilet with enough drugs to take down an elephant. Kellan came home in time to witness me flushing his contraband down the porcelain throne in his en-suite bathroom.

He punched me. I took the swing like a champ. I could've brought him down, easy. He was tall and lanky; I was taller and built. But I didn't. I let him take everything out on me. His very own living, breathing punching bag. Mostly because I deserved it for allowing him to develop a goddamn drug habit under my own roof.

I didn't, however, take into account how wired he'd be. Pupils so dilated, black eclipsed the white, blue, and gray. Kellan never stopped. Even when I began to resemble the Brundlefly.

It finished when I fought back for once. And I never fought with Kel. Not like this.

I used my words. Underhanded methods. Overhanded methods. Revoked his allowance. Gave him a curfew. Issued a bedtime. Hired a shady-as-hell hacker in Bushwick to place a tracker on his phone. You name it.

But I never, ever laid hands on him.

Until that night.

I wrapped my arms across his shoulder and chest, hugging him like a seatbelt. Then, I lifted him, dropped him to his knees, and hovered above him from behind until he stopped thrashing. Hannah returned home from work to a symphony of thumps and ran into the bathroom screaming.

I ended up in the ER for stitches. Nine of them, to be exact. Still have a scar just past my hairline as a shiny trophy. And Hannah became obsessed with the idea of shipping my little brother off to military school. She wanted to wash her hands of him. She didn't realize his departure would mean hers, too.

In the end, it'd been for nothing. I couldn't save Kellan. But Charlie... She knew. And damn it, I couldn't get over it.

I realized I'd gotten up sometime in the past ten minutes and made it to the corner store two blocks away. The street buzzed with traffic. I could hail a cab and change at the clinic, but Charlie... I turned.

The walk back passed at turtle speeds. Heavy pellets of water struck every inch of me. There was nothing dry by the time I reached the steps of my home. I sat down, gathering myself before I entered and... I don't know... apologized for being an ass? It was a start on a long list of sins I needed to atone for.

Behind me, the door cracked open. As if she'd been waiting for me. The rain had picked up speed in the past twenty minutes. I couldn't see through the curtain of water weighing down my lashes.

The onslaught over me ceasefired. I looked up to find Charlie on the step above. She held a polka dot umbrella over my head. It covered all of me and half of her, leaving her matching dress at the mercy of Mother Nature.

The fabric turned translucent in a second. Water doused the thin cotton. It hugged her curves, exposing everything, including her bare breasts. I swallowed and nudged her hand until the umbrella protected all of her.

She shoved it back over me. "Your hands are freezing. Come inside."

"Pass." I deserved the cold. I deserved worse.

"Come on." Her hand reached for my arm, startling at the touch. "Jesus, Tate. You're gonna get sick."

I said nothing. Didn't care to. Why did I come back?

When it became clear I had no intention of moving, she kneeled and rubbed my arm with her free hand to warm me up. She invaded my senses. Sugar, cookies, cypress. *Charlie.* I backed away from her like she was venom, and I didn't have an antidote.

She's Kel's. Kellan's, Kellan's, Kellan's.

If I said it enough, would it stop this craving? I doubted it. But it took a special piece of shit to fail his brother, then steal something he loved when he wasn't around to enjoy it.

Charlie's hand dropped to her side. She scowled at me. "What is your problem, Tate? I thought we were over this. You're acting like you hate me."

I don't hate you. That's the problem.

Actually, I did. But for all the wrong reasons.

"I do." My mouth ignored my brain's command to shut the fuck up. "I hate you for knowing Kellan wanted to kill himself and keeping it from me. I hate you for not saving him. And most of all, I hate myself for still wanting you."

Rain pelleted down on us. Fat drops tumbled from her lashes to her cheeks like tears. She looked broken and beautiful in this moment. More so than I'd ever seen her. She still had the umbrella over me. And she still had pain in her heart, using the organ for batting practice. And she was selfless, and fuck-hot, and the opposite of everything my words suggested. If I could take them back, I would.

"I'm sorry," she whispered.

"So, it's true. You knew."

"I did." She sat down beside me, keeping her distance, even if it meant more rain hammered down on her. "I'm also sorry I didn't tell you."

"Why'd you lie?"

"Because... I don't know. Lies hurt. Truth slays." She squeezed her thigh as she used my own words against me. I couldn't believe she remembered them.

"And still, I ended up hurt." I could admit that, at least.

"Because you found out the truth," she pointed out. "There's no excuse. We met on Valentine's Day in eighth grade. I went to St. Paul's roof, where I found Kellan. He was about to jump. I yelled at him to stop, and he did. We talked the rest of the night. Ended up making a pact to check up on one another on the same day at the same time every year until we graduated."

"Just once a year?"

"Kellan's idea. He wanted to limit the time we spent together in public. I think he didn't want me near him in school because he was a social pariah by that point. If I talked to him, I'd be their next target. And like a coward, I accepted his terms. I think I felt relief." Rain tracked down her cheek, blurring her freckles. Or maybe it was a tear.

"You should've come to me."

"I thought I had it under control. Actually, I lied to myself that I did. I think, deep down, I knew I didn't, but I was too consumed with my own issues and too hesitant to take extreme measures to help Kellan. Eventually, I tried. I talked to him at school, but he humiliated me in front of the other students. I went to the principal and wrote a letter, but whatever she did, it made Kellan madder. I texted him, but he blocked my number. I showed up in front of your house and waited for you for hours, but Kellan called the cops to kick me out."

"He didn't want to be saved."

"No, he didn't. But it shouldn't have stopped me. I kept trying, even after that, but nothing worked. I guess... I know I tried. Hard. But I also know there were more things I could have done. I should have tracked you down and told you. Forced you to make him get help. Maybe sought out Terry. He's rough around the edges, but I know he would've at least helped me get in touch with you. There were so many options, and I didn't do enough. And then I lied to you about it when we met and I had the opportunity to come clean."

"Charlie."

She shook her head. "Wait. I need to say this." She turned her body to face me entirely. Her hand reached out, touching mine. "I'm sorry, Tate. You don't need to accept my apology. Just know I'm sorry. That I cared about him. That he was worth saving. That I will regret not saving him for the rest of my life."

I slipped my hand out from under hers. "I don't know if it's worse that you knew and didn't save him or that I lived with him and didn't know. Either way, Kellan is gone." I scoffed. "Foresight is better than hindsight."

We settled into a stretch of silence.

She broke it first. "Leah blames herself for our parents' deaths. At least partially. It's obviously my fault. All of it. But sometimes, I let her share the blame even though I know it's wrong, because shouldering the burden is tiring."

"You were thirteen," I muttered.

"Maybe. But I still knew better." Her voice came out so low, it was barely a whisper beneath the onslaught. "You're Leah in this situation, Tate. I wanted to blame you to make myself feel better, but the truth is, you didn't know. You had a moody teenager pushed onto you by a father who was never in your life. Yet, you fed him, housed him, and did your best to raise him. You had a demanding job, which was necessary in order to afford caring for Kellan."

I shot up. My head knocked the umbrella from her hands. It tumbled to the ground a foot away from us. Neither of us moved to grab it.

I stabbed my chest with my thumb. "And I knew he turned to drugs, that he wanted to see his father, that he hated going to school."

She rose to her feet, getting in my face. "Give yourself a break."

"That's exactly what I told myself when I came home every day, exhausted, knowing I had to set Kellan straight but putting it off until the next day because I couldn't muster the energy."

She shook her head and backed onto the step above her, bringing her closer to my eye level.

"Actually, I *could* muster the energy," I snarled, angry at myself. "I just didn't."

"You deserve forgiveness."

"Well, I'll be waiting for the rest of my life."

Another tear slipped down her cheek.

"Poor Tate," she mimicked my words in the library, drawing my gaze to her lips. "You share your body with your demons, and they're hungry. Let me feed them."

Her breaths matched mine. Our chests rose and fell to the same beat. She settled her fingertips above my heart. My palm curved around her neck.

This was not the time to do this. On the tail of guilt. In front of a house I'd shared with Kellan. Beneath a sky that no longer sheltered him.

She made the decision for me. Her mouth descended on mine. I tugged her closer, gluing our bodies together. Our tongues fought for dominance.

I lifted her in my arms, gripping handfuls of her ass. This time, she folded her legs around my waist, letting me carry her to my front door. I pressed her against it and dug my erection between her thighs.

Her head fell back against the wood. A loud groan traveled up her throat. I trailed my tongue down her neck, sucking hard on the skin between her collarbone and breast.

"More." She was panting, begging, clawing at my shirt. "More, more, more."

I pinched her nipple through her dress and brought my hand between us, dipping below the skirt and into her panties. My finger slipped in easily. She claimed my lips again, sucking my tongue into her mouth, hands cradling both sides of my face.

"More," she begged again, resting her forehead on mine.

She reached down and stroked my hard-on through my pants. I thrust against her, groaning. Rain battered down on us. Her walls clenched around my fingers. I added another one and slammed my mouth onto hers. She groaned into me, riding my hand.

I was pissed off, and hurt, and not thinking clearly, but I needed more, too. We kissed, and kissed, and kissed. I dug my palm against her clit and skimmed her jaw with my teeth. She scratched the nape of my neck, toying with the hair there.

"Inside me," she gasped, conquering my demons as her own, chanting over and over again like her need would exorcise them. "I want you inside me."

She tasted of rainwater and coffee and pure, feral need. I curled my fingers, hitting exactly where I wanted to. My thumb brushed her clit. She cried out and gripped my shoulders. Her nails dug in deep. Scratched me. Claimed me as hers.

And she fell apart, coming around me.

"So perfect," I whispered against her lips. My teeth grazed the sensitive skin, nipping it.

Her head fell to my shoulder, tongue slipping out to sample my neck. A car whizzed past us, honking. Someone whooped and catcalled through its window.

We tore apart. Her chest rose and fell with her breaths. Her nipples jutted out of her drenched dress. I brought my finger to her lower lip, parting it from its neighbor. It glazed with her wetness before the rain washed it away.

"Beautiful."

She smiled, dazed and still on a high. "Sandalwood, bonfire, citrus... sex."

"Sugar, cookies, cypress."

"I drank coffee," she pointed out.

"I changed my body wash."

"Liar."

I did lie.

I kept everything exactly the same as the last time we kissed.

Too afraid to change a thing.

Chapter Sixty-Four

Charlotte

Hornily deserved to become an official word, because it described my kiss with Tate Marchetti perfectly.

I considered submitting a request to Webster's and pulled the site up, only to realize it already existed. Reagan's voice pierced the veil of silence through a broadcast on the intercom.

A new (and unwelcome) addition to the office.

She sought a way to talk to us without leaving her young unattended.

As a result, our ears were collectively punished.

"Charlotte!" She still hadn't gotten the memo that the intercom negated her need to yell. "I need you in here! Please!"

I shot out of my chair, rushing to her before she prolonged the torture-by-intercom.

Nothing good came out of that thing.

Plus, after she'd installed it, Abigail pointed out that she could just text or call when she needed us. Rich as she was, Reagan didn't want the money to go to waste, which meant she used the system.

Often.

I let myself inside her office without knocking. (The babies cried each time any of us did. They also cried at the sound of paper shredding, sighs, coughs, sneezes, and general signs of life.)

"Everything okay?" I peered at Ethan over the edge of the self-rocking bassinet.

He was my favorite twin. He cried a little less than Noah, who needed an ark to weather all his tears.

"Just tired." She lifted Noah to her chest, adjusted a towel over her shoulder, and began to burp him. "I had to change my shirt twice yesterday, so this time, I brought an entire suitcase. Four changes, and I haven't run out of blouses. Silver linings and all."

"Tate mentioned you shouldn't be working so soon."

Her brows shot up. "Tate?"

"Dr. Marchetti," I corrected, but it was too late. "Actually, I've been meaning to tell you..." I fidgeted, hand drifting to my leg.

Did I have to tell her?

Would the world end if I didn't?

Reagan's eyes narrowed on my hand. "Spit it out, Charlotte. Noah has a sixth sense for anxiety, and I can't deal with another minute of crying," she joked, but on cue, he vomited on the burping towel.

I forced my arm behind my back, circling the wrist with the opposite hand. The position reminded me of the one I assumed whenever Mom would scold Leah over her grades. Like I was guilty by association and needed to make myself as small as possible before she realized it.

"The manuscript isn't from the unaddressed slush pile," I admitted.

"It isn't?" She straightened in a flash, rocking Noah in the process. "Hmm... You wouldn't poach it from another agent. Is it yours? Now that I think about it, I never asked about the author. Pregnancy brain. Then, the new-mom brain kicked in."

Reagan lifted the baby as proof, a few inches shy of holding him out Simba-style.

"It's not mine. I mean, it is. It was given to me. But I didn't write it."

She raised her brow again, as if to say, *Well? Who did?*

"Kellan Marchetti."

There was a pause, followed by a few blinks. "Dr. Marchetti's brother?"

"Yes."

"And Terry Marchetti's son." She did the math, rubbing at her chin. "Okay. Wow."

"Yup."

"Helen called. She sounded like a woman obsessed. I've never heard her so happy. Now I know why. I bet she's seeing dollar signs right now."

"I wouldn't blame her if she did."

"Is the book actually good, or is she blinded by the marketability?" She winced. "Sorry. Have to ask."

"It's good," I promised. "Better than good. It's great. *The Imperfections* on steroids. The writing is more mature, the storyline more original, everything about it crafted to detonate a grenade on the emotions of its readers. I didn't even tell Helen who the author was when I handed it to her. I left that part blank."

"You sound protective of it."

"I am." There was a good dose of shame in this admission.

"I heard how Kellan died when it happened, the publishing community being as small as it is. You're doing a great thing for him."

"I'm trying."

"Helen mentioned she plans to send over an offer this week."

I stilled. "Really?"

"It's your book. Your choice whether to accept it. Let me know if you need help reviewing the contract."

"Wow." I meant it. Really. "Thank you."

"Between us, I have a feeling you can push the envelope on the advance for this one." She winked at me.

And suddenly, publishing Kellan's book felt real.

Chapter Sixty-Five

Charlotte

I arrived home in a stupidly good mood.

Sure, Tate and I were interrupted before we could go all the way.

And yeah, I'd nearly lost my virginity on his doorstep, in public.

And okay, maybe I got flustered and bailed with a dumb excuse no one, let alone Tate, would believe.

You need to run to the dry cleaner's before the rain stains your thrift-shop dress? You couldn't think of anything better, Charlotte?

But I was one step closer to executing my vow to Kellan, and that had to count for something. And maybe if I fulfilled my promise to him, I wouldn't feel like a sack of crap for doing all the things I did with his brother.

The door to Leah's room creaked open. I didn't even know she was home. Which was stupid now that I thought about it.

It was Leah.

Of course.

She was always home.

The good news was, if she ever committed a crime, house arrest wouldn't change her lifestyle one bit.

I pretended I wasn't super on edge in her presence, flipping through channels from my spot on the couch. She strode into the living room in a gold off-the-shoulder bandage dress and flawless smoky makeup.

A hanger hung from each wrist. One with a black blazer. The other, a knee-length coat.

A question tingled my tongue. I held it back, plucking at my leg. Suddenly anxious, like only she made me.

My eyes shifted to the TV, drifting back and forth between rotten corpses on some detective drama and Leah dressed up for the first time in almost nine years.

Leah won out. I couldn't stop staring. If we were talking, I would've run to my room and offered her my favorite hair clip. The one Mom bought me after I won the scholarship to St. Paul's. It matched the shade of gold on her dress and paired well with the pea coat.

I sighed. Louder than I'd intended.

Leah's eyes drifted to me.

I wondered when we'd chop up our beef and share the stew, but it didn't seem like anytime soon. We hadn't talked since I found the letter, and this—her looking at me, and me eyeballing the heck out of her eleven-out-of-ten getup—was the closest we'd gotten to acknowledging one another's existence in ages.

"I'm going on a date with Jonah."

On the screen, one of the medical examiners pulled out a rolled cut-and-paste letter from the victim's mouth. Something lodged in my throat. A scream. Of happiness or anxiety, I didn't know.

"I said I'm going on a date with Jonah."

I scrunched my nose and shook my head before it sank in that I wasn't hallucinating and LEAH JUST TALKED TO ME.

And holy crap, she was going on a date with Jonah.

"Oh." I swiveled to face her.

Oh, Charlotte?

Really?

My first word to her was "Oh"? After everything that went down?

"Yeah. I figured it was time for me to start dating." She fiddled with the hem of her dress. "Why? Is it a bad idea?"

"No. Not at all. He's been wanting to go out with you for ages. You're putting this guy out of his misery."

"If you say so." She held up both hangers. "Which one?"

This was so insanely normal. The old normal. The good normal.

"The coat."

She slipped back into her room, clicking the door shut behind her. A gruesome Cold War, ended with less than twenty words from me. Somewhere up there, Dad must've been facepalming.

I approached my bedroom and wedged the door open like it was a jack-in-the-box toy and I expected something to pop out. My most valuable possessions lived in a fireproof box beneath my bed.

I flipped it open and dug around until I found it. The clip. Pearl-shaped emeralds set in a bed of gold leaves.

I curled my fist around it, feeling it for the first time since The Night Of, which marked the end of my streak. Before the fire, I wore the clip every day. It was on my head the night Mom and Dad died. The night I ruined Leah's face.

It was only fair that I let her wear it.

Backing out of my room, I knocked on her door.

There was a long pause before she answered. "Come in."

I stepped inside and set the clip on the edge of her vanity. "For your date. Put your hair in a messy low bun and tuck it into the crown."

Her fingertips traced a leaf. "It's the one Mom gave you."

"Yeah."

We stayed silent, digesting it. Us. Them.

Finally, she lifted it flat in her palm, offering it to me. "Will you help me put it on?"

And I did.

Chapter Sixty-Six

Charlotte

I bribed Terry to spend the night at a fancy hotel in SoHo. Handed him a giant gift card I spent half my promotion bonus on, noting that it expired tonight. (It didn't, but I needed him gone.) Three aces slid down my sleeve.

Complimentary Wi-Fi. A stocked library. Soundproof walls.

None of them worked.

"What's your angle, little thing?" He chewed a piece of cinnamon gum at the volume you'd use to blast music. "You do something to the manuscript?"

"No." I folded my arms behind my back, grabbing onto my wrist and squeezing, trying my damnedest to look innocent to the second most jaded man alive. The first being his son. "My sister's expecting me home early, and I didn't want the gift card to go to waste. Maybe you'll hammer something out if you get a taste of the luxury penthouse lifestyle again."

"Easy, Miss Richards." He waved the gift card next to his ear. "This'll get me a junior suite at best. You couldn't spring for something better?"

"You know what? Forget it. I'll give it to my neighbor." I moved to take it back.

"Never said I didn't want it." He dodged me, holding it above my head like a taunting teenager. "Just needed to see there aren't any strings attached. I've seen. I get it. You don't have any other friends."

"You don't have to be so brash about it."

He cackled, waving off my sass. "Let's see what one grand gets me in SoHo."

I didn't know what I was expecting, but it definitely wasn't a thank you. Which was good for me, since I didn't receive one. Classic Terry. He left, tugging along his bulky typewriter case and a suitcase he informed me was a necessity for commandeering hotel goods.

And that left me alone at Tate's, keeping myself busy with housework until he arrived. It seemed to be the only thing that could clear my mind these days. Plus, Tate obviously needed the help. His place used to resemble the underside of a seat on the subway, caked with more grime than reasonable for two inhabitants. (To be fair, it was all Terry. He left a trail of trash large enough to single-handedly explain New York's one-to-four rat-to-human ratio.)

Leah would leave on her second date with Jonah in an hour or two, so I expected her to arrive home late and assume I'd gone to bed. I had this house to myself and a limitless amount of time to stay. A limitless amount of time to wait for Tate to arrive. And wait. And wait. And wait some more.

By the time I gave up and made it back to Morris Heights, it was way past midnight, Leah had probably gone to bed long ago, and I felt dumber than the dude who sold his ten percent stake in Apple for eight-hundred bucks. I walked the path to my complex, bathed in darkness. The streetlights couldn't stay lit for more than a second before they flickered off again. A shadowy figure waited on one of the steep steps leading to my street. I hovered just out of sight at the base of the stairs, biding my time until the person moved. He didn't.

I yawned, worried I'd fall asleep standing. I could go around to the next street and hike that set of steps up the hill, but I'd still cross paths with him once I rounded back toward my apartment on the top end. Might as well do it now and get it over with.

The sleek smart phone lit up in my hand. I debated whom to call. The cops seemed like an obvious bet, but Jonah would get here faster. So Jonah it was.

With my trigger-happy thumb hovered over the green call button, I bounded up the stairs. Half-convinced Leah would wake up to find me on the news. Headline: Body Found at Galileo Playground, Sprawled Across the Uranus Globe. The streetlamp winked in and out. I switched on the phone's flashlight, hoping I hadn't provoked the dude on the steps by shining it in his face.

"Charlie?"

It was Tate. He squinted and blocked the glare with his palm, dropping it when I pocketed the device.

I came to a halt beside him. "What are you doing here?"

"Waiting for you." He sounded bewildered himself. As if this was a first for him, too. I watched as he stood and dusted off the back of his suit. Three pieces. Each one well-acquainted with his lean body. And not the type of outfit you wore on this side of the city to wait around for a twenty-two-year-old girl you weren't dating. "Took you a while," he noted.

"How long have you been here?"

"Since I got off work."

Chill out, heart.

I sucked in a ragged breath. "Which was..."

"Three hours ago, give or take a few minutes."

Silence blanketed us as we let that sink in. He waited three hours for me. HE WAITED THREE HOURS FOR ME. Then again, I did, too. But at his place. We were in the same book, just stuck in different chapters. Would we ever reach the same page?

I tucked hair behind my ear, playing it cool. "You could have called me."

You could've called him, too.

"I did."

"Oh." I brought up my lock screen and found it empty of notifications.

"I must've been on the train."

He said nothing. I didn't, either.

We were such an odd match. Fixated on one another. Unwilling to admit it. At this point, we'd created a new dance. Where I ducked, and he dodged. He opened; I closed. Denial. Doubt. Desire. Whatever we called it, it sucked.

"You're out late today." He raised a brow.

I adjusted the strap of my messenger bag, shifting from foot to foot. "I was at your house."

"Working on the book?"

"Yeah," I lied. Let's go with that. "Working hard."

Or hardly working. On the bright side, your grouting is the cleanest it's ever been.

He stared into the night. "You wanna go for a walk?"

"It's two in the morning."

And we are liable to go for round two of that kiss if this drags out.

Not sure how I'd explain that to Leah if she happened to catch us. Tate eclipsed me in age and stature and basically every unit of measure besides tragedy, and even that one was a close match.

"That's not a no."

"Galileo Playground?" I suggested.

My eyes shuttered as I awaited his answer. A morsel of what I wanted to happen flashed behind my lids. Us. Tangled in the jungle gym. Screwing on the swings. Him, eating me out on the slide. I needed to run straight to my room, do fifty Hail Marys, and bathe in holy water. This was the playground I brought Jonah's daughter to once a week. I'd never be able to play with Rowling there again.

"Sure."

My eyes shot open. My heart thumped against its cage like a battering ram.

Open up, it demanded. *Let Tate in. I promise I'll keep beating when he hurts you.*

Guess I was never taking Rowling to the playground again. I couldn't even bring myself to feel bad.

We walked there in silence, passing looming brick buildings and quirky shops along the way. The magic I loved about the city could be summed up through this path, and I was sharing it with Tate Marchetti. Surreal.

My pinky brushed his. I stuck it out, letting it drag along his skin before retreating. His bumped mine. Was it sad that I considered this foreplay? By the time we reached the fenced playground ten minutes later, I was panting in anticipation.

Tate hopped over the gate first, catching my messenger bag when I tossed it over. I climbed the iron bars, hyperaware of his eyes on my body like a hawk. The metal was cold and damp under my palms. Tate's hands met my waist at the last stretch, picking me up with ease and lowering me onto leveled ground.

The streetlight lent us its orangey glow. I disconnected from him, bending to grab my bag. Giant concrete spheres littered the park, each painted a different bold color and labeled with their namesake planet. I passed Jupiter, Saturn, and Venus, setting my belongings against the jungle gym slide and plopping onto a swing. I tensed when Tate positioned himself behind me. His hands wrapped around both chains, drawing me closer to him. My back molded to his front. His chin rested on top of my head.

"I don't know what I'm doing," he whispered into my hair.

"It's easy. You push, and I fly."

"I meant with you."

"So did I."

"Cute," he drawled, but his palms met my waist, and soon enough, wind lapped at my cheeks.

It didn't seem real. Us here. Him pushing me on the swings. The domestic type of scene women swooned over in viral young-adult novels with guaranteed happily ever afters.

"I'm out of my comfort zone, Charlie."

Me, too.

Since when did we talk about us in a way that demanded answers? I wasn't ready for this. For risk.

"You're doing fine. But if you're that unsure, maybe we should switch." I hopped off the swing set, gesturing to the now-empty seat. "I've been skimping on arms day. It's time I worked out something other than my legs."

His eyes dipped to said legs, scanning their entire length. He took his sweet time. His throat bobbed. When he spoke, it came out husky. "Don't change a thing."

I'd been joking, but his tone said he wasn't.

Looking at him overwhelmed me, so I reclaimed the swing. He picked up where we'd left off, sending me gliding through the air.

"I go here when I need to clear my head."

When the guilt gets to be too much. When the ghosts swirl together around me, and I feel suffocated.

"Of Kellan," he concluded.

It struck me how well he knew my broken pieces. So much so, fear spiked inside me. Shot from my heart to my head. The people I cared about either died or hated me. This was not a young-adult romance. My life did not inspire happy endings.

I fought through the doubt, marveling when I managed it. Goosebumps lined my arms. From the cold air. From him. From my rare show of strength.

"You ever think Kellan was strong?" I let the wind carry my words to Tate. "So fucking strong to deal with it as long as he did? Because that's what I think."

As much as I pitied him while he lived, it intensified by the end of *Darling Venom.* I knew his life story now. His fears. His triumphs. His losses. But there was something that struck me once I reached the last page. He'd sewn a thread of hope into his words. The kind that didn't speak of a man on the brink of ending his life. Or maybe the hope was that he'd end his life.

"The book." Tate cleared his throat. "Does it say why?"

"No." I swallowed, happy I couldn't see him because I knew there'd be disappointment on his face, and it'd gut me.

He swore, losing the rhythm of his pushes. "We'll never find peace, will we?"

I couldn't accept that. Couldn't stomach Tate's suffering when he wore the weight of Kellan's decision on his shoulders every day, and it left him battered before the sun set.

"Kellan wanted to die. He planned his death long before I entered his life, and even after he met me, he knew he would go through with it. You couldn't have prevented it." As I said the words, I realized they didn't feel like a lie told to temper Tate's pain. Maybe it was wishful thinking, yet I couldn't shake the idea that they were true.

And if they are...?

It meant I couldn't have prevented Kellan's death, either. A tear dropped to my lip and bled across the surface. I swiped my tongue out, collecting the evidence. My shoulders shook. Clutching the chains tighter, I tried to hide it as Tate continued to push me, but I knew he saw. He always saw me.

I couldn't have prevented Kellan's death.

The more I thought it, the more I wanted it to be true. The more I *believed* it to be true. I was a bookmark in the middle of a novel already written. Delaying the inevitable. It was as if Kellan had written *Darling Venom* knowing he would end his life, that I would blame myself for his death, and that he didn't want me to. If Tate wanted to heal, he needed to read it, too.

"You should read it," I whispered. Reluctantly. Knowing if he did, he might end our relationship before it ever began.

Kellan made a compelling case for him and me becoming a couple. As if we were destiny. And Tate was such a black-and-white person, I didn't

337

think he'd be able to accept the beauty in gray.

"I can't." The words were spoken quietly, carried away from us by the breeze. This was Tate Marchetti at his rawest. At his realest. Scared, and regretful, and broken.

I pushed the chains out, widening their wingspan to slow the swing. Behind me, he stepped forward, reading my move. I collided with his front. He wrapped an arm around my waist, steadying me. His large palm covered my stomach and the curve of my breast. I waited for him to move it. He didn't. We stayed like that. Silent.

I settled my hand on his, sliding it upward into dangerous territory before I pulled it off me and landed on the ground. Tate took over, choosing an area by the slides. He scanned his options and parked on the edge of Neptune. I balanced on top of Uranus, criss-cross applesauce. A green slide divided us.

I'd never been big on astrology, but I once looked up each planet for Rowling. I remembered their symbolism by heart. Their rules. Their magic. It wasn't lost on me that Neptune was associated with dreams, illusions, vagueness, and uncertainty. And Uranus? Sudden changes. Whether these were good changes or bad ones, I feared the path to discovery. There was something perpetually tragic about us. Even in moments of peace. We were two empty planets, bound by grief and a gravitational pull neither of us could deny. Destined to collide and end in a fiery death.

"Why did you come?" I asked when it became clear he wouldn't be the one breaking the silence.

"I don't know." Tate kicked one leg over the other and crossed his arms. I liked how out of place he looked in his suit on the playground. How he could command even this space.

I didn't want to admit why I was desperate enough to shell out a thousand bucks to send Terry to a hotel for the night. Why I waited all night for Tate. Invisible threads tethered us together. We were marionettes, our strings tightening by the day.

"I want you, Tate." The words flew out before I could stop them. "Near me. Next to me. Inside me. I'll take what I can get."

He needed time to adapt to wanting something. To accept that he deserved it. To be honest, I needed it, too. But it didn't mean we couldn't enjoy each other in the meantime.

One look at his face reminded me why I was so far out of my depth. But it was too late to swim to the shallow end. Tate straightened from Neptune and stalked toward me. My throat tightened. He wore a carnivorous scowl, tracking every inch of me with each step.

When he reached me, he moved between my legs. His finger met my chin, the other brushing my lower lip.

"I don't know what is happening to me," he admitted, tipping my head up, forcing me to look at him. "I'm so fucking obsessed with you, V."

V.

His venom.

Tate's arm curved around my neck, fingers gliding through my hair, tugging my head back. He leaned down, whispering into my ear, "I'm going to kiss you now."

"Please, do."

He seared my lips with his, and it was tragic and illicit and beautiful, like precious art stolen during a bloody war.

"Again," I pleaded.

He did.

"Again."

Another kiss.

"Again, and again, and again."

That night, in a field of planets absent of stars, he granted my demands, kissing me until my lips bruised and the sun rose over the horizon. I panted, resting my forehead against his.

Leah's words from The Night Of shotgunned through my head.

Falling in love makes you feel immortal. Don't you want that?

Yes, I thought. *Yes, I do.*

Chapter Sixty-Seven

Charlotte

I came to Tate's bearing good news.

The second Terry saw me, he staggered back against the couch, looking like he'd seen a ghost.

My brows pressed together. I waved a hand in front of his face, waiting for him to snap out of it.

"You good, Ter?"

Yes, we'd graduated to nicknames, and this one was light years better than the one I'd given him junior year of high school—Terry-ble.

He recovered after a minute, fingering a chain on Kellan's jacket. A typewriter charm glinted from the loop. "Where did you get this?"

"Kellan left it on the roof one night."

He didn't ask me to explain.

He knew about the roof.

After reading *Darling Venom*, he knew about everything.

And if Tate reads it, he will, too.

That bitter thought seized me. It jumped at any opportunity to remind me we were destined for doom.

"His mom bought it for him." Terry flipped through some notes before him, sliding one on the coffee table between us. He hammered his pointer finger into the center of the page. "It happened around this time."

I stared down at the paper. They were bullet-pointed. Marked in his signature thin strokes that always started neat and ended in illegible scrawls. Just beneath the edge of his fingertips, a comment Terry wrote about *The Imperfections* pre-release press tour glared back at me.

Re-read chapter three. Things fell apart when I returned from the tour. Kellan lashed out often. Piece together what happened. Did someone tell him something? Is it my fault?

The rest eluded me, too messy to make out. With Terry, it could either be unintentional or by design. I once spotted notes he didn't want me to read. He'd kept them close to his body at all times since.

"Really?" I plucked at a chain, this one with two charms in the same beaded holder. An actual cartoon vagina charm and a middle finger. An ode to Tate, I figured. And not a favorable one. "I always thought it was old," I added, rotating the middle finger, so it flipped me off and not the vagina.

"Christie shopped at designer thrift shops. She blew through her money pretty fast." He tapped his nose, indicating he meant it literally. "Since she retired from modeling after Kel's birth and I... Well, at that point, *The Imperfections* hadn't released, and my advances topped out in the five-grand range."

Christie Bowman, otherwise known as the greatest fashion icon in modern history, a former swimsuit model, and Kellan's mom, cared for him throughout his childhood. Until she overdosed.

In the most chilling passage of *Darling Venom*, Kellan describes finding his mother dead, covered in blood and white powder. Followed by the days that came after, which he spent alone.

His father, nowhere to be found.

His mother, dead.

His brother, someone he refused to lean on.

"I had no idea. I would've given it back if I'd known."

"He knew you had it."

"How do you figure?"

"Were you wearing a jacket that day?"

I tried to remember. "I don't think so."

"He left his jacket on purpose. He wanted you to have it," Terry said it with conviction, and though it was pure conjecture, it made me feel fuzzy inside, replaced by a sharp jolt to the heart. He stacked the notes. "Do you think we can finish in time?"

We wanted to release on Valentine's Day, preferably the next one, which marked the fifth anniversary of Kellan's death. A super tight turnaround, but I'd slipped it into the contract, and Helen agreed, given the context.

I'd come here to tell Terry that I'd officially sold the rights of *Darling Venom* to Helen and the Big Five company she worked for. But I held back. The pressure seemed to mount on his shoulders each time we spoke. I didn't want him to topple over from the weight. At least until we finished this round of edits.

Instead, I slipped him a packet. "I know we can. These are the last two chapters. He didn't write an epilogue. Told me he doesn't believe in them."

"He's the opposite of me."

"*The Imperfections* doesn't have an epilogue," I pointed out. "Maybe you're more alike than you think."

"Or maybe that's why people liked it."

As opposed to the other books.

He didn't say it, but I saw the words in his eyes. The sight triggered a distant memory of his backlist. The one full of stories readers hated. For all his pessimistic, woe-is-me, doom-upon-us-all Terry-ness, his other books finished with neat conclusions. But *The Imperfections* didn't get an ending wrapped in a red satin bow. People liked that it stayed messy. That life stayed messy.

We dove into these chapters. When we worked, Terry transformed. He became animated. Less depressed. And sober. Very sober. I hadn't seen him drunk since the day I'd asked him to help me with *Darling Venom*. Even after he broke down his first time reading the manuscript. It was uncomfortable to see such a combative man crumble. Like witnessing your dad crying for the first time.

By the time we finished for the night, we'd gravitated to Kellan's room to capture the setting of the penultimate chapter. Aches stretched all over my body from hovering over the pages. I fought off hunger, accepting the chapters Terry slid my way.

He watched as I slipped them into my messenger bag and closed the flap. "Do you think it's okay?"

I'd come to realize self-doubt in Terrence Marchetti wasn't as rare as I'd thought. He masked it with snark and addictions, but the more I looked, the more I saw someone lost and seeking direction.

Unfortunately for him, I was the only one willing to give it. And well, I didn't exactly have my shit together, either. Certainly not enough to help someone four decades older than me.

"I sold the manuscript."

There was a beat of silence. Disbelief? Anger? Shock? All the above?

Then Terry punched his fist above him, whooping like his favorite team just scored a goal. "To a Big Five?"

I bit my lip, hiding a smile. "Yeah."

"My boy." He shook his head. "My boy, my boy, my boy. A published author. Wow." He paused. "His name will be on it?"

"Of course."

"Nice and big?"

"Bigger than the title. I included the clause in the contract."

"In several countries?"

"Shopping the sub-rights as we speak."

"My boy," he whispered again, and I realized, not for the first time, that when Terry was passionate and soft, he transformed into a man worth looking up to.

"I can see why he admired you."

Terry froze. "He didn't. At least not in the end."

"He never stopped. I was there. On the roof. And while I never understood why he idolized you, beyond the fact that you fathered him, I think I understand it now. Yeah, you're rough around the edges... but you're also talented, obsessed with your craft, and oddly soft, like underbaked cookie dough."

His cheeks turned ruddy, but he coughed, playing it cool. "Bad for your health?"

"Was that all you got from that?"

"I ignored the rest because I'm holding on to hope that you're not as delusional as you sound."

"Or maybe you're not the monster you think you are. Maybe you're not the fraud you think you are, either. Are you afraid to accept that?"

"Don't tell me you're as naïve as my boy."

"It's the truth."

"I did him dirty, and we both know that."

"You were struggling with your own demons."

"That's an excuse. I raised him in a hellscape. The fact that he lasted almost eighteen years is a damn miracle."

"He still loved you."

It was there. In the book. Proof Kellan didn't harbor resentment for any of his family. Not Christie. Not Terry. Not Tate.

"He grew up watching Christie and me snort more coke than the entire cast did in *The Wolf of Wallstreet*. Before *The Imperfections* released, when he needed new clothes, sports tuition, a stable fucking childhood, I couldn't afford it because I spent all of Christie's modeling fortune and my shitty advances on blow and booze. Did he ever tell you that? Oh, wait. He didn't have to. It's all in his book."

"So is his love for you," I insisted.

"Kellan had dreams, and goals, and desires. Things to live for. The kid made friends everywhere he went, wrote stories editors would drool over, ran home to Christie and me excited for the next day. His teachers all said he'd become something. Just a damn good kid all around. He used to have the brightest fucking future I'd ever seen, and I killed it. I killed *him*."

"His mom died, and he spiraled."

"I gave her the drugs."

"Kellan knew it, and he didn't resent you for it."

"I left her there for Kel to find, just so I wouldn't have to deal with the press. Because I plagiarized a book and I was so damn scared of any and all scrutiny."

"It's awful, what you did. There are amends to be made. But he forgave you. The words are there, inked in the pages forever."

"Like I said. Too naïve for his own good."

"You're not giving your son enough credit. He has agency to make his own choices on whom to forgive."

"Had. He *had* agency. Until I killed him, Charlotte. He needed me after his mom died, and I sent him away."

"You were struggling with her death, too."

Kellan noted it. In *Darling Venom*. That he never questioned Terry's love for Christie again after he found him hands clasped, kneeling before his bed, begging for a higher power to take him, too.

"That wasn't why I sent him to Tate."

My head blew back like whiplash. "What?"

"I abandoned him because I couldn't stand to look at him!"

I didn't dare ask. I felt like I'd stepped on glass, and if I moved, it would sink deeper into my skin and bleed me dry.

He must've taken my silence as backpedaling because coarse laughter ripped out of his throat. Broken, twisted, and pained. "You saw my sins in those pages, and you still think I'm worth a dime?"

"It doesn't matter what I think. I'm not the one you hurt. That's Kellan. His opinion is the one that's relevant, and he thought you were worth idolizing. Worth forgiving. There's something inside you Kellan liked and wanted for himself. I can't tell you how to live your life, but if I knew Kellan thought of me like that, I'd find the thread of me he loved and honor him by using it to the fullest extent."

"I'm a terrible father, Charlotte. I will die a terrible father. It's too late."

"It's not. You still have Tate. Tate is alive and breathing."

And in so much pain, he is drowning.

"That ship has sailed. It's halfway across the world, sinking to the bottom of the Pacific."

"You have to try."

"Tatum would sooner part with his balls than make amends with me." He swiped a palm down his face. "And Kellan—"

I shook my head, not letting him finish the thought. "Maybe I didn't know Kellan as well as I thought, but I know him well enough to see *Darling Venom* is your redemption. He would have thought so."

"You're right, Miss Richards. You don't know Kellan as well as you thought."

"I can't force you to believe me, but you'll see. When his book is out in the wild for everyone to read, to acknowledge his sheer talent that only we've had the privilege of witnessing, you will see. It is the greatest gift you can give him right now. And Tate... It's not too late to make it right with Tate, either."

"You think I don't want to make it up to Tate? That he isn't the only reason I'm still breathing? Death is too generous for a bastard like me. So, no. It's too late to patch things up with Tate. I don't deserve it. The least I can do is be alive for him to hate. To remind him the real person to blame for Kellan's death isn't him. It's me."

There was the slightest noise.

A single footstep.

My eyes snapped to the door.

I met Tate's gaze through the gap.

Terry's confession was an arrow, and it landed right in his oldest son's heart.

Chapter Sixty-Eight

Charlotte

Happy streaks always ended.

So, it didn't surprise me when Leah arrived home from her date with a bang.

Literally.

She slammed the door behind her. Loud. As if she were making a point. And well, there were only two people it could be for.

And I didn't think it was me.

She kicked off her shoes at the door. The heels ricocheted off the wall and landed a foot away.

She was muttering something under her breath.

All I could make out was *Jonah*, and *desperate*, and *should have known.*

Oh, no, Jonah. What did you do?

I pulled out my phone to text him while Leah ripped off her sweater, shoving it down her arms. I watched my neat-freak sister toss her clothes on the living room carpet.

The horror.

"How did the date go?"

"Perfect," she snarled.

"Okay. If you say so." I angry-texted a string of exclamation marks to Jonah. "Do you mind talking about why you're upset?"

"I'm insecure!" She blew up on me suddenly, like a dormant volcano erupting out of nowhere. "Is that what you want to hear? It's not Jonah's fault girls hit on him while he's on a date with me. It's my stupid face's fault, but definitely not his."

This was bad. So bad.

"Did he pay them any attention?"

"No. 'Charlie Hunnam Jr.' didn't have to. They are pretty and perfect. With their skin intact. Unmarked. Flawless. Everything I will never be." She choked out the words, tearing off her hair tie, letting her curls fall around her face.

A bag of makeup wipes crumpled in her hand. It tumbled to the floor after she yanked out the last, swiping the damp tissue violently across her scars.

A knock sounded at the door.

Leah growled. "Can you take this?"

I pointed to my towel, pulling it tighter around my boobs. "I'd rather not. I'm not decent."

"I don't have makeup on."

"Leah!" I tried to put a little sense into her brain. She couldn't go on wearing a literal mask every time she walked out of the house and out to the world.

Leah sighed heavily, stomped to the door, and rose to her tiptoes to look through the peephole. She groaned, spun, and pressed the back of her head to the tiny stretch of wall beside it. "Shit."

And another knock.

This time, it thundered and didn't stop.

Leah didn't move, no doubt praying that the visitor would turn around and walk away. The pounding stopped.

"I heard you saying shit," Jonah said from the other end. "So, I know you know that I'm out here. A little unhappy about my nickname, but here we are. Are we going to be adults about this, or are you going to hide in there? A little help, Char?"

I suppressed a snort of laughter, leaning against the doorframe of my bedroom.

"Fine," Leah bit out. "Give me five. I'll open in a second."

"No. Now."

"Excuse me?"

"I want to see your face right now. Bare."

"You don't know what you are asking." Her voice shook. My heart broke in my chest.

"Fucking try me, Teacup."

There was silence.

She took a step back, staring at the door. Something tightened in my throat. I wanted to scream at her, to urge her to do this, to take the leap, but I knew it was her moment. Her decision. Her story to write for herself.

Because that was what we were, essentially. Authors of our own stories. A curveball in the form of a dark twist had spilled onto Leah's story, an ink-stained hole in her happily ever after, but she could still turn a corner. A page. She could still ride into the sunset with the prince with the shining tattoo sleeve. Not on a horse, but on a Harley.

Leah took another step away from Jonah.

"Leah." His voice broke.

And another one.

No. Please, no.

She turned her back on the door, walking away from him. Tears blurred my vision.

Jonah sighed. "You are so stubborn. I would take all your scars in a heartbeat and wear them like fucking Levi's if I could."

Leah stopped. I twisted my fingers, begging her to see the truth. His truth. That he cared. That her scars didn't define her.

Her eyes widened.

In realization?

I didn't dare breathe. A tear slipped down her cheek.

That's it, Leah. Listen to him. He's telling the truth.

All Jonah saw was this hot, sweet girl from across the hall who fed an orphaned baby fox, raised her sister when she was eighteen, walked through fire for the people she loved, and took care of his kid. I'd always known this.

He'd always known this.

But it looked like she'd just now figured it out.

She spun around and ran to the door. Unlatched the lock and flung it open. They stood in front of each other. Both panting.

He was so hot.

She was so beautiful.

I felt like a total intruder, but I didn't even care, because this was the chapter I'd been waiting to read in Leah's story since the night that changed everything.

Jonah took a step in. He cupped Leah's head with his huge, dirty mechanic paws and walked her backwards, toward the wall.

"Perfect," he growled into her face, his thumb brushing the purple skin of her right cheek. Her back hit the wall. His face sloped down, his lips parallel with hers. "Fucking perfect."

Then he kissed her so hard, I got secondhand dizziness. I took a step back and closed my door, giving them some privacy.

No matter what happened between Jonah and Leah, I felt lighter now. Like some of my responsibility for her state of aloneness no longer existed.

She was falling back into life.

Rewriting those bad chapters.

More importantly—she was finally coming to terms with the cover she'd been dealt with in life and remembering what the most important part of the book was.

The spine.

Chapter Sixty-Nine

Charlotte

"A penny for your thoughts."

Leah flipped a coin my way.

I didn't have time to catch it, I was so stunned. She hadn't done this in... well, let's see, close to nine years now. I thought she'd forgotten all about our tradition.

I looked up from my book, nestled on the couch. Row was tucked under Leah's arm on the opposite armrest, reading her a fairytale.

"Why are you asking?"

"You're reading *Heartburn* by Nora Ephron. There's no more ice cream left in the fridge, and your hair looks like you poured grease all over it. I think it's safe to say you are heartbroken." Leah looked down at the mass of blonde curls under her arm and kissed Row's temple. "Whaddaya think, Row?"

"Super-duper heartbroken," Rowling, who would have agreed with Leah about anything, including a theory claiming the sun was purple and clouds were made of armpit hair, confirmed with an eager nod.

I still couldn't get over the penny.

"I thought you forgot about the whole 'penny for your thoughts' thingy."

The oven dinged. Leah released Row, getting up from the couch to check on the chocolate chip cookies they were making.

I loved our apartment. The whiteness and cream of the furniture and colorfulness of the throws and paintings. Everything was exactly where it should be. Tidy and clean and perfect. Everything other than my sister's face.

But today, it finally felt like it would be okay.

"Why would I?"

She was in a good mood lately. Probably because she'd started to see she could be loved despite her biggest fear—her face.

She wore full makeup now, because Rowling was here, but I could tell she felt more comfortable without it. In fact, she'd gone au natural in front of Jonah three times now. The second, to test him. The third, because she still couldn't believe it didn't bother him.

"I don't know." I shrugged, flipping through the book without reading it. "I thought you were mad at me."

She knew what I meant. Leah grabbed a mitt and opened the oven. The scent of warm dough and chocolate filled the air, making my mouth water. Hand wrapped in a kitchen towel, she slid the cookie tray back.

"I am. I mean, I was. I'm still mad. At the world. At God. And maybe... I don't know... Myself. For smoking. But after that happened, not much else could give me back what I lost, so I kind of decided to stick to the bad habit."

"It is eating me alive," I mouthed without words, not wanting Rowling to hear.

She returned to the couch and bent down until she and Row were eye level. "The cookies will be done in a bit. Want to head into the shower? By the time you get out, they'll be nice and cool, so you don't burn your tongue."

Row nodded, taking off to the bathroom. Jonah was raising her well. I don't know why, but it gave me hope for his relationship with my sister. He was a good egg. Truly.

Leah turned back to me. "What is? My smoking habit? Or whatever's eating your head."

"You'll kick the habit," I declared. My way of answering. And skirting the subject.

"How are you so sure? Some people try and fail."

"Because you never fail, Leah. At anything." I bumped her shoulder with mine. "And because you're dating Jonah, it's serious, and he has Row."

She sighed, biting back a smile. "You're right. I've already started patches. Haven't had a cigarette since date number two."

"I'm happy for you."

"It's your turn to be happy. You gonna tell me what's eating you?"

"Guilt. It flares up sometimes."

"About Mom and Dad?"

"No. That flares up often, too, of course. But I remind myself they loved me. That they wouldn't want me to hold back in life for their sake."

"You're right." She bit her hair. "God, I wish I told you that sooner."

I almost said it was okay. That she was struggling, and I held fault in this, too. But I didn't. I decided to accept the apology with no conditions. I wanted to be seen, and for once, I felt like I deserved to be.

"It wasn't okay," I admitted.

Leah's eyes popped wide open, like she never thought she'd see the day where I stood up for myself. But then her lips broke into a grin, and she love-tapped my waist with her elbow.

"You're right. It wasn't." She shook her head, planting a hand on each of my shoulders, twisting me to face her. "What happened that night was an accident. And I should have told you that, but every time I looked at my face, I fell back into the pit of self-loathing. I haven't been a sister to you in a long time."

"You saved my life." I squeezed her hand, trying my hardest not to collapse into tears. "You raised me."

She folded me into her arms, hugging me close. I clung to her, feeling light and airy despite the heaviness of my guilt.

After a few minutes, I felt her whisper into my hair. "Where's the guilt from, Charlotte? I'll beat 'em up."

"Kellan. I think I will always feel guilty about being happy when Kellan doesn't have that same opportunity."

I left out the other half of it. Being happy with Tate. It was the deepest betrayal. A hurdle I tried and failed to run around. And it wasn't just me. I knew Tate felt the same. Through the way he stared at me and Terry together. The way his eyes lingered on Kellan's room each time he passed, and he turned away. The way we clicked with one another on some days, only to drift into awkward silence on others.

"Oh." The word escaped Leah's mouth in one gut-wrenching breath. "Oh, Charlotte. I'm so sorry."

I knew what she meant. What she apologized for. The letter. That wasn't okay either, but I understood. Intentions mattered. And while Leah suffered, she would never have intentionally hurt Kellan to hurt me.

She pulled back. "Tate came to see me. He yelled at me, actually."

"He *what?!*"

"Okay, it wasn't exactly a yell. More like a strongly worded conversation."

"What did he say?"

"He gave me an earful, telling me all the ways I mistreated you."

"I didn't tell him to do that," I rushed out.

"I'm not mad. I mean, at first, I was, but I realized after that he was correct. I did mistreat you." She offered me a sheepish smile, squeezing my hand. "Jonah was right outside. Which, in hindsight, is double the confirmation Tate did the right thing. Jonah would've stopped him otherwise."

"Still..." My heart jackhammered so fast, I wouldn't be surprised if I ended up in the ER.

"He wouldn't have come to see me if he didn't feel something for you." She held a question in her eyes, like she wanted to ask me about him, but she didn't want to step on any toes so soon into the revival of our friendship.

"Yes, I'm falling for him," I answered the unspoken question. "And yes, I think he feels something for me, too. But Kellan will always be between us, both as glue and a divider, and I feel like the worst person in the world for even saying this."

"It's okay to have feelings. It makes you normal. But it's not okay to live in the past. Trust me. I tried. And it only made me angry, bitter, and full of regret." She brought her legs to her chest, wrapping her arms around her knees. "We can never change the past. The only way to move forward is to heal. And that's an order." She winked at me. "I'm your big sister. You have to listen to me, Lottie."

Lottie. She called me Lottie again.

Leah got up to grab the cookies while I stared at the kids' show she'd put on for Row. Some high schoolers were singing and dancing before the boy looped an arm around the girl's waist, declaring his love for her. Just like that. So simple.

People fall in love every day. Good people. Bad people. All the colors in between. They love fast, and hard, and deeply. And sometimes, they are lucky enough to be loved back.

And maybe... maybe I was worthy of love, too.

Row rushed out of the bathroom in fresh pajamas, wet hair flinging droplets everywhere. Leah squealed when they landed on her, pulled Row into a hug, and lifted her high into the air in circles. Jonah let himself in, all greased up from an evening in the shop. Row ran to him, sprinting in circles when he tried to grab her with his dirty fingers. He paused briefly to kiss Leah's forehead. She was beaming. Blossoming under the crown of Jonah's affection.

Tate deserves the same relief.

I decided something then and there. Something big, and daunting, and possibly impossible.

I vowed to save Tate Marchetti from himself.

Chapter Seventy

Tate

The American Obstetrics Association decided it would be a good idea to invite me as the keynote speaker at their annual conference for obstetricians and gynecologists.

Despite the obvious fact that Bernard and Marchetti had a waiting list big enough to sell out Madison Square Garden and needed free publicity like Bezos needed money, Walter took it upon himself to accept the invitation on my behalf.

"It's an honor," he'd informed me, sounding way too salty for someone who planned on retiring within the next two years.

I was to motivational speaking what Tommy Wiseau was to acting. Just didn't have it in me to spend an hour telling strangers to get their shit together when the thing I wanted most, aside from my brother resurrected from the dead, was to screw his high school crush and possibly the love of his life in ways that would make a porn star blush.

Which meant, an hour before the speech at the Black Hotel in Midtown Manhattan, I found myself in a dive bar I didn't know the name of, downing a double shot of bottom-shelf vodka. I chased it with a sampler of organic, fluoride-free mouthwash (doctor perks), spitting out the green liquid into a sink permanently stained yellow.

By the time my cab arrived at the hotel, I had enough of a buzz going to try my hand at hypocrisy. Sylvia had written the speech, which meant it read like inspiration porn straight out of a *Sisterhood of the Traveling Pants* flick. Full of goodies like:

Don't wait until a moment becomes a memory to appreciate its value.

Push through the rain to find the rainbow.

You are the most important patient you will ever have.

Chop off my balls and blend them if this speech gets leaked.

The last one was all me. And, unfortunately, not in the cards for tonight since I didn't want to be the next YouTube sensation. Titled— *New York Doctor's Public Meltdown: Begs Room Full of Gynos to Touch His Genitals.*

Walter clapped me on the shoulder when I arrived. He buckled into his seat, like he'd expected me not to come. I sat through a painful dinner, talked to colleagues whose names I didn't remember, and delivered Sylvia's speech without vomiting from the cheesiness. I felt like Terry on that podium. Using alcohol as a crutch. Buzzed in public. Everything I'd vowed never to be.

As soon as I hopped off the stage, the country's finest gynos passed me around the room like a tray of hors d'oeuvres no one wanted.

"Hey, man, I read your profile in *American Obstetrics.* Is it true your dad is Terry Marchetti?"

Nah. Sperm donation. Not unlike some of the ones our IVF patients acquire, only theirs come from men that aren't pieces of shit.

"I heard your mom was Christie Bowman. Wish I knew that while we were at Harvard, bro. Had a *Playboy* poster of her on my walls growing up."

One—Nope. That's my brother's mom. Terrence gets around. If he actually had any money to dole out, I'd probably find myself in a crowded room during the will hearing. And two—why would you tell me that?

"Nice to see you again, man. It's been years, hasn't it? I heard about your brother. I'm so sorry for your loss."

If you were truly sorry, you would have shown up for the funeral. Four years ago. Could've brought the attendance tally up to a whopping seven.

As always, the reminder of Kel's death soured my mood. I left the conference early. Ignored Walter when he texted me, asking where I'd gone. Lately, I couldn't think about Kellan without thinking about the girl he loved. It was easy to hate myself. For being a hypocrite. For being like my father. For wanting Charlie. And that's how I found myself in another dive bar after the speech. This one worse than the last. Grime-coated tables. Liquor with the labels peeled off. Thick humidity from the broken air conditioner.

I was getting drunk, and I was doing it on purpose, knowing it made me just like my useless father and hating the fuck out of myself for it.

The bartender planted a hand on my shoulder as soon as I stood. "You're swaying in your seat. I'm not letting you leave like this."

I didn't answer on account of the fact that I'd somehow landed myself on a boat, and it was rocking the hell out of me.

"You got anyone to call?" he added, reaching for my phone between us. I guess even this place had morals. More morals than I did, at least. "Or I can call you a cab."

"Charlie," I mumbled. "Call Charlie."

He plucked my finger from its death grip on the dirty bartop and used it to unlock my phone, speaking into it after a moment. "Is this Charlie...? No, it's Luke. I'm a bartender... Your friend is here with me. He's plastered. Told me to call Charlie to come get him. You're the only Charlie in his phone. Actually, you're one of two numbers in his phone. Not a popular guy, is he...? We're at The Office... No, The Office... No, the bar is called The Office... All right. See ya, Charles."

He dropped the device back in my palm, and I didn't remember when he'd taken it. My head fell to the bartop. Sticky. So fucking sticky. I breathed in the scent of booze and peanuts, wondering what this place did when someone with a nut allergy walked in. Seemed like a lawsuit waiting to happen.

Fingertips grazed my shoulder. Scratched it. Then pinched it when

I didn't budge. I groaned out a curse, blinking my eyes against the bar top. When had I fallen asleep? I lifted my head. Turned to the owner of the fingers.

Charlie.

I blinked, trying to figure out if I was imagining her. I did that sometimes. Imagined her near me when she wasn't. Especially looking like she did now. So beautiful, she couldn't be real. Why was she here? I didn't need her to mother hen me. Or see me behaving like Terry.

"Oh, Tate." She sighed, and yes, she was here.

Charlie actually came. So *this* was what it felt like to have someone to depend on. It took me a while to recognize the feeling as happiness because I'd spent the past four or so years devoid of it.

"Charlie."

She reached out. Her knuckles grazed my cheek. "Let's get you home, Dr. Marchetti."

"He's a doctor?" the bartender chimed in. "Wouldn't want him to be my doctor."

"Wrong reproductive system," I mumbled, turning back to Charlie. "You're not gonna ask why I'm here?"

"I have a feeling I already know."

Of course, she did. She was the only one who understood me.

Charlie slipped under my shoulder and flung my arm across her back, helping me up. I tried keeping as much weight off her as I could, which was none. We struggled with the twenty feet to the door. The icy wind hit me like a tackle. I staggered back into Charlie, sending us both against the ribbed wall. I bracketed my hands on either side of her head, barely managing to hold myself. My body pinned hers.

Some asshole whistled. "Give us a show, baby!"

I stuck my middle finger up and waved it in his direction, gaze still fixed on her.

A different asshole shouted back, "Other side, dipshit!"

The rest of their friends dissolved into laughter, moving on from us. Charlie held her breath in, head tilted back, doing her damnedest not to lose the staring contest we found ourselves in.

She licked her lips. "It's hard to breathe."

I held my position for another second before I backed up. Didn't go how I'd intended. I swayed. Might've started to fall. Okay, definitely falling. Charlie reached out before I stumbled to the pavement, steadying me. If this was how Terry felt ninety percent of the time, I'd never be able to understand why he did it.

"Come on, Tate." She nudged my forehead off her, holding me up as much as she could.

"My car." I paused and brought her to a halt with me. "What about my car?"

She patted down her pockets, stopping when her hand connected with a square lump. "I have my driver's license in my wallet."

"What car-less New Yorker has a license?"

"It's a long story." The hazy double vision retreated just enough for me to catch her brows colliding. "Is that really important right now?"

"Yes." I took a breather at the crosswalk, wrapping my arms around the base of a traffic light so she didn't have to bear my weight. "Everything about you is important."

Charlie turned away for a moment, patting her cheeks with the back of her hands before sighing. "I thought I'd need it for college. Princeton as the dream, and Yale as the safety school. I ended up at a cheap school in Kentucky."

"That was three sentences," I pointed out. "You said long. I was expecting a little speech."

"When people say something is a long story, it means they don't want to talk about it."

"That makes no sense. Just say what you want to say. Then again, Yale as a safety and Princeton as a reach doesn't make sense. Yale's the better school."

"Are we really doing this right now?"

"Yes."

"Fine." She stabbed the crosswalk button, even though there was an eighty percent chance it was non-functional. Probably pictured me as she did it, too. "Princeton's acceptance rate is lower. Not that I should entertain this conversation with a man who betrayed his undergrad for its rival school."

"I guess betrayal comes easy for me."

We both knew what I meant.

Her fingers pried me off the pole. "Where'd you park your car?"

"I don't know."

She tugged me along the block, craning her neck in search of my Lexus. "I don't see it."

"Me neither."

"Where are your keys?"

Then I remembered. "I took a cab."

"*Tate.*"

"Hey, you're here. That means things have been going not-so-well tonight."

She sank to a nearby step, panting, hand raised. "Give me a second."

I sat beside her.

"Who's the other person?" she finally asked.

"Huh?"

"On your phone. Luke the Bartender said there are two."

"Walter Bernard."

"You don't have Terry's number?"

"Why would I have my sperm donor's number?"

"Ugh." Charlie groaned, resting her head on my shoulder. "He's your father, and he's getting old. He won't be around forever. If he apologizes and tries to make amends, I hope you take him up on his offer."

"Hard pass," I slurred.

"Why?"

The words I'd overheard last week bounced around in my head.

The least I can do is be alive for him to hate. To remind him the real person to blame for Kellan's death isn't him. It's me.

I scoffed. Terrence Marchetti: The Martyr. As. Fucking. If.

"I'll never forgive him." I shook my head, stopping as soon as waves of dizziness crashed into me. "There's no point in talking to him, let alone giving him yet *another* chance."

"There's so much hate inside you."

"It's the only thing Terry is capable of inspiring." I popped a brow up, facing her. "You're the word expert. Does that make him inspirational?"

"It says more about you than it does about him." Her hand wrapped around my fist, bringing it onto her lap. She uncurled my fingers one by one and pressed my palm to my heart. "Hatred comes from here. When you hate someone, a piece of them is lodged in your heart. If you don't let the hate go, you live with that person inside you forever."

"Are you telling me there's a piece of Terrence Marchetti inside me?"

"Yes."

"It's called DNA, Charlie, and unfortunately, he's about half of mine. I'm not an expert on reproduction, but I hear it comes with the sperm donor territory."

"Ha. Ha. Funny." She released my hand to gesture at me, top to bottom, as if she found something concerning with every inch of me. "This isn't sustainable, Tate. You're drowning. Let me be your life raft."

"I don't need saving."

"I think you do. You are a walking, talking cry for help. You loathe drinking and drugs, yet you're the drunkest I've ever seen you. You harbor so much hate for the only remaining family you have."

"And I imagine fucking the love of my brother's life often. Very often. Occasionally with my dick in my hands, like a fucking pervert."

Her breath hitched. I expected her to flinch, but she didn't.

Instead, she flipped my hand over on her knee and toyed with my palm, following the lines from one side to the other. Her fingertips traced a scar along the curve between my thumb and pointer finger. I got it from a surgical knife screw up in med school. It matched the one on her wrist in length, but mine was considerably thinner. I watched as she lined our scars up perfectly and pressed them together.

"Scars are supposed to heal. You're not supposed to pick at the scab."

"I don't know where you got your medical degree, Miss Richards, but I strongly suggest you request a refund." I pulled my hand back and let it rest on the steps, feeling oddly empty at the missing contact. "As someone who's actually performed surgery, I can tell you... Scars are permanent. Most will fade, but they don't disappear. If they're gone, it's not a scar."

That's another sign you missed. The long sleeves Kel wore to hide his scars.

Allow me to repeat that—it took my little brother dying for me to realize he'd been cutting himself for years.

Fuck. Fuck. Fucking fuck.

Charlie stood, brushing herself off. She held her hand out to me. "I couldn't save your brother, but I will save you, Tate. Even if I have to lose myself in the process."

No doubt words she'd never speak aloud if she thought I'd remember them tomorrow.

I accepted her hand, but only because I didn't trust myself not to stumble over both of us. I already had one death on my hands, two if you counted my soul, and adding another one just seemed greedy. "You're welcome to try, Miss Richards."

"I like it better when you call me Charlie." She started to walk, stealing glances at me. "I know you visited Leah for me. Thank you."

"I didn't do it for you."

"Sure, you didn't."

I liked that she called me out on my bull. In fact, I liked a lot about her.

Fuck, fuck, fuck.

We walked to a busy street, where Charlie flagged down a cab. She helped me in, giving the driver my address. Most of the ride passed in silence until she broke it a few blocks away from my brownstone.

"I'm taking you up on that offer, Tate."

"To fuck?" And that was how I knew I was plastered. *What the hell, Tate?*

The cabbie swerved, flicking his eyes at us through the rearview mirror.

Charlie groaned, shaking her head. "To save you."

"When did I ask for that?"

"Ten minutes ago. Your memory is shot." She relaxed against the worn leather seat. "Word of advice, Dr. Marchetti. Drunk talk will never do you any favors."

I wanted to tell her I wasn't that drunk. That she shouldn't be saying these things to me, because I would remember them tomorrow. But I couldn't. Not because I didn't think I'd wake up with her words seared in my brain, but because I wanted to hear her with her walls lowered. I was so fucked.

A sudden sharp turn rocked her shoulder against mine. She swayed into me and didn't move away.

"I expect you to keep your word." It came out as a soft whisper I strained to hear. "Regardless of your state of mind when you spoke."

The car pulled to a stop. Charlie stared at me, unmoving, waiting for a reply. One I couldn't give her. I didn't trust myself to speak. Something dark leaked out of her feverish eyes. Expectation. Desire. Desperation. They shot through her, right into me. She wouldn't stop until she got an answer, but I'd already forgotten the question. All that lingered was this feeling. Of anticipation. Like my life was about to change. Like I wanted it to happen.

The cabbie cleared his throat. I produced my wallet and slipped him an extra fifty for bailing me out of this shit show of my making. Charlie leaned closer, lips brushing my ear. I swallowed. Hard.

"I'm going to save you, Tate."

No. You're gonna make me lose control.

And for the first time, I wanted to lose it all.

Chapter Seventy-One

Charlotte

True to my word, I showed up at Tate's office the next day with two bags of Lao takeout.

If I wanted to save Tate Marchetti, I needed to be a permanent fixture in his life. Helen sent me the final round of proofing to approve, so tomorrow marked the end of my read-throughs with Terry.

We were reaching the last grains in the hourglass.

I needed to find a way to flip it over.

To my surprise, Sylvia didn't appear unhappy to see me. If anything, I read relief on her face. And more exhaustion than I'd ever seen. Brand-new dark rims lined her eyes.

The professionally dyed, ultra-tight ponytail she usually sported now hung limp, an inch of blonde roots circling her hairline. Even her outfit lacked the normal effort.

This time, she didn't bother with a fake smile. Just pointed in the general direction behind me.

"He's in his office."

I hesitated. "Is everything okay?"

It came out as a whisper. Mostly, because I wouldn't put it past Tate to fire someone for breathing too loud.

Talking about her boss behind his back?

Definitely a fireable offense.

"He's been... a lot lately. He hasn't been like this since I started working here."

"How long ago was that?"

"Almost four years, give or take a few months."

After Kellan's death, I noted.

I doubt anyone told her, too. Suicide was like that. A taboo subject. When someone took their own life, people spoke about it in euphemisms. I knew all the phrases well.

Passed too soon. At peace now. Died of a tragic incident.

Or, the alternative—refusing to speak about it at all. Either way, it was a hard thing to confirm. One look at her, and I could tell she had no clue. That she found Tate to be a live wire without a source.

She scratched her cheek, opening and closing her mouth.

I put her out of her misery. "Do you have something you want to ask?"

"Do you know Dr. Marchetti well?"

I shrugged. "Well enough."

"Is he always like this? He's been cold from the start, occasionally taxing, yet he still managed to be fair. But the past few months..."

He's spiraling.

"It's me," I lied. Well, partly. I'd barged into Tate's life and pushed every single button, every single boundary I could. That spiral had bits and pieces of my name written on it. It was up to me to fix.

"Seriously?"

"Seriously. I gave him a hard time. He's reacting to it. I'm sorry if it's been making the office situation tense. I'll do my best to make it better."

"Are you guys, like... dating?"

Are we?

I tilted my head, aware of our age gap for the first time in a while. "We're... something." I lifted the takeout and pointed to Tate's office. "Food's getting cold."

"Will you let Dr. Marchetti know I'm taking my lunch break now?"

I nodded, watching her leave.

Tate didn't seem surprised when I entered. Only resigned. I set the bag on a chair and pulled out tray after tray, spreading them across every inch of his desk.

He leaned against the leather wingback. "What is this?"

"Sai oua with sticky rice, seen savanh, look seen, khao piak sen, and a complimentary dessert." I broke apart a pair of chopsticks and stuck them out for him to take. "Hope you like your food spicy."

"I was referring to your presence." He returned to the monitor, clicking away at his mouse. "I already ate."

"What a ridiculous thing to lie about."

"When people say they already ate, it means they don't want to eat," he drawled, using my words against me. He made me so furious I couldn't breathe. That couldn't be right. How someone else had power over your lungs.

"You remember last night?"

"Of course."

He would be that type of drunk. The insufferable kind.

I set my chopsticks down. "You were intoxicated."

Plastered, actually.

He spared me a glance. "It won't happen again."

"It's okay if it does." I pulled my lower lip into my mouth. "You can also call me again when you need to. It's okay to lean on others."

Technically, Luke the Bartender had been the one to call, but Tate told him to. That counted. Right?

Tate pressed his fingertips together, studying me over them. I squirmed under the intensity of his stare.

"That may be true," he finally said, "but I cannot and will not lean on alcohol again. You have my word."

"It's okay if you do that, too. You're far from addicted. You won't turn into Terry if you drink every once in a while."

"Twice in one year is more than enough. Two times too many, in fact."

"Are you that scared of becoming Terry?"

He shifted his attention back to the computer. A bluish hue radiated from the monitor, slashing across his sharp cheekbones and illuminating half his face. Little clicks filled the room. I'd wait all day for an answer if I had to. It finally came, and it only took a minute.

"Addiction can be hereditary."

"Is being an asshole hereditary?"

"In the Marchetti household? Yes."

The corner of his lips rose in that lopsided grin. We were in safe territory when we bantered, which I suspected was why we did it. Sometimes, you just need to smile and laugh. Even if it's at yourself.

His eyes dipped to my palm, which cradled my stomach. "Have you eaten?"

"Yes."

Not. I'd lost my appetite around the time he admitted to remembering the night before. The second I noticed his intoxication, I let my guard down and said things I wouldn't have otherwise.

And you warned him about drunk words? Should've warned yourself about sober ones.

He powered his desktop off, pinning me with his full attention. It hammered me down. I sank into the tough pleather like a nail.

"Now who's lying?"

"I'll eat when I get home," I promised.

Starvation was not in my arsenal of self-destruction. Accidental orgasms, painful memories, and putting myself through Tate's predictably unpredictable mood swings, on the other hand?

Check, check, check.

He peered inside each takeout lid before selecting a dessert with coconut, mango, and condensed milk. "At least eat this."

I picked up the chopsticks and ate on autopilot without paying attention to the food. It was hard to with Tate watching me, reclined like an emperor in his oversized luxury chair. Pure full-grain leather. The kind that sold for thousands and offered a painless sitting experience.

Meanwhile, I fidgeted in my seat. Made of some synthetic blend with a talent for extracting sweat out of my thighs. It was so like him to make the people around him as uncomfortable as possible without even trying.

After my last bite, he emptied rows of bottles from the mini fridge in the corner and replaced them with the remaining takeout containers.

"There's something different about you today," I noted.

Tate set a water in front of me. "Perhaps my sudden optimism?"

I snapped my fingers when I figured it out. "Gratitude."

He gave me a look that suggested he thought I was dumb and pitied me for it.

I continued, undeterred, "Are you touched that I'm here?" I brought my hand to my cheek. A grin eclipsed my face. I must've looked stupid, smiling at him like I was auditioning for Jack Torrance's role in *The Shining*.

His silence said it all.

"You are," I whispered, awestruck and childish enough to tease him about it.

Those softened eyes. I should've noticed them the moment he caught sight of the food and avoided staring at me.

More silence. I tapped my fingers against the armrest, waiting. I had no intention of making this easy for him. Finally, Tate offered a simple thank you, but I accepted it like I was on the receiving end of an Olympic gold medal. Minus the grace.

I sipped the water, studying him above the rim. He ran a finger along the built-in shelf, which was large for someone who didn't read for pleasure. Full of thick textbook volumes with titles like *Rediscovering the Vagina*, *Past the Labia*, and *The Art of Making Babies*.

This could be the film set for a porno.

"Do you always react this way when people feed you?" I asked before I did something stupid, like volunteer as tribute.

"People don't feed me."

"Now they do."

"Considering this is your first time... Yes, I've reacted this way every time."

I flushed. I couldn't be in this office and hear the words "first" and "time" used together without remembering what also happened for the first time a few rooms over. Especially not with his proximity.

"It's not my first time." I cleared my throat, husky all of a sudden. His eyes snapped to mine. "I filled your fridge," I explained.

"So, it was you."

"Terry is broke."

I realized belatedly that, if he read between the lines, I'd just rubbed in his face the fact that he had no one else in his life but his father and me. He wanted nothing to do with Terry, and anything to do with me came with the sobering aftertaste of guilt.

Quite a rotten pickle.

His fingers paused. "Seems that way."

Those were the same words he'd used when I came on his fingers.

My breath hitched. The temperature skyrocketed. I stripped off my sweater, leaving me in a black cropped BIGBANG tee, high-waisted jean shorts, and fishnets peeking over the waistband.

His eyes met the strip of skin at my stomach. An earthquake rattled my insides. Followed by a tsunami. And an avalanche.

I stretched, flashing more skin for him to see.

His throat bobbed. He perched on the edge of his desk, leg brushing against my thigh. He didn't move it, and again, I found myself relishing his touch, no matter how brief and casual.

"Thank you."

It took me a second too long to realize he wasn't thanking me for the peep show. A ruddy flush spread across my cheeks. "You're welcome."

"Don't do it again in the future. Save your money."

"I got a raise after my promotion."

"The request still stands." He straightened, outstretched fingertips grazing the bare skin of my waist with the movement. *On purpose?* When he took a seat on the other side of the desk, he gave no indication he'd even noticed. "I have the means to buy my own food," he said casually. As if he hadn't just touched me. Lit a match. Left me to burn. "If I wanted to, I would have."

"I know." I tried to control my heartbeats. "But I wanted to buy you food, so I did, and you can't say no to it because I bought it on my *measly* salary."

"Reagan's not enough of an asshole to pay you a measly salary."

"You don't know that."

"What happened to the girl who claimed to be Reagan's favorite?"

"Do you always have an answer for everything?"

"Only Monday through Sunday." His knuckles grazed his chin. "I'll eat the leftovers later."

"Good."

I believed him. Couldn't keep the smile off my face, too. A yawn extinguished it, catching me by surprise.

"Did you sleep?"

"Had a late night." I popped a brow. "I wonder why."

"What happened to 'call me whenever you want'?"

"Didn't say I regret it. Just pointed out a fact. I stayed out late, and now I'm tired." I made my way to the lounger by the floor-to-ceiling windows, plopping onto it with another yawn. This time, I managed to cover my mouth. "Offer still stands."

Which brought me to my other offer. To save him. Did he remember that, too?

I opened my mouth to ask him, but he beat me to the punch.

"Go home. Get some rest."

"I'm fine," I swore, scoring a hat trick with the yawns. "Not even tired."

What a crowning achievement, my ability to get everything wrong.

Chapter Seventy-Two

Charlotte

I woke up with Tate in my face, pulling a thick blanket over me. The sun shone behind him like a halo. The urge to kiss him crashed into me hard. I reached out, grazing his jaw. His eyes pitched to mine. His long fingers stilled at the edge of the fleece, so close to touching me.

"Tate."

"You fell asleep." A raised brow followed up his words, as if to say, *I told you so.*

"Oh." I cleared my throat, unsure whether to stay down or sit up. "I forgot to tell you. Sylvia took her lunch break."

"She returned an hour ago."

"An hour?" I shot up. "That can't be right. How long have I been asleep?"

"It's two in the afternoon now, so about an hour and a half."

"Don't you have any appointments?"

"I did. Last one ended fifteen minutes ago. Next one starts in an hour."

"Why didn't you wake me?"

"I'm the source of your sleepless night. It made sense to let you rest."

Such a clinical answer.

Nights, I corrected. *Plural. This is not the first time I've lost sleep over you, Tate Marchetti. I doubt it will be the last, too.*

Voices crept beneath the door. I made out Sylvia's, along with the nurse who helped me before my exam. Grace. They were discussing a sale at Bloomie's. If we could hear them, I wondered if they could hear us.

"Do you work all your staff on weekends? Aren't there labor laws?"

"I'm always on call. Walter and I have enough staff to rotate, keeping them at four to five days a week and forty hours max." He raised a single brow. "Are you actually interested in hearing this?"

"I am. When it comes to you, I want to know everything."

I'd resigned myself to the fact a while ago. They say love is ten percent falling and ninety percent picking yourself back up. What they never tell you is how quick that ten percent passes and how long that ninety percent lasts. Judging by how fast I'd fallen for Tate Marchetti, when we reached the end of our shelf life, I'd be totally, utterly fucked.

Our proximity struck me. My face inches from his. Our breaths tangling. He had kneeled to cover me with the blanket, but he hadn't gotten up. His nearness rattled me. Excited me. *Consumed* me. He was the type of big that didn't bend to the confines of physical size. Tate sucked all the oxygen out of the room, and the fact that I could even breathe around him defied biology. He caught me staring at his lips. I licked mine, releasing an unsteady breath. I don't know who moved first. One second, we were inches apart. The next, our bodies melded together, everything glued from chest up. Nothing between us but clothes I wanted to tear off.

I sank my teeth into his lower lip, sucking it into my mouth. One of his hands grabbed my ass and squeezed. The other curved around my waist and tugged me closer. His body was smooth, hard concrete. Skillfully chiseled. His erection, long and thick. I climbed on top of him, wrapping my legs around his back. He rolled his hips, hands palming my ass as he carried me from the couch, his lips fused to mine. Our tongues danced. Tangled. Fought for dominance. He won, but so did I. My back met the door, pushing my core against his length.

I groaned. "You have a habit of pinning me against things."

"Don't remind me, Charlie."

Charlie. Goosebumps peppered my arms. The hand gripping my ass traveled between us and popped the button from my shorts. I scratched my nails down his back, kicking my shoes off. He thrust against me, the friction delicious even through the fabric. Another thrust. My body rattled the door. Behind me, the talking halted before kicking up again.

"Your... um, staff," I pointed out, hoping it wouldn't stop him.

I didn't think he heard me. He was too far gone, his scorching tongue rolling down my neck. A growl vibrated against my collarbone. His teeth followed it with a nip before he backed up. I watched with hooded eyes as he yanked the rough fabric of my shorts down to my ankles. My shirt came off next, leaving me in lace lingerie and waist-high fishnet tights.

His hands came to my sides, tearing the panties and slipping them past the net. He kneeled before me, grabbed my leg, and hooked it over his shoulder, baring me to him. The large diamond-shaped holes of the tights gave him easy access. I felt his breath there. Impossibly warm.

"You owe me all the pennies in your purse." He stared at my core. The wetness pooled, running down my thigh. "I made you drip before I even used my tongue or cock."

It took me a few seconds too long to realize he was referring to the bet we'd made months ago. When I'd stupidly questioned his dirty talk.

He seemed more pliable than usual, so even though my cheeks burned, I mustered all my courage to push him over the edge. "Double or nothing: if you make me come on your tongue, I'll give you all the pennies in the world." I couldn't believe I'd just said that.

But it worked. Tate gripped my thigh tighter. "Deal." He leaned forward, talking directly to my pussy. "I'm about to be a very rich man."

His nose nudged my clit, teeth grazing the lips that bracketed it. He sucked one into his mouth before moving on to the bundle of nerves between them. Then he licked the outline of my sex with the tip of his tongue—slowly, slowly, so, so slowly—until he finally plunged, thrusting into me. My palms hit the door. Sylvia and Grace paused their chatter again. I heard snippets of phrases—*Dr. Marchetti, some girl, lucky bitch*—

but it was impossible to focus with Tate driving his tongue inside me. His finger looped around one of the diamond nets, drew it back, and released, snapping it against my skin.

I moaned at the sting, chanting his name. Pleading for more. "Inside me. I need you inside me."

"Come on my lips, and maybe I'll reward you."

"You just want all the pennies in the world." I laughed, but it quickly turned into another moan.

He added two fingers inside me, snug against his tongue. My breath hitched at the tight fit. And then he curved them, hitting a spot I thought was just a myth.

I came. So hard, my eyes slammed shut. I still saw Tate behind them. Ruggedly handsome. Devilish satisfaction shining in his eyes. I clenched around his fingers, drawing them in deeper. Tate's tongue licked my clit in soft, teasing strokes until I floated down from the high.

I opened my eyes and peered down at him, watching as he pulled back and swiped his lower lip with his thumb. He was fully clothed, and I was nearly naked, and we were so different and so similar, it pained me.

Tate rose to his feet. I held my breath, not sure what to expect. Certainly not the kiss he planted on my lips. The taste of me lingered on them, faintly sweet. He moved back, but I looped my palm behind his neck and held him close.

"Charlotte," he warned. "You already owe me more pennies than you can afford."

"Please fuck me."

"Jesus."

I sealed our lips together. He returned my kiss and picked me up with ease, setting me on the edge of his desk. I grabbed his shirt, fumbled with the buttons, and yanked the last one, tearing it open. Tightly packed abs rippled the surface of his stomach. He stole my breath. Ripped it right out of my chest and took it as his.

"That's so unfair." I groaned.

He grinned. I took his silence as an invitation to hop off the desk and kneel before him. He watched me fumble for his pants button, content to observe my struggle without offering to help. I gave in and broke that, too, shoving his slacks and boxers down in one go.

His erection bobbed, hitting his stomach.

Um. Wow. It was difficult to reconcile the existence of fairness when Tate Marchetti had been born with an assault rifle for a cock. Thick, hard, and longer than should be legal.

"If you keep staring at my cock with your mouth open like that, I'm going to take it as an invitation to enter."

My mouth watered. "Please, do."

His eyes met mine, throat rolling. I hopped onto the desk again, lay on my back, and admired him from this angle. His fingers traced the netting of my tights, stopping to run one along my slit before he ripped the net. It tore around my pussy.

He palmed his cock, gave it a tug from the base to the head, and dragged it along the length until he reached my clit. He circled around the bud. I reached up and pinched my nipple. His eyes blackened and tangled with mine. Lust layered with need surged between us.

The crown lined up with my entrance. I jerked forward, trying to catch him. The tip slid inside me. My eyes rolled back, a groan escaping my throat.

Holy crap.

We were doing this.

We were really doing this.

I felt the absence immediately. My eyes shot open. He'd stepped back, putting space between us.

I inventoried him, from the hand gripping his erection tight to the pained expression pasted on his face. "What's wrong?"

"I'm not taking your virginity like this, Charlie."

"I'm not a candles and roses kind of girl. It doesn't matter."

"It does to me." He looked like he couldn't believe what he was saying.

His dick looked like it couldn't either, so strained, it jerked on its own. I wanted it in me. Needed it. Any way possible. I also knew winning an argument with Tate was a rare feat.

"But..."

"I'm going to fuck your mouth, Charlie."

I curled my fists, mortified that I was negotiating this. Begging for him. "My pussy would be a tighter, more pleasurable ride."

He arched his brow, as if to say, *are we really going there?* "So would your ass."

My cheeks pinked. I was not entirely opposed to the idea. "Let's try my mouth first."

"That's what I thought."

"Well? I'm waiting."

He swore, all but rolling his eyes as he stepped forward. He stared down at me sprawled across his desk, fixated on the view. "You're a fucking vision, Charlie."

He was staring at my face, not my body, and something about it made every cell in me turn gooey like toasted marshmallows. He planned on making this easy for me. I saw it in his eyes. Knew him well enough to realize it. But I wanted dirty, and gritty, and raw. The real him.

"Don't hold back," I pleaded. "Give me everything."

"It'll hurt."

I hoisted myself onto my elbows. "Try me."

He lifted me and set me on the rug. I grabbed a pillow from the couch and slid it under my shoulders, propping my upper body up. He kneeled before me, legs on either side of my chest, scooting until his erection stood right in front my face.

I licked my lips, grazing the tip of his cock.

"Fuck," he hissed, hands resting on the couch behind me to hold his weight up.

The movement thrust the smooth head of his cock against my lips. I parted them, drawing him as far into my mouth as I could in one go. I managed to take half of him. My fingers wrapped around the base, guiding more of him past my lips.

He thrust into my mouth, giving me exactly what I asked for. His fingers tangled with my hair, pushing my head forward until he hit the back of my throat. "Good girl."

My pussy clenched at his words, hips thrusting up. I wanted him to fill me. Devour me. Render me unable to walk for days. My tongue swept the underside of his cock with each of his thrusts.

He pumped into my mouth, his movements jerky and erratic. I was greedy for him, taking everything he'd give me, begging for more with my eyes. A knock interrupted us.

Sylvia's voice invaded the room. "Dr. Marchetti? Your three o'clock is here."

"Coming," he grunted back, jerking out of me.

And, well, he sure was.

"Wait." I reached for his hip. "I wanna know what it tastes like." I licked my lips. "I've never..."

He groaned, stroking his length from base to tip. I opened my mouth wide. He pumped his cock in front of me, jerking himself off with his crown pressed against my tongue. Thick, white ropes shot out of him, landing on my lips, tongue, teeth.

He palmed the back of my head, guiding me forward. My lips wrapped around the tip of his cock to accept the rest. He filled my mouth, tasting earthy and warm. I swallowed, unable to get enough of him.

When he pulled back, I couldn't stop staring at him. He slid down my body until our faces were level. He was mine in a way that made me primal. Coiled with grief, and lust, and every version of need that existed. He was mine, and I was his, and no amount of guilt would ever change that.

"I love you," I whispered against his lips. I'd never meant anything more.

He reared back as if I'd slapped him. I ached at the sudden loss. A wall slammed down his face. Bricks made of repulsion and guilt. Like I'd thrown a glass of cold water on him.

"You don't know me, Charlie. If you did, you wouldn't love me."

He meant every word. Hopelessness surged inside me. It was like watching the saddest movie you'd ever seen, knowing you couldn't change the plot.

"As much as I bet you'd like to, you can't dictate my feelings. I love you, Tate Marchetti. It's as simple as that."

Tate believed he wasn't worthy of love. I could see it in his ragged exhales. It tore me to shreds.

But I thought of Leah. Of the past couple of weeks we'd spent dipping our toes into sisterhood again. Wading in shallow waters. Convincing one another we deserved good things. Some people need to hear the words over and over again before they believe it.

He moved off me and stood, but I got in his face, forcing him to see me. I refused to give up, and I wanted him to know it.

I think you love me back. I think you love me, and it scares you. But that's okay. If you run, I will, too. With you.

I pressed my palm over his heart. "You don't have to say it back. I'm patient."

"You can't chase me forever."

I smiled. "I can."

"You'll get sick of it."

"Tell you what," I said, already knowing I'd break this promise if he decided to be stubborn. "One year. I'll chase you for one year, and in that year, you'll say it back."

"No."

"I love you, Tate. And I'll say it over and over again until you no longer feel guilty when you hear it."

It was a promise I shouldn't have made. One that defied the hardest lesson I'd ever learned: Love is expensive. Its currency is grief.

And sometimes, it costs more than you can afford.

Chapter Seventy-Three

Charlotte

I made the mistake of mentioning the plagiarism to Terry. We sat at Tate's kitchen island, hovered around my laptop screen. Staring at *Darling Venom*'s cover. Of chains embracing a journal, joined at the lock.

I tilted my head. "It suits him, doesn't it?"

"He would've said a cover doesn't make a book," Terry pointed out, and he was right.

Kellan possessed what he self-dubbed *literary ethics*, which technically referred to moral principles intrinsic to literature. But I preferred his version. Where the appreciation for words reigned supreme over the other bullshit—covers, social media frenzy, and press junkets.

Terry zoomed until his son's name filled the entire seventeen-inch screen. "But, secretly, he would've kept a copy just to stare at it. And yes, the cover does suit him."

"I meant being an author."

He opened the manuscript doc. "We should get back to *Darling Venom*." It was due tomorrow. The final version.

"Have you figured out what the line in chapter eighteen is about?"

The human capacity to forgive in the name of love breeds doormats. Unless, of course, the person doing the forgiving is someone you love and the person being forgiven is you. Then, it's called personal growth, and that stench of hypocrisy? Plug your nose, darling. It ain't going anywhere.

It stuck out like a sore thumb. A passage directed, for the first time, to the reader, as if Kellan needed to cement the message. Only, in the context of the chapter, it made no sense. Terry had insisted it stay, which led to a terse debate with Helen. I took Terry's side, but only because it was also Kellan's side. My gut led me there. And a heavy dose of logic. As an economic writer, he wouldn't have added the line without a reason. We couldn't brush the fact aside just because he wasn't around to make his case.

"No. It's staying."

"I know." I scrolled to the passage in question. A streak of red highlighted the entire paragraph, courtesy of Track Changes. "Helen will need an answer she can stomach to justify the break in narrative consistency."

"How about—I'm Kellan's father, and I don't want his words cut?"

"She's not as sentimental as we are."

"Are you? Sentimental?"

"Unfortunately."

Terry snorted.

I reread the passage. "We still need a reason to offer to Helen."

And this was where it went to shit. Where I broke my Do-Not-Bring-Up-the-Plagiarism rule. Which existed for everyone's sake, including my own plausible deniability as Kellan's agent.

"You're a broken record, Miss Richards."

"You can do better than cliché analogies, Mr. Marchetti."

He flipped a page, not once looking at me. "Apparently not, according to David Arnault of *The Literary Plague*."

"One—that is well-known to be the only negative critic review *The Imperfections* received. Two—there's a reason it's called *The Literary Plague*; they're notoriously incapable of human emotions over there. Reagan blacklists them from advance review copies for half her authors.

And three—technically, you didn't even wri—" I couldn't see them, but I knew my cheeks were turning a shade of red that would make Clifford jealous.

"I didn't even write it." Finally, he gifted me the full force of his attention. "That what you wanted to say?"

Unlike me, he didn't turn a shade of red more suitable for a stop sign. But, for the first time, I detected something lurking beneath his surface. Not regret. That had always been there. Maybe... I reared back, a little shocked at what I picked up. Terry seemed *less* regretful.

It was such a roadblock in the progress I thought we'd made that I found it difficult to say anything to him in the hours that followed, choosing to drop the subject forever. We worked at opposite corners of the island, hovered over two different halves of the manuscript—his printed, mine electronic. I didn't expect Terry to make *negative* progress on our last day working together, but the Marchetti family was nothing if not unpredictable. With only a few pages left, I found my mind drifting, teeth gnawing on the end of a cheap pen as I mulled over his reaction.

Terry frowned, tapping a section of the book with the back of his pen. "Did you forget to make the edits on this paragraph?"

I glanced at the passage, upside down, not really having to look to know which he was referring to. It had to be the one on Tate. What else could it be? "I declined your edits on the paragraph." The highlighted lines blurred before my eyes came into focus. The word *hate* glared back at me.

"Care to elaborate?"

"If Tate ever reads *Darling Venom*, I want him to read the words exactly as they were written by Kellan." Especially this paragraph. The first mention of Tate in the novel.

Terry nodded. "Okay."

And that was that. Only, it didn't scream of a man regressing in his journey away from douchedom.

I finished the manuscript first and continued gnawing on the pen, stopping just before ink painted my teeth crimson. "Can I ask you something?"

Terry didn't look up from the pages. "Would saying no stop you?"

I flushed. "No."

"Go on."

"What happened with *The Imperfections*?"

He milked his workload, finishing the final page before he closed the manuscript, piercing blue-grays meeting my mint greens. "I'm surprised it took you this long to ask."

"Is that a deflection?"

"That's question number two, darlin'." He capped his fountain pen and tossed it beside his notepad. "You're racking up a bill, and last I checked, you're more broke than I am."

"I was scared to ask. I'm afraid of what your answer may be."

I'm afraid it will cross a line. I'm afraid if it does, that will mean I can't work on Darling Venom with you, and I need this book to be perfect.

Now that we'd finished, my concerns evaporated. I still felt on edge. All it took was one tiny change for everything we'd built to collapse.

"I was high when I stumbled on the first draft of *The Imperfections*. So high, I thought it was mine. Thought I'd get to flip the finger at every judgmental dick who told me not to write drunk, edit sober, 'cause something I wrote turned out to be a fucking masterpiece. Point is, I was convinced I hit the fucking jackpot, it was that goddamn good. Rough around the edges and in need of some major edits, but innovative as hell with bones better than 99.999% of polished final drafts out there."

"So, you sent it to your agent?"

"Not at that point." He patted his pockets for his smokes before remembering I confiscated them each time we met. There were few things I loathed more than cigarettes. By now, he knew it, too. Terry collected his fountain pen and tapped it against the table instead, continuing, "I realized as soon as I sobered up that the manuscript wasn't mine." *Tap. Tap.* "Actually, once the drugs and booze flushed out, it was pretty fucking

PARKER S. HUNTINGTON

obvious it didn't come from my brain."

Tap, tap.

Tap.

"Do you still have the original?" I doubted he did, but I needed to try. *The Imperfections* sat at the top of my list of all-time faves, right after *Darling Venom*. The unedited version? It would unearth the writer's mind. I itched to get my hands on it.

He waved me off. "I had too much pride to steal it. Swear. But my agent called, told me my publisher didn't want the manuscript she tried to shop to them, and suggested I write something more *marketable*." He spat the last word as if it were profanity.

"She wasn't wrong." I felt defensive over someone I didn't know, but Abigail and Reagan often dished the same advice to their authors. Without a big name or connections, publishers didn't take risks unless the manuscript deserved it. Unless it was *The Imperfections*.

"She was wrong," he insisted. *Tap. Tap.* "Never tried hard enough to sell my shit, that one. Questionable, at best. Bat shit, most certainly. The worst thing is, she's no longer my agent, but the witch still gets a cut of every sale of *The Imperfections*."

"She sold the book to the publisher. She's entitled to a cut of the proceeds."

"Anyone with a functioning mouth could sell that book." He paused. "Actually, you don't even need to say a damn word to sell it. Just hand it to any paper pusher at a Big Five, and the rest'll be history." *Tap. Tap. Tap.* "Anyway, point is, she shouldn't have told me to write something marketable."

"Agree to disagree."

He snorted. Agreeing to disagree was the only thing we ever agreed on. But it worked. We finished *Darling Venom* without a hitch. I didn't count chapter eighteen on account of the fact that I backed his decision to keep the passage. I just wish he'd give me an explanation, but my expectations of Terry hovered somewhere below the dude who engineered the Leaning

384

Tower of Pisa and above Joe Exotic. He did, however, grow on me.

Tap. Tap.

His fountain pen broke. Midnight ink spurted everywhere, dripping down the side of the island and splashing onto the hardwood. It would stain soon, and I might have worried over it if Tate hadn't mentioned that his plan to renovate the brownstone had gone up in flames after Kellan died. The more Terry trashed this place, the higher the chances Tate would finally do something for himself. Guess I was in the mood to push everyone today.

Terry curled his upper lip, a telltale sign he was about to go on the defensive. "If she hadn't told me to go marketable, to sell out, I wouldn't have done what I did."

Personal accountability seemed to be a lost cause when it came to the great Terrence Marchetti, so I didn't press him.

Not true, I reminded myself. *He came through on Darling Venom. He just needs a nudge. Someone to point out his flaws, give him some tough love, and push him in the right direction.*

Since Terrence Marchetti had no friends, I guess that someone would be me.

I raised a brow. "So, you stole the manuscript because you needed one at that moment, and you didn't want to write something marketable."

He shrugged. "I'm no sell-out."

"Just a thief."

"The book wouldn't have been published if I didn't take it." He held both palms up. "The author I took *The Imperfections* from never debuted and didn't have plans to. It's like *Darling Venom.* If I didn't intervene, Kellan's book would've died right alongside him, and that would have been an even bigger travesty. To lose a son is unbearable. To lose his words—unsurpassable."

Stealing an unknown author's work was not at all similar to polishing his son's final manuscript to fulfill his dying wish. Not even close.

I pushed back at the false equivalency. "So, you did the guy a favor?"

"Hey, I wrote *The Imperfections*, too," he protested. "The edits I did were heavy. Twenty-fucking-thousand words. So damn heavy, I think it fucked with his head. I changed so much of the original manuscript, it made him second-guess every word he wrote after that."

"So, you *didn't* do him a favor."

He scooted his chair back. "I don't have to sit here and deal with this."

I stopped the stool with my leg and held still, even when the impact stung my shin. "I think you do, Terry, because it seems to me that this is the first time you've ever been honest about the plagiarism. About your mistakes, in general. How does it feel to be honest for once? How does it feel to confront your struggles head-on?"

His fingers reached for the broken pen, pulling back when one of the jagged edges pinched his skin. Ink stretched across his fingertips like zebra stripes. He rubbed at the raw flesh. "This isn't an episode of *60 Minutes*."

No, but I felt like a knockoff Lesley Stahl, Oprah, and Dr. Phil rolled into one. I intended to do what I could for Terry. Not for him, but for his sons. By some stroke of magic, some wild miracle, he managed to father two incredible people. I had to believe Kellan was watching us, witnessing the effort Terry put into *Darling Venom*, and feeling some vindication. But Tate? Terry had given up before he even started, and I refused to accept it.

"You scared a newbie author into never publishing again." I stood, rounded Terry's chair, and forced myself into his line of sight. "There is a weight on you. I see it every day. If you want to lift it, you need to make amends. I think the author you stole from is a good place to start."

And then maybe you can try with Tate before there's nothing left to salvage.

Terry shook his head. "It's too late. What's done is done."

A wall slammed down in front of him. I'd pushed too hard. Disappointment sank into my skin like claws. I returned to my seat, giving up... for now. I guess moments like this were why people said you should never meet your idols.

"Well, that's a damn shame. *The Imperfections...*" I closed my eyes, recalling every night I'd spent pouring over the book after my parents died. For most of the past decade, I had nothing to turn to but its pages. "It's a gift to literature. To humanity."

"Isn't that the fucking truth," Terry muttered.

He moved to the fridge and dug around before I could continue hounding him. I pulled up my phone, emailing Helen to inform her we finished the manuscript. Thoughts of Tate consumed me. We never put a label on our relationship, and I doubted he would feel comfortable with one if I broached the subject. This was the same man who refused to touch Kellan's room for over four years.

I toyed with my phone, wondering how to approach this. A heavy breath rushed out of me. "Can you do me a favor?"

Terry turned. A stick of string cheese dangled from the corner of his lips like an oversized cigarette. He spoke around it, "Another one?"

"Can you keep the fact that we finished to yourself?"

His hand connected with the cheese and yanked, decapitating half of it in one go. "'Cause you need a reason to keep coming over here?"

Tate and I were a fragile ecosystem of ill-fated decisions. Each one had the potential to destroy us. Nothing good would happen once I no longer had an excuse to show up. I feared our future like people feared a natural disaster, unable to predict it. I could either prevent damage or leave myself vulnerable when it strikes. I had more self-preservation than that.

"Yes," I admitted.

"You want me to lie to my son?"

I held back a groan. When I said I wanted Terrence Marchetti to assume the role of the dependable parent, I hadn't expected it to backfire so soon. Especially when he possessed the moral aptitude of the Grinch.

"If he asks, tell him we're done with the book, but if he doesn't..." I scratched the back of my neck, having the decency to appear sheepish. "Can you just not volunteer the information?"

It wouldn't be a lie, per se. Just an omission of truth. In the grand scheme of things, it hardly counted as a sin.

Sure. And the Manson Family wasn't a cult.

"Well, well, well... Aren't you the pillar of morality?"

That wasn't an answer, and we both knew it. I waited for Terry to finish. He didn't. I tried to figure out his endgame. He knew I could run to the press and offer an exclusive on his plagiarism, but the last thing I wanted was negative press for the Marchetti name before Kellan's release. And that, I decided, gave Terry the winning hand.

The silence stretched another minute. I took it as his answer. Fine. I'd find another way. Another excuse to keep myself in Tate's life. After all, time is a deadbeat parent. Once it's gone, that asshole is never coming back. With Tate, I had no intention of sitting around.

I packed up my things, heading to the door with the envelope containing the manuscript pressed tightly to my chest for safekeeping. My palm planted on a chunk of peeling wallpaper, the other hand moving to zip up my ankle boots.

"I've been meaning to ask..."

Terry's words stopped me just shy of the doorknob. I pivoted to face him. He dragged a hand down the leg of his sweats. Ran a palm over his face. Cleared his throat.

"Go on," I pressed when he didn't.

"The credits on *Darling Venom*..." He palmed the back of his neck. "Can you leave my name off them? No editing credits, no proofing credits, not even the damn foreword."

I didn't know what I expected him to say, but it wasn't that.

"Okay." I already had no intention of putting Terry's name on this. It was Kellan's turn to shine.

"You do that, and I'll keep it to myself that we finished." He blew his cheeks out and released the air. "Wouldn't be the worst thing if you stuck around and dislodged that stick from Tate's ass."

"Poetic."

He belched, rubbing his belly, right above an unidentifiable stain. "That's why they pay me the big bucks."

Since Terry was the one to bring Tate up this time, I decided to leap over the line between walking toward progress and racing toward it. "If you won't apologize to the author you stole *The Imperfections* from, at least try apologizing to Tate. Whatever it takes." Maybe I was reaching, but he did just agree to keep me in Tate's life.

"It's pointless. He won't forgive me."

"You won't know if you don't try."

"I'm not worthy of redemption."

"That's Tate's decision to make." I shook my head. "The goal shouldn't be redemption. It should be telling Tate you care enough to repair your relationship. A real apology isn't given with the intention of healing yourself. That's just a side effect."

"I'll think about it."

I sucked my lower lip past my teeth, biting down. "After my parents died, I realized something I should have known earlier. I think you've realized it, too, but you're having trouble admitting it because it means you'll have to change your life from the bottom up."

"Yeah? What's that?"

"Love is just being there for someone. It's that simple."

His brows pulled together. A crease developed between them. The air felt charged, but neither of us dared to drain it. I turned to leave but stopped again when I realized Terry looked like he wanted to say something else.

"This is really it, huh?" To his credit, he seemed to dread the idea. His hands dipped into his pockets, feet rocking back. I didn't know if he was referring to the book, Tate, or our meetings. Maybe all the above.

I waited for him to clarify.

"We finished."

Ah. The book. He meant the book.

Terry said *finished* like he never expected it to happen. Since *The*

Imperfections, he'd never released again. This marked his first novel in nearly a decade. And it wasn't his own.

"We finished," I rasped back. I selected my next words with caution, knowing I was treading dangerous waters with someone who had a tendency of turning to substances to cure his problems. "You're not a fraud, Ter."

"Of course not." He lifted some fingers up, pretending to count them, wiggling all ten digits when he ran out. "I wrote thirteen books before *The Imperfections* ever happened."

"I mean it. I know you pretend you don't care about the plagiarism, that it doesn't affect the way you think about yourself, but it's obvious that it does. Finishing Kellan's book while staying true to his voice and vision proves what you're capable of. You are not a fraud."

"Anyone could have done that."

"No. Not at all. There's a reason I came to you."

"Free labor."

I quirked a brow. "The money saved isn't enough incentive to deal with you, especially when Helen would've offered someone far more tolerable to help."

"I'm that bad, eh?"

I smiled. "The worst."

He shook his head. "I'm still a fraud."

"Have you ever tried saying otherwise?"

"Why would I?"

"Because when you say you're a fraud, you justify acting like one. You justify hating yourself. You justify bad behavior. It's an insult to Kellan's memory when he idolized the hell out of you."

Terry had no answer to that, but I refused to let him off the hook.

"You're not a fraud, Terry," I said with so much conviction, it had to rattle him. "You helped finish Kellan's book, and it's a damn perfect book. You are not a fraud. Why don't you try saying *that* aloud for once?"

"This is dumb."

"Just do it. For Kellan."

For yourself.

He swallowed, looked away, and mumbled, "I'm not a fraud."

"Louder."

"I'm not a fraud." His eyes hit the door as if he wanted to be anywhere but here. "This isn't a children's flick."

"You're right. This is real life, and you're an adult. It's time to act like one." I crossed my arms. "Again."

"I'm not a fraud," he deadpanned, sarcasm so thick I could slather it on sliced bread like peanut butter. Extra crunchy.

"You're right. You're not." I waved the envelope with the manuscript. "You finished *Darling Venom.* You are not a fraud. Say it again."

He repeated it, over and over, and I knew why he was entertaining me. Terrence Marchetti was sick of hating himself. Of living with a weight on his shoulders that rendered him unable to move.

He desperately wanted to believe he was not a fraud, so he could start acting like he wasn't one.

"Again," I urged. But I didn't need to. He was saying it on his own now. Without me asking. Stronger. Louder. Faster.

He rocked back on his heels. The nerves left him one by one. His shoulders squared, chin tipping up. That permanent frown dissolved. Terry looked me dead in the eyes. And finally—*finally*—he repeated, "I'm not a fraud."

This time, he meant it. I could tell. And it took a hell of a lot for him to admit that. Years. Ten of them.

Maybe more.

I flashed him a smile. Terry returned it. Under the failing bulb of Tate Marchetti's neglected entryway, suffering in the feverish summer heat, it felt as if something monumental had just happened.

A milestone I never thought we'd reach.

Maybe, just maybe, I felt Kellan here with us.

And maybe, just maybe, he was smiling, too.

Chapter Seventy-Four

Charlotte

Lately, Uranus had become acquainted with, well, mine.

I sat on the planet in the middle of Galileo Playground. Tate chose Mars. I flushed, remembering its astrological meaning. Sex. Desire. Passion.

Or war.

I tabled the volatile thought before my mind ruined the mood. By some unspoken agreement, this had turned into our place.

I couldn't step inside my apartment without walking into Jonah all over Leah in a soft-core porn reenactment, knitting needles included.

Terry lacked the ability to take a hint, which made Tate's brownstone off-limits if we wanted privacy.

And we always did.

So, this marked our sixth night in a row meeting here. Like two teenage punks stealing kisses and collecting cigarette butts, our mere interaction a rebellion against the world.

"How's the book?"

The question took me by surprise. Tate never broached the subject of *Darling Venom*. Bringing up Kellan was rare enough without the addition of a manuscript he refused to read.

One that happened to feature me as his brother's love interest.

Not that he knew.

And when he finds out, how do you think he'll react?

Not very well. And that made every second together a gift.

I studied Tate as much as I could under the blanket of darkness. The streetlamp still flickered on and off, so my eyes never adjusted. It stayed on long enough to illuminate his silhouette. He had his arms folded across his chest, as if he needed to brace himself for the answer.

I went for casual.

"It's a good book." I waited a beat, debating whether I should look this gift horse in the mouth and shoo it away. "You should read it."

And buh-bye went the horsie.

I knew if Tate read *Darling Venom*, it might spell The End for us. And that he was my favorite source of happiness. Which, I realized, might've been a new type of self-destruction. Guess old habits die hard.

"I don't read." He hopped off Mars and moved onto Saturn.

Structure. Restriction. Obligation.

Not that I thought his planetary decisions were his way of telling me something, but still... I wanted to bulldoze past his walls and send him to Pluto—transformation, rebirth, evolution.

I rested my hands behind me on the globe, using them to support my weight as I leaned back. "Your patients would be appalled to learn you made it through med school without cracking open a book."

"Textbooks and medical journals don't count as reading."

"Pretend it's a textbook. A textbook on Kellan's soul."

He leaned forward, eyes tangling with mine. "Is it autobiographical?"

"In a sense..." I shrugged. Or tried to with my arms still stretched behind me. "Some things are fictionalized."

"Such as...?"

My happy ending with Kellan. One where he's alive and together with me. One where you're not in the picture.

"The happy ending."

I bit my lip, closing my eyes. The breeze lapped at my cheeks. Tate and I *would* choose the coldest, darkest time of day to meet. Everything we did bore the not-so-subtle stench of masochism.

"Kellan isn't the type to write happy endings."

"It's happy by his standard."

"That sounds more accurate."

It tore out of him. My eyes popped open, zeroing in on Tate. He stared up at the sky, his lips parted. The bottom one crept forward, as if he held words in his head desperate to spill out. In the span of a few minutes, Tate had gone from casual to stricken. I guess that's why they call grief an unforgiving bitch. She can sucker punch you at any time.

I slid my jacket off my shoulders and let it fall to the ground so I could enjoy the chill. Or maybe it would spur Tate to come here and warm me. I didn't know what I wanted. I just knew, whatever warmth I received, I needed to know it wasn't artificial. Or temporary.

"What are you thinking right now?" I asked.

"I'm thinking life is cruel, and whoever designed it is crueler." He slanted his head, staring at the night sky. A frown touched his lips. "And that's only on days I'm willing to suspend my disbelief in favor of the possibility of a world where Kel still exists."

I tried to swallow around the boulder in my throat. Tate wore a Kellan-shaped hole in his chest. I wanted to fill it up. To step inside his body and see the world as he saw it. So I could experience the pain he felt and shoulder it for him.

"You're right." The wind carried his words to me like a love letter being passed in secret. "Kellan was so strong to last as long as he did."

I stared at my toes, wiggled them because it gave me something to do other than cry, and returned my attention to Tate when I remembered how to breathe.

His eyes were already on me. I felt the full force of them and sucked in a breath. They bore a question. I had a hunch as to what it was, but I didn't know whether I wanted him to ask it or bury it six feet under, never to be heard from again.

Ask it, I decided.

Ask me what I was doing on that roof the night I met Kellan. Please, Tate. You already know.

I swallowed. "I used to think about his last moments. The ones before the fall. What ran through his mind? Was he scared? Was he excited? Or was he just plain... over it? Maybe even all the above."

"And now you don't?"

"Now I know better." I propped both feet on the globe, pulled my knees to my chest, and locked my arms around them once I found my balance. Physically, at least. "For starters, it's the worst form of torture to imagine the moments before someone you love died. I don't recommend it. Not even to the dude who invented the guillotine. But also, I think Kellan planned his death far before either of us ever knew, and in that plan, he included a path for us to heal."

Tate held a palm out. "Please cough up the directions and a map, because I'm feeling left the fuck out."

I reached out toward his hand as if I could touch it from this distance. "*Darling Venom*. That's the map. The apology. The plan."

Tate had moved, almost as if to meet my outstretched fingers, but at my words, he veered to Jupiter.

Luck. Optimism. Abundance.

I'd take any of those right now, please and thank you.

He settled on top of the half-orange, half-green globe. Not that I could make the colors out at this hour. But I knew. Just as I knew he would decline any invitation to read his brother's words.

"I'll pass."

See?

I decided then and there that I would not give up until Tate Marchetti read *Darling Venom*. It was my only weapon in this war to heal him.

I lowered my hand. "I think Kellan wrote the book for you to read. With you in mind, Tate."

395

"Doubt he left me anything other than a big fuck-you laundry pile. We weren't close. Besides, he gave the keys to the drawers to you."

I rested my chin on my knees, studying him. Tate's blue-grays glittered with turmoil. He parked a fist on his thigh. Two feet and an ocean of doubt separated us. I suspected he was keeping something from me.

We were going around in circles. Hiding things from each other. Unable to seek peace without truth. It would be hypocritical to demand that Tate cough up his secret without offering mine, and yet...

I planned on doing exactly that.

Because my secret might end us.

It shouldn't, but it might.

"I don't believe it. I don't believe, for a second, that Kellan left you nothing. I think you're keeping something from me."

Tate's mouth pressed in a tight line. I bit the inside of my cheek, waiting. Just when I thought he'd dropped the subject, he spoke. "The night he died, Kel left me a voicemail."

It took a beat for his words to sink in, but when they did, I found myself slipping off Uranus. My arms found purchase around the orb. Tate offered a hand, which I took just to touch him.

"What..." I dusted myself off and cleared the shakiness out of my voice, only half succeeding. "What did he say?"

I didn't dare sit. I didn't dare *move*.

"I don't know."

Translation: I've never listened to it.

It took a special kind of willpower to have in your possession the parting words from someone you loved and wanted, more than anything, to see again and not listen to them. I had lasted about a second before I tore open Kellan's letter, forcing myself to wait until I reached the roof to read it.

It's not willpower, I realized. *It's fear.*

I almost offered to listen to the voicemail for him, but I was afraid he'd say yes. Instead, I made my way to the jungle gym, climbed the steps, and sat by the opening for the sliding pole, legs dangling over the ledge.

"I don't know what's in the voicemail, Tate, but I do know what is in *Darling Venom.*" I kicked at the pole, the bottom of my Chucks scuffing it. "A roadmap. There isn't a map key or labels or even borders, but the highways, landmarks, and roads are there. If you read between the lines, you'll see the message."

"Which is?"

"That we couldn't have stopped it. I think, if Kellan knew what his suicide would do to the people he loved, he wouldn't have done it." If I sounded certain, it was because I was. Some things you just knew. With your gut. With your head. With your heart. I looped an arm around the railing, resting my head on the cool metal. "I think he genuinely thought *Darling Venom* would be enough for us to absolve ourselves of guilt. He didn't bank on Leah not giving me the letter or the sheer level of self-loathing you possess."

Tate didn't correct my assertions. What could he say? I don't hate myself? *Yeah, and pigs fly, the Earth is flat, and JFK is the Illuminati's headquarters.*

Our gazes collided. My heart galloped with every step he took toward me. I didn't expect him to answer, so I asked the question that plagued my mind every day. "Are you doing okay, Tate?"

He paused mid-step. "I'm fine."

"It's a universally known fact that 'I'm fine' is the only phrase in the English language with indefinite meanings. I'm not okay. I'm okay. I'm sad. I'm happy. I can't do this anymore. I'll be okay. I'm lost." I paused, emphasizing, "Please, help me."

"Maybe it just means I'm fine."

"Does it?"

"No."

It volleyed between us. The inconvenient truth. Large and demanding. Only, we treated it like it was fragile. Bubble-wrapped it, then locked it in a vault. I braced myself for what came next. The only thing that could follow up his confession.

"I never asked you why you were on the roof the first time you and Kel met."

I swallowed, looking away. He didn't press me to answer, but I felt his presence all around me. I felt *him*. Instead of suffocating me, it enveloped me like a hug. When I returned my gaze to him, he looked serious. More serious than I'd ever seen him.

Tate squeezed into the space between the pole and me. The tight fit pressed us flush together. With my body propped on the jungle gym, he stood just above eye level with me. His fingers met my chin, forcing me to meet his blue-grays. An inferno raged inside them.

He looked me straight in the eyes, unwavering. "You're breathing, Charlie. You are breathing, and it is beautiful, and I am so grateful for that."

It might've been better than the L-word.

My heart threatened to break out of its cage and tackle Tate if I didn't touch him right now. His lips descended on mine, and just like that, I felt like I was living again.

I wondered when Tate's kisses had gone from stealing my breaths to giving them back. I clutched the lapels of his suit, drawing him nearer. Greedy for everything he could give me and more.

I wished I could lock this moment in a time capsule, bury it deep where it was safe, and return to it the inevitable moment we ended. At least then, I'd have something beautiful to remember our love by.

His lips grazed my temple. "The world is better with you in it, Charlie."

And I believed him.

Neither of us was okay, but we had each other. I was healing, day by day, and I'd drag him with me. No matter what it took. Tate Marchetti purged the loneliness from me. He cured me.

I grinned. "You really are a doctor."

"Last I checked." He raised a brow, dipping down for another kiss.

My phone buzzed in my pocket. I fished it out. The screen flashed with a message from Leah.

Leah: Where are you?! I got up to get water and didn't see you.

Leah: It's three in the morning! Who are you and what have you done to my sister?! [Princess Diaries Eyebrows GIF]

I did the math. My bedroom was not the kitchen, and I left the door closed, which meant Leah actively checked in on me. It felt like I'd escaped my body and drifted to another plane where happiness existed. Where Leah Richards loved me and Tate Marchetti showered me with midnight kisses on a meadow of planets.

Me: On my way home. See you in ten. [I'm Horny Workout GIF]

I waved my phone. "Leah texted, wanting to know where I am. I think that's my cue to leave."

"God help me, we really are teenagers, aren't we?" He groaned.

I tossed my hair behind my back. "Race you to the park's gate."

Hopping off the jungle gym, I flushed as I brushed down Tate's body. His arm looped around my waist and deposited me on solid ground.

"Hi, Charlie."

"Hi, Tate."

I edged back and claimed his hand. Like always, Tate walked me to the apartment, stopping just shy of the top step to the third floor. I pushed past that invisible barrier he never broke, but he spun me and pressed his mouth to mine.

He pulled away. "Now, you can go."

"Such a tease."

I made my way to my place, unable to wipe the stupid grin off my face. I pushed the door open, moved through the threshold, and poked my head out to look at Tate one last time. He was still staring at me.

"Oh, and Tate? I love you."

I fled before I could see his reaction, closing the door behind me and not looking back.

Chapter Seventy-Five

Tate

There were a million and one reasons not to ride the subway.

The smells.

The grime.

The inability to find a goddamn seat.

And on the wild stroke of luck that you did, the 99.99% chance of someone's ass landing on your face.

But today's reason came in the form of a digital billboard with Kellan's name on it. It smacked me in the face on my way out of the station. Not literally, but might as well have.

There were twelve of them. They stretched the wall from where I stood at the service booth all the way to the staircase I needed to climb to escape this hellscape. Lit up like a wildfire. Taking up just as much oxygen, too.

Fuck, it was getting hard to breathe.

Not like I didn't put in an effort to ignore it. The universe made it impossible. Every time I tried to veer left to place some distance between the boards and me, half of Manhattan jostled me back like a human pinball.

I found myself staring.

At the cover.

At his name.

At the praises that littered each poster from people who sounded important.

"*A celebration of two lost souls finding each other. Peppered with social commentary on love, loss, and the state of society, Marchetti's words present a convincing case for making bad choices and enjoying them.*" — The New York Examiner

"*Kellan Marchetti is Holden Caulfield, if Caulfield were to fall in wild, unrestrained love. This book became my lover, one I never wanted to be without again. Each page left me desperate for more.*" — L.T. Moon, New York Times *Bestselling Author*

"*Darling Venom reminds me why I read.*" — Publishers Daily

By the time I made it to my brownstone, I couldn't pinpoint why an anchor had settled in my stomach. Doubt. Regret. Nostalgia. All the above? If the ads were to be believed, people loved the book, which should've made me happy. All it did was pummel the reminder into me that Kel wasn't around to witness it.

And that's what you get for trying to save the planet. You bought a car for a fucking reason. Use it.

The idea to burn the world down before it had the opportunity to burn me seized my mind. I slammed the front door, ending the fantasy before I could draw up a blueprint.

Charlie sat on the couch, her laptop balanced on her knee. When she caught sight of me through the slot connecting the kitchen and living room, she slipped her earbuds out, closed the screen, and approached me.

We met at the center, where the ends of both rooms kissed.

I cleared my throat. "I saw ads for *Darling Venom* when I got out of my stop in the subway."

"They're amazing, aren't they?" She stood on her tiptoes, pressing her lips to the column of my throat because she could. "Someone at Kirkus said they haven't enjoyed a book that much since Viet Thanh Nguyen's *The Sympathizer*."

"Never read it."

"'Course you haven't." Her brow arched. "I never took you as the subway type."

"My Lexus is getting a tire change, and I made the mistake of passing up on a cab."

She kissed my Adam's apple and stepped back, just as footsteps thundered into the hallway above us.

Terry materialized at the base of the staircase with a packed bag and the handle of his typewriter case clutched in his other fist. He looped the duffel around his shoulder and turned to Charlie. "See you in a few days, Miss Richards."

I eyed his get-up, noting the slicked-back hair and a scent I'd never smelled on him before. Soap. "Aren't you supposed to be working on Kellan's manuscript like you promised Charlie?"

"This a new addendum to the terms of my stay?" He waited for me to answer.

I didn't. Neither did Charlie.

"Well, then." He tipped an imaginary cap to me. "I'll be going now. I hope that's okay with you, officer."

Charlie nodded toward his bag. "Where are you going?"

"A writer's conference."

I narrowed my eyes. "Which one?"

"Why?" He sent me a wink. "You worried 'bout me?"

"Worried about *them*. It might be my moral duty to call them up and warn the attendees to keep their eyes peeled for you and your favorite ten-finger discount."

Charlie elbowed my ribs. Or tried to. With our height difference, it landed right in the gut. I rubbed at my side. Terry left with a two-fingered salute that turned into one finger—the middle one—when Charlie turned her back to us, drifting toward the kitchen.

It occurred to me that he might've done this on purpose. Given Charlie and me alone time. But it also occurred to me that moments of civility between us were less likely than a serial killer finding Jesus.

When I turned, Charlie held a glass of water to her lips, smiling over the rim.

I popped a brow. "Yes?"

"Humans are so weird." She didn't elaborate.

I watched, feeling a little strung-out as she took sip after sip, marinating us in silence. "Spit it out, Charlie."

She laughed and set the cup down onto the counter.

"Kellan villainized you. You villainize Terry. What's the point? Where did it get him? Where does it get you?" She stalked toward me. "We either lionize or villainize the people who most impact our lives. There isn't an in between. A gray area that allows for complexity. For accountability without cancelation. For healing without rage. The gray holds the truth, but we only see black and white."

"What are you saying?"

"Make up with your father, Tate."

"I don't have a father."

"Oh? How were you born? Immaculate conception?"

"Must've been found with the storks." I flashed her a smile.

"That smile..." She groaned. "It eviscerates my train of thought."

We settled into silence. She pinned me with her full attention, waiting. Just waiting. Something had changed between us, but it happened so slow. Like water leaking from a faucet, drop by drop. Next thing you know, you're hit with a utility bill you can't afford.

"I'll think about it," I finally relented, remembering what I'd overhead Terry say. That he existed to give me something to hate. To blame.

"Please, do."

403

"That's not a promise," I warned.

"I know."

The words held too much optimism, and like a dick, I wanted to extinguish it for the sake of my sanity. I didn't, however. A decision I chalked up to the smile that swept over her face.

Tatum Marchetti, you are so damn screwed.

We ended up in the kitchen with a stack of takeout menus before us.

"I love you," Charlie said casually. So fucking casually, it took a second to register.

I was getting used to hearing it. Worse, I liked it. Craved it, even.

She plopped down on the barstool, picked up the menu for yakitori, and turned it over, studying the back. "Any suggestions?"

"Yeah." I tapped her temple. "Some ginkgo for your brain. You already said you love me."

Again. And again. And again.

But there was an itch in my chest that only those words were able to scratch. I tried to figure out what was different between Charlie and Hannah that made me only want to hear Charlie utter the three-word phrase. Why couldn't I go for the more appropriate relationship? The one without the age gap? The one that didn't make me feel like I needed to do fifty Hail Marys a night to avoid an eternity in Hell?

The answer was obvious. The odd taste in music, clothes, and people. The way she brought books to her nose and inhaled as if they offered their secrets to her when she got close enough. Her laughter that was rare but wicked and racked her whole frame with its intensity. Whatever made her the only person at St. Paul's to befriend my weird kid brother, who wore kilts and fishnet gloves and frowns.

It was everything. Just... *her*. Charlie.

Sweet, loving Charlie.

At any given second, Charlotte Richards stared at me like she was ten seconds away from offering to burn herself to keep me warm.

And like a bastard, I lit the match.

Chapter Seventy-Six

Tate

Charlie's theory—that I would get used to being told I love you and actually like it—was spot-on. No other explanation existed for why I found myself doing things I promised I'd never do.

This time, I let her enter my room. My space. My bed. A few hours after we finished the takeout, she dove onto my sheets, landing on her back, eyes closed. I took a moment to watch her.

Here.

In the only place in my world that felt untouched by life's bullshit.

She wore a dress that would've been at home in Wednesday Addams' closet—black with a white collar, stopping halfway down her thighs. Her bare legs stretched before me. Long and pale and tempting.

I wanted to flip the slip of fabric over and bury myself inside her. I held back, joining her on my mattress but staying on my half of it.

Her chest rose and fell. "Leah is sleeping over at Jonah's."

"Good for her."

She peeked an eye open. "You were drunk when I told you this, so I'll say it again—I know you went to see her." I cursed. "I'm not mad," she added. "I'm grateful."

Maybe it was her ability to forgive, or the fact that she saw me in a better light than I saw myself. Either way, it might've been the last thing to snap my remaining thread of decency. All I wanted now was to sink into her. She turned onto her side. My eyes snapped down to her round ass.

She peered over her shoulder. A devilish grin snuck onto her face. "Caught you."

"Don't give a fuck." I gripped her hip, just above the place where her ass began to curve. If she gave me the green light, I'd sink my teeth there, too.

She returned to her back. My hand shifted with her, coming to her upper thigh, dangerously close to a piece of her I'd been dying to explore. I told my dick to calm the hell down, but I kept my hand where it was. We both lay there, above the sheets, staring at the parts of each other we wanted to touch. Eventually, she grabbed us ice cream while I dumped my shirt in the hamper and changed into sweats. I turned in time to see her settle into my bed with a tub of mint chip. She offered me a spoon, eyes lingering on my bare chest.

I shook my head, snorting. "I would gargle mouthwash if I wanted that taste in my mouth."

"Mint chip does not taste like mouthwash."

"Sure it doesn't."

I watched her shovel spoon after spoon of ice cream past her lips.

"Have you read Paul Beatty's *The Sellout?*" She set the finished pint onto the nightstand and waited for my answer, continuing when it became clear I wouldn't give one. "Right. You don't read."

"That's what you're here for."

"Really? I thought it was for this." She leaned over and licked below my navel, tracing a trail to my sweats.

Before she could pull back, I looped an arm around her waist and tugged her on top of me, invading her mouth with my tongue. Her hands went to my biceps. She used them for leverage, grinding herself against my thigh.

"Please, Tate." Her pleas danced around us.

I wouldn't entertain them, but I didn't want them to stop, either. I'd get us both off, taking this as far as last time, but no farther.

406

I knew she would ask more of me, so I lifted the skirt of her dress and pressed the hem to her lips. "Bite down."

She complied. With the bottom half of her dress pulled up, I got a front-row view of Charlotte Richards in a black lace thong, her curves almost sinful.

"I'm going to ask you a series of questions. Don't release the dress. Understood?"

She nodded.

"Do you want my fingers in your pussy or your ass?"

"Tate!"

I caught the hem, tsking. "You released the dress."

"That was a test?"

"And you failed it." I arched an eyebrow. "I thought you were an A-student."

As if to shut me up, her hand slipped past the waistband of my sweats and palmed my hard-on. It pulsed against her. She still had mint chip on the corner of her lips. I swiped the ice cream along her lower lip and tugged down, parting her mouth. Her tongue darted out and teased my skin. Then she leaned forward and sucked the tip of my thumb.

"Fuck," I cursed. Pushed it all the way past her lips. Imagined my dick in its stead.

Her fingers flew to my base. I lifted her off me. She watched through hooded eyes as I tore off my sweats and boxer briefs in one move and lay back down. Charlie climbed on top of me again, resuming our earlier position. I tucked the bottom of her dress back between her teeth, stealing a peek at her thong. Her wetness could be seen from satellites. She was that fucking hot for this.

"Let's try again. Rub your clit against my thigh."

Her nails dug into my chest, finding purchase as she see-sawed back and forth, grinding herself on my leg.

"Would you like me to pinch your nipple or your clit? Nod for nipple. Shake for clit."

She shook her head. I reached forward, slid her thong to the side, and dove past her lips, pinching the slick bud. The fabric in her mouth muffled her moans.

"A-plus."

She rolled her eyes, teeth still clamped around the dress' edge.

"Would you like me to watch you get yourself off? Or would you like to watch *me* jerk off?"

Charlie shook her head. Then nodded.

I forced back a laugh. "Don't be greedy. Nod for you. Shake for me."

She nodded, and fuck, I was so down for this. My cock pulsed like it had a heart of its own. It pressed against her ass. She wiggled against it, looking pleased with herself. I wanted to cave. To take this all the way. To make her come around my cock, not her fingers. But I also knew the second I did, she'd whisper the same three words she loved to tell me, and I'd crumble. Lose all control.

She repositioned herself so she was closer, on my abs this time, giving me a better view. Her fingers went to her slit, disappearing into the folds. *Fuck. Me.* She was so wet, I felt her all over my stomach. Her fingertips grazed her clit. She rocked on top of me, chasing a high I wanted to join. Her legs tightened against my sides as she rubbed furiously, moaning into the hem of her dress. Even though I knew it was asking for trouble, I toyed with her zipper, tugging. Charlie released the fabric from her teeth, and the dress pooled around her waist. She straightened, slipped it over her head, and tossed it behind her. Her bra and panties came off next, discarded on the floor across the room. Then her thighs returned to bracketing my hips, her fingers pumping in and out of her pussy.

My dick bobbed against her ass, obliterating the last of my willpower.

"Charlie." I groaned.

She rolled her hips, quaking on top of me. "Just the tip," she bargained, and never in the history of Planet Fucking Earth has it ever been just the tip.

"I don't have a condom."

"No way."

"Seriously."

Contrary to what the way we met suggested, I didn't sleep around, nor did I have sex often. Didn't find it enjoyable. Or life, in general. Though Charlie seemed to defy both these preferences.

"Well, as my doctor—"

"Former doctor," I corrected. "If even."

"—you know I'm on the pill. And that I'm clean." She popped a brow. "Are you clean?"

"Charlie, no."

"You're not?"

"No, we're not doing this," I clarified.

"So, you *are* clean."

"Yes, but it doesn't matter, since we're not doing this."

"Just the tip."

I shook my head, but it somehow shifted into a nod, and what the fuck was I doing? Her grin did things to me I'd never admit. She moved back, her pussy gliding along my rigid cock.

"Just the tip," I warned, lining us up.

The head of my cock slipped past her folds for a moment. A fucking flash, I swear. But her body arched into mine. And that was it. The last straw. I flipped her onto her back and positioned myself at her entrance.

My eyes trailed a path up her body, past her tits, along the curve of her neck, over her lips, to those seafoam eyes. "Look at you, Charlie. I never stood a fucking chance."

And then I pushed inside her. Her walls clamped around me in a vise grip. I'd broken her during my exam, but she was still a virgin and, therefore, so fucking tight, I almost came at first contact like a goddamn teenager.

"Tate." Her hands gripped my biceps. "Move."

"Give me a sec." My head dropped to her shoulder, burrowing into her neck. I ran my tongue along the curve and—finally, fucking *finally*— moved deeper inside her.

She met each of my thrusts like she feared I wouldn't be inside her again, her hips coming at me with so much energy, I hit the back of her pussy each time. "More," she begged. "Faster."

I obeyed, giving her everything she asked for, except the words I could never say. She clung to me. Her nails sank into my shoulder as her walls clenched around me.

"Fuck," I muttered against her skin, too close to coming.

My hand reached between us, fingers rubbing her clit in circles. She chanted my name again and again, like a prayer. Like an answer. Like she loved me. Her hand drifted to the nape of my neck. I grabbed it, brought her wrist to my lips, and kissed the scar there.

"Tate."

I moved my lips to her ear, whispering, "Come, Charlie."

She fell apart around me, nails breaking skin, walls tightening. I followed after her with a growl and collapsed onto her before rolling onto my back. She rested her head on my chest, tracing a path in the center. "I love you."

I parted my lips. She zeroed in on them, something like hope burgeoning in her eyes. But then I closed them again, and she deflated like a popped balloon. A tear slipped down her cheek and pooled onto my chest. It was almost enough to tell her. It was the truth, after all. But I couldn't bring myself to. Instead, we sat in silence, marinating in our thoughts.

At midnight, Charlie checked the time and got up to leave like she was Cinderella, had a curfew, and feared her carriage would pop back into a pumpkin any second. I leaned against my headboard, watching her dress. Her eyes were bloodshot, though she'd only shed one tear. I felt like a dickwad. And still, I didn't tell her what we both wanted me to say.

Instead, I followed her hands as they hooked her bra back on. "Will you be okay alone?"

"I've officially been an adult for four years, Tate." She pretended to count, wiggling four fingers and following it up with a smile I wanted to kiss off her face. "I think I can survive another night."

"I'll drive you home."

Fully clothed now, she stopped at my door, turned to face me, and waved her phone. "I already ordered an Uber."

"Cancel."

"It's a ride share."

"The only ride you participated in tonight was on my dick."

She stared down at the lock screen, glancing up. "Cameron is here."

Cameron could go fuck himself.

"Charlie."

"Tate." She smiled. Strode to me. Pressed her lips to mine. Took something from me each time she did. "I'll see you tomorrow."

I said nothing for a moment. Just stared at her, hoping the longer I drew this out, the greater the chance Cameron, the douche outside, would take off. She knew what I was doing. Her head shook. A smile ghosted her lips.

"I can't hold up the ride share, Tate." She raised a brow, bringing my attention back to her eyes. Still red-rimmed. I was the douche here. Not Cameron. And certainly not her. "It's an asshole move," she finished.

"Fine. Text me when you get home."

"I will."

And then she left.

I leaned back, staring at the ceiling. Alone this time. If this were a racetrack, I'd be on the last leg. Careening toward the finish line. If I told Charlie what she wanted to hear, there'd be no turning back. Once the floodgates opened, they wouldn't close. What else would I end up feeling? How much more pain could I handle?

You're an asshole, Tate Marchetti. And your brother can no longer be your crutch. Your excuse.

The words sat on the tip of my tongue. All three. Short and unassuming. I toyed with them, trying to bring myself to conjure them aloud for the first time. To convince myself their weight would lift with the release. That they would be easy to say without an audience to hear.

In the end, I said nothing.

411

Chapter Seventy-Seven

Tate

The house felt haunted without Charlie here.

Too silent.

Too cold.

Too lonely.

I heard her Uber take off. I lasted a few minutes before I hopped off my bed and cracked my blinds open, catching the mist on the glass. It would rain soon.

And that was enough for me to justify grabbing my coat and sliding into my Lexus, hightailing it to Morris Heights.

I made it there before her ride share. The skyscraper of steps leading to her street gave me more than enough time to question my sanity. I trekked to her building and spent the next twenty minutes under the rain before I realized I'd forgotten to grab an umbrella in my rush here.

There went my excuse for showing up.

You've lost your damn mind, Tate.

By the time Cameron The Asshat pulled to the curb, there wasn't a dry spot left on me. Charlie hopped out of the Yukon and slowed in front of me, eyes dragging a path down my sopping-wet body. "Tate. What are you doing here?"

"It's raining," I said as if it explained everything.

God, I needed to get it together.

I raked my fingers through my hair, flinging fat drops down my back, admitting, "I don't know."

I might've laughed. Probably. I felt unhinged. Out of my mind. Past a point of return. Whatever we were, I liked it. I wanted to hold on to this, but I didn't feel capable.

Not without ruining us both.

The sound of rain hitting surfaces filled the silence. It pounded on the pavement.

The cars.

Us.

So much rain, I could barely see her.

Probably for the best. As it was, I could make out the traces of anticipation on her face. I had no intention of telling her I love her.

Not today.

Not ever.

And still, I showed up. It was a special kind of cruel to string her along like this. I knew it, but I couldn't help myself.

You're no better than Terry.

Charlie sighed and approached me until we stood toe to toe. Her fingertips brushed my cheek, pulling back upon contact. "You're freezing."

"I can't feel my hands."

She reached into my pockets, pulled out my palms, and brought them to her lips, blowing hot air onto the frozen flesh. We were both soaking wet now, racing toward a cold.

The doctor in me knew this was a horrible idea, and the (dwindling) conscience in me agreed, but I couldn't relay that to my feet. They stood still.

Was I betraying them, or were they betraying me?

"Let's go inside." She dropped one of my hands, using the other to yank me toward the door to her complex.

Finally—fucking finally—my feet moved.

In the wrong direction.

One step.

And another.

I followed her up the stairs, the only sound the squishy thuds of our wet shoes. She brought a finger to her lips. I stopped in the hall between her door and her neighbor's.

The one she'd mentioned wanted her sister.

"They're probably already in Jonah's bedroom." Charlie waggled her brows, unable to stop the smile on her face as she thrust her key into the lock and twisted.

I held the door open for her. We both piled inside, kicking our heavy shoes off. She held my hand, tugging me along like a leashed dog. And I followed her. My proverbial tail wagged so hard, I felt particularly pathetic in this moment.

She brought me into the bathroom. We tumbled into the shower with our clothes still on. My fingers fumbled with the spigot until ice-cold spikes pelted us. I spun her, covering her body from the arctic water until the torrent turned hot.

I don't know who moved first.

Our lips collided, teeth clashing.

I gripped her hair, tilting her head up to meet mine. She pawed at my body. My chest. My clothes.

I let her tear everything off me, picked her up, and pressed her against the tiled wall, slowing our kisses. Savoring the taste of her.

This time, when I sank inside Charlie, it was tender.

Soft.

Slow.

And this time, I said the words.

In my head.

Where the demons feasted on my weaknesses and told me I didn't deserve her.

Chapter Seventy-Eight

Tate

"Penny for your thoughts?" Terry swaggered into the kitchen. Something landed on my lap.

Not a penny.

A poker chip. Warm from Terry's palm.

I lifted it, studying the engraving.

To thine own self be true.

Fake gold rimmed the green token. The words "unity", "service", and "recovery" arched along the border. A big two stamped the center.

Two months.

Terry had been sober for two months. I wasn't sure how to take this, or whether I believed the currency beyond its prop value.

"That's what the cool kids say these days, right?" he followed up. "Saw little Miss Richards flipping pennies around the house."

My fingers toyed with the smooth edges of the chip before I tossed it back at him. It bounced off his chest and landed in his open palm. I don't think I'd ever seen Terry with enough hand-eye coordination to tie his shoes, let alone catch a coin mid-fall.

"Well?" Terry settled onto the barstool beside me and slid the token across the counter. It slowed inches from my cereal bowl. "I gave you one hell of a penny. Now give me one of your thoughts."

I ignored his words and the chip, swiveling my seat until I faced him. He'd combed his hair. Cut it, too.

A thick layer of gel slicked the strands back, pressed tight to his scalp. The salt-and-pepper bristles that once covered his cheeks and chin were no longer there.

He wore a clean t-shirt that didn't look like something you'd find in a dumpster outside your local Goodwill. In fact, put him in a lineup with a dozen aging nine-to-fivers, and he'd fit right in.

Weird shit.

"You've really been sober." I didn't feel as much of a fool as I thought I would after saying it.

"Unfortunately."

"Why?"

"Terms and conditions of my stay."

I believed that like I believed the Old New World Order theory. "Give me the real reason."

I downed half my glass of water and bit into an ice cube, crushing it into dust between my molars. I don't know what I was waiting for.

For me to hate him more? Less? For an opportunity to let him know I'd heard his words that night to Charlie? That I knew he had suicidal thoughts and stayed alive for my sake?

Maybe I wanted to offer him my permission to die.

My head throbbed. I contemplated retreating to my room before he could worsen it, but I decided his sobriety merited my attention. Hippocratic Oath and all.

At the very least, I wanted an answer.

Naturally, he didn't give me one. His knuckles rapped the laminate countertop, then found purchase on the peeling edge. He picked at the coating. I didn't stop him. This place needed a gut job, anyway.

"I saw *Darling Venom* before." His fingers pinched the laminate, husking it off the substrate. "Got tempted."

"When?"

"Must've been six years ago." He paused. "I was drunk."

"'Course you were."

"Yeah. Of course, I was." He shook his head, laughing. "Dad of the year, right?"

If this is good parenting, I don't want to see bad parenting.

I bit my tongue, remembering Charlie's words. Healing without rage, she'd said. Not sure if I was capable. But if I couldn't give her the other thing she wanted, I could at least try to give her this.

"Have you read *Darling Venom*?" Terry tore a chunk of laminate clean off the counter.

I wanted to be that scrap. Free of all the ugly dead weight. He flicked it to the hardwood. It sailed away from us, zigzagging to the mahogany planks like a floating feather.

I ripped my eyes away from it. "No, and I have no plans to."

"It's a damn good book."

I set my glass down and watched the ice cubes rattle against the walls. "So is *The Imperfections*, I hear. Be sure to congratulate the real author on my behalf."

I considered rubbing my deadbeat father's long list of failures in his face a favorite hobby. But this time, a bitter taste spread across my tongue. Copper, actually. I'd bitten it.

Fuck.

The least I can do is be alive for him to hate.

Terry's words haunted me. A poltergeist I couldn't exorcise. I sealed my lips together, wary that nonsense would spill out if I gave my mouth free rein.

He scratched his temple, releasing a bitter laugh. "Guess I deserved that." He swung in his stool to face me. "You should read *Darling Venom*. Might do you some good. At the very least, I think Kel wanted you to."

"Maybe," I said to shut him up. I still had no intention of subjecting myself to that mental torture on top of my daily overdose.

He eyed the chip in front of me, opening and closing his mouth

Finally, he spoke. "I've been seeing things clearer lately. The past, mostly." He ran a palm along his jaw. "It's long overdue."

"See anything good?"

"Yeah."

I stilled.

Held my breath.

Waited for him to continue.

"Some of it was good. But most of it..." He shook his head. "It's too late. The shit we can't change changes us. I've fought it as long as I could, but this is a cage I deserve to be in. A prison of my own making."

I saw it for what it was.

The real reason he was sober.

He considered it punishment for his sins. Hearing this didn't make me happy like I thought it would.

Fuck.

I finally realized what I was waiting for. It wasn't to hate him more. Or to give him my permission to die. It was much, much worse. I wanted him to live. To forget about my feelings and exist without misery. To relieve me of the burden of dragging another life down with me.

Terry stood, gathered his coat over the crook of his elbow, and pushed his chair in. Civilized behavior. So unlike him. It was hard to reconcile the man in front of me with the one who showed up on my front step, drunk and drugged, with a sullen Kellan in tow.

"Wait." I latched onto the chip, turned it over in my hand so the two side faced up, and offered it to Terry.

He shook his head. "It's yours. I'll keep the next."

The next.

He planned on staying sober. And for the first time, I believed him.

"Don't live," I told him once his hand hit the handle to my front door, his back still to me, "to give me something to hate. Live for yourself."

One of us needed to.

Chapter Seventy-Nine

Charlotte

I stood in the empty elevator, fixed on the books in my arms. Reagan had gifted me three copies of *Darling Venom* early, printing them herself with Helen's permission. One for me. One for Terry. One for Tate.

When the metal doors split, I entered the revolving door and went an extra round, contemplating where Terry would be. I knew of two possible places. Exit left for Old Town Bar. (Leave it to Terry to surround himself with booze while attempting sobriety. He called it people-watching; I called it unnecessary temptation.) Exit right for St. Francis de Sales Cathedral near Loeb Boathouse.

Last week, I bumped into him in front of its pointed tympanum on my way home from the Society Library next door. Terry attended AA meetings in the church's thumb-shaped basement. According to him, no matter where he sat, the thumb pointed down.

Another rotation, and I made my decision. I hid the books inside my coat and slipped through the door wing, dipping right. Thumbs-down it was.

I bet wrong. St. Francis' basement was empty when I entered, save for a lone priest. He slapped the lap of a folding chair. It snapped together, pretzeling into a thin rectangle. Tucking it beneath his arm, he glanced up at me. "Can I help you, ma'am?"

"Is there an AA meeting here?"

"It ended an hour ago. The next one starts tomorrow morning at seven. There'll be donuts."

I left the basement. (Definitely thumb-shaped, by the way. And pointed down. Not sure how anyone could heal in such a depressing environment.) Climbing the last steps, I adjusted the books beneath my coat and hugged them through the thick fabric. A nun passed me, did a double take at my bundle, and side-eyed me as if I were hiding contraband inside it. I strode to the cathedral's entrance, dodged a signicade that read *sugar-free sacramental wine available upon request*, and burst onto the busy sidewalk. Since I was here, might as well stop by the Society Library.

I greeted Doris and Faye on my way to the stacks, stopping at a quiet corner with some of my favorite books. I found Terry sitting at a table, hunched over Danez Smith's *Don't Call Us Dead*. He cradled it between both palms as if it were a book of hymn. I cleared my throat.

Terry flattened the corner of a page some heathen had dog-eared, without glancing up. "How'd you find me here?"

"There aren't many places to roam for free. You traded one vice for another. At least this one's not destructive."

"Destructive in a different way," he corrected and shut his book. "Now that we've established I'm broke, jobless, and an addict, what do you want?"

"I come bearing gifts. Gift, actually. Singular." I set the hardcover onto the wooden table.

Terry yawned, peering down at the book. His jaw snapped shut. He bit his tongue, but I knew that wasn't the reason for the tears forming. He stroked the hardcover with a single finger, then proceeded to rip off the shrink wrap in one go, flinging it behind him. He was crying now. Full-on bawling. The sound echoed around the room, filling the corridors between shelves, bouncing off books I knew and loved. I didn't stop him. I didn't say anything. Instead, I placed a hand on his shaking shoulder as he clutched his son's book—his son's soul—to his chest.

Tears are the language of grief. And grief is the language of love.

Chapter Eighty

Charlotte

Thanks to a two-hour stint babysitting Row, I made it to Tate's late. The sun had long-since vanished. He'd be home soon, so I raced to his room, a blueprint tube hooked over my shoulder. It contained three giant posters with the same passage from *Darling Venom*.

Blown up.

Impossible to ignore.

I needed to hang them somewhere Tate couldn't look away from. He could pass a wall without a glance. But his ceiling? I stared at the spot above his mattress. Unless he wanted to suffocate, he would sleep on his side or back.

After setting a copy of *Darling Venom* on the nightstand, I bracketed the bed with posters. One on the left wall. One on the right. One on the ceiling. I hobbled onto his duvet, standing on my tiptoes. An empty trash basket stretched above my head, upside down, its base smoothing out the poster.

"I'd like to report a break-in."

I froze.

The trashcan tumbled to the sheets.

Tate stood at the door, propped against the frame, his phone pressed against the opposite ear. His eyes struck me like two sharpened arrows. Amusement danced behind them.

A smile crept up my face. I played along and kneeled on his duvet, thrusting out my joined wrists. "Ask the cops if they have fuzzy cuffs. I've always wanted to try them."

He stalked forward, grabbed my hands, and lowered me to the mattress, holding them above my head. I wrapped my leg around his back. He didn't bother removing my dress before he entered me, lips meeting mine, hand dipping to my clit. His thrusts were rough. Deep. Fast.

I came first, pulsing around him. When he finished, he collapsed beside me, staring at the ceiling. "Furnishing my place now?" He tilted his head, voice carrying an edge of humor. "Interesting choice of décor."

"Took you a while to notice."

"You distracted me." Flipping onto his side, he walked his fingers down my leg and traced lazy circles on my inner thigh, staring past me. "You surrounded my bed with them like a prayer circle."

"I have a habit of being thorough."

"Are they the same?"

"Yeah." I paused. "It's a passage from *Darling Venom*."

His fingertips stilled. "Charlie."

I couldn't gauge his tone. I knew what it wasn't—guttural, warning, broken. But that didn't get me very far.

"Are you mad?"

"I'm never mad at you, Charlie." It rolled off his tongue in a whisper.

"You make it sound like that's a bad thing."

He didn't answer. Just kissed my nose, strode to the en-suite bathroom, and switched the sink on. I followed, accepting the wet napkin he handed me. We cleaned ourselves and straightened our clothes. His arms traveled to the vanity, trapping me against it. A tie dangled around his neck like a noose.

I took in the tufts of hair sticking out in different directions. "Long day?"

"Better now."

"Want to talk about it?"

"IVF failed on a patient. Again. She turns forty-nine next week. Her reproductive endocrinologist advised her to stop. She came to me for a second opinion."

"You're not a fertility specialist."

"No, but I'm her gynecologist and an obstetrician that specializes in high-risk pregnancies, so she trusts me." He tangled his fingers in my hair, lips drifting to my shoulder. "I didn't tell her what she wanted to hear. She shattered in front of me, Charlie. Said she will never forgive herself for not trying sooner."

"Opportunity lasts a moment. Regret lasts a lifetime. It's something my mom used to say."

"You don't talk about her often."

"No, but I think about my parents every night." My hands felt restless. I freed Tate from his half-Windsor and dropped the dotted tie to the tiles. "I lost everything in the fire, so there's nothing physical to remember them by. All I have is a barrette and what's in here." I tapped my temple. "I'm scared that, one day, I'll forget what they looked like. So, I take the time to replay my favorite memories with them before I sleep."

His lips ghosted over the spot I'd touched. "You can share the memories with me. Consider me your personal cloud."

That implied a future together. It was the first hint of commitment he'd ever given me. Cruel hope scorched me. We'd reached an addictive level of domesticity. I planned on squeezing as much out of him as I could. Dinner. A date. Promises.

Anything to latch on to.

"Oh, yeah? How's your memory?"

"What was the question again?"

Laughter bubbled up my throat. "You're the one that needs ginkgo." I followed him back to the room. "I left a copy of *Darling Venom* on your nightstand."

His eyes lingered on it. "Thanks."

"You don't sound thankful."

"I don't read. That's what you're here for. Remember?"

"You won't suddenly catch the writer's bug if you read one book. Somehow, I highly doubt you're liable for a mid-life career change."

"Mid-life? I'm in my mid-*thirties*."

I scrunched my nose. "Positively geriatric."

"I'll remember that when you reach the big three-oh." The words came out casually, but holy crap, they implied we'd be something to each other eight years from now. He listened to my stomach grumble. "Have you eaten?"

"Nope. Wanna grab some food? I know a place that makes a mean tsukemen."

"It's late."

"There are restaurants still open. It's a Friday in New York City."

"Let's order in." He led the way to the kitchen. To the overused takeout menus I'd probably memorize by heart before he ever admitted his intentions.

I deflated, shoulders slumping forward. It would be better if he were mean. If he told me straight-up that I'd get nothing from him. As it was, Tate fed me everything I wanted... except the thing I craved most. Love.

I snatched the pizza menu from him, realizing for the first time that we never went anywhere in public. "You avoid taking me out."

"Not true." I'd spoken without real heat, but he sounded defensive. Too defensive. *Wow.* Did he really avoid taking me out?

I focused on him, cataloging his rigid posture. "Oh? Where have we been?"

"The playground."

"Past midnight."

"The library."

"In the corner, where no one could see."

"The bar."

"You were drunk."

"Don't remind me."

"I'm sensing a pattern here. Prove me wrong. Take me somewhere, Tate. Right now. Anywhere that isn't cloaked in darkness."

"You're pushing for too much," he warned.

Was I? The menu dropped. Slipped from my hand and collided with the floor. I felt stupid. Like a lamb running toward a slaughterhouse. I gave Tate all I could, reaching further even when it drained me. The more I replayed his words, the more pissed I got.

Tate Marchetti would never admit he loved me. Despite everything we'd been through, he would never come around. Never promise me a future. Never give me the unconditional love my parents shared. So many nevers.

I let him walk all over me, and he'd left a deep set of footprints. Well, he could go fuck himself. I was done. Trying to salvage us would be like rearranging deck chairs while the *Titanic* sank. I deserved better than this.

"It's dinner, not a marriage proposal and June wedding," I spat out, bumping his shoulder as I tore past him.

We both went rigid at the contact. I scowled when I heard his exhale, spinning to face him. Slowly, so slowly, Tate turned to me. He managed to look put together. Cold and unflappable. It occurred to me that he might genuinely believe I was overreacting.

Asshole.

He stepped forward.

I matched his stride back.

He stilled. "If you want a marriage proposal and a June wedding, that's fine. But it's not something that'll happen between us, and the faster you sober up, the quicker you understand I'm just a coffee stain in your autobiography, Charlie. Not a chapter. Certainly not the hero. I can't take you out. Can't be seen with you. Cannot love you the way you deserve to be loved." He shook his head, rubbing the nape of his neck. "You grew up with two parents who loved you and a sister who would give her life for yours. I didn't. I have never been good at giving and receiving love."

"That's a cop-out. An excuse." I threw my hands up. "You haven't even tried."

"My mom and I barely talk, Terry is as reliable as spoiled milk, and Kel hated me from the start. The Marchetti men aren't made for healthy relationships. The second we lose control, we spiral. This is the closest I'll ever get, Charlotte."

Charlotte.

We were both panting, standing on opposite ends of the kitchen. Half a dozen worn mahogany planks and an ocean of history separated us. Neither of us dared to cross the unyielding tides and frothing whitecaps.

"Fine." I crossed my arms. "Just so we're clear, I'm saying this for Kellan. I can't stop you from ignoring your brother's book or his voicemail, but I can guilt you over it." I glared at Tate with nearly nine years of pent-up anger. "It is a privilege to have parting gifts from someone you love. For there to be something to latch onto each time you miss him. Read Darling Venom, Tate. Read it even if it feels like your soul is ripping in two. At the end of the day, it is part of your story."

At the door, I stared at Tate one final time. His hands curled into fists by his sides. A knee jerked forward before it straightened again. As if he wanted to come to me but couldn't bring himself to.

He reminded me of a swan. So graceful above water, but beneath the surface, he was paddling like hell to stay afloat.

He will only love me in the dark. He will never love me in daylight.

"Don't go, Charlie."

It was, perhaps, the most vulnerable I'd ever seen him. But it was selfish, and cruel, and not enough. I deserved to receive the love I gave him. I shook my head.

This was goodbye.

"Losing Kellan taught you his worth. I apologize in advance for what losing me will teach you."

Chapter Eighty-One

Tate

Charlie left.

Charlie is gone.

I lost Charlie.

I patted my mouth, my throat, my chest, inventorying my body.

Initial diagnosis: it hurts, but I'll get over the pain.

Chapter Eighty-Two

Tate

Follow-up diagnosis: still hurts like a motherfucker. Operation Forget Charlie kicked off two weeks ago and failed every day since. Here was the weird thing. I knew I'd be okay. That the unsettling, phantom-limb feeling would evaporate with time. It sucked, but it was what it was.

And still. *Still.* Her number tempted me whenever I passed it on my phone. An act of torture that could only be considered intentional, seeing as only one other contact sat in the device, and calling Walter Bernard at three in the morning sounded as appealing as joining *The Bachelor.*

My alarm went off, reminding me I had a job, babies to deliver, a woman I'd no longer see. Not that I'd slept a wink. I glared at the red digital numbers on the clock. When was the last time I'd gotten more than four hours of sleep? Charlotte Richards had exited my life, yet she still managed to be here. In my space. I woke surrounded by the scent of lemons. Of Charlie. (She'd switched the detergent from unscented to citrus a few months ago, and it smelled like her. I could change it, but I didn't.)

A crease marred my forehead from lying facedown. A common occurrence, since I'd changed my habits to accommodate the monstrosity on my ceiling. Not that I couldn't read a mere paragraph. I just knew better than to kick myself while down. Couldn't bring myself to tear down the poster, too.

Terry entered the room without knocking, setting a grease trap on my nightstand. Whatever hid inside the brown brag had leaked through the kraft paper. He nodded at it. "From Mike's."

I stared at the unidentifiable lump. Dark stains littered the sack. Oil spread onto my wood. "Pass. I prefer my arteries unclogged."

Though the idea of death by food had merit. On the scale of miserable deaths, it ranked far lower than getting trampled by an elephant stampede, falling into a sewage tank and drowning in literal shit, and other unpleasant options.

He pulled the cheesesteak from the bag and set it on my duvet, bleeding grease onto the Egyptian cotton. "Eat."

I tore into the sandwich, but only because it saved me the time it would've taken to jog downstairs and consume half a box of expired cereal. (Spoiler alert: it's been a while since I bought groceries, too.) Plus, eating this got Terry out of my hair. Birds, meet stone.

He tipped his head toward the ceiling and clutched his stomach, wheezing out raucous laughter. "Little Miss Richards do that?"

"The one and only."

After I finished, Terry collected the trash (note to self: check the sky for flying pigs later) and headed for the door. He stopped just shy of it, pointing at the poster. "You know, we almost got rid of this passage. That editor lady claimed it impeded the flow of the narrative. Miss Richards fought to keep it."

He left me with that morsel. I jerked the oil-stained covers off the bed and fell onto my back, staring up at the giant print. Made it through the first line before I flicked my lamp off, blacking out the world.

The words I'd read echoed in my head. Over and over. A broken record stuck on a piercing note. I covered my face with a pillow, smashing it over both ears. And still, I heard Kel's words. Not in his voice, oddly. But in hers.

It's time to talk about my brother.

No, it wasn't.

Chapter Eighty-Three

Tate

I delivered a stillborn today.

His mother bawled, clutching onto him as if her pain could breathe life into him. Sweat leaked down her temples. Tears showered her cheeks.

Her husband hovered beside her, peering at their lifeless baby. Comforting his wife despite his own grief. Something I saw often in my line of work, yet never seemed able to duplicate.

This was the worst part of my job.

The part that usually sent memories of losing Kel rocketing through me.

But this time, I felt Charlie's absence. She would know what to say right now. How to use her losses to help the people around her. Even a stranger.

I nodded to a nurse, who signaled the staff to clear the room so the parents could grieve in private. We stood just outside, lined against the wall, heads bowed.

A symphony of wails crept past the closed door and whistled down the corridor.

By the time I arrived home, I felt like the collar of my dress shirt was out to choke me. I tore off the buttons, wanting them gone faster than I could unfasten them.

The light switch was far, and I was too exhausted to cross my bedroom and flip it off. I was so sick of struggling to breathe, so I lay on my back. Kellan's words glared at me from their perch above, but Charlie's words were the ones that haunted me.

It is a privilege to have parting gifts from someone you love after a sudden death. For there to be something to latch onto each time you miss him.

The fire left her with nothing of her parents.

As for the parents of the stillborn child I'd delivered this evening, they would never know the sound of his cries, never see him take his first steps, never feel the anxiety of sending him off on his first day of school.

Charlie was right.

Kellan's words were a privilege.

I stared at the poster above me.

And this time, I read.

Chapter Eighty-Four

It's time to talk about my brother.

I hate my brother in the way you hate milk growing up, knowing it's good for you yet unable to stomach the taste.

In other words, I hate my brother for the wrong reasons. That Asshole gave me hope. In a weird, fucked-up way, I thrived on his control-freak manner of handling me.

I'm no psychologist, but if I had to self-diagnose, I'd say I have a heavy dose of mommy issues that Big (and Overbearing) Brother Dearest managed to cook into something palatable and serve in the flowery dishware his Martha Stewart-wannabe fiancée bought from Williams Fucking Sonoma. With a heaping side of hope and the warm and fuzzies.

He was still That Asshole to me.

Always would be.

But in the same way you'd call your best friend a dipshit for doing dipshit things.

This will be the only time I admit I love my brother. So, savor it, folks. It's all you're gonna get.

Now that we got that out of the way, here's why I hate That Asshole...

Chapter Eighty-Five

Tate

The passage ended there.

With an ellipsis.

Three tiny dots that might as well be a taunt.

I shifted on my side, coming face-to-face with *Darling Venom*. On my nightstand. Exactly where Charlie had set it.

The pages teased me, shielded by the thick cover. I wanted to open it, devour it, discover everything else Kellan had written about me.

The good. The bad. The ugly.

I wanted it all.

I reached out. Collected the hardback. Freed the pages from the cover and read. The dedication sucker punched me first.

For the Marchetti men, without whom I wouldn't be fucked-up enough to write this book. May we one day get our shit together.

Classic Kel.

It was like he was here. Talking to me. Slinging accusations with his half-grin and eyes that matched mine. Not hidden inside black ink on white pages.

I turned to chapter one, sucked in a breath, and committed the first line to memory.

How convenient it is to have the villain and victim laid out before me in such a pretty, perfect bow.

An hour passed.

Then another.

I lost track of time, swallowing each word, unable to savor them in my greed to reach the next. Until I hit that point.

Where shit got real.

That Asshole would tell you he's doing me a favor. Preventing me from a spiral that will turn me into our piece-of-shit father. (His words, not mine.) What a cop-out. I made sure he knew, too, in the form of a fuck-you key to his Lexus' brand-new paint job.

The next day, Martha Stewart Jr. pulled me aside on my way out the door. I humored her, mostly because I'd rather receive a lecture from MSJ than an ass-whooping from some jock on steroids whose goal in life required peaking in high school.

She crossed her arms, a habit of hers, and launched into her spiel. "There are two types of love—easy and tough. Easy love is just like breathing. Anyone can do it. But tough love? It hurts way more to give it than it does to receive it."

"'Anyone' cannot breathe, or you'd be out of a job as a nurse," I pointed out, then fished a notepad and pen from my bag. "Need a note for my homeroom teacher, now that I'm late for class, thanks to you. Make it out to Mr. Wilson."

Tears slid past my lips.

I swiped my tongue out, clearing them. I barely registered Terry as he slipped into the room. He set a glass of water on the nightstand and left, clicking the door shut behind him.

I gripped the book tighter, reading faster.

In reality, Wilson taught sixth period art history. I used the note to ditch five out of six of my classes that day, somehow ending up in front of That Asshole's clinic. I wandered into the hospital and watched my brother cut into some woman through an observation window connected to the operating theater. He lifted a baby out of her. It cried. Kicked. Screeched. I had to admit, That Asshole had his moments. If he'd just asked me if I wanted to move in with him instead of forcing me to, maybe we wouldn't be in this mess.

Here's the thing about my brother. He's a natural-born caregiver. Sends me to the top schools, forces me to eat nutrient-packed meals that taste like cardboard, and shacks up with MSJ, just for little ol' me. But he's never received as much love as he's given. Unconditionally. Without expecting a damn thing in return. One day, it'll happen, and he won't know how to react. Without even trying, That Asshole will ruin the woman he loves.

I peeled the pages open and forced myself to finish. Even though it hurt like a motherfucker. And when I finished, there was nothing left of me but bones, flesh, and blood.

I sprawled across the hardwood planks, loose-limbed and exhausted.

Charlie kissed Kellan.

Correction: Charlie kissed Kellan, and he wrote an entire book about it. Named it after her taste. Immortalized her inside the same coffin he'd locked his soul.

And above all, he'd given them a happy ending.

Chapter Eighty-Six

Tate

My excuse for showing up at Charlie's apartment consisted of returning *Darling Venom* and not much else.

I knew treating her like a public library suggested I had the IQ of a pencil—it's not like she didn't have any copies of the book. Still, I came on autopilot. Careening toward a cliff, the train wreck that I was.

Leah stood in the hallway, keys dangling from her fingertips. She took me in, a sight that no doubt differed from the previous version of me she'd met.

I hadn't changed out of my torn button-down. Stains from upchucking my dinner peppered my dress pants.

I probably reeked, too.

She set her key in the doorknob, then turned to face me. "Lottie's at the playground."

Let it be a metaphor, asshat. Since you are now, apparently, catching feelings for a child.

"So, she's Lottie now."

"Yes. Thank you for snapping some sense into me." She crossed her arms. "But it doesn't excuse the hell you've put her through."

"She told you that?"

"No. You just did. She, on the other hand, told me not to worry. She didn't want to burden me. Lottie's like that. Always thinking about others before herself."

Her foot tapped a chaotic rhythm beneath her sensible shoe. She wore a collared tunic. Some sort of work uniform, I surmised. For a job Charlie once mentioned she never wanted.

Every sacrifice a person makes paves the way for the next one. Until they come so easily, they no longer consider them sacrifices. I knew because it'd been the same with Kel and me.

Leah sighed. "Since you offered unsolicited advice last time we talked, it's my turn. If you can't get your shit together and treat Lottie right, don't string her along. She's gone through enough pain and suffering to last a lifetime, and I'll be damned if you add to it."

She twisted the door handle, slinking into her apartment before I could answer. I hightailed it out of there.

On the walk to Galileo Playground, I accepted two indisputable facts:

1) Kellan claimed Charlie in *Darling Venom*.

And 2) I was stealing his girl, and I was the scum of the earth for it, but I vowed to never take it to the next level. If he couldn't have her all the way, neither could I.

Maybe a meteor would fall.

Level me.

Put me out of my misery.

Because Leah was right. I was not okay, and I couldn't string Charlie along, forcing her to wait for me to get my shit together.

I knew as soon as I saw Charlie that I shouldn't have come. Delivering hope with no intention of following through should be a criminal offense. At least then I'd be jailed and far less likely to show up here on a whim.

Charlie's intense green eyes tracked me from her perch on Mars.

The god of war, I noted.

She sent me a weird look. Maybe a little hopeful. Maybe a little confused.

"Are you here to apologize?"

If she wanted an apology, she was going to have to be more specific. In that department, I'd racked up a list longer than Santa's.

"Save it," she continued, turning back to watch a park squirrel dart down the slide. "I don't want to hear it."

I remembered my excuse, lifting the book. "I came to return this to you."

Her shoulders deflated, but she held her head high. "It's yours to keep." She sounded resigned.

"I read it."

"Impressive."

"Charlie."

"Charlotte."

"*Charlie.*"

"Fine." She pointed in the general direction of the jungle gym, still not looking at me. "Set the book on the slide. I'll grab it later." Charlie didn't want to chance touching me. Message received.

"For the squirrel to use as a landing pad?"

She ignored me. "Is that all? Or do you have something else you'd like to hand me? To say?"

Leave, Tate, the sole remaining thread of rationality inside me demanded. *That's all you came to do. Speaking of, a courier would have done the trick.*

My feet didn't budge.

Damn it.

"It was the first book I've read since college."

She paused. I could tell she didn't want to talk to me. I could also tell curiosity was going to kill this kitty.

"How was it?" The words rushed out of her, finally.

"Beautiful. Ugly. Hard to finish." I sat on Saturn because it was the closest planet to her. "I've hit rock bottom."

"Rock is one of the best foundations to build on. But it won't be with me." She was back to pulling her leg. I wondered when she'd started the habit again. Funny how I only now realized that she'd stopped.

I moved off Saturn to comfort her, but she jerked back. It dawned on me that Charlie was not mine anymore.

Not mine to comfort.

Not mine to love.

"I can't love you, Charlotte." The words ripped out of me.

She sighed, shaking her head. "You tried to tell me that in so many ways. I finally believe you."

I felt, for a moment, as if I'd stepped outside my body.

Or maybe died a little inside.

"It's the truth," I insisted. "I can't."

Silence from her.

"I read *Darling Venom*. He loved you. I can't ignore that."

The words did the trick.

Charlie snapped.

"How convenient for you to have read that right on the heels of our breakup. The perfect excuse. Actually, it's not a breakup. We were never official. You wouldn't even go to dinner with me!" This time, she came to me. With a vengeance. She halted just shy of touching me, her breaths escaping in jerks. "And you know what, Tate? You're a real bastard for using your dead brother as an excuse not to love me."

She turned to leave, but something stopped her.

Her hand gestured up and down the length of me. "Do you see yourself? When was the last time you slept?" It didn't help my case that I looked like I'd spent a decade on Mötley Crüe's tour bus. Her voice went from a boil to a simmer. "You are spiraling, and you are too stubborn to admit you need me."

If her tongue were a bullet, she would have killed me already. It was bad enough that I hadn't come here for closure, yet ended up having it force-fed to me with a shovel.

She was being mean. On purpose. It didn't suit her, but I wasn't in a position to tell her that. Worse, I didn't want her to stop. My favorite thing about Charlie was her ability to see past my bullshit. How fitting was it that, to the end, she stayed true to herself?

She offered me a sad smile, shaking her head. "This is not about my history with Kellan."

"It is."

"No, it's not. It's about your fear. Your inability to lose control. You've always been the person others depend on, and now it's your turn to depend on me. It scares you. You don't want to tell me you love me because you think it gives me power over you. But you've also clung onto me for so long, because no matter how much you try to deny it, you love me. So, you use Kellan as an excuse to stay in this limbo with me instead of saying the words we both know are true." She paused, staring into my fucking soul. "Tell me I'm wrong."

I couldn't. It occurred to me that Charlie did that often. Got all up in my business. Consumed me. Forced me to confront things I wouldn't otherwise.

"You are frozen in place, Tate. Stuck in slow motion and unwilling to take a step forward. Have you even listened to the voicemail Kellan sent you that night?"

No. And I have no plans to.

"That's what I thought."

She plucked something from her pocket and offered it to me. When I didn't take it, she touched me for the first time in weeks, uncurling my fist, setting the object on my palm, and wrapping my fingers around it.

The key to Kel's second drawer.

Now there really was nothing left of us.

I staggered back and tumbled past the gate circling the playground, feeling as if I'd left a piece of myself in the park.

It was time to return to my old way of living.

At a distance.

Turns out, life is a tragedy up close.

Part Three:
The Antidote

Chapter Eighty-Seven

Tate

Today's unexpected dose of Charlotte Richards came from Reagan. I didn't need the reminder that I hadn't seen or talked to Charlie in months, but leave it to Reagan to dish it to me free of charge.

"Kellan received eight starred reviews on *Darling Venom*." She read my face. "You have no clue what a starred review is, do you?"

"No, but it sounds important."

"It is. This is major for a debut book shopped by a newbie agent. This will make Charlotte's career."

I snapped my gloves off, reminding myself to smile.

My half-grin worked on Reagan, who returned it and straightened her paper gown, hopping off the exam table. "So, I'm all clear to have sex this time? At this point, I'm convinced you're afraid I'll get knocked up and add to your workload."

"I'm giving you the green light. Take it slow, and if you experience any pain or discomfort, be sure to call." I moved to give her privacy to change, pausing once my hand hit the doorknob. "How's Charlie been?"

Reagan tipped her head to the side, taking her time to answer. "She's Charlotte. Strong. Dependable. Caring. And yet, she's different."

"Sadder?"

"No. I think she's healing."

It was a good thing.

I told myself it sweetened my sour mood, yet I lashed out at Sylvia for being unprofessional when she came back from her lunch break with an Italy-sized marinara stain on her blouse.

Walter shoved me into my office as if I were a bomb he needed to disarm.

After Kellan died, we'd cleaned house at Bernard and Marchetti. I didn't want anyone to talk or even think about his death. Walter protested at first, but once I began snapping at everyone who dared to offer condolences, he let the entire staff go, gave them generous severance packages, and set them up with new jobs at his colleagues' practices. (Unlike me, he managed to socialize and make friends in the industry.)

This time around, I wanted to do the same.

I'd lost Charlie.

This, too, felt like parting from a limb without warning.

I kept the key she'd given me in my pocket just to torture myself. To remind me of our final moments together.

Rather than hitting up a bar like I wanted, I ended up on my couch. Beside Terry. Watching a rerun of some eighties show neither of us enjoyed.

I knew he had something he wanted to say, on account of the fact that, every time a commercial break hit, his lips parted and he huffed out a breath from the back of his throat, only for nothing but hissy air to escape.

The show resumed.

We went back to watching characters we didn't know the names of doing things that made no sense since we'd started the episode midway.

Did this count as father-son bonding?

If so, I wanted a refund.

Finally, Terry put us out of our misery, latching on to the remote and shutting off the television. "You have something you wanna say?"

"Sounds like you're the one with something to say. Huff any harder, and they'll need to recast you as the wolf in *The Three Little Pigs*."

"It's a crowning achievement in my life, the fact that the only book my adult son has ever referenced to me is a children's tale."

"You're welcome."

He tossed the remote aside. "I noticed you read *Darling Venom*."

"A while ago."

I swallowed, recalling the water Terry had left me that day. Such a little thing, yet I couldn't shake it.

They say there's no such thing as a small act of kindness. Someone should've warned me better before I invited my father into my house.

"Miss Richards fought to preserve every part that mentions you as Kellan wrote it. Those are his words, untouched. Just thought you should know."

"You want us together."

"*You* want the two of you together," he corrected. "I'm just an exhausted bystander."

"The fact that she worked hard to preserve Kellan's vision of me changes nothing."

In fact, I figured she would.

After all, she was warm, sweet Charlie.

Reliable to a fault.

Until our breakup.

Terry ran his knuckles along his jaw, head tilted. "And what would?"

"If I knew, I wouldn't be in this situation."

"If it's not about Kellan, it's about... Oh." He laughed, patting me on the shoulder. "Your brother was right."

"About?"

"About what you'd be like in a real relationship—unable to commit. Fine. I share some blame in this. Why would you let yourself lose control when it's all you've seen me do, only to end up a deadbeat addict?"

He pulled out his most recent AA chip and winked, flashing it at me.

Five months.

I guess a leopard *could* change its spots.

"The good news is," he pressed the token into my palm, "it's never too late to change."

Maybe it's your turn, Tate.

I headed to bed, pausing in the hallway in front of Kel's room. That boulder that normally fell to the pit of my stomach at the sight of it had disappeared.

Whatever he'd left didn't intimidate me as much as *Darling Venom* once did.

My foot slid forward.

I took a step.

And another.

Creaked his door open.

Approached the desk.

Stuck the key into the slot and turned, holding my breath.

A plume of dust assaulted my nostrils. I inventoried the drawer.

Two pennies. A single gold-dusted frame.

The metal felt cold and heavy in my hands. A picture was tucked beneath the glass. One of Kel and me on his sixteenth birthday. I had my head thrown back in laughter while he tried and failed to scale the ruins of Renwick Smallpox Hospital.

I'd thought there were no more pictures of us, but I shouldn't have been surprised. Memories are like long-distance relationships. The farther you travel, the weaker they become.

I collected the coins, brought them to my room, and set them and the vintage frame on my nightstand, right beside the photo Mom took.

Falling back onto my mattress, I palmed my phone and toggled to the voicemail.

It was time to hear what Kel had to say to me.

Chapter Eighty-Eight

Hey, Tate.
It's Kel.

I still think you're an asshole, but you're an asshole I need a favor from. There's this girl I know. Her name is Charlotte Richards.

She's strong. Stronger than she thinks she is. Made of the toughest stuff. Like the coating on an old-as-fuck Nokia phone. Or the shit they use to launch rockets into space.

Tough as hell, Dicks is.

But I worry about her, ya know?

I'm going some place far, and I need you to make sure she's okay. Look over her every now and then. Check that she has a pulse. That she's not taking shit from that sister of hers. We both have assholes for siblings, FYI.

If you do that for me, it'll make you a little less of an asshole in my book, which is an offer you may wanna take me up on, because I seem like the type that would come back as a poltergeist.

So, yeah.

That's my favor.

It's not even a big favor, all things considered, which means you're a dickwad if you don't do it...

What else do I say...?

Oh. Yeah.

What the hell was up with Hannah? The chick believes domestic bliss is knitting Christmas sweaters with your face on it. Your face. Being shackled to her is like getting stuck in an episode of Doctor Foster *that won't fucking end. Even you can do better. Came to your senses late there. Good riddance.*

Guess this is where I should say something nice to wrap this up. Fucking barf.

Here goes nothing...

I could've handled being dumped on your steps better. For the record, you could have, too. In our collective defense, it's hard to start a relationship on good footing when it begins with literal shit.

But living with you only sucked a bit, though Hannah's the absolute fucking worst. I know I'm kinda awful to deal with, but you tried. I saw that. I really did.

Aw, fuck it.

I don't hate you, Tate.

I might even like you a little.

See you in the next life.

Maybe we'll actually be brothers in that one.

Chapter Eighty-Nine

Tate

Nothing said you've hit rock bottom like being greeted by name by the staff of Worm Welcome, whose entire menu contained earthworms.

"Mr. Marchetti. You again." Sammy moved from the register.

Mister. I'd worked pretty damn hard on my medical degree, but I didn't correct her. The less she knew about me, the better. As it was, I found it hard to digest the fact that I frequented a place known for serving up creatures that eat dead bodies.

The bell above the door jingled as it shut behind me. I settled at my usual table, slipping on aviators when the sun hit my face.

Sammy parked next to my seat by the window. We both stared outside at the playground across the street. She pocketed her pen and notepad. "Let me guess—you're gonna order a bottled water and take an hour of prime Worm Welcome seating to gawk at that woman." Pink bubblegum snapped against her lips. Her tongue slithered out to gather it back inside her mouth. Good thing this place only carried worms, because I'd effectively lost my appetite. "I should report you for stalking," she added.

And I should report you to the health inspector.

I flashed a smile. "And miss out on my stellar tips?"

"Stellar?" She scoffed. For the record, I skimped *once* when I ran out of cash. Doubled my tip the next visit, too. But Sammy held a grudge like Wall Street assholes held offshore bank accounts.

"Keep talking, and there'll be one less zero behind whatever bill I give you today."

"Yeah, yeah." She waved me off. "What can I get for ya?"

"A bottled water."

Her brow lifted, as if to say, *see?* Nodding, she returned with my order, then left me alone to stare at Galileo Playground. It was empty, except for a rando snuffing a cigarette butt on Neptune. I palmed my phone and replayed Kellan's voicemail, something I found myself doing often. What did it mean that Kellan asked me to look out for Charlie? I knew what I wanted it to mean—permission to be with her. Permission to be happy. His blessing. But I also knew Charlie was right. Our problems didn't come from Kel. They came from me. I needed to learn to accept love. To lose control.

Like clockwork, Charlie arrived with Rowling. I watched her push Jonah's daughter on the swings before planet hopping as if they were bars and she was pre-sobriety Terry. I wondered if she knew each planet's meaning and realized I could no longer ask. There were a lot of things I wanted to do with Charlie that I would never get the chance to. She'd told me we were over. And still... I almost walked up to her. I almost kissed her. I almost told her I love her. Almost.

Sammy returned with a plate of food I never ordered, setting it down in front of me. I stared at it. Looked normal enough. A pretzel. Golden dough, a little burnt, and bent in the shape of a heart with a lopsided X in the middle. "We dehydrate the earthworms, blend them, and mix 'em right into the flour. Great source of protein."

It might've been a sign I needed to get the hell out of here. Probably stop showing up in the first place. But I didn't. I told myself I was fulfilling a promise to Kel. That I was watching over Charlie, just as he'd intended, in the way he'd intended. But after reading *Darling Venom*, one thing became clear: Kellan regretted missing his chance with Charlie.

I knew I would, too.

Chapter Ninety

Charlotte, 23

February 14th

Today marked nine years since Kellan saved me.

Five years since he died.

One year since I met Tate Marchetti.

February fourteenth was a day of firsts.

Just not today.

I told myself it didn't matter that Leah had forgotten my birthday.

After all, I'd spent the past ten of them without a single congratulation from her.

Plus, to be fair, things were hectic with her recent success. She posted a tutorial on YouTube for scar makeup, which ended up racking up more views than that dancing dog compilation.

I found myself on the subway, riding the path from Kellan's cemetery to a familiar station. The cabin rocked me. I swayed, deciding not to resist the waves. My phone buzzed with a text.

Leah: I promise you I did NOT forget about your birthday. Jonah and I drove all the way to Jersey to get you your favorite menemen, and

some asshole decided to rear-end us.
Me: Are you okay?
Leah: Yes, but pissed. Jonah says he can fix it easy. Still...
Leah: [Rob Lowe Screaming in a Desert GIF]
Me: Don't worry about it. Can't wait to eat the menemen tonight!
Thank you.

I slid my phone into my pocket, mood lifted. Leah and I were officially back to normal. It felt right. As if no time had passed. Which scared me, in a good way, because while it meant I had something to lose again, it also meant I had something to fight for.

The subway doors whooshed open, flashing a peek of one of Kellan's many MTA billboards. Helen had set up an early release in three major retailers to ramp up buzz, but *Darling Venom* ended up selling out before midnight yesterday. Which meant, this morning, the official day of release, there were no physical books to sell.

Helen ordered another print—four-hundred thousand copies. Meanwhile, indie bookstores flooded with customers. Kellan would have loved it.

By the time I reached St. Paul's, I wore a smile on my face. The same chain-link dangled from two hooks, barring entrance to the rooftop stairs. I shimmied under it, climbing the steps with less dread than I'd expected.

Maybe because I'd come for a good reason.

To celebrate Kel's release with him.

Just like that day nine years ago, I saw something I didn't expect to see.

A person.

He sat close to the ledge, his legs dangling over the rafters.

"Tate," I whispered, not expecting him to hear it.

I must've been seeing things, because I could've sworn I also saw Tate the other day, near Galileo Playground. And again at an advance reading of *Darling Venom*.

My imagination tended to run wild. I often googled Tate Marchetti, knowing I'd find nothing. I couldn't bring myself to visit him, because if I did, I'd break, and if I broke, I'd let him piece me back together, and if he pieced me back together, I'd stay. And if I stayed and he didn't relinquish his carefully crafted control, the cycle would begin again.

I decided not to risk it on the off-chance this wasn't a mirage. Turning, I moved for the staircase, ready to torpedo down.

"Wait!"

I froze, swallowed a deep breath, and faced him. Then pinched my leg. This was real. He was here. Holy crap. The shingles rattled as I strode toward him. I looped an arm around a chimney to steady myself, sitting about a foot away from Tate. The familiar suit he wore did things to my stomach, as it always did. Nothing had changed. From his hair, to his clothes, to his shoes, he'd stayed the same. I didn't know how I felt about that.

I shifted on the tile, getting comfortable. Tate held something in his fist. A carrot cake, I realized. But he wasn't eating it.

He followed my line of sight to the orange, Saran-wrapped block. "I don't like carrot cake," he admitted.

I held my hand out. "Cough it up."

He offered it to me. "Happy birthday, Charlie."

I flushed, unwrapping the cake and biting into the corner. The schoolyard seemed brighter below us.

"I've never seen this view in broad daylight." I curled the plastic back over the pastry. "It's better than I imagined."

It wasn't what I wanted to say. I wanted to ask why he'd shown up, but I knew the answer. Held it in my hand. Why else would he appear with a carrot cake? My palms grew so clammy I could open a water park with the sweat.

"I thought of what to say on the drive here, in case I saw you."

"Yeah? What did you come up with?"

"Nothing. I ruled everything out."

"What were the candidates?"

"I'm sorry."

"A good start, but too short," I agreed.

"I'm selfish."

"That simplifies our relationship. It's unfair to both of us."

"I miss you."

My heartbeat kicked up, pulsing in my ears. "I don't see anything wrong with that one."

Except the fact that I could already feel myself waning, and I'd vowed to respect myself enough to not let anyone drag me around.

"Charlie." I turned to face him. Tate held a penny in his hand, flipping it over and over. He tossed it to me. "Penny for your thoughts."

"I miss you," I admitted. I flipped the coin back, waiting for him to catch it. "Penny for yours."

"You're it."

"What?"

He slid closer, brushing shoulders with me. Sweet determination lit a fire in his eyes. "You said you wished you could find the thing to keep me going. You're it, Charlie. You're the thing that keeps me going."

I remembered that day. We'd talked on the phone for the first time, then I showed up at his house. I was already falling back then.

"I love you, Charlotte Richards. I can't promise you I'll always be okay, but I can promise you I'll always love you and I'll never be ashamed to say it. Over the past five years, I lost myself in grief. But then I found the most precious thing in the world—you."

His mouth claimed mine, forcing away years of loneliness and replacing them with him. I felt him everywhere. Inhaled the familiar sandalwood, bonfire, and citrus. Tangled my tongue with his.

I pulled back, panting, resting my forehead against his. "You come up with all that in the car?"

"It was a productive ride."

He leaned in for another kiss. I smiled against his lips, realizing today's first.

Being told I love you by someone I loved back.

Epilogue

Charlie

"Charlotte, *dahr-ling*, you're doing it again." Reagan struts into my office (yes, office, with four walls and even a window), dropping a magazine onto my overloaded desk.

I *hmm*, still typing away, in the middle of an email to a foreign publisher looking to buy the Italian rights for a book I recently sold. "Doing what?"

"Holding back on me. Why is it I have to find out you signed a five-book deal with Random House for Marshall Clive through this?" She picks up the copy of *Publishers Daily* and waves it in the air. "It's my agency, after all."

But there's not a trace of anger in her voice. How can there be? This contract kisses seven figures. Since I work for her as a full-fledged agent, her cut could fund an entire year of tuition for one twin at their bougie preschool. Preferably for Noah. Ethan turned out to be an asshole, who *still* cries at the sight of me.

"It wasn't supposed to be published until Monday." I pluck the magazine from between her manicured fingers, shoving it into one of my drawers so I can message a picture to Marshall later. "I'm s—" I stop. I'm not sorry. There is nothing to be sorry for. I made a kick-ass deal and forgot to send her the memo. I'm learning to let go of my guilt. Of my need to apologize to the entire world. It's a process, but I'm definitely taking baby steps.

"No, you're not sorry." A smile spreads over Reagan's face. "And you shouldn't be. Tell me all about this deal. Over lunch." She claps.

Now is a good time to apologize.

"Can't. Sorry." But for the first time in years, the word doesn't carry that added weight. Of someone afraid to let the other person down. "I'm meeting Tate for an early lunch. Dinner or a raincheck?"

In the background, the boys have woken from their nap, evidenced by their screams. I hear people outside trying to offer them food three-year-olds have no business eating. It's weird, but I kind of got used to writing with two screaming kids in my ear. If this secondhand experience with twins has taught me anything, it's that motherhood is life's boot camp. I have renewed respect for mothers everywhere.

"Tate." Reagan wiggles her brows. "Where's he taking you?"

I can't tell her. Not because Tate told me not to. He didn't. But because I'm pretty confident it's a private matter. I can't explain it. I just have a hunch.

"Not sure." I stand, pick up a printed contract, and head to the filing cabinet. "We're going to meet on Fifth and see what's available and good." That's a flat-out lie. I don't like lying, but it feels like a necessary evil at this point.

Reagan nods. Her smile says she knows something she isn't telling me, but since I lied to her not even a second ago, I'm in no position to pry. "Right. Of course. Well, I hope you enjoy it."

"Sure, I will. Dinner, then?"

"Oh, I don't know. Let's talk tomorrow. It's not that urgent, anyway." Then she knocks my desk twice—the sliver of space not covered with papers, that is—and ushers out of my office.

I finish the email, take a picture of the article about the deal and send it to Marshall, then grab my jacket, wrapping my neck in a cashmere scarf

Leah and Jonah gifted me for Christmas. It's an ugly, orange thing, but it means so much to me, I rarely leave it in the house.

In Tate's new house.

In *my* house, in a lot of ways.

Not officially, though. It was more of a natural progression. The way a spider weaves what starts as an unassuming web that takes over an entire garage wall after a few months. I'm not sure who the spider is in our scenario. I just know that one sleepover a week turned into four. And before I knew it, I needed my own toothbrush, and toothpaste, and hairbrush, and deodorant, and body lotion, because going to my apartment before work became too much of a hassle.

And then Jonah asked Leah to buy a home with him. Not before checking if I was okay with it (of course, I was). And she said yes. It came at a good time, because Reagan had just promoted me, and that promotion came with a serious raise. But now I'm paying for a studio apartment I don't sleep in. Tate's place is closer to my office, and the only time I venture back to my studio is to collect the mail.

I take the train to St. Paul, people-watching as I do. New York is shedding itself from the leftovers of winter. You can see it on the naked trees that are not so naked anymore. In the way the onion effect makes people peel their clothes on the subway. In the fact that city workers have a bit more spring in their step. I get off at the station. My heart lodges in my throat. I don't know why I'm nervous. The last time I came, something good happened. But... I hate that roof. The ugliness of the life it took. That gut-punch of memories that hits me when I pass the same spot where Kellan plummeted. And now Tate wants us to meet there. A part of me resents him for that because he is about to take another Kellan thing and taint it with Tate. That roof belongs to Kellan and me. But saying no seems too big. Too dramatic. Especially after we chipped away a piece of Kellan that Valentine's Day and replaced it with us.

I race up the emergency steps, wondering what it will take for St. Paul to restrict access to these stairs. I'm fifteen minutes early. This was planned. I need time to gather myself before Tate shows.

When I reach the roof, I'm surprised at how familiar it is. How it hasn't changed. I'm also surprised to find Tate already here. His back is to me. The wind whips his dark hair. Seeing him like this, his coat hanging perfectly on his imperial body, I forgive myself for drowning in him. For taking the bait. For falling in love with my dead best friend's brother. My dead best friend who was in love with me and who left me the most precious gift of all—a brilliant, heartfelt book.

"Yes." Tate's voice booms. He knows I'm here, yet I don't think I made a sound. It's funny how even though we're together—been together for a while now—he is still formidable. Still cold to people around him who are not me. "Yes, it had to be here. I know you've been wondering. But it had to."

"Why?" I don't ask what it entails. It's less important than why we're here.

Tate spins, pinning me with a look. "Because so many of your memories from this place are all wrong, and it's not fair to you. Because it's time to build good memories on top of the bad ones. It doesn't mean we're forgetting Kellan. It means we're honoring him."

I'm surprised to find myself not completely on defense where Kellan is concerned. That, too, is a welcome change. I think what caused it is that Tate and I are a team now. That I no longer doubt his emotions toward his little brother.

"Okay." I incline my head. "We're here now. Is this where we're having lunch?"

Tate is not the picnic type, but stranger things have happened. Like the fact that he is now on good terms with Terry, who took Tate's old house when he traded up to the new one closer to the clinic.

Tate makes his way toward me, moving with the grace and composure of a nocturnal predator. My heart jackhammers in my chest. I reach to pluck at my leg, but instead squeeze my jacket pocket. It always carries a paperback of *Darling Venom*. Wrinkled and read to death, but there. My tribute to Kellan.

Tate stops two feet from me. I have so much adrenaline in my body, I want to scream. What's happening?

"Charlie."

"Tate."

"Did Reagan really not tell you why you're here today?"

I scrunch my forehead. "No. And I'm getting real tired of being in the dark, so you may wanna jump ahead and tell me what's happening."

He laughs, and in this moment, I can see Kellan in him. In the bashfulness. In the youth. But also something that's uniquely and completely Tate. The man I fell in love with. The force to be reckoned with. The storm that caught me in its eye.

"Charlotte. Lottie. Charlie." He shakes his head, sticking his hand in his hair and tousling it. "I'm not good with this bullshit. Listen. Here it is—when I met you, I was a mess. No. A mess is an understatement. I was a train wreck. A sinking ship. A danger to myself and those around me. You typhooned into my life and changed it. Flipped it upside down. And now? Now I can't imagine my life without you." He pauses. "No. That's not right. I can imagine my life without you. And I would be fucking miserable. Actually, I'm not sure it would be worth living at all. We already live together, though we've never made it official, and I think it's time you make an honest man out of me."

With that, he lowers himself to one knee. I cup my mouth. I might be screaming, but I can't hear anything. Tate brought me here to propose to me. He took me to the place I experienced one of the most traumatic things in my life and turned it into the most beautiful. He wants to pick up my pieces and help me mend them together. Like I did for him.

He plucks a blue velvet box from his coat pocket and pops it open. It's a gorgeous ring, the diamond stark-black. Shimmering around it are tiny, polished gems. The band itself is thin and elegant. It is so me, I want to cry. No, wait, I do cry. Hot tears run down my freezing face. I shake my head.

"No? Is that a no?" His voice takes a sharp edge. He's trying to keep together. *Oh, crap.* He thinks I'm refusing him.

458

I laugh and lower myself to my knees, grabbing his face. "No, idiot. That's a yes. That's one hundred percent yes. I just can't believe you were so thoughtful as to bring me here."

Without answering me, he picks up my left hand and slips the ring onto my finger. It's quick. Like he doesn't want me to change my mind. Tate kisses the diamond on my hand, his eyes holding mine. "Really? Because I can't believe my dumb ass has waited for so long."

Then we're flung over each other. I don't know who started it, or who will end it. The kiss is sloppy and full of emotions and laughter and saliva. My tears mix with our lips, and we devour them. We're both used to this simple fact of life—any pleasure worth having is always laced with a bit of pain.

Darling Venom.

Beauty wrapped in ugliness.

Love disguised as hate.

We clutch each other's shoulders. It seems like we'll never let go.

"I'm going to make you happy, Charlie."

And you know what? He already has.

Tate

One year after

"It's going to be a shit show," I drawl as I slip out of my car, rounding it to open the door for Charlie.

She wobbles to her feet, cradling her pregnant belly. She's doing great for late first trimester. Hardly any morning sickness. No mood swings. Not even an enhanced sense of smell. I warned her this could change at any moment. That pregnancy is not a walk in the park for everyone.

"It's going to be fine."

I wrap a shawl over her shoulders and lace our fingers. We make our way to the Literary Museum of Art in Brooklyn, where Kellan is about to be honored. Another print of *Darling Venom* hit shelves last week. Terry weeps whenever he hears the book's official sale count (ten million units and rising), which makes him an interesting choice to accept the award.

"You don't really believe that," I groan, squeezing her hand in mine.

"No, I don't. But we have to respect his wishes. This is how he wants to do this. He owes it to himself, and to Kellan. We can't stop it. And anyway, it's not our place to."

My wife has a point. She always has a point.

I hate it.

In the museum, it's more of the same. I've gotten used to this literary mumbo jumbo from being Charlie's plus one for countless events. The highbrow conversation. The flutes of champagne. The in-depth pondering about texts written while the author was high as fuck. An entire hour passes before the organizer of the event—a woman whose name I can't pronounce, who looks as if she's tried every single plastic surgery available on the market—clinks her glass with a fork. Classic. She asks for everyone's attention, her scarlet smile dark and big. Oblivious to what she's in for. I sit back, watching her call Terry to the stage with a mixture of satisfaction and dread. My father gets up from our table and walks over.

The woman onstage bangs on about *Darling Venom*. About how well it did in stores. How kids are learning about it in high school now. Behind her, Terry pales. He shoots me a look, waiting for assurance that he's doing the right thing. I incline my head slightly, as if to say, *go for it*.

The speaker talks for another twenty minutes. Charlie grabs my hand and squeezes. She knows I'm nervous. I'm sure she's nervous, too. And then the woman finally gives Terry the microphone.

He cuts straight to the point, like he told us he would earlier, when he came for a pregame drink at our house. Coffee, in case you were wondering. Asshole has been sober for a while now.

He clears his throat. "Thank you. For the support. For buying *Darling Venom*. Reading it. Loving it. For telling your friends to buy it. For sending me pictures of it in bookstores. I don't think you know how much that means to me. How... how fucking freaky it feels. That you pour something that's in your head onto a page, and that thing that you thought about becomes so popular, everyone wants to hear it and read about it."

He takes a breath. Closes his eyes. His shoulders are shaking, but he doesn't cry. "Only I'm afraid I cannot feel any of those things that make a writer proud. See, there's a reason I declined any public speaking until now. It's not because I value my privacy—fuck my privacy. It's not because I have nothing to say. I have too much to say. It's because saying what I have to say is frightening, yet necessary." I have a bad feeling about his next words. Or a good one, depending on how I look at it.

The event coordinator weaves through the tables, almost plowing herself to the stage. "This is supposed to be about Mr. Marchetti."

"That's me," Terry points out. The crowd dissolves into laughter.

"The other Marchetti."

"I'm getting there."

More laughter. Charlie and I exchange glances. Neither of us is amused. We're concerned for Terry. She gestures for me to grab the car. I move, still paying close attention to Terry's speech as he returns to the mic and starts up again.

"Where was I? Right. Kellan Marchetti was a lot of things. An author. A prodigy. A brother. A son. And the writer of a book I stole from him and called my own. *The Imperfections.*"

A collective gasp sucks the air out of the room. I freeze by the doorway, turning back to face Terry. I expected him to come clean about plagiarism, but I never expected the writer to be Kel. But it makes sense. So much sense.

My father closes his eyes, but he soldiers through. And for that, for the first time—maybe for the only time—I am proud of him. "I didn't write *The Imperfections.* Not most of it, anyway. I stole from my own boy. From my flesh and blood. He was brilliant, and special, and talented, and I was a fraud. He did incredible things with his mind, and I pretended they were mine. This is why you never got a second book. This is why I went under the radar. This is the naked, ugly, maddening truth. That I stole *The*

Imperfections. Plagiarized, if you will. I don't deserve this. This love. This support. This adoration. Kellan does. His second book, *Darling Venom*, is out there. Go read it. Borrow it. Libby it. Tell your friends. Tell them to tell *their* friends. Give him the respect I didn't. God knows he deserves it."

He takes a step back from the microphone. My eyes shut. I can feel Kellan here. Around us. Maybe even inside this room. His spirit. I think, wherever he is, he's okay now.

"I won't be taking questions. Thank you."

Charlie grabs my hand. I don't know when she got here, but it's classic Charlie to be dependable in every situation. I catch up with her pace. "Tate. Get the car real quick." She shoves me in the chest.

I make a break for it, turning once to make sure she's safe. She rushes toward Terry, who is trying to sneak out of the back door. Charlie clutches his hand and tugs. I want to urge her to slow down. She is pregnant. With my baby. But there's no stopping her. I dart to the valet, watching as my wife pushes my father beneath a tree to hide. The mob is after him. It's less scary than it looks. Just a bunch of old farts in suits and satin dresses, wanting to know what it means for the signed hardcover they purchased with their meal for this occasion, shelling out a cool four thousand bucks for the pleasure. I slide into my Lexus and round the building to fetch Terry and Charlie. A laugh escapes me. I feel like a kid misbehaving. All this running around. Making a mess. I pull to a stop when I see Charlie and Terry racing toward my car from the rearview mirror. Charlie is laughing. Her eyes glitter under the night sky.

And I know Kellan loved me, too. He did, because he gave me the most wonderful gift before he died.

He gave me Venom.

For a free bonus scene, join my mailing list at: shor.by/VenomFreebie - XOXO, Parker

462

Acknowledgments

Chlo, I miss you. I love you. Bau and Rose, you four-legged terrors. L, thanks for keeping me functional. Sorry I'm a mediocre girlfriend. (I'm not really sorry. You knew what you signed up for.)

To Heidi Jones, who married a professional golfer. Basically. Maybe. Probably. To Heather Pollock, who puts up with a lot of my BS. To the people who helped whip this book into shape—Emily, Michelle, Vanessa, and Paige. To my BFFs from G.A.—Libra and Boom Boom. Thanks for putting up with my anxiety, prepubescent humor, and limitless array of pics you'll never be able to unsee. To Elan. You still haven't told me if the ninja and dancer who fell in love after that tripping-over-a-ball-of-yarn fiasco really married in a chapel made of watermelons. Asshole.

And to the API community. It's been a tough year, but dammit, we're strong. I'm so proud of our resilience.

I'd like to pay tribute to two beautiful, important people the world lost too soon. Janice Owen was a reader and a proofer, and it was in both capacities that we met. Janice worked with me on every book I've ever published, quickly becoming a friend I relied on—not just for her keen eye, but also for her positive, cheerful personality. Janice, you brought me great comfort over the years, lending me your warmth and allowing me to lean on you whenever I needed someone to depend on. I will miss your light. Thank you for being in my life.

Kamel Dupuis-Perez was my Amazon rep. I'd never spoken to anyone as passionate about his wife and children. He valued people, dedicating himself to inclusion in publishing. Kamel, thanks for making me feel seen. For dealing with my excessive and obnoxiously long emails. I never got to DoorDash you my favorite xiao long bao or overnight a lì xì. Sorry I never thanked you for your kinds words. For listening to me. For being there.

For more books from Parker, visit www.parkershuntington.com/

Made in the USA
Middletown, DE
17 September 2023